DARK ROMEO

SIENNA BLAKE

Dark Romeo by Sienna Blake. – 2nd Ed.
First Edition: January 2018
Published by SB Publishing
Copyright 2018 Sienna Blake
Cover art copyright 2018 Cosmic Letterz. All rights reserved Sienna Blake. Stock
images: depositphotos, shutterstock
Development editing and proofreading services by Book Detailing.
Proofreading services by Proof Positive: http://proofpositivepro.com.

For Terrie,
Who called dibs on Roman.
And for being your bad-ass miracle-worker multi-tasking ninja self.
Love you.

"My only love sprung from my only hate!
Too early seen unknown, and known too late!
Prodigious birth of love it is to me,
That I must love a loathèd enemy."

~ *Romeo & Juliet* by William Shakespeare
Act 1, Scene 5

ROMAN

I was being hunted down like a dog at my brother's own funeral. I ran bent over, weaving through the rows of gray and bone-white gravestones. Praying angels with pitying eyes stared down at me from their tall moss-covered pedestals, their eerie silence making my heavy breath seem like screaming. My polished black leather shoes sank in places. My tailored Armani suit pants were edged with mud.

It would be too easy for him to find me. I was leaving too many tracks.

What did you expect, Roman? I growled internally. *That you could sneak into the back of your brother's funeral and no one would notice you? That you could come back here to Verona and not have to face* him?

I didn't have a choice but to come back. Even though Jacob and I hadn't spoken in years, he was still my older brother. Flashes of when we were younger entered my mind, causing a touch of softness in my cold heart. He'd protected me from schoolyard bullies, read stories to me at night. He'd been my friend, my protector. That was before we grew up and he morphed into a bully himself. That was before I learned to take care of myself. That was before I ran away.

I thought I could live the rest of my worthless life in my self-inflicted exile in Europe. The plan was perfect. Until my eldest brother got himself killed. *Why did you have to die, Jacob?*

"Roman," a male voice barked out from somewhere behind me—too close behind me—the irritation clear in his gruff tone. "Don't be so tiresome."

I thought I could sneak into the back of the service without being spotted. I thought I could then sneak out before it ended.

I had been so wrong.

Abel Montero had seen me. My father's "dog".

That's why I had to run. I wanted to swoop in and out of Verona quietly, without a big mess. Shooting Abel, as much as I'd enjoy it, would be a big fucking mess.

I zig-zagged through the gravestones, grateful for the large ornate slabs and crypts the size of small cottages that provided me with some cover. Waverley Cemetery was Verona's oldest, dating back over 300 years, and most prestigious, spanning across almost fifty acres. Large enough for me to lose Abel in. Hopefully.

I skidded around a corner and ducked behind a large mausoleum, pressing against the cold stone, slimy with moss. I heard a soft gasp. I came face to face with a young woman standing meters away in front of one of the gravestones.

I thought I'd been alone in this graveyard on this watery late Saturday afternoon.

I was wrong.

Her almond eyes widened as they locked with mine, two orbs of amber whiskey. My heart began to hammer in my chest. I found myself gripping the mausoleum to keep my balance. I guessed she was about my age. Her long honey-and-wheat hair fell over her slim shoulders and over her round breasts, their shape visible through her fitted white summer dress printed with large sunflowers. It showcased her tiny waist, just wide enough that I could wrap both my hands around it. She had sharp cheekbones and a slim neck, her skin a lovely tanned color. Her red rosebud mouth parted on a gasp. I instantly imagined myself licking those lips before pushing past them to enter her with my tongue. I almost groaned as the image stabbed me like a hot poker in the lower belly.

She was one of the most stunning creatures I'd ever seen in my life. She exuded sexuality but not in a fake, obvious way. She was natural and classy: her full, naked lips; her alert, intelligent stare; the way her hair swooped partly over one eye, as if she were playing peek-a-boo with me. The way her dress dropped past her knees and yet tucked in at all the right places, hinting at the glorious body underneath, slim yet curvy with the perfect hint of muscle on her arms. A lady on the outside, a sexual creature on the inside.

She was lovely. Perfect.

For a second I forgot I was hiding. Hell, I forgot who I was running from. And why.

JULIANNA

Almost fourteen years... and I still haven't gotten her justice.

I'm sorry, mama.

I laid down white peonies against her pale headstone and stepped back to stand at the base of her plot. I folded my fingers together in front of me, staring at the elegant clusters of still-closed petals, a brush of pink at the tips. They had been her favorite. She used to dress the house in them, generous bunches spilling over the tops of clear vases set on the surface of every table. She'd brush the petals lovingly every time she passed them, the same way she used to brush against my cheek. My heart squeezed. For a second my emotions threatened to spill over.

I wrestled them into control in a tight space in my chest. Fourteen years. Fourteen years and it still hurt that she wasn't here anymore, the wound as raw as it was when my heart was first torn open. It could not heal without answers, answers I'd failed to deliver. There was no moving on without closure. The need for justice still burned through my veins.

"Happy birthday," I whispered to the silent earth. She would have been forty-seven today if fate hadn't taken her away from

4

me. I would have woken up early and snuck over to my parents' house. My father and I would have made a huge stack of blueberry pancakes and fresh coffee and crowded them onto a tray. My father would have carried it into the room that my parents' shared, me in front holding the pot of milk and jug of maple syrup. She would have pretended to still be sleeping as we burst in, waking her up with my off-key singing and my father's magnificent alto voice, one that rivalled Pavarotti. My mother was always up at the crack of dawn, except for her birthday, when she "slept in" to let us surprise her. She would have sat up in bed, the most beautiful woman in the world, even without a stitch of makeup, clapping her hands and laughing as we jumped in around her and spoiled her with flowers, gifts and breakfast in bed that we shared from one plate using three forks.

I never heard my father sing again after she died.

I glanced at my watch before looking around the deserted cemetery. Where was my father? He was supposed to be here by now.

On sunny days this place looked peaceful, but on days like today, the overcast clouds made the gravestones seem all the more solemn and dull. I felt very, very alone, the only heart beating in a field of dust and silent memories.

A sound made me turn my head. Someone was approaching and approaching fast. A tall, dark figure came leaping out past the corner of the huge mausoleum before me. I opened my mouth to let out a noise of surprise. Until I saw him.

My breath was trapped under the thick knot that developed in my throat. Everything above it—my mouth, my tongue, my lips—all went dry. My heart began to thump against my ribs. I could hear the glugging sound of my blood in my own ears. Suddenly I felt dizzy, my mind going blank except to focus solely on the sight of him. Was I having a heart attack? Surely not. I was only twenty-five for God's sakes. What was happening to me?

Somewhere deep inside, I was vaguely aware that I was staring. I should look away. I should say something. Anything.

I opened my mouth and...

Nope, nothing. How curious. My voice seemed to have stopped working.

My eyes kept working, though. They drank in the sight of him from head to toe as he pressed his back against the mausoleum, his hands gripping the stone. He was so beautiful that it hurt to look at him. Like I was staring at the sun, his image burning a permanent mark on my brain.

His dark hair was long, almost too long, curling over his collar, tousled and messy like he'd run his hands through it a few too many times today. It was done in a way that looked incredibly sexy, like he'd just rolled out of bed. His deep-set, hooded eyes were dark, either deep chocolate or black; I couldn't tell from where I was standing. Framed by thick black lashes and dark brows, they were much too intense, like two black holes drawing my awareness towards him. The features of his face were expertly put together like an artist had sculpted him: straight nose, high cheekbones, smooth light-brown skin, a hint of stubble shadowing his strong square jaw.

He was tall, his wide shoulders and thick torso evident even through the tailored black suit jacket he wore unbuttoned, showing a white shirt underneath and a slim black tie which sat slightly askew. Even this didn't make him look unkempt but rather roguish instead. His trousers matched, fitting perfectly, showcasing strong thighs. His black leather round-toed shoes were expensive; I guessed Armani or Gucci.

He had a sophisticated polish to his air, like he was born wearing a suit and yet... there was something dark about his demeanor. Something rough. Aggressive. Like he'd fit just as well in a boxing ring or wearing a black leather jacket and straddling a bike. Like he'd give me a run for my money in a shoot-out.

What a curious combination. One I'd never seen before. I'd

met plenty of men. They were always one or the other. Either educated and well-mannered yet almost feminine in their polish. Or coarse and brutishly aggressive without a scrap of sophistication.

He raised a hand and pressed a finger to his lips, making a shushing motion. God, those lips. Even from here I could see they were thick and pillowy; the kind of lips that were made to suck and nibble on.

Whoa. Julianna. Where did that thought come from?

Heavy footsteps came towards us, echoing off the gravestones. I tore my eyes off this curious stranger. On one side of the mausoleum a wiry man in a dark suit and black leather gloves approached, a nasty-looking scar going from his left ear across his cheek and to the corner of his lip.

Instinctively I leaned back. All my years as a trained police officer gave me a second sense for bad men. He was one of them. It was something in the cruel whip of his mouth, in his eyes... they were dull and flat, like no spark of life or humanity was left.

I fought a shiver, my fingers going to my hip. Shit. No gun. I was off-duty today. I had a piece in my car parked in the lot about a ten-minute walk from here, but it was no use to me now.

Scarface halted at the sight of me, pausing for a second, probably wondering what to do now. I dropped my gaze, hoping he would ignore me.

"You." His voice was harsh and rough like someone who'd spent too many years smoking cigarettes. He spat out his words as if he was angry that I was even here.

I looked back up to him, willing myself to remain calm even as he glared at me as if he was picturing cutting me into little pieces. I would not attack first, but I would defend myself.

"Did you see a man coming by here?"

It clicked into place. Scarface had been chasing the beautiful man still hiding against the mausoleum wall right in front of me. A man that Scarface would see if he took two steps forward.

A protectiveness rose inside me. Scarface could not have him. "I did," I said. Even though I took pains not to glance in his direction, I could sense the beautiful stranger flinching, no doubt wondering if I was going to give him away. I had to speak fast so he wouldn't do anything stupid. "He went running that way." I pointed out towards my left, towards the other side of the cemetery.

Scarface glanced over to where I had pointed. He looked back to me, doubt clear in his narrowed eyes. "That way? You're sure?"

"Good-looking guy in a black suit, running bent over? He went that way," I said casually as if I didn't care whether Scarface believed me or not.

"Good-looking," Scarface muttered. He snorted. "Yeah, that's the bastard."

He turned and ran through the gravestones in the false direction I had given him. He didn't even say thanks. Rude prick. In case he decided to glance back, I lowered my eyes back to my mother's grave.

My awareness drew back to the beautiful stranger. I could feel his eyes on me, making every inch of my skin become super-aware; I could sense where the air met my bare forearms, feel my hairs standing on end, feel the way my breath caught in my lungs. Or was I just imagining that he was looking?

I glanced up. Sure enough, his eyes were focused on me. My stomach did a shaky little flip. Why was he staring? It was making me feel…weird.

I forced my eyes back down to the grave. I wasn't sure I could stand to maintain eye contact with him while he was looking at me like *that*. Maybe if I ignored him he'd go away?

Not a chance. The stranger pushed off the stone and strode towards me, causing my gaze to jerk involuntarily up to him again. He moved like a panther, proud and prowling, powerful strides making me want to back up. My heels wobbled in the grass and I longed for something to grab on to.

He stopped at the back of my mother's headstone and placed his hands lightly on the top of the gray stone. We were only meters away from each other now, separated only by a grave's length. It felt too close. His eyes were intense, focused on me, yet revealing nothing, while I felt like an exposed wire, an open book.

Say something, Julianna. Something. Anything!

Weirdly, my voice had stopped working. Why was I reacting this way to him? I had never reacted like this to anyone before.

He spoke, breaking the silence. "You didn't have to help me."

Holy shit. That voice.

I learned in high school science about how sounds at certain pitches could make a tuning fork hum, but only at the perfect frequency. Whatever frequency his voice was, I had been tuned to it. It sent a vibration through my body unlike anything I've ever felt before. Deep and raspy, it was the kind of voice you'd hear on an old-time jazz vocalist. The kind of voice that induced images of sultry summer nights, soft sheets and nothing but skin on skin. It wasn't fair. That voice on this man. It was too much. Too much beauty. Too much...sex.

Somehow my voice kicked in. "I know I didn't have to help you." I gave him a half-smile. "Obviously, I have a soft spot for damsels in distress."

He laughed. The sound was glorious, rich and rolling and full. I wanted to weave his laughter into a blanket and wrap it around me. I grinned at him like a fool, pleased at myself that I could elicit such a warm response from such a stunning-looking man.

"Well," he said after his laughter had faded, "thank you, my valiant knight." He bowed low, making me blush.

I turned my face towards the direction where Scarface had disappeared to. "I don't suppose you'd tell me why you're running from him?"

"You wouldn't believe me even if I told you."

"Try me."

SIENNA BLAKE

His lips twitched before he spoke. "I just arrived in town for a funeral. I thought I could fly in, come straight here and fly out tomorrow without having to see my father but…he's determined to pin me down."

His father? I tried to picture Scarface birthing the god before me. I couldn't. How could such beauty come from such ugliness? "You're right. I don't believe you. That man looked nothing like your father."

He looked like he was about to say something else about it, but he didn't. "Are you here visiting someone?" He indicated the grave between us, firmly changing the subject.

The sadness I'd been feeling before he showed up leaked back in. Funny how it seemed to have disappeared around him. I nodded down at the grave, pinpricks behind my eyes. "Yes."

"You loved…*him?*"

"Her. My mother. Deeply."

"I know what that's like." His voice was tight and low, pain squeezing out between his words. "I lost my mother too."

Strangely, my pain eased, soothed by the silence that descended over us. A shared silence. A moment of perfect understanding, when you both spoke without words. I'd only ever shared these moments with my mother, who had been my best friend when she'd been alive. Now I was having this moment with a perfect stranger…a beautiful, intriguing stranger.

I was about to blurt out everything I had been thinking about perfect moments when my phone rang, saving me from myself. My heart sank when I saw the name across the screen. I knew what was coming. I should have expected it.

I answered the call, feeling the beautiful man's eyes on me. "You're not coming, are you?" I said into the receiver, my voice working around the golf ball at the base of my neck.

"Sorry, honey," my father said. "Work."

"Of course." It was always work. My chest tightened.

"I'll come by later for dinner, okay? Your place? About sevenish?" Which meant I'd be lucky if he arrived by nine p.m.

"Sure." I hung up, staring at my mother's grave again, gripping my cell in my hand. Her fucking birthday and he couldn't make this one day a priority. He couldn't make *me* a priority. Work needed him so he went. Work always needed him. What about when I needed him?

I let out a curse as bitterness flooded over the back of my tongue. Before I could stop myself, I threw my phone. It hit the ground and bounced once before half disappearing in a cluster of untrimmed grass. I could feel the beautiful man's gaze on me like a cloak. I pressed my hands into my face to avoid his scrutiny, embarrassed that I had let a stranger witness this rare show of emotion from me. He probably thought I was mental.

"Are you okay?" The concern in his voice was a finger plucking on my heart strings.

I sucked in a breath and wiped under my eyes before lifting my head. He'd walked between the gravestones over to my phone, picking it out of the grass. I didn't move to take it from him.

"It's my father," I blurted out before I could stop myself. "He was supposed to meet me here. It's her birthday. *Was* her birthday today." I didn't know why I was telling him. I didn't even know his name.

"But he's not coming."

I shook my head, a fresh wave of anger causing me to grit my teeth.

"I'd be angry too."

"I'm not angry…" I was lying. It was probably so obvious to him. I sighed. "Fine. I am angry."

"And you have a right to be." He paused. "My father…angers me too."

"Which is why you run away from him." I shook my hair out

of my face. "I only wish that my father noticed me enough to chase after me."

I had said too much. I had said too much to a beautiful stranger who made me feel unsteady, like my world was tipping, who somehow made me talk so openly. If I spent any more time with him I just might spill all the deepest, darkest secrets of my heart.

"I should go," I said suddenly.

Something in my chest let out a disappointed thud, even though *I* was the one instigating goodbye. I realized I wanted him to stop me.

He nodded. "Thanks again for throwing him off my trail. You didn't have to. I'm glad you did."

I sagged a little. He wasn't going to stop me. How silly. Saying one thing, wanting another.

"You can pay it forward." I turned to walk away. Before I could take a step, I heard him clear his throat. When I looked back he was holding out my phone, a tiny smirk on his face.

Right. I needed that.

He didn't move, forcing me to close the distance between us. I walked on unsteady feet, choosing my heel placements carefully so that I didn't trip, the tightness in my chest growing the nearer I got to him.

I stopped before him. This close I could see his eyes were a deep, rich chocolate, tiny flecks of amber in them. I could smell him, an intoxicating mix of spicy wood and a hint of citrus; pure masculinity. I was suddenly overcome with a ridiculous urge to push my nose into his jacket.

He dangled my phone out in front of me. I reached out to take it. He snatched it out of my reach. "First, your name," he said, his eyes twinkling with playfulness.

"Julianna Capulet," I said.

He spoke my first name, drawing out the ahhh in Julianna like a moan. It caused a strange sensation in my lower belly.

"And yours?" I managed to squeak out.

"Roman. Roman...Lettiere."

Roman. I repeated the name in my head, trying to taste it on my tongue but daring not to speak it, like perhaps saying his name would somehow curse me, binding my soul to this beautiful devil forever.

"I suppose I owe you your phone back." With his eyes still on mine, he held his hand in front of him and opened his fingers. My phone was sitting in his palm like a treat. I was a dog being coaxed to come closer. *I will not be intimidated*, I lectured myself. *He's just a man.*

No, not a man. A god and a devil in one.

As I closed my fingers around the phone, I brushed his palm with my fingertips. An electrical current leaped from his skin, traveling up my arm. Before I could yank my hand away, his other hand closed over mine, trapping me in his large, warm hands.

"Julianna?" The way he said my name sounded like a caress. I sucked in a breath as a strange wave of heat ran through my body, radiating from the place where he touched me. "A few of us are having a few drinks tonight at Club Luxe at ten o'clock. You should stop by."

I felt like I was floating on a sea of his voice and his touch. I think I gave him a shaky, uncommitted nod/shake of my head.

"Words, Julianna. I need words."

I managed to snap partially out of my reverie. It was his touch! How could anyone concentrate with this man's hands on them? "Maybe." It was all I could promise. I wasn't sure if I could handle being so affected like this.

"If you don't show up, I'll be incredibly disappointed. I'll have to come get you," he said, in a calm yet firm tone.

What? a part of my brain screamed at me. His casual dominance was unnerving. Usually, I was put off by such cocky, domineering alpha-hole men. He made it seem...sexy. He did it in a way that made me feel...wanted. Not owned.

"What do you say, Jules?"

Jules. He had nicknamed me. I loved it.

No, how dare he presume to nickname me. I should be offended.

"Fine," I said, so he would let me leave. I wouldn't go. Going to a club alone, in a sea of faces, to meet him? He'd probably forget about me the second I walked out of his sight. His casual threat was empty anyway. He had no idea where I lived. Because of my job, my address was unlisted.

"'Fine' what?" he asked, still not letting go of me.

This man was sharp. I doubted anyone ever pulled the wool over his eyes.

"Fine, I'll come."

He grinned, revealing a set of perfect white teeth. I realized too late that what I'd said had been taken the wrong way. "Oh," he said with a chuckle, "I have no doubt you will."

A hot flush went through me. Liquid heat pooled between my legs, making me tense. This wasn't a heart attack. This was early menopause. Can a woman get menopause in her twenties?

He bent over, his eyes still drilling into mine, to brush his full lips across each one of my knuckles. That single touch was enough to elicit a soft moan from me. I promptly cut it off by snapping my mouth together. *Jesus Christ. A heart attack* and *menopause.*

I snatched my hand holding my phone from his. "Well. Bye, then." I spun and walked off as fast as I could without toppling over in my heels. Well, that was...odd. Glad that was over. I felt his gaze burning into my back.

ROMAN

"Roman Giovanni Tyrell, is that you?" a familiar female voice called out. Low and soothing with the tremor of age, it was like the wrap of a blanket on a cold night.

"Hey, Nonna," I called back as I opened the back door of her low brick two-bedroom cottage out in the eastern suburbs of Verona. Nonna had lived here for as long as I could remember and my best friend, Mercutio, had practically grown up here.

I was older than Merc, just. By only six months. He always seemed to act the older brother to me. He and I had often been mistaken for brothers; we had the same thick dark hair and olive skin. That's where the similarities ended. Merc was almost as tall as me, over six feet, but his frame was lean muscles like a basketball player where I had grown thick like a rugby player. Despite my somewhat crazy lifestyle in Europe, I'd found a constant in boxing and lifting weights.

Nonna Sheree was Mercutio's grandmother, a pint-sized woman with a soft smile and fierce temper when we boys had disobeyed her, stealing bites of cherry pie while it was cooling on the window sill or using up too much water spraying each other (and the house through open windows) with water from the hose in the sticky depths of summer.

She appeared at the kitchen entrance, wiping her hands on a dish towel tucked into her apron. She'd aged in the last eight years, her hair almost completely white, wrinkles softening her paper skin. But her eyes, a dark earthy color, just like Mercutio's, were alive and sparkling with youth. "You boys never use the front door. You know it's a bigger doorway."

"The front door is for guests," called Merc from behind me. "We're family."

I eased my head and shoulders through the low doorway. I was still dressed in the suit I had worn to the funeral sans jacket and tie. My top two buttons were open. "This isn't a doorway," I muttered. "It's a cat flap."

Nonna made a tsking noise and shook her head, a soft smile on her wizened face. "I swear, one of these days you're going to get stuck in the frame."

I stepped right into her kitchen, a warm glow coming from the oven, the smell of roasting chicken and garlic already permeating the rooms of the house. "Damn that smells good." I leaned down and gave her a hug, my arms wrapping all the way around her tiny frame. "You've shrunk, Nonna," I teased gently.

"It's *you* that has gotten taller and wider," she said with a soft swat to my arm with her dishcloth. "Holy Mother of Mary, look at you."

"Yeah," added Merc. "Now he's an even bigger pain in the ass."

"Language, Mercutio," said Nonna.

"Sorry."

Nonna gave me another proud look-over. "You were a boy when you left. You've grown into such a handsome man now." She reached up and pinched both my cheeks.

"Nonna," I complained, feeling my cheeks flush. Only she could get away with pinching me like I was still eight.

She patted my cheek. "It's good to see you again." My frosty heart felt like it warmed for the first time in eight years. She turned back to the oven. "Dinner's almost ready, so go on into the dining room and sit down. Mercutio, can you help bring this roast out?"

"On it," he said, slipping his hands into a pair of pastel floral mitts.

Within minutes we were sitting around Nonna's round wooden table. I groaned with pleasure as the taste of rosemary roasted chicken and garlic potatoes exploded in my mouth. "I haven't eaten this good..." I mused between mouthfuls of food, "since I left, Nonna."

"I don't believe that for a second, Roman," said Nonna, but her smile said she was pleased. "Europe has great food. Tell us all about it."

I shrugged. "Europe was..." as far away from Verona as I could get. "Good."

Merc snorted. "Yeah, I heard it was *good*."

I shot him a *shut the fuck up* look. "How have you been, Nonna?" I asked, quickly changing the subject from me.

I ate and listened as she talked about the studies that Mercutio had completed, pride in her voice. Then about her garden, the new varieties of tomatoes and herbs she was growing. All the while my mind kept going back to the woman from the graveyard.

Julianna Capulet. The most stunning creature I'd ever seen.

Perhaps if I had just seen her, if I'd not spoken to her, I might have had enough grace to leave her alone. The second we'd touched, it sealed her fate. Electricity had lashed up my arm. I didn't want her to let go. Ever. I had grabbed her hand with my other, trapping her tiny soft fingers between my palms, my hands doing to hers what I wanted to do to her body. To cover her completely. To own her, possess her. Dominate her.

I wanted her.

I wanted her with a force that surprised me. That was almost painful.

I would have her.

She had been shocked by it too, her beautiful eyes widening and her breath hitching. Her nipples hardened through her dress. Good to see she was as affected by me as I was by her. I had to use all my willpower not to bend over and take those tiny buds into my mouth through the material. Or rip that damn dress off right there. Instead, I was a gentleman. No use scaring her off on our first meeting. I brushed my lips on her knuckles in a kiss, letting myself taste her skin, sweet as honey. She had let out a soft moan. That one little noise had me so hard that it hurt. I vowed then and there, I'd coax more of those noises from her before this day was over.

"Roman?"

I snapped out of my head, shifting in my seat to adjust my semi-erection under the table. Had someone asked me something? I hadn't heard a single word in... I glanced between Merc and Nonna. "Yeah?"

Nonna lifted a bowl. "More potatoes?"

Twenty minutes later, Nonna and Mercutio had put aside their plates while I was helping myself to a third serving.

Nonna watched me with an affectionate smile on her face as I tore into a chicken leg with my teeth. "I forgot how much food you can put away."

"That's because he's a growing boy." Merc punched my arm. "Still."

I swatted back at him, which instigated a mini punching war, like when we were kids. Except now our punches hurt a damn sight more. And threatened to knock over the table.

"Boys," said Nonna with a warning tone.

"He started it," Merc and I both said together, fingers pointed at the other.

Nonna rolled her eyes but there was a smile on her face. "It's like you never left," she said quietly, her eyes brimming with tears.

Guilt flooded my belly. I stared down at my plate, picking at the remains of the chicken leg I had only half-devoured. Suddenly I wasn't hungry anymore.

I had been eighteen when I left Verona. It felt like a lifetime ago. And yet, it felt like yesterday. On the plane from Verona to London I'd shed hidden tears into my airline-provided blanket for Nonna and Merc. I'd missed them immediately, feeling like two pieces of me had been torn from my soul. They had been the last tears I'd shed.

After the plates were cleared away, Nonna brought out hot drinks and ginger snap cookies.

"I have gifts for you," I announced.

"Gifts?" Nonna asked.

"From Europe." I riffled through my brown aged-leather duffel sitting on the empty chair beside me, the only luggage I had brought with me. I found Merc's present, gift-wrapped by the store in matte gold paper and a matching bow, and threw it at him. He caught it and stared at the square box. "If this is an engagement ring, I will hit you."

I rolled my eyes. "Just open it, fool."

I found Nonna's present, a larger box, also gift-wrapped to perfection in silver paper with a black ribbon. I walked around the table to hand it to her, placing it in her hands with a sheepish grin.

"Roman, what have you done?" she said, surprise in her tone.

"Open it."

There was a moment where the only sound was the tearing of paper. My stomach flipped as I waited for their reactions.

Nonna set the black suede box on the table beside her cup of tea before opening it. "Good lord." She sank back into her chair with her hand over her heart. "Roman, it's beautiful!" She stared at the necklace inside, a circle of metal links meant to be worn around the base of the neck. She brushed the stones set into the metal with a shaking finger. "Look at it sparkling. Roman, don't tell me it's real."

Merc hid a snort with a cough.

I hid a smile. "I won't, then."

It *was* real. Pavé diamonds set in pink gold. But it wasn't about the damn diamonds. I knew it would go with her favorite earrings, a pair she'd owned forever that Pablo, her deceased husband, gave her for their first wedding anniversary.

"Let me help you put it on."

She held aside her white hair, soft like baby-fluff and cut short into a classic bob, as I secured the necklace around her neck.

"Oh," she stammered. "It will go perfectly with those earrings from Pablo."

I grinned. "What a great idea, Nonna."

"Let me go look at them in my bedroom mirror properly." She hurried out of the room.

Merc pulled his gold Rolex out of his demolition site of cardboard and paper. He raised an eyebrow at me, considerably less impressed than Nonna. "What the fuck am I going to do with a fancy gold watch?"

"You don't like it?"

"Sure, it's nice. But I won't get two steps out of this house without someone trying to mug me for it."

"Then pawn it, I don't give a shit."

He set the watch down and frowned. "You didn't have to buy us anything."

I felt pricks of anger across my skin. I fisted my arms over my chest. "I haven't seen you in eight fucking years and I wanted to give you something."

"You didn't have to spend my annual salary on it," Merc said quietly.

"I have money," I said gruffly as if it were a curse. It was a curse. A shackle. I'd been receiving a generous monthly allowance from the man who had fathered me since I was sixteen. I hated every penny although I spent it all. "You two are the only two people I care to spend it on, alright? So shut the fuck up and say 'thanks', you ungrateful ass."

Merc snorted but his demeanour softened. He slipped his new watch on his wrist before giving me a lopsided grin. "Thanks, man."

I grunted back in reply. He knew it meant that I accepted his apology.

I sank back into my chair, wrapping my hands around my mug full of coffee, black like my heart. It was the same mug that Nonna always gave me when I came over. White enamel, large handle, chipped from use, always filled with hot drinks lovingly prepared for me over the years. Hot chocolate when I was a kid, coffee as I got older.

I looked around the cottage. The wallpaper of vintage white tea roses was even more faded than last time. It looked like a small roof leak had stained part of the ceiling. Some of the knobs on the cupboards had been replaced, making them all mismatched. The mantelpiece was filled with framed photos, some with me in them, and several bookshelves housed books with well-worn spines. The couch was covered with soft pastel throws to cover where they'd been worn thin, but they were comfortable and just large enough to hold the three of us. This place might not look like much, but it shone from my fond memories.

It was a stark contrast to my Tyrell family home, only a few blocks from here, a mansion of cold marble and white walls, stuffed with obnoxious, uncomfortable furniture. A home that I refused to visit. A home that I'd be happy never to step inside again.

I glanced over to Merc as he fiddled with his watch. I wondered if he ever knew that I had been insanely jealous of him growing up. This place was more of a home for me than mine was. These two right here were more family than I'd ever had after my mother died.

I glanced over to Nonna's bedroom where I could hear her calls of appreciation as she admired the necklace in the mirror. There was something I needed to ask Merc before she came back in the room.

I leaned over to him. "Have you heard from your dad?" I said in a low voice.

Merc's father, Tito "Goldfish" Brevio, had been an accountant who had worked part-time for my father. That's how Merc and I knew each other as kids. Over a decade ago Tito was forced to testify against my family. He famously changed his statement in court and screwed up the prosecutor's case against my father at the time. Then he disappeared, leaving Nonna to look after thirteen-year-old Merc at the time. Nonna had never forgiven Tito for abandoning Merc.

That's how he earned the nickname Goldfish, because of his eight-second memory stunt in court. Some even speculated that it had all been planned by my father. Double jeopardy and all. After the Goldfish case was thrown out, my father couldn't be tried for those crimes again. It was a nice big fuck you to the legal system which he'd evaded even to this day.

As far as Nonna was concerned, Tito was dead. His name was not to be uttered or spoken in this house. At least, not in front of her.

Merc glanced away. "You know I can't tell you that."

I stiffened. Merc used to tell me everything.

That was before you left him eight years ago.

"Come on, man," I said softly, nudging his elbow. "It's me."

Merc let out a sigh and glanced at Nonna's bedroom door before leaning in. "He's around. Doing okay. Still underground."

"He hasn't surfaced yet? It's way past the statute of limitations for him. The feds can't charge him with anything now."

"Yeah, but…" Merc paused and a look of guilt crept into his eyes as he glanced at me, then looked away.

"What? Spit it out."

Merc shrugged. "I think…I think he's still scared of your father. What he might do if…"

I swallowed. My father was not a man to be crossed. "Do you think he'll ever come home, then?" It's what Mercutio had been dreaming of since he was thirteen, the only thing he ever asked for on every birthday and every Christmas.

"One day, he'll come home," Merc said quietly. "One day."

JULIANNA

He had such damn deep-set eyes. Too dark. Annoyingly intense. The way he had looked at me. Like I was prey. His gaze rolling so obviously over my body, not even bothering to hide that he was imagining doing all sorts of wicked, unwanted things. My body flushed. Completely unwanted things.

And those lips. The most beautiful wide, thickest lips I had ever seen wasted on a man. I bet they'd feel terrible against mine. I bet he'd be a bad kisser. Totally unskilled. Not that I was imagining him kissing me.

And that voice. So rough and indecent. The way he had demanded my name. Demanded that I meet him again tonight. So shameless. What kind of woman did he think I was? If I had any sense I'd go to the club tonight just to tell him off for being so…so…presumptuous.

"Julianna, you okay, honey?"

I glanced up from my dinner plate of fettuccine marinara to my father's concerned face, his thick, bushy salt-and-pepper brows furrowed over familiar whiskey-colored eyes. Those were my eyes. I looked like my mother—same curvy build, same long hair that couldn't decide if it was honey or wheat, same full bottom lip—but I had his eyes. Once upon a time, when my mother's love painted color on his cheeks and injected his smile with warmth, he would have been handsome. Since she died, the lines had deepened into a permanent frown and a set of purple shadows remained under his eyes.

I forced a smile. "I'm fine."

His frown didn't smooth out. "You sure? Because I've been talking to you for a few minutes now and you've just been staring at your dinner."

I pushed my plate away. "I'm not hungry."

"Is it…because of today?" he said, a little quieter.

My heart tugged. I may have lost my mother, but my father lost the love of his life. Despite how busy my father was, I knew he would have remembered Mama's birthday today. He never forgot things like that when she'd been alive. Despite being so furious with him earlier, I knew that part of the reason he buried himself in work was to keep from remembering her and hurting even more.

I reached out across our small wooden dining table to grab his hand. "A little. Are you okay?"

"Fine," he said.

"I miss her," I admitted.

His fingers squeezed mine. He looked like he was about to say something when his phone on the tabletop by his elbow began to ring. He pulled back his hand and answered it. "Hello?" *Sorry, it's work*, he mouthed at me. Of course, it was. His face pulled into a frown. "What? Where?"

I sighed and stabbed at a piece of pasta. I already knew that our family dinner was going to get cut short.

When my father hung up, he was already pushing his chair out. "Sorry, honey. They need me to manage some stuff at work."

I dropped the napkin from my lips. "Do you need me to—"

"No," he said a little too abruptly. "It's fine."

"It's not a homicide?"

He paused. It was. Bastard. "I already have Pierce and Ramirez on it."

I crossed my arms as the familiar argument began to swirl heat around under my skin. "You're never going to give me a chance to prove myself, are you?"

"When you're ready."

"Ready?" I yelled. "I've been a detective for over six months and you haven't let me handle a single case."

"Yes, I have."

"Not any *real* cases. I'm stuck going through paperwork and old cold cases." I hovered around him as he gathered his things. "I scored the highest on my detective's exam in the whole damn state."

"I know. But...you shouldn't be working today."

"Then by the same argument, neither should you."

He let out a sigh as he grabbed his jacket from the hook near my front door. "Julianna, I don't want to argue about this now. It's an election year and the mayor is putting the pressure on me to get the streets cleaned up."

"So, it's another gang-related homicide."

"I can't discuss the case."

I slammed my palm on my front door, preventing him from leaving. "You hate that I'm a detective."

His features turned sour. "You're my only daughter. You should have gone to law school. Your mother, God rest her soul, would hate the idea of you putting yourself in the firing line of killers and rapists. She'd be turning over in her—"

"*You* hate the idea. Mama would have been proud that I followed in your footsteps." It was a shitty thing, using my dead mother as a point of argument between us. Neither of us could ever seem to just let her rest.

"You're damn right *I* hate the idea!" He took a deep breath and let it out, his face softening. "There are some bad, *bad* people out there in the world, Julu." I couldn't say my name properly when I was learning how to speak. I could only say Julu. My parents thought it was adorable. The nickname stuck even as I grew up. "If anything ever happened to you…"

I would not be swayed by his attempt at a guilt trip. After my mother died, my father became so protective it was stifling. He yelled and spat and threatened when I announced I was moving out after I graduated high school. Again when I announced I was joining the police academy. There was nothing he could do because at eighteen I was legally an adult. Even now at the age of twenty-five, he hated that he couldn't wrap me in cotton. He still wanted to keep me caged and "safe".

"Why do you think I became a detective? To put those bad people away. I'm trained to do just that."

"Honey—"

"Put me on the next major homicide case or I'll transfer to another city. No, I'll transfer to another state."

He flinched, a growing panic clear in his eyes. *I* was the one card that I could play. "You wouldn't."

I lifted my chin. "I won't have my career stifled because I'm your daughter and you want to protect me." There. I said it.

"Julu, you're my *only* daughter." The hitch in his tone sent a stab of guilt through me. "You're the only one I have left."

Was I being too hard on him? Was I being unreasonable? My resolve began to soften. After my mother died my father had dove into his work and never resurfaced. His efforts had earned him promotion after promotion until he was promoted to the top position in the city as Verona's chief of police. But it meant that his friendships had suffered. He had no family left, except me. He hadn't even dated again as far as I was aware. If I left Verona…

I shoved this thought away. I could not let him guilt me into giving up my dream. I wasn't a scared little girl. I was an adult with a gun and a badge.

I stepped in front of the door, blocking his way out. "Dad, I'm not a child anymore. I can protect myself. Let me work real cases."

"You haven't seen the horrors I have," he said in a reverent whisper I knew was meant to scare me. "You haven't seen how dark the human psyche can get, how twisted…"

"I can take it."

"Once you see those things, you can't unsee them." He shook his head. "It's my job as a father to protect you." He didn't look like he was going to budge.

Neither was I. I straightened to my full height and looked him right in the eyes. "You can either let me work as a homicide detective here, under your command, under your…protection," I chose my words carefully, "or you can watch me do it from another state."

A look of surprise flashed across his face. Then his features softened. "You're as stubborn as she was," he said, a hint of affection in his tone. He sighed. "Fine. The next major case is yours."

Finally. I couldn't stop the grin from bursting across my face. I lunged for him and wrapped my arms around him in a hug. "Thanks, Dad."

He kissed my forehead. "Stay safe, baby girl." Then he left.

I let out a huge breath and leaned against the inside of my front door. I did it. I had won that argument. I would get my chance to work on a real case. So why did I suddenly feel so anxious? *This is your chance to prove yourself, Julianna. Don't blow it.*

I ate the rest of my dinner alone, staring at my phone, the clock on my wall ticking loudly into the room. I lived alone in a rented apartment on the top floor of a five-story building in Verona's east side inner city. It was a cozy apartment, old wooden floors that creaked, heating that was temperamental in winter and the occasional drunken row heard from the streets below. But it was mine.

I had filled it with a mix of decent second-hand furniture, like my comfy two-piece chocolate leather couch, and cheap basics, a light wooden dining room set and DIY-shelves.

My father hated that I lived in the inner city; he still lived in our old house in an outer suburb, a safe, respectable and utterly boring neighborhood. I understood why; the towering chaos of buildings bathing the city in shadows, the dirty, well-worn streets jammed full of smells, the unknown hidden in the dark corners. Perhaps, it was all these things. But I saw the raw uncut gem underneath.

I felt a thrill every time I walked the streets, each corner beckoning with possibilities or something new to be discovered. I felt the city humming away around me, even at night. Here, I felt a part of something. The inner city was Verona's beating heart, as tough and black as it was. It was gritty and alive and...*real*. And I loved it.

My phone dinged as I chewed on my pasta. I swiped it open with my pinkie.

Unknown: Remember. 10pm. Club Luxe.

It was sent from a private number. No signature. Who...?

Roman. It was from Roman. A little thrill shot up my spine like a tiny electrocution. He hadn't just forgotten about me. He still wanted me to meet him. The nerve.

How did he get my number? A memory of him picking up my phone at the graveyard flashed through my mind. He'd held on to it for a long time. At the time, I had been so distracted I hadn't thought anything of it. He must have texted himself my number or something. I should feel indignant. I *did* feel indignant.

I glanced up at the clock. Twenty past nine. If I dressed now I could be there on time. Club Luxe was only twenty minutes away in the trendy downtown area. In less than an hour I could be seeing him again. My body seemed to vibrate awake at the thought.

No. I wouldn't go. He obviously wanted certain *things* from me and… and… giving in to these feelings, however *nice* they might be, were for other women. Not me. I had a reputation to uphold. A career to focus on. Paperwork to do.

I placed my phone face down on the table so I couldn't stare at the screen and returned to my food. My appetite was gone. My eyes kept being drawn to the phone, tiny butterflies fluttering around my stomach.

I still hadn't replied to Roman's text. One, I wasn't sure I had the strength to tell him I wasn't coming. And two, I thought it better not to reply rather than get dragged into a debate I was scared I'd end up giving in to.

I pushed my half-finished dinner away and grabbed my phone. My finger hovered over the message reply button.

Dammit. I wasn't replying, remember?

I opened my recent calls. The only two contacts that came up were my father and Luiz Espinoza, the partner I'd been assigned to when I made homicide. I hit call on Espinoza's name before I could change my mind. I chewed my lip as I listened to the ring tone. I needed a distraction. Something to take my mind off intense eyes and electric touches.

He picked up after three rings. "Espinoza," he yelled into the phone, muffled thudding and thrashing of an electric guitar in the background.

"It's me," I said. "Where are you?"

"Yo, Capi," he said, using his nickname for me. "I'm at Dixie's. The No Name Band is playing tonight."

I frowned. "Why don't they have a name?"

"What? No, the band's name is the 'No Name Band'."

"Oh, right. What do they sing?"

There was a small pause. "You didn't call me to talk about my awesome taste in music. What's up?"

"Has there, um, been any calls?"

"From who?"

"Work."

He snorted. "It's a Saturday night, Capi. It's our day off. Go have some *fun*," he emphasized the word over the music in the background. "I'll see you Monday."

Fun. Right. I know what fun is.

I hung up and saw that another message had come through. My heart fluttered. Another one from Roman?

It wasn't. It was from Christian.

Christian: I tried to call you. What are you up to tonight?

Christian Price was the son of Senator Price, my father's childhood friend. Christian and I would sometimes see each other when my father dragged me to dinners at the senator's mansion. If Christian was texting, he must be home from Princeton where he was finishing a bachelor of business or politics or something. My father didn't hide that he encouraged Christian and me getting together.

Me: Sorry, I have plans tonight.

I felt a little bad for my lie. It was kinder than telling him the truth. I just didn't want to date him.

Christian: Another time then.

. . .

It wasn't that I didn't like Christian, just that I never felt 100% comfortable around him. Our silences felt stilted. Our conversations were just...bland. I mean, what did a homicide detective have to say to the silver-spooned son of a senator? I didn't feel any chemistry. That zing. The electricity and fireworks that my mother promised I would feel when I'd found the right one.

Like you did with Roman. I shoved that thought away.

Almost like he knew I was thinking of him, my phone dinged with another text message.

Roman: Don't make me come get you.

I chewed on my lip and my eyes went involuntarily to my front door as if he might come barreling through at any second. I shivered at the thought.

My front door remained silent.

I shook my head. Silly. He was bluffing. He didn't know where I lived. How could he possibly find out?

I washed the dishes, dried them and put them away. All the while Roman's face kept intruding into my mind. I threw the dish towel aside and folded my arms as I leaned against the counter. The clock read twenty minutes to ten...

Maybe there was something good on TV?

It was still twenty damn minutes to ten.

Dammit, I couldn't sit around staring at the clock. I walked out of my apartment, leaving the door unlocked behind me. I was about to knock on the door opposite when it swung open.

Nora, my sixty-something-year-old neighbor, was dressed in a powder blue skirt suit trimmed with black and shiny black pumps a la Jackie Kennedy. It looked stunning against her dark chocolate skin. Her light gray hair was coiffed into a French bun. She had a dash of deep red lipstick across her thick lips.

"Wow, Nora, you look great!" I said.

She beamed at me. "Thank you, honey. Can't chat now. I'm late. Ta-ta," she called back at me as she strode down the hall to the elevator.

Damn. Even senior citizens had more of a life than I did.

I slunk back into my apartment, shutting the door behind me. What now? I could go over cold case files from work like I did most nights. For some reason, this didn't appeal to me right now. I sighed. I was officially the lamest single twenty-five-year-old in all of Verona, home alone on her Saturday night off.

The silence of my apartment seemed so stark and empty, the echoing of my clock reminding me that every second was getting closer to ten p.m. and my chance to see Roman again was slipping away.

My phone dinged again.

Roman: Don't break my heart, Jules...

My chest felt funny again. I stared at my phone. Perhaps, it wouldn't hurt to meet him for a few minutes. Five. Ten at most. Just to let him know in person that us spending time together was a bad idea. I had a career to focus on. It seemed so rude to reject him over a text message.

A shiver ran down my spine at the thought of seeing Roman again. These strange feelings... the odd way my body reacted... I shouldn't go.

Screw it. It wasn't like I had anything better to do.

I dropped my phone on the table as I half-strode, half-ran into my bedroom to get ready.

ROMAN

Three text messages and still no response from Julianna.

I frowned at my silent phone that I was threatening to break by gripping onto it too hard. The connection we had at the graveyard was unmistakable. Sparks, fireworks and all that clichéd bullshit. It had caught me off guard. I hadn't been as smooth as I usually was. I knew she'd felt it too by the way her breath hitched and her nipples hardened through her cotton dress. How could she feel it too and *not* come to meet me? Didn't she feel this *pull*?

I fantasized about storming over to her apartment, breaking open her door and carrying her out of there over my damn shoulder. My cock stirred. On second thought, maybe I'd carry her to her bedroom. We were going to end up there anyway. At least that was the plan. I already had her address.

Most people didn't realize that their phones were like GPS trackers. All I needed was her phone number and my connections at the phone company. Sometimes it helped to be a Tyrell.

I was standing with a group of people that I knew from high school in a roped off VIP section of Club Luxe. I haven't seen these guys in almost eight years. I barely noticed them, forcing small talk and fielding uninspired questions about Europe. I was being a rude prick but I couldn't seem to snap myself out of it. Usually, I was so good at this small talk shit.

Ten Twenty-three p.m. and she hadn't fucking shown up.

I had pegged her to show up. On time. Women usually did. So why the fuck hadn't she? Why the hell did I give so much of a shit?

I glared around the club, my eyes seeking her out, scanning each curve and honey shade of long hair for her. There was something about her...

Something...different.

It was like every single cell and fiber of her had been calibrated to strike at every single one of mine, making them all vibrate awake all at once. Fuck, every time I thought about how soft the skin on her neck looked or how silky her hair might feel I got hard.

And she was making me act...different.

I wasn't even interested in the scantily clad girls pawing at my shirt, rubbing their breasts against my arm, tugging at my collar. I swatted them aside like they were flies. They weren't *her*. I wanted her. I wanted her like I'd never wanted a woman before.

I would have her.

I drank down the rest of my scotch and slammed down my glass onto a side table. I stabbed out another text message to her and hit send.

Me: I'm coming to get you.

JULIANNA

I was going to hunt down the asshole who invented high heels and kill him. Yes, it was definitely a *him*. Because no woman in her right mind would have created such torture instruments and called them fashion. I'd beat him senseless with these platform soles, then stab him to death with the spiky heels of his own demonic creations.

Death by Manolos.

I wondered if that would be considered good or bad publicity?

I had made the mistake of walking to Club Luxe. It was only a twenty-minute walk from where I lived, but I wasn't used to walking in these things. My feet were already killing me.

I didn't know what had been going through my mind when I chose this outfit. The dress was a slim-fitting black bandage dress with lace detailing that fell to mid-thigh. Nora had bought me this dress and these shoes a few years ago in the hopes that I might actually have a hot date to wear them on. Out of everything I owned I thought it would be the most appropriate thing to wear to a club, seeing as they had a dress code. It had *nothing* to do with how Roman might react when he saw me again.

I stepped into the main room of Club Luxe and froze. It was set inside a refurbished old warehouse, the colored lights ricocheting off the exposed pipes along the open ceiling. The ultramodern décor was all chrome and black lines. The music, a funky house beat with husky vocals in French, thumped through my body like a second heartbeat. Bodies wriggled like a blurry sexual mass on a small dance floor. There were booths and tables along the edges, beautiful people draped across the couches with cocktail glasses in hand, people who looked like they were comfortable here, people having fun.

I didn't belong here. What a dumb idea to come. Someone bumped me from behind and made a rude noise. I realized I was standing there like an idiot in the entranceway.

"Sorry," I muttered to no one in particular, the offended party having already disappeared into the throng. I lunged for the closest bar that ran most of the way along the right side and clutched at the onyx countertop as if it'd stop me from falling over. What now?

Well, I'd find Roman, tell him I couldn't see him again and leave.

I searched the crowd for him, trying not to catch anyone's eye or draw attention to myself. Pretty hard in a dress that felt like it kept riding up my thighs like a horny teenager's hand. It wasn't as skimpy as the daring barely-covering-the-ass uniform in here but it was still shorter than I usually wore my skirts.

Where was he? I couldn't see him from here.

Okay. One walk around. If he wasn't here, I was leaving.

I turned around with my back to the bar and lifted my chin, preparing myself to push my way through the club. I didn't move. There he was, standing across the room in a loose circle of guys and girls. I couldn't tell you what they looked like. The only thing that was in focus was him.

He was more beautiful than I remembered. A dark god among mortals. He looked like a fighter out of his suit, a boxer or

MMA fighter, his fitted black t-shirt showing off his sculpted torso. His hips, encased in fitted designer jeans, swayed lightly to the music. I bet he was as hard as granite underneath those clothes. I bet every muscle was defined. Not that I cared anything about *that*.

That same ache I felt earlier today flared deep in my lower belly, this time harder and stronger. Dear God. I wanted him. I wanted him in a way I'd never wanted anyone before. The sudden realization made me shiver.

Go up to him. Talk to him. He's waiting for you.

I didn't move. What if he thought I was a desperate slut for coming here? What if I *was* a desperate slut for coming here? This wasn't me. I wasn't a girl who slept with strangers. I never chased after guys; I was never interested. Was this my repressed sexuality all coming out now with a bang, like Nora always threatened?

The others in his group all laughed at something, catching my attention. He smiled curtly and nodded. The laughter died down quickly as if they'd quashed it because he didn't approve of the joke. I could see them all turned towards him, facing him, leaning in, the other women around him eyeing him up. He barely noticed them. He had a slight frown on his face. He looked agitated or bored like he didn't want to be here. *You and me both.* Unlike me, he looked like he belonged.

I watched him search the club like a sniper studying his area. Two girls gyrated in front of him, smiles only for him, trying to catch his attention. He ignored them and continued to scan the crowd. I could taste their disappointment from here.

He was exactly the kind of man my mother would warn me about if she were alive. Dominant without trying, coiled power in his thick muscles. It wasn't just about his intimidating frame. There was an inherent leadership in the way he stood, self-assuredness and confidence, which made women want him and men want to be him. He was a born leader. People followed him without ever knowing why.

He'd be the best worst idea. I'd let him get close to me, I'd fall for him and he'd break my heart. Damn if it wouldn't be one hell of a ride down. I let out the breath I'd been holding. I was way out of my depth. I had to leave now before he spotted me.

He pulled out his phone and I watched, mesmerized as he typed out a text. My phone in my bag buzzed. Holy shit. That text was for me. I had to go. Now!

Before I could move, he looked up. Our gazes fused together and a thrill rushed down my body. My heart jumped up into my throat and started beating so loudly that the music dulled. Too late to leave now. He'd seen me. Just say hello then leave.

Or go home with him and never leave.

Shit. He was coming over here.

ROMAN

There she was.

Julianna. Leaning against the bar on the other side of the room. For a moment, I wondered if I had dreamed her out of thin air.

Sweet mother of God, she looked incredible. The sight of her hit me like a fist in my gut. The music seemed to go funny in my ears. The body that her outfit earlier only hinted at was now on display: taut legs in a black dress that clung to her curves and fell several inches above her knee. Her hair was loose and fell in soft waves over her shoulders, down the sides of her breasts.

She was stunning. More stunning than I'd imagined her, and trust me, I'd imagined her in all sorts of ways all evening. I stepped out of the VIP section, ignoring my friends calling out for me. I pushed my way through the crowd. It seemed like every motherfucker wanted to get between her and me.

She broke eye contact with me and turned to the guy who had sidled up to her, trying to speak to her. My blood simmered. Now he was touching her, playing with the ends of her hair close to her breasts. Too fucking close to her breasts. He grabbed her wrist, yanking her closer to him. Instant fury like a torrent of fire rose in me. Nobody fucking touched her. Nobody hurt her. She was *mine*.

"Get your fucking hands off her," I yelled, rage booming though my voice, startling the club-goers around me, not that I gave a shit. I shoved the people in my way aside. I would kill the fucking son of a bitch who dared lay a hand on her.

Julianna twisted her arm, rolling it aside so that the asshole was forced to let go. She stabbed her heel into his toe causing him to hop before he tilted off balance. She shoved him down over the bar, pinning him by twisting his arm around his back. He let out a yelp.

Holy. Shit.

I skidded to a halt beside them, my anger turning to red-hot lust. I had never seen a woman handle herself like that before. I could do nothing but stare open-mouthed and mute at this powerful, gorgeous creature, respect building in my gut.

"Don't you dare touch me again, asshole," she said to him, her voice hard and fierce. The sound of her cursing made my dick harden.

Julianna looked up to me as the guy she had in an armlock made whining noises against the bar. She gave me a smile like nothing was the matter. Unbelievable.

"Oh. Hi," she said, almost shyly. "Again."

I gave her my best charming grin. "I was just coming over to save you..."

She raised an eyebrow. That tiny movement was a challenge. "Why?" she said sweetly. She applied the slightest pressure to the unfortunate guy's wrist and he let out a low pained cry. She jutted her chin out and a defiance flared in her feline eyes. "Because I'm a *girl* and all I need is a big strong man to come save me?"

"No, because you're a human being. I don't like it when I see other human beings being treated without respect. Not when I can do something about it."

She shifted, seemingly surprised by my honest comment, embarrassed even. "Well...I don't need saving."

"I can see that." I indicated her unfortunate victim. I spotted a bouncer heading towards us. I held my hand up to signal to him that I had it under control. He nodded and kept his distance. The bouncer was a low-level street thug who'd been trying to climb my family's ranks for years. Part of the reason why I could score the VIP treatment here at the last minute.

Julianna spotted this exchange. "Do you own this place or something?" she asked.

I shrugged. "I know some of the guys who work here." Here and pretty much every hot spot of Verona. I didn't want to explain to her how I knew them. Tonight, I wasn't Roman Tyrell. Tonight, I was just a guy and she was a girl...

"Can you let go of me now?" the man whose face was squashed up against the bar interrupted in a whining tone.

I shot Julianna a grin and leaned in close to him. "Tell the lady, you're sorry and *maybe* she'll let you go."

The man's eyes widened when he saw me, recognition flaring in his eyes. "Y-y-you."

That's right, stupid fucker. You just pissed off a Tyrell. "Tell her you're sorry," I repeated.

"I'm sorry," he cried out.

I stared up at Julianna and was struck again by how stunning she was. She raised an eyebrow at me as if she knew what I was thinking. I gave her one of my trademark half-smirks. "Are you satisfied with his apology, milady?"

"Only if you *don't* try and touch up a girl without her permission again," she said to him.

The idiot was silent.

I leaned in closer and growled. "When the lady speaks to you, you answer her."

He let out a whine. "Okay, okay. I'll never do it again."

Julianna applied some more pressure to the guy's arm and he

let out a louder cry. She was staring at me, a half angry, half lustful look in her dark eyes. "Tell Roman," she said, her voice coming out low and heated, "that I don't need him to fight my battles for me."

"What?" the guy cried.

"Tell Julianna," I said, matching her stare, "that she should learn that it's okay for a man to help her. It doesn't make her weak."

"Tell Roman, that he's an arrogant ass who has no idea what it's like to be a woman in a man's world."

"Tell Julianna, that I can't tell if she wants to fight me or fuck me tonight."

Julianna's red lips pulled up into a smirk. "Why can't it be both?"

Jesus, fuck. I felt my cock surge with blood and I swallowed back a groan. I wasn't finished. "Tell Julianna that she's the most stunning creature I have ever seen."

"What the fuck?" the guy stuttered against the bar.

"Ever?" Julianna asked, an amused eyebrow raised.

"Ever." And I fucking meant it. She was captivating. Intoxicating. A lioness among sheep. This wasn't a woman who'd fall at my feet and gaze adoringly up at me. She'd demand to stand beside me. She'd demand to be pleased. She'd deserve to be pleased.

I had to have her. Here. Now. Anywhere. I'd take her here on the fucking bar if she'd let me.

I nodded down at the single annoying thing standing between her and me; the asshole she'd thoroughly put in his place. "Maybe you should let him go. Before you break something. We both know it's really me you want to get your hands on."

Julianna snatched her hands off him. He stumbled back off the bar, rubbing his shoulder and his wrist.

"Get out of here," she told him, her eyes still pinned on me.

"You two are fucked up," he muttered before he hurried into the crowd.

We both eased closer as if out of instinct, our eyes eating each other up. My cock was hard as a stone, painful against my jeans, and I didn't give a shit who noticed.

"You're very sure of yourself," she said.

"Doesn't mean I'm not right." I took the final step towards her, filling up the space between us. In heels, she came up to my eye-line. I could smell her perfume of pears and musk, an intoxicating combination. Sweet yet fierce. Like she was.

"Do you think we made our point?" she asked. "To him, I mean.

"I think you put the fear of God into him."

"Are you kidding? I just disarmed him. He was pissing his pants when he saw your face up close."

"Well," I folded my arms, knowing that it showed off my biceps. Look at me, like a fucking peacock preening myself in front of her. "I am pretty scary."

She smirked and copied my stance, folding her arms over her chest, making her breasts push in and up. Jesus, I could fall into those fucking breasts.

Eyes up, Roman. She's a fucking lady. It took all my willpower not to follow those curves down farther. I tore my eyes away and looked up. Even under the dim light, I could see her cheeks were flushed.

"Maybe you're scary to *some* people," she said, her voice low and teasing.

I grinned. The lioness wasn't scared of me. Interesting. I leaned in closer like I was about to tell her a secret. "Maybe, I should scare you."

She stepped right up to me and lifted her chin as if to make a point. "If you want me to run away in fear, you're going to have to do a better job than that."

I lowered my face so close we were breathing in the same air.

She had peppermint on her breath, and I noticed the gold flecks in her amber-colored eyes before they dilated into large black holes I was falling into. Everything about her was drawing me in, closer, closer. "Maybe, I want to watch you run."

"Maybe, I want you to chase me."

My hands found her tiny waist. I pulled her against me, our bodies pressing together, her breasts so wonderfully soft against my chest I could have cried, my hard erection nestled against her belly. My body vibrated with need. Her. I needed her. I knew she could feel what she was doing to me. Her mouth parted as she sucked in a breath. Those fucking lips, so plump and inviting, so pink and juicy. I needed those lips.

I closed my mouth on hers before I knew what I was doing. She was soft, so fucking soft, as I sucked on her bottom lip. She tasted like strawberries, her lip balm perhaps, and mint. I licked at the seam of her lips, desperately trying to get inside her. More. I wanted more of her. All of her. *Give me what I want.*

She parted her mouth for me. My tongue found hers and suddenly we were all groans and hands, exploring, wild. I think I may have lost my mind right then and there. My hands roamed over the curve of her back, demanding, tugging her closer. I couldn't get her close enough. She arched into me, melding to me, her arms around my neck, her breasts pressing against my chest, making my body burn like she was on fire.

My hotel was only a few blocks from here. It housed a very comfortable, very large bed that she would look incredible in. Naked. So very fucking naked. Not that we'd make it much past the door, or the wall or the floor. I grinned against her mouth.

She tugged back. With regret, I released her lips from mine, but I kept my hands flattened around her back, keeping her flush with my body. The world rushed back into my head. Suddenly I missed the emptiness she'd closed around me when I had my mouth on hers. It'd been the closest thing I'd felt to peace in... years. Maybe ever.

She better have a good reason for stopping this kiss.

"Let's get out of here," she whispered, her words vibrating against my lips, her arms still around my neck.

Damn good reason.

I groaned into her mouth as a response. "Isn't that my line?"

"If you want, I can take it back so you get to say it."

"No, no. It's fine. I'm an equal opportunities man."

She bit her bottom lip with her teeth and the sight of it shot a flare of lust straight to my cock. "So?"

I swallowed. Fuck. I was leaving tomorrow...

What the fuck is wrong with you Roman? Just say yes!

"Roman?" Her tongue flicked out and licked the center of my top lip. It sent a direct line of electricity to my cock, making the aching almost unbearable. There were all sorts of ways she could put that tongue to use.

Focus, Roman, focus.

I gently pushed her out of reach of my mouth. "You're going to have to stop that if I'm going to think clearly."

"Oh." She frowned. "You have a girlfriend?"

"No."

"Wife?"

"Fuck, no."

She let out a sigh. "Then you really shouldn't have to think this hard. You either want to or not." She tried to pull away.

I pinned her to the bar with my body to stop her from leaving.

Why was I being such a limp dick? Why was I hesitating on taking this gorgeous woman home and doing all the dirty things I wanted to with her. I never fucking hesitated.

Because I was leaving tomorrow. Usually, I wouldn't care about setting expectations, but I wanted to be straight up with her. I was hesitating because it already felt like more than just a night club hookup. Because we shared something earlier today. Fuck, we were sharing something now, even if it was as simple as lust at first sight. It already felt like more. I already knew I would think of her on the plane on the way to London. I'd remember her name—I never remembered names. I'd recall the way she smelled, and the taste of her and all those little details. She needed to know this.

"I think...that maybe there's something I need to tell you before we continue."

She raised an eyebrow. "Sounds serious. Should I sit down?" she asked with a light note in her voice.

"I don't live here. I live in London. I came home for a funeral. I'm flying out tomorrow night, so..."

Her shoulders sank a little. Her disappointment tasted almost as strong as mine. "We would only have tonight," she finished for me.

I let out a breath. "And now you have all the facts ..." Well, not *all* the facts.

I studied her face for a reaction, feeling like my heart was on a knife's edge. Why did I care so much how she would react? She tilted her head, watching me as she chewed on her lip.

"What are you thinking?" I blurted out. "You can tell me."

She released her lip along with a breath. "I'm not sure, with you, if a night would be enough..."

I groaned and tucked her into my arms. Her hair smelled like the vanilla cookies my mother used to bake. "I know what you mean."

"What time do you leave Verona?" Her voice vibrated against my chest.

"Ten p.m. tomorrow night."

"Which gives us less than twenty-four hours to try to make it...enough."

I pulled back and looked at her. Her eyes were shiny with fear and exhilaration. "Really?" I asked. "Would one night be enough?"

She swallowed. "I don't know. I just know I want...you."

She wanted me. Not my surname. Not my money. Not my

reputation, or my family's power. Not for a walk on the wild side, or a chance to brag that she'd fucked a Tyrell.

Just…me.

I slid my fingers into hers. Electricity ran up my arm and into my body, kicking my heart into a racing pace. "Let's get out of here."

JULIANNA

"**M**y hotel's only a minute away," Roman said, as we walked the quiet streets, lit by watery streetlights. His shoulder brushed against mine again, and another rush of heat flooded through me.

"That's what you said five minutes ago," I said. I glanced over to him, eager to discreetly study his stunning lines again. He was already staring at me, a sexy half-smirk on his beautiful lips. He half-stepped, half-turned towards me, and I bumped into him. In the dimness between streetlights, he grabbed my face in his hands and swooped his lips onto mine. Ignoring the passerbys, we kissed, hungry and desperate, hands and tongues, bodies pressing into each other as my insides burned and my core ached. Everything was spinning. I didn't even have a single drink. What the hell was happening to me?

He groaned as I pushed him away, my body screaming at me to find his mouth again, the other part screaming at me to hurry up to his hotel room so I could put his mouth to work on other needier parts of me. "At this rate, we won't get to your hotel room," I complained half-heartedly. I wasn't kidding.

"Whose fault is that?" he said, his hands still roaming my body, threatening to tip me over into a full-blown distraction.

"Yours. Stop kissing me like that—"

"Stop being so kissable."

"—and touching me like that."

"Stop being so sexy."

Damn him and his perfect comebacks. "It's taken us almost twenty minutes to get three stupid blocks."

He looked down at me, his top lip pulled up in a half-smirk so adorable I almost lunged for him again. "I have a solution."

"You do?"

He picked me up around the waist and hoisted me over his shoulder like I weighed nothing. My world tipped upside down. Air flitted up my skirt. I let out a scream. "Put me down. My ass is showing."

"Holy sweet Jesus."

"What?"

"It's a sensational ass." He pressed his palm across the area where the backs of my thighs met my ass. The warmth of his hand sent tingles all through the insides of me. "What are you doing?" I gasped.

"Trying to preserve your modesty."

"What?"

"I'm holding your skirt down. No one is allowed to look at this magnificent ass except me."

"Take your hand off me."

He grunted. "Okay then. It's your fault if I have to kill someone for staring."

He released me. The wind took this opportunity to blow up my legs. I felt my skirt lift and cold air on my ass. I let out a yelp.

He let out a groan. "You're wearing red lacy underwear?" His voice came out tight, almost pained. "Please tell me the bra matches."

The wind was obviously on his side because it blew my skirt up again. "Ok, ok. Put your hand back."

"I'm confused. Did you want my hand on your ass or—"

"Put your damn hand back."

He chuckled. The low vibration went right through me. "My pleasure."

This time his hand pressed right on my ass, his large palm feeling like it was encasing both cheeks. I knew he had shifted his hand higher on purpose. I felt the tips of his fingers dig in a little, like a cat testing its claws. Holy shit. My core had turned into one of those globes filled with electricity you see in magic shops, and the sparks were following his hands.

He began to walk, my body swaying gently in time with his gait. From this angle, I had a wonderful view of his ass. Dear God, it was a glorious ass, round and firm and so slappable. I let my body relax over him in submission as he carried me like a conquest to his hotel. Even the feminist in me shut the hell up.

"You have no idea what I'm going to do to this ass when I get you alone," he said.

"Why don't you tell me?" I replied in a voice I barely recognized. All the blood was rushing to my head, making me dizzy.

"I'm going to bend you over, peel your underwear off." He paused. "Peel it off," he repeated. "I'll be lucky not to hurt you when I tear them off." He almost sounded pissed off, like it was my fault for how he was feeling. Like my lacy red underwear offended him. "I'll be gentle first, lull you into a false sense of security; I'll knead these gorgeous globes, kiss them, lick them, give them a love bite or two..."

I gulped.

"Then when you least expect it..." A crack sounded and a flare of pain spread across my left ass cheek. Then warm pleasure flooded through me replacing the pain. I let out a low moan. "I'll slap both cheeks 'til they're red and hot, and your pussy is swollen and dripping."

I shivered as the images he promised me assaulted my mind. "And then?" I begged, the desperation clear in my voice.

I could almost feel him grinning.

"Then I'm going to part your cheeks and bury my face into your wet folds. I'm going to lick along your crease, spreading your juices until you're wet from front to back.

The blood had stopped rushing to my head. It was all going to my core now, that whole area swelling, filling with blood, throbbing like a second heartbeat. I stifled a moan as he walked into the hotel lobby, ignoring the surprised greeting of the doorman. The sudden change of light and the image of his tongue between my legs blinded me. He walked past the late-night hotel staff on reception. I was grateful my face was hidden by my hair.

"Jesus," he muttered. "I can *smell* how much you want me and I haven't even touched you. You smell so fucking sweet. I can't wait to taste you."

Dear God. Could these hotel staff smell my lust too? Could they hear him? My cheeks burned with heat. Which only added to the internal fire.

He rode up in the elevator with me still over his shoulder. He only put me down once we arrived in front of what I suspected was his hotel suite. Right on the top floor. My head spun and not just because the blood in my body was trying to re-figure out which way was up.

He held me up against the door with his arms on either side of me, preventing me from falling over. "Once we get in there, you're mine."

I licked my lips and stared into his hooded eyes, burning like black fire. "What does that mean?"

"That means, *whatever* I want, you're giving me. Is that clear?"

"Whatever you want?" I squeaked out.

"I can see you, Julianna. You like to control every aspect of your life. It will be hard for you to give it up. You'll fight me.

That's okay, I like a little fight. But fight me knowing that I will win."

Through my fog of desire rose the first sign of hesitation. A realization that if I said yes, I would be giving in to a man, a fully matured man, powerful and aggressive. He was nothing like the boys I dallied with before. I was in way over my head.

There was a part of me that sensed the darkness that lay within the depths of this beautiful creature. *Run!* a voice inside me screamed before it was lost in a wave of heat as he parted my legs with his knee and pressed his thigh against my sensitive core. With his hands on my hips, he ground me onto him. "I could make it so, *so* good for you. Only if you just...give in to me." He had to stop that, what he was doing with his thigh, with his hips against me. I could feel the length of his hardness between us. I ached for it to be inside me. "This is your last chance to say *no*."

I grabbed his shirt, crushing it in my hands, rocking myself against his thigh, in complete awe of this wild woman he had turned me into. "No fucking chance."

His face split into that gorgeous grin. He lunged for me.

We poured into that hotel suite, door banging against the wall behind me, his hands going up the hem of my skirt and gripping my ass, pulling me up onto him, my legs hooking around his waist, his hard length against my belly. I was near insane, tugging at his shirt and his belt. I barely noticed the suite as we ricocheted off walls and furniture, a single beast of tongues and hands, all the way to the large bedroom, pouring our groans into each other's mouths. Somewhere along the way my heels had been kicked off.

At the foot of the bed, he placed me down on the plush carpet. He tore his mouth off me and placed his forehead on mine, our chests heaving in and out, begging for the air that we'd stolen from each other. It was the calm before the storm. A pause. A moment. We both needed it.

He spun me around. With one hand flat on my back, bent me over to kneel on the bed, like he promised. The gush of wetness added to my already soaking underwear. His hands pushed the hem of my dress up over my hips, cold air swirling around my bare legs. His hands traced the small of my back, over my curves and down my thighs.

"Red. Lacy. Like," he muttered. He'd become incoherent.

I looked back at him over one shoulder. He was staring at my ass up in the air for him. I felt so dirty and vulnerable in this position. I'd never let myself be this vulnerable in front of any man. I shouldn't like it. But I did. I fucking did. "Are you trying to say that you like my panties?"

He looked up and caught my eye. "I fucking love them. And I'm really, really sorry." Before I could ask why, he ripped my underwear right off me, the room filling with the noise of tearing lace and the sound of my gasp.

Oh. Right. He had warned me earlier he was going to do that.

Cool air rushed across my wet exposed sex, making it tingle. I heard him groan. It sounded so close to my naked lips. I should feel degraded having a stranger's face practically in my pussy. But the way he was looking at me, a mixture of lust and awe, I felt powerful. I felt sexy.

"Jesus Christ," he said, "your ass looks incredible from this angle."

"Sensational, magnificent...now incredible?" I teased.

I could hear him shifting behind me. "Your ass has turned me into a fucking thesaurus."

I could feel his presence right behind me. It made all the hairs on my body stand on end. I bit my lip. He had promised me kneading and kissing and biting next.

Crack. His hand came down on my ass so hard that I cried out, the pain flaring then followed by a rush of heated pleasure. "I thought you were going to—"

"Can't wait."

His hand came down again. Then again. I moaned into the sheets as I gripped on to them for dear life, every smack lifting the pain and the pleasure higher than the one before it. My body became a live wire, a taut bundle of fire and electricity. My pussy was throbbing now, swollen and wet, overripe from his assault. I braced for the next hit.

His hands spread my cheeks apart and his face pushed into me. The instant his tongue touched my folds I almost leaped off the bed. I was so sensitive it was almost unbearable.

His hands clamped on my hips. "Hold still. Or I'll have to tie you down." His threat sent a shiver through me, a mix of fear and desire. Me, tied down and completely in his power. I shouldn't want that. But I did. How could I want something I feared?

He licked me again, this time with a firmer touch. Waves of pleasure knocked through my spine like a row of dominos. He groaned, the vibration rumbling through me. "You taste so good." His flat, wet, warm tongue stroked along my crease. The pleasure rolling through me made my toes curl, drawing moans from my lips.

I had never really enjoyed oral sex. I had always felt too dirty, too exposed. It was too intimate to have a man's nose and lips and eyes right there, pushing into my hidden pink flesh, taking my secret taste into his mouth and my woman's scent into his lungs. Not with him. Not with Roman.

I gave in to the pleasure, to the vulnerability of having his face in my most private of parts, his nose and breath tickling my ass crack. He began to lick further and further back, painting me with the moisture of my sex and his mouth.

His tongue drew across the pucker of my behind. "No," I gasped and clenched my ass, yanking my hips away from his face.

He tensed. "What did I say at the door?"

I squeezed my eyes shut. "But I—"

"What did you agree to?"

Give in.

Jesus, was I really doing this? I inhaled long and deep and forced my muscles to relax. I eased my hips back towards him.

"Good girl. For that, you're going to get a reward."

Before I could speak his finger slid up my slit and found my clit, circling the sensitive spot in tiny circles. I let out a low moan and my body melted further towards him. His fingertip played at my entrance, strumming my pleasure strings like I was an instrument.

"Look at you. So wet. So needy."

I moaned back in response, my ass tipping higher towards him so he could have more access to me.

"You ready for your reward now?"

My reward? I thought this was my reward.

He slid two fingers into me. I sucked in a breath. My width squeezed around them as he paused to give me a moment to settle. He curled his fingers towards the front of me and began to rub. A thick, tight pulse of intensity began to grow, originating from his fingertips. Magic fucking fingertips. I heard moaning, wild and wanton and careless to whoever heard them. It was coming from me. My hips jerked back towards him, begging for more as this ball of energy expanded and consumed me.

This time when he parted my ass cheeks with the fingers of his other hand and I felt his breath on my ass, I pushed back onto his tongue. He flicked it around the sensitive rim of my rosebud. The waves expanded from front and back, meeting together in an explosion of pleasure. I couldn't take it anymore.

An orgasm thundered over me before I knew what was happening, my body shuddering and my cries muffled into the sheets. His fingers played hard and fast inside me, urging me on further as he hummed with approval against me, the vibration skimming across my skin.

It felt like forever as the waves flowed over me again and again. I collapsed, my mind a complete blank. His fingers slid from my body and I let out a low moan. *Come back.* I felt empty without him.

Dear God. What the fuck just happened to me?

I felt his hands on me pulling me up to sit on my heels, leaning against his firm chest. I realized he was still clothed. We hadn't even waited to get naked yet. He traced my lips with his fingers still wet with me. "Suck them. See how good you taste."

I paused. I'd never done that. I'd never tasted myself.

"Jules?"

I remembered what I had agreed to. *Yes to whatever he wants.*

Gingerly, I licked the tips of his fingers. Musky with a hint of sweetness.

"More," he demanded.

I opened my mouth and he slid his fingers inside of me, stroking my tongue and wiping my arousal all over my taste buds. I could almost feel his fingers inside my pussy again. It felt so dirty and bad, and I fucking loved it. I groaned, lapping at his fingers with my tongue, sucking them as he dragged his fingers out. I felt his length twitch against the small of my back.

Yes, that. That was what I wanted inside me. It felt so big and hard. I was more than ready.

"Lift up your arms."

I did, my limbs still weak from my orgasm. I felt awkward and clumsy like a child. He pulled my dress up all the way off, careful not to pull my hair, before he dropped it off the side of the bed onto the carpet with a satisfying ripple of sound.

He made a satisfied noise in his throat. "Matching. I knew it." His fingers traced the front of my bra, and I found myself arching into his palms, wanting his touch on me without the lace between us. "You knew before you came to meet me that we'd end up here."

"I..." I couldn't lie to him. He'd already seen right through me. My cheeks heated at his insight.

He didn't give me time to be embarrassed. With one flick of

his fingers, my bra was unhooked and I was fully naked, kneeling on the bed for him. "Fuck," he hissed. I could feel his eyes on me, drinking me in, rolling openly and unashamedly over my body, leaving scorching trails across my already sensitive skin.

I heard his belt buckle clink behind me and I froze. My ear tuned in to the whispers of clothing being removed and discarded on the floor, every noise causing my skin to become even more sensitized until I couldn't take it anymore. I shifted around to look at him.

He was glorious. Wide rounded shoulders to match his muscular arms, firm chest and a stomach of defined abs. And that V. Oh God, he had that V, a small birthmark on his lower left hip. His skin was smooth, tanned and taut, marked only by a puckered scar on his left chest.

My eyes fixed on his length. He was thick, straight, not too long. I felt my thighs begin to shake and I collapsed back on the bed, my arms barely holding me up as he towered over me now.

"I was going to drag this out," he admitted, a foil packet already in his hand. "But you've had me hard since I first saw you." He grinned. "That's what the rest of the night is for. For now, I just need to fuck you." He rolled the condom on his length and flicked the empty foil aside. He drew himself over me like a blanket, pushing my thighs apart, his strong arms wrapping around me and pulling me close. He shifted himself so that his tip was at my entrance and paused.

Everything around me came into sharp focus. I realized with a gasp that I was *here* with this man, a man so beautiful he would make angels cry. This wasn't just possibility or a wistful daydream I had conjured up. This was truly happening. Somehow possibility and reality had twisted together to become one. What I was experiencing in the moment—his earthy cologne mixed with sweat, the weight of his body crushing mine, the pinwheels of electricity crackling through my body—was *real*. I was here. With Roman.

He sheathed himself inside me in one smooth movement. I gasped as I felt myself stretch to my limit. I'd never been so awake in my whole life. I felt thrust suddenly into a world of song and fire I never knew existed.

"Sweet Jesus," he muttered. "I'm not going to last."

He began to drive in and out of me, hard and relentless. Just like our attraction, there was no easing into this. I could feel every inch of him. Our flesh slid and tugged, delicious friction beginning to reignite me again.

Oh my God. Was I going to come *again*?

He seemed to sense it. He pulled one leg up over his shoulder and pushed in deeper. I tensed, my body already starting to tighten and clench around him as he drilled into me.

The second orgasm slammed through me, starting almost abruptly. I cried out partly from surprise, but mostly from the intensity of the feeling thundering through me. Every muscle in my body tensed as if electricity was shooting through me. My fingers and toes curled. He let out a loud groan and his body jerked. I felt him pulsing inside me. It felt like he was feeding me his orgasm, doubling it. Waves of pleasure knocked back and forth between us, on and on, our twin cries and our breaths twisting around each other.

If I'd known sex could be *this* good, perhaps I would have had more sex instead of applying myself to my career. Even as I had this thought, I dismissed it. I knew, deep down, this was not *just* sex.

He let my leg down and collapsed onto me, holding his weight up with his elbows so he wouldn't crush me. I closed my eyes and wrapped my arms around his wide, warm back. I breathed in his spicy woody cologne and the hint of sweat and sex, letting the deepest, fullest sense of satisfaction cover me like a blanket. His nose brushed lightly along my neck. He was smelling me too. He let out a low long sigh.

"That's never happened before," I whispered to myself.

He lifted himself up and pulled off the condom before coming down beside me. His eyes roamed over me, still naked, making me want to pull the sheets up over me.

"You mean..." he leaned in closer as if he were about to share a secret, our faces enclosed in this private space of our warm, sweet breaths. There was a sparkle in his beautiful dark eyes. "Actual sex?"

I poked his side and he flinched with a short laugh. The man was ticklish. Interesting.

"No, you ass." I poked him again.

"Stop that or I'll be forced to punish you."

"Don't make fun of me again or I'll be forced to punish *you*." I poked him again to make a point. I really enjoyed watching him squirm.

He rolled on top of me. "I think we need to call a truce."

"The only time someone calls the truce is when he's about to lose." I tried to poke him again.

He grabbed my hand, threading his fingers through mine and holding it down over my head so I couldn't do it again. "I'm merely giving you an option of a truce to be a gentleman. I don't lose."

He was too strong. And he was cheating, using his weight to hold me down. Being pinned down should inspire fear in me. Instead, I felt the heat rushing to my core. Again. Dear God. What was he doing to me?

He smirked at me, smugness clear on his face.

I rolled my eyes, but a small smile pulled at my lips.

"Now that I've clearly *lost* against you," he said, "you were saying... what hadn't you ever done before?"

I chewed my lip, wondering if I dared to reveal my secret.

He raised his eyebrow. "I've been inside you, Jules. I've had my fingers, drenched in your come, shoved down your throat and my tongue in your asshole. Are you really going to be self-conscious now?"

Fair enough. "Coming twice," I blurted out. "I've never come twice in a night."

A smirk appeared on his face. "Safe to say then you've never come three times in a night."

"No," I squeaked as his hips began to grind against me again, his length hardening. He grinned, wicked and salacious, the hunger clear in his eyes. I wasn't the only one ready to go again.

"Challenge accepted."

ROMAN

I had the most incredible dream. I dreamed I had an angel in my arms. She saw past the darkness that shrouded me. She wrapped her light around me and bathed me in warmth. She absolved me of all my sins.

I slept more soundly than I had in a long time.

I woke to the feeling of a warm body against me, silky hair against my chest, soft warmth along my side making a heat trickle into my lower body.

Julianna.

I let her stay the night.

I never let them stay.

Sometime during the night, I had grabbed her and pulled her against me. And I hadn't let her go. I opened my eyes. The early afternoon light was streaming through the window, highlighting the Presidential Suite's honey wood and cream décor in a soft glow. The expensive sheets were twisted around us. Half the blankets and pillows had been kicked off the bed. I spotted the broken lamp I'd knocked off the bedside table last night. Last night… Already my mind was filling with images from last night, making my cock ache. Jesus Christ. Last night…

I'd had my fair share of one night stands and flings. Last night blew them all away. Meeting someone who set your body on fire with one touch—one searing look, one whispered word—came along less than a handful of times in a lifetime. She would not be someone I'd forget that easily.

I looked down at her sleeping face, careful not to move so as not to wake her. I wondered if she knew how gorgeous she was. I doubted it. Despite her bravado and confidence last night, I could sense she was unaware of how devastatingly beautiful she truly was. Her long dark lashes almost reached the top of her polished cheekbones, a perfect tiny brown mole over her pouty mouth, naturally crimson and slightly parted. She barely had any makeup on her face, I realized. None of that foundation shit that always smeared across my pillows. Just a touch of mascara darkened her lashes.

She looked younger when she slept. Her features were soft and full. Without her shields up, she was as vulnerable as a babe in my arms. My heart clenched. If only I could protect this very part of her. She wouldn't need her shields if she had me. She wouldn't need to be so tough all the time. Or in control all the time.

"Are you watching me sleep?" she mumbled even as her eyelids remained closed.

I grinned. Busted. "That depends."

"On what?"

"On whether you find it sweet or creepy."

Her eyes flickered open and she blinked a few times before she glanced around. "Damn, this is a nice hotel suite."

"Funny enough, it's the same suite as last night," I teased.

She rolled her eyes. "I was too busy last night to notice it."

Damn straight. "You did seem very distracted."

"Whose fault was that?" She rubbed her eyes and pushed the hair from her cheeks. She stretched out her legs, the soft skin of her toned thighs brushing along my side, stirring the need for her again. "What time is it?"

I stiffened and my fingers gripped onto her involuntarily. "You have somewhere to be?"

She glanced over to me. "No...but it's not very productive laying around in bed all day."

"I can think of a few productive things to do to you in bed today."

"Roman—"

I shut her up with a deep kiss. I'd fuck her until she forgot that she needed to be anywhere but right here with me. Over me. Under me. All around me. It took a second before she melted against me. Her submission sent a surge of blood to my lower half. She *was* mine.

Not for long, an annoying voice inside me said. *You're leaving tonight.*

Fuck tonight. There was only *now*.

I rolled over her, my erection against her soft folds, my chest pressing against her breasts. I latched my mouth onto hers like she was my only source of oxygen. When her soft tongue rubbed against mine, it sent my head spinning. I rubbed my aching cock against her growing wetness, her little moans urging me on. I could feel the animal inside me breaking loose. I was going to lose my fucking mind.

Everything about her, the way my fingers sank into her soft skin, the shape of her as she fit against me, the taste of her come still on my tongue, all conspired to drive me crazy. I wanted to fuck every single one of her holes until she was hoarse from screaming. I wanted to bury myself so deep inside her that the stains would never wash off. I wanted to tear her beautiful body apart.

Slow down, you selfish fucker.

I tore my mouth off her, sucking in air, trying to take hold of my senses. I didn't want to scare her. I don't know why I cared so much but I did. I needed a new plan. A new position. Before I totally lost my shit and ripped her apart.

"Roman?" I could hear the question in her voice. Why did I stop?

If you only knew what you were doing to me.

I rolled us over, crushing her to me with my arm until I was on my back and she was straddled over me. She pushed herself up so she could look at me, her eyes on me, waiting, like such a good girl, for my next instructions. She had fought me last night when I had pushed against her boundaries. This morning, she was as open and curious as a newborn doe. Last night I had given her body what it needed and more. Now she trusted me with it completely. She'd let me do anything to her now.

I reached up to cup her breast, rolling a thumb over her nipple, making it pebble. She let out a moan. "I want to watch you fuck me," I said.

A look of happiness stole across her face in the form of a shy smile. My heart gave out a little kick. She reached between us and wrapped her soft hand around my erection. I was already wet from the juices soaking out of her. She used her fist to spread it all along my length. I grinned to myself. There was a dirty girl inside of her. She just needed me to coax it out.

She positioned herself over me and slid herself down. My eyes rolled into the back of my head. Sweet mother of mercy, she was so damn tight and warm, the only piece of sweet heaven reserved for a devil like me.

She settled her hips down to the hilt and gasped. "I don't know whether I'll ever get used to the size of you."

I fucking hoped not.

She moved slowly at first, her hips lifting and rolling down onto me, her tiny soft hands running over my chest and abs as if she didn't know which part of me to hold on to. I loved the way she bit her lip as she tried to hold in her groans, the way her perfect round breasts bounced, her lickable nipples peeking through her hair.

She began to speed up, causing the pressure in my body to build. I kneaded her ass and ground my hips up to meet hers. Fuck, I had to stop touching her before I lost control. Usually, I'd be grabbing her hips and slamming her down onto me faster. I didn't. I reached up, grabbed the headboard and held on, my knuckles going white.

She slammed down onto me harder and faster until her breaths were my name coming out in curses, over and over.

I was so damn close I was seeing stars behind my eyelids. "Fuck yes marry me," I muttered, my growling becoming incoherent, my brain completely shorting out. I wasn't sure what I was saying to her, I just knew I didn't want her to stop. Ever.

Her pussy clenched. I felt her orgasm rumbling all around me. I couldn't fucking take it anymore. I grabbed her thighs and spurred her on as she rode us both over the edge. An orgasm tore through me like an earthquake, my vision turning into a sea of white.

Her scream faded and she collapsed on my chest, her sweat mixing with mine. I crushed her into me like I could pull her into my body. Like I could keep her. Her perfume of pears and musk, mixed with the musk of sex, filled my nose. She was intoxicating, every part of her. Every time I sank into her warm, soft folds I went in a little deeper, I lost myself a little further. For the first time in my life I wondered, would I ever get enough?

"I should go," she said, sitting up, startling me out of my reverie. "Let you get ready to leave. I'm sure you have other people you want to catch up with while you're here."

No. My stomach tightened. I didn't want her to leave.

She has to leave eventually.

But not now.

I forced a smile and tried in the most casual voice I could. "Do you want to use the shower?"

She bit her lip. I knew she was wondering about my offer. "Thanks, but I can shower at home."

I gripped her thighs, not letting her rise off me, scared that if I let her up, I wouldn't find a way to make her stay a little bit longer. *Don't you want to stay?* "There's a huge high-pressure showerhead in there that I've paid for already, so you might as well use it."

"I don't know."

I screwed up my nose. "Look, I really didn't want to have to say this, but you really, *really* need a shower."

She laughed and poked my side, the vulnerable part of me that she had somehow ferreted out. Not even Jacob had known I was ticklish there. "I do *not* stink."

I pinched my nose. "Like high heaven."

She poked me again. I grabbed her hand, laughing, rolling over her to pin her down. Her hair flowed out across the pillow like spilled wheat. Fuck, she looked so damn beautiful staring up at me with her sharp whiskey-colored eyes and her breasts pressing up against my chest. I leaned down and covered her mouth with mine. This woman was like a drug. I wanted to have her over and over again.

She tore her lips from mine and pushed at my chest. "Roman, let me up."

I felt my face tighten. I'd never had to work so fucking hard to get a woman to stay with me. "Shower first," I commanded.

"So bossy."

"Deal with it. That's what you signed up for when you entered my bedroom."

She rolled her eyes but there was a small smile on her lips. "Fine. Shower first."

I rolled my hips against hers, my body heating up again, my dick swelling already. The thought of being inside her again was enough. "I'll join you."

She gasped as I rubbed my length against her slit. "Are you serious? Again?"

I grinned, rolled us up to the edge of the bed and stood with her clinging to my torso. I held her to me with my hands on her ass and thighs as I walked us into the bathroom.

"I'm never going to leave if you keep this up," she mused against my neck.

That's the plan.

JULIANNA

What was I doing? I let the hot water wash the shampoo out of my hair. It ran over my head and body, swirling white suds disappearing into the drain. I had already stayed longer than I'd planned. Roman had fucked me in the shower up against the marble tiles, making me come hard again, before giving his beautiful body a quick clean while I leaned against the wall, studying him with greedy eyes. Now I was alone *actually* having a shower and yet thinking of him.

He was such a contradiction. Domineering and fierce, yet funny and playful. He managed to inspire such trust in me so quickly. More than that, I could see the watchful, observant man underneath the charming exterior, the kind of man whose thoughts ran deep. The kind of man who knew exactly what was going on around him at all times. He was so fucking beautiful it almost hurt to look at him.

He was dangerous. Dangerous for my heart. I had only known him less than a day and already... already I didn't want to leave.

He is *leaving. Tonight.*

The more time I spent with him, the more attached I'd get. I had to go before this feeling got any stronger. I needed to protect myself. Every time he'd sunk his length into me, my body shook with such soul-deep pleasure unlike I'd ever thought possible. He'd awakened something inside me. Now I wasn't sure if I could live without it. Without him.

Don't be stupid, Julianna. You barely know the guy.

It was only one night. That was the deal. I knew this when I agreed to come home with him. I couldn't stay any longer. I couldn't let myself get any more addicted. I was leaving. Right after this shower. No exceptions. I nodded slightly to myself with determination. Mind made up, I turned off the water.

I came out of the bathroom, dried and wrapped in a bathrobe. I'd have to collect my clothes where ever they had been thrown around the room last night. I frowned as I looked over the empty bedroom. There were my bag and shoes. I couldn't see my clothes anywhere.

"Roman, have you seen my—?" I stepped into the living room of the suite and froze. There was a huge buffet of eggs, fruits, granola, yogurts, cheeses and cold meats as well as pastries and croissants on a silver trolley beside a laid-out circular marble-topped table with matching cream Elizabethan chairs. Roman was sitting in one of those chairs wearing only his Georgio Armani briefs, looking like a king sitting on a throne. He just needed a crown. Hell, he didn't need a crown. One look at him and you could feel the royalty oozing off him. "What's this?" I asked.

"Breakfast. Although, with the current time, it's technically lunch. Sit. Eat." He waved at the other seat at the table.

I frowned. "But you're leaving Verona in..." I looked at the stylish clock on the wall, the silver hands reading 1:53, "in about eight hours."

"That's still eight hours…"

I folded my arms across me. "This can't go anywhere," I said, wondering if it was me or him I was trying to convince.

"I know," he said, his voice going quiet.

"So, what are you doing?"

"I don't know," he said gruffly. "Just… eat breakfast with me."

My heart did a flip in my chest. This was dangerous. Every second I let him keep me here was only going to make the inevitable goodbye ever the more painful.

Apparently, I was a sucker for pain.

"Besides," he said, "I had your clothes sent out for cleaning. They should be back in four hours."

"Four hours." I blinked. "What the hell am I supposed to wear in the meantime."

He grinned. "That bathrobe is perfect. Or nothing. I don't mind."

Asshole. He was giving me no choice. "You did this on purpose."

He didn't confirm or deny my statement. He pointed again to the chair opposite him. "Sit. Now. Or did you forget the rules?"

I snorted. "I thought your bossiness only extended to sex."

"You thought wrong."

Forcing me into the shower, ordering breakfast, sending my only clothes to be cleaned… He was finding excuses to keep me here. Didn't men do their best to get rid of you after a one-night stand?

Does this feel like a one-night stand?

No, it didn't. But he was leaving soon. A one-night stand was *all* that it could be.

He was still staring at me, waiting for me to follow his instructions. I let out a sigh and sat down in my robe at the breakfast table, crossing one leg over the other. I noticed his gaze drift down to my thigh and realized my robe was flashing him a decent amount of leg. I yanked my bathrobe closed before he decided he was hungry for something other than breakfast. I shook my head as I stared at the spread. "Seriously Roman, there's enough food here to feed an army."

"I didn't know what you liked. So, I ordered one of everything." I could sense him studying me. "What would you choose to eat for breakfast?"

I grabbed the plate of eggs, bacon, fried mushrooms, grilled tomatoes and hash browns, placing it in front of me. It smelled amazing. My tummy gave out a little rumble in agreement. I cut up a bite-sized piece of each item on the plate, then carefully skewered them onto my fork into one large, perfect bite. I glanced over to him and he raised an eyebrow.

Normally I would be too self-conscious to let any man watch me eating like this.

"I've been inside you, Jules. I've had my fingers, drenched in your come, shoved down your throat, and my tongue in your asshole."

I grinned before I placed the entire contents of my fork into my mouth. His mouth dropped open. I groaned with pleasure as I chewed, then swallowed.

He pointed at my plate. "You're going to eat all of that."

"Why not?" I began to cut up another perfect bite.

He shook his head. "Looks like I'm eating the rabbit food." He grabbed the bowl of berries, yogurt, and granola. "I'll know not to order you a salad for dinner."

Dinner?

I stopped chewing. "I'm not staying for dinner."

"It wasn't a request."

"Roman, you can't keep me here."

"I'm not. Feel free to leave. Without your clothes."

Damn him. He had me there. I lowered my fork and crossed my arms over my chest. "If we're going to spend the day with each other, we need some rules."

He grinned. "It's a bit late for hard limits, Jules."

I fought a rising flush. "No personal questions." If we kept things impersonal, then it would stop me from getting too attached. Right?

"What do you mean by 'personal' questions?"

"You know, family, work…personal stuff."

"If I asked you if you liked maple syrup, is that too personal?" He indicated the small pot of maple syrup sitting beside the stack of pancakes.

I shifted in my chair. "No."

"That's good to know." He dug into his bowl of granola.

I frowned. I was missing something. "Why is that good to know?"

"Because you're going to suck it off my cock."

My eyes dropped to his briefs. He was already hard. Again.

Dear God, this man was going to be the death of me.

Hours later, we lay naked and sticky from maple syrup on the plush rug on the carpet of the living area, a few cushions strewn about, a soft jazz playing from the radio. I had long since given up fighting him. I had given up trying to leave because deep down I didn't want to. I was here, staying with him for as long as he'd let me.

"Why did you move to London eight years ago?" I asked Roman as I traced his bare chest with my finger.

He had one hand behind his head and the other brushing my side. "I thought you said no personal questions."

I pouted. "I may have been a bit harsh."

He studied me before saying, "Let's make a deal. I'll answer a personal question for every one of mine that you answer."

I swallowed down a knot of apprehension. "Deal. So…why did you move?"

He inhaled deeply. "My father is a difficult man. My family

is…complicated. We have a family business and the politics… The politics are killer. I didn't want to be a part of it. I wanted to be my own person."

"That's very brave of you."

He let out a humorless laugh. "Or desperate."

I shook my head. "Brave," I confirmed. "I don't know if I could ever get the courage to leave Verona, even though…even though part of me wants to. To get out from my father's shadow."

He shifted closer and brushed a lock of hair from my cheek. "Why don't you?"

I shook my head. "I'm the only one that he has left."

"You can't live your life for your father."

"You can't live your life to avoid yours," I snapped back.

We both stared at each other, the silence growing thick. I thought for a second that I may have crossed the line. Then his face softened and he nodded. "Touché."

I suddenly felt like a jerk. "I'm sorry, I shouldn't have said that. I don't know the first thing about your relationship with your father."

"You're still right. I am living my life to avoid him." Roman inhaled deeply and let out a long sigh. "He was never the same since my mother died," he said quietly. His eyes flashed with sadness that he wasn't even trying to hide.

My heart clenched. "Was that her funeral you went to yesterday?"

"No. My mother died fourteen years ago." His voice trailed off.

Fourteen years. His mother died the same year that mine did. "So did mine."

"That was the gravesite you were visiting yesterday." It wasn't a question.

I nodded.

"Tell me about her."

I shouldn't. My mother lived in a deep, safe space in the depths of my heart that no one, *no one* ever got to see. She was mine and my memories of her were mine.

"I'll tell you about my mother," he said softly.

That, apparently, was enough for me.

ROMAN

" I 'll tell you about my mother," I said before I could stop
myself.

I was treading on dangerous territory. If I said too
much about my family, then she might guess that I was Roman
Tyrell, not Roman Lettiere as I had told her yesterday. I don't
know why I had lied about my surname. No, I do. I hadn't
wanted to see her eyes fill with judgment at the cursed name
Tyrell. Besides, it wasn't that much of a lie. Lettiere had been my
mother's maiden name. I had always felt like a Lettiere instead of
a Tyrell.

"My mother was fierce," Julianna said softly, "she stood up for
what she believed in. She loved me and my father with a steady
ferocity. She'd do anything for us."

Julianna could have been speaking about herself. "It sounds
like your mother was an incredible woman."

She nodded, her eyes still facing forward. "I struggle to follow
in her shadow."

"I doubt that."

She let out a long breath. "Your turn," she said quietly.

My turn. I had agreed to give her a piece of my soul for one of hers. I felt my heart turn to steel the way it did when things hurt too much. "My mother was a good woman who was cursed to fall in love and marry the wrong man." Even I could hear the bitterness in my own voice.

She had been cursed to love my father, a man whose ambition endangered her life and eventually killed her. "I've never stopped missing her," I admitted.

"Me too," she said.

"I don't think you ever really get used to it."

She nodded. "Every event for the rest of my life will be over-shadowed by the hole she left behind."

"Every birthday."

"Each Christmas," she agreed. Something flashed in her eyes. "Whose funeral did you go to yesterday?"

"My eldest brother."

Her face fell. "I'm so sorry."

I shrugged, even though the loss of him fisted in my belly. Jacob and I had not seen eye to eye for a long time, but I loved him like only a brother could. Once upon a time I had worshiped him like only a younger brother could.

"Were you close?"

"Once. When we were younger. Then he changed. I didn't like what he became." The man they buried yesterday wasn't the Jacob I knew and loved. The truth was, I had missed him for over a decade. For me, the *real* Jacob died that summer he turned sixteen—the summer my mother died—and my father began to groom him to take over our family business. I had been twelve.

Through my youthful eyes, Jacob became something I didn't recognize. I watched him morph into one of the monsters that crawled out of one of the stories that he used to read to me before bed. He became a ball of learned rage and hatred. Of eye-for-an-eye justice. Of self-righteous fury.

Our relationship changed. I was no longer the little brother he would protect with his life. He no longer trusted me, taught by our father never to trust anyone, not even his own blood. I became a threat to his future throne.

It was only a matter of time for me to follow him down that dark path...

Julianna's hand fell upon my arm. Her touch sent waves of heat through my body. She was like a ray of sunshine cutting through the fog I'd been drifting around in for the last fourteen years. If she knew what she was doing to me, she didn't show it.

"Sometimes that's harder," she said. "Trying to mourn someone still alive who doesn't look like the person you loved."

I looked up at her and studied her face. Underneath the flawless features was a sadness, an empathy beyond sensing another person's sadness. She *knew*. She understood.

"My brother and I," I began, "...it's complicated."

"It always is with family."

"Do you have brothers? Sisters?" I asked.

"No. It's just me and my father now."

"And as the only child, the weight of family expectations falls right on your pretty little shoulders."

"Indeed," she said quietly.

JULIANNA

I wanted to change the subject off my father. I wasn't uncomfortable talking about him. I was uncomfortable that Roman seemed to *understand* too much. This strange intimacy was unnerving. It went against every logical thought of how close I could feel to a man who was practically a stranger, how connected I should feel to a man I'd only just met.

I found that small puckered scar on his shoulder and ran my finger over it. "What's this?"

For a second it seemed a flash of something dark went across his eyes. Then it was gone. "It's a scar."

I almost rolled my eyes. "Obviously. How did you get it?"

He said nothing.

"It looks like…" I frowned as I leaned in closer. The shape, round with a slight crater, the size of a penny. I'd seen it before. I'd seen it before at work. "Is that…a *bullet wound?*"

Roman grabbed my hand and pulled it off his scar. He didn't seem to like me touching it. "It's nothing."

Nothing?

I stared at him. His face was totally closed off, his gaze avoiding mine. Except now I could see a glimpse of the darkness that simmered under the surface. It didn't really come as a shock to me. I'd sensed it even from the moment we met.

I opened my mouth to ask him more. A ringing cut me off. Roman grabbed his phone from above his head and pressed a button, cutting it off.

"My alarm," he explained, his voice sounding strained. "It's seven. I have to be at the airport by eight. My ride will be here in ten minutes."

I nodded and forced myself to pull away from him. I felt so cold and empty at the thought of never seeing him again. I stood and turned, walking back to the bedroom where my clothes were waiting. They had arrived freshly laundered hours ago. By then neither of us mentioned my leaving early.

Roman called my name. I didn't stop or turn to acknowledge him. I was struggling with a sudden flood of emotion, unexpected in its intensity. This was unfair. Why did I have to meet him, to glimpse the kind of intimacy and closeness I could have, only to have him disappear out of my life forever?

Roman and I dressed side by side, the silence growing thicker. Out of the corner of my eye, I watched him as he pulled on jeans over his hard body. I tried to memorize the lines of his beautiful torso before he shrugged on a button up shirt over it. Even putting *on* clothes he was mesmerizing. I leaned against the drawers as he pulled out a duffel bag, still half packed, and threw a few more things in.

"You pack light."

"I wasn't planning on staying."

That stung. I turned away to slip on my other heel. "Of course, you weren't." *How stupid are you, Julianna? Did you expect him to stay in Verona for you after one night?*

I felt his hand on my arm. He turned me to face him. When I glanced up his features were drawn and dark. "I don't want to leave you."

"But you have to. Right?"

"Right." He paused, then licked his lips, lips that I would miss like crazy. Lips that gave me soul-consuming, brain-dizzying kisses that I would, from this day forward, compare all other kisses to. His eyes shone with a sudden light. "Come with me."

This took me by such surprise that I laughed out loud. "Sure," I joked. "I'll call in sick to work and skip town."

"I'm serious." His features grew hard and set.

I blinked. "What?"

"Come with me right now. We could go to Paris. You told me you've always wanted to see it." I had, earlier when we'd been talking about the things we'd always wanted to do but never done. "There are always spare seats in first class."

Paris? First class? Right now? I'd never even left the country, let alone traveled in an airplane first class.

"I don't have anything with me," I said weakly.

"I'll buy you whatever you need. We can stop by your place, pick up your passport."

"What about your studies? What about London?"

"They're not going anywhere." He shrugged. "I take time off all the time."

I shook my head, unable to believe what he was suggesting. "You're crazy."

He grabbed me by the upper arms, searching my face. "But it's the best kind of crazy."

"I…" Me, go to Paris with him?

He let out a growl. "Why are you fighting me again? I don't want this to end yet. Neither do you. Leave Verona with me. I promise, the second that you want to come home I'll have you on the next flight back, no questions asked. Let's not say goodbye yet."

I could. I could leave with him. Take off like I've always wanted to.

We'd go to Paris for a long weekend, maybe a week, then what? I'd come back to Verona and he'd go back to London? It would kill me. Letting him leave now was already painful. If I spent another day with him, another two, three...

Better to cut this off at the pass. I shook my head. "I'm sorry. I can't."

His mouth pinched. "Who said I was giving you a choice?"

I rolled my eyes. "What are you going to do? Carry me over your shoulder onto the plane."

His eyes flashed with possibility.

Shit. "Why don't you stay in Verona a bit longer?" I asked, before he got any ideas.

He shook his head, his lip curling. "I can't stay here."

"Why not?"

"I just can't."

I crossed my arms over my chest. "And I can't leave."

He let go of me and stepped back, the cold air rushing in between us like a jolt of reality.

"It was a stupid idea anyway."

"Roman, please..." I pleaded. I hated that he was angry at me. I hated that we were saying goodbye like this.

His phone beeped. "My ride is here." Roman slipped it into his pocket and grabbed his duffel bag. He turned to walk out.

"Please don't leave angry with me," I said, quietly.

He froze. He glanced over his shoulder and his gaze caught mine. I could see it, the sadness and regret underneath the anger. The same things that were burning inside of me.

For a second I thought he might turn around and walk across the room towards me, closing the distance like I desperately wanted him to do.

"The room has been paid for until tomorrow," he said.

Then he was gone.

No goodbyes.

No last kiss.

Just gone.

ROMAN

I threw myself into the passenger side and slammed Mercutio's car door, my duffel dropped at my feet. Weird emotions swirled around inside me. I hated myself for walking out on Julianna the way I did, as if she had meant nothing. But I knew, if I had crossed that room to kiss her one last time the way I'd wanted to, I'd never fucking leave. And I had to leave.

I could feel Mercutio staring at me. He still hadn't pulled away from the curb. I glared at him. "What?" I snapped.

He snorted. "Hello to you, too, motherfucker. Thanks for making your excuses to everyone last night. You're the fucking best for picking me up and taking me to the airport."

I slumped into my seat. "Sorry, Merc," I said, my voice soft and genuine.

He made a grunting sound and I knew it was his way of accepting my apology. "You look like shit."

That was him telling me we were okay. "Thanks."

He pulled away from the curb and into traffic. I sat in silence. I could feel his eyes glancing over to me every few seconds. "Who was she anyway?"

I shook my head. "The girl of my dreams, Merc. The girl of my fucking dreams."

"Seriously?"

"She makes me laugh, she's so fucking easy to talk to. And the sex…"

"TMI, bro. I don't need to know."

"Jesus fucking Christ, Merc." I let out a growl. "Every woman before her and after her is going to pale in comparison."

He raised an eyebrow at me. "Does this mean you're only fucking dudes from now on?"

I punched him in the arm, causing him to swerve. The car next to us beeped loudly.

Merc cursed and straightened the car. "Shit, you know I'd support you even if you did fuck dudes. Wouldn't be into it, but I'd still love you, man."

"I'm not turning gay," I muttered. "Maybe joining the fucking priesthood."

Merc laughed. Until he glanced over at me. I was furious. Furious at life for dealing me the family I had. Furious at my father for being the tyrant that he was. Furious at my brother for dying, causing the spotlight to shine firmly onto me, meaning that I *had* to get away from Verona, now more than ever. Most of all I was furious at myself for walking away from Julianna.

"Jesus," Merc said, "you're really cut up about this girl."

"No shit, Sherlock."

"She's really that perfect."

"More than perfect."

"And you're letting her get away?"

"I asked her to come with me. Offered her a ticket to Paris…" I gritted my teeth. That's what really fucking hurt. I was alone in feeling like our connection was worth pursuing until the wheels fell off.

"And she said no."

"She said no. Just like you. Both of you bitches. I'm not good enough for either of you to leave this piece of shit city. Even if I pay for it."

"Roman..."

I growled. "Yeah, I know. You have your fucking reasons." Mercutio may have grown up with me, but his family was not well off like mine. Mercutio had refused to get involved in the "life". He was too proud to take a handout from me. He worked a steady job in IT after taking night classes while working a menial job at a factory. He refused to let me help him out with money. He'd always said, he'd come visit me in Europe when he could afford to pay for his own damn ticket. Proud fucker. I loved him like a brother.

I stared out the window, watching the city flash past me. Verona was like an old prison, the buildings its bars, blackened with soot and mold, barely letting the light seep down to the crumbling streets. The alleyways were in a constant haze from all the white smoke puffing out of open exhausts, and the pipes webbing across the sides of buildings cracked like joints. This was a place where the rules were harsh and unwritten. Where hidden players held the dice and decent people had no idea that they were merely sheep in a valley of wolves.

The next time I came back, it'd be for my father's funeral.

Once I got to London I had to figure out what to do with myself. Maybe, get a job at the boxing gym I'd attended for the last eight years. Learn how to save and shit. I couldn't keep living off my father's allowance. Especially now.

"So..." Merc's voice broke into my thoughts, "girl of your dreams, huh? What was her name?"

"Her name's—"

"Holy fuck." Mercutio slammed on the brakes. I jerked forward and my seatbelt caught me across the chest. A chorus of beeps blared around us. The car skidded to a halt. A black Escalade had driven across the lane to barricade the road in front of us. Another black SUV blocked the road behind us. The few cars behind us began trickling around us in the farthest lane, slowly. I could feel their eyes and curiosity peering at the blockage in the road.

My heart began thumping in my chest. Either this was a planned hit from the Veronesis or my father's men had finally found me. I don't know which one I feared more.

Of all the times to be without a fucking gun.

"Are you packing, Merc?" I opened the glove compartment and rummaged through it, finding only papers and a small black torch.

"What? Hell no."

Damn him and his no gun policy. I slammed the compartment shut. The passenger door of the front Escalade opened. A figure stepped out.

Fuck. It was Abel.

Which meant my father was here for me.

I inhaled deeply and cursed my last name. I couldn't put my father off any longer. It was better to get out of the car and see what he wanted. I was cornered now. I took a deep breath and braced myself to face the dark presence that had been waiting here to catch me.

"Stay here," I said to Merc. "They want me, not you."

"I'm coming with—"

"Merc, it's my father. He won't hurt me." At least, I hoped not. "He probably just wants to talk to me." I hoped. I wouldn't put anything past my father.

I opened the car door and stepped out.

"Roman," Merc called.

"Yeah?"

"Call me if you need me, k?"

I nodded, patting my jeans pocket to make sure my phone was with me. Then shut the door so I could face Abel.

They say that you should never judge a book by its cover. With Abel, he was every bit the monster on the inside as on the out. He was a wiry man, a few inches shorter than my six foot two, a scar that ran down from his left ear, down to the corner of his lip, as if he had once been caught in a fish hook and torn away from it. For almost as long as I could remember, he wore black leather gloves so he'd never leave a fingerprint anywhere. It wasn't his strength or fists you ever had to worry about. It was the various knives he always had in his possession and his ability to wield them like scalpels. And the fact that he had no soul. No remorse. No conscience. He would gut his sister's baby in front of her if it suited him.

He strode towards me, hatred rolling off him. I stood my ground. If there was one thing my father taught me, never let them see you flinch. If you flinch, you're dead.

Abel sneered and his scar puckered. "Your father wants you."

A black limousine rolled up beside us and stopped, the passenger side door by my side. Abel opened the door, holding it wide open for me. "Get in."

"I have a plane to catch."

Abel pulled out a gun and cocked the weapon, pointing the black barrel at my head. I had no doubt he'd shoot given half the chance. "Get. In."

JULIANNA

I stepped in through my front door and dropped my keys into the bowl on the side table.

"Where the hell have you been?" a voice behind me demanded, making me jump. A tiny figure stood in my doorway, hands on hips.

"Nora." I let out a breath of relief, stepping aside to let her in. "Jesus Christ, you scared me."

I walked towards my kitchen for a glass of water. She swatted my ass as I passed her.

"Ow. What was that for?"

"That was for making me worry when you didn't come home last night."

I stiffened. "How did you know I didn't come home last night?"

She gave me a look. "Firstly, I waited up for you so long here that I fell asleep on your couch. I wanted to tell you about my date."

"Oh."

"And secondly," she waved her finger at my tight black dress, the one that I had been wearing for almost twenty-four hours, "that is a walk of shame outfit if I ever saw one."

"Nora! How do you even know what a walk of shame is? Wait...wait. I don't want to know."

She snorted. "Please, I might be old but I'm not dead."

I turned back to my glass of water, hoping to avoid all further conversation.

When I didn't answer, she swatted me again, making me hiss. "And that is for making me wait to get all the dirty details."

I rubbed my ass, glaring at her. "Remind me to get my spare keys from you."

"Don't change the subject. Who was he and how good was he in bed?" A wide toothy grin spread across her face.

I felt my cheeks heat up as the memories of the last twenty-four hours assaulted my mind.

Nora's grin grew wider. "Dear Lord, the man has made you speechless. Tell me everything. Did you meet him out somewhere?"

"Well...not exactly."

"Through a friend?"

"No."

She let out a huff. "So? Where'd you met him?"

"Um, at Mom's?"

Nora's mouth dropped open. "Are you actually telling me that you picked up a guy at the *cemetery*?"

I winced. "No. He asked *me* out."

"So, you allowed yourself to be picked up by some guy you met at a graveyard?"

"Kinda?"

"I knew it. You," she waggled her finger at me, "are a closet freak."

"What? I am not."

"Freaky deacky leather squeaky."

I laughed, mostly out of embarrassment. I was *not* having this conversation with a woman who was old enough to be my grandmother. "It's not like that."

"Did you make out with him at the cemetery?"

"Ew, Nora, we were at a *cemetery*."

"Didn't stop you from thinking about it, did it?"

I had more than thought about it. I remembered how Roman had pressed his finger to his mouth in a shushing motion, drawing my eyes to his lips. Those perfect lips, the most beautiful lips I had ever seen on a man. I had wanted to pull them against my mouth and taste them. I had wanted it with a fierceness that had taken my breath away.

"I knew it." Nora was grinning at me, her head nodding slightly. "I could see it all over your face."

I didn't bother denying it. I gulped down water, trying to quell the heat rising up my body.

"Did you sleep with him?"

I choked, spluttering water everywhere. "Nora!" I admonished, my cheeks flushing red-hot as images of the last twenty-four hours with him—his skin, his tongue, his body—washed over me.

"Oh my lolly gobble bliss bomb! You did sleep with him!" she screamed.

"Nora, shhh." I cringed as I imagined my other neighbors hearing.

"Tell. Me. Everything. Height, specs, penis size."

"I don't know his penis size!"

"Lame." She huffed out a breath of air. "Tell me everything anyway."

My stomach fluttered, forcing a grin out of me. "Okay."

We sat on my couch. I launched into a recap of what had happened with Roman, leaving out the sexy specifics despite Nora's attempts to tease them out of me. "Every second with him felt so incredible, so natural, like breathing. It was unlike anything I've ever experienced, unlike anything I even thought possible."

Nora clasped her hands together and let out a sigh, her eyes going all misty. My belly clenched tighter as I spoke about him.

I missed him.

I missed his touch, his voice, I missed laughing with him.

When I told Nora about his offer to take me to Paris, she let out a shriek. "*What*? Why are you still here?" Her eyes bulged. She looked like she might hit me. "You said *no*?"

"I couldn't have just taken off like that."

She rolled her eyes. "Yes, you could have. That's an excuse because you," she glared at me, "are scared."

I tried shrugging off her words, but they had settled like tiny knives in my belly. "What was the point anyway if I did say yes? My life is here in Verona and his is in London. It'd never work out."

"When you get my age, you realize that life is short. Sometimes you don't need to know the 'point' of it before you jump in. If it feels right, then do it. Carpe the fuck out of that diem."

I bit my lip. I wasn't scared. I was just being responsible. Right?

So why did it feel like I had done the wrong thing by not taking a chance with Roman?

My stomach sank as I realized I could never make it right. He was gone. I was never going to see him again.

ROMAN

In the limousine, my father sat facing forward in the middle of the black leather seat, waiting for me. I slid into the seat opposite him, my stomach knotting into a ball. I hadn't seen my father since I left Verona at eighteen. His dominating presence hadn't changed.

He was in his early fifties now but he looked as though he still worked out regularly. His shoulders were linebacker broad, his barrel waist showing little signs of flab in an expensive Armani black pinstripe suit, black shirt and a red silk tie with a matching pocket hankie. He cut an imposing figure, one arm outstretched across the luxuriously soft leather seat, his ankle holster showing a little under the hem of his slacks as he sat with one leg resting on his other knee. I knew he'd probably have a pistol tucked under his suit jacket too.

His dark hair was slicked back. His goatee was showing the first signs of silver hairs. His black hooded eyes that looked so much like mine bore into me, the lines between his brows set in a permanent frown. I should be used to his look of barely disguised disgust, of bitter disappointment. It never failed to feel like a knife twisting into my gut. I hated him, but for some fucked up reason, I still needed him to approve of me.

Hi, son. Nice to see you see you again after eight long years. Gee, you've grown into a man now. He didn't bother with such niceties. He rolled his gaze over me, assessing me. Probably wondering why he'd been cursed with such a disappointment.

"No," my father said, as Abel tried to get in the back with us. "Get in front." He turned towards me, his eyes flashing like a storm. "I want to speak to my son, alone." His voice hadn't changed; heavy and gravelly, it was the voice of my childhood nightmares.

Abel shut the door. My father and I were left alone. The bulletproof and soundproof partition was up between us and the front cab. I bit down the growing apprehension in my gut.

The limo began to move. I shifted in my seat and tried to unclench my jaw. "Where are we going?" I asked my father, the first thing I'd said to his face in eight years.

"For a drive."

I swallowed as I stared out the tinted windows, Verona flashing past us as we turned off from the highway. "I need to be at the airport by eight to catch a flight."

My father smiled but it was not friendly. "You thought you could come to Verona, slip in and out of your brother's funeral without saying hello to your old man? What did I do to deserve such disrespect?" I could hear the cold anger in his voice. He was pissed. More pissed at me than I think he'd ever been.

I cringed. "I ran out of time. I had too many friends to see and..." I glanced over to him. He was still glaring at me. "I wasn't sure you'd want to see me," I said, trying to keep the bitterness out of my voice. "You seemed happy when I left Verona."

"Family comes first," he said. "Family is the most important thing. I'd think that even *you'*d have learned that by now."

I tried to ignore his dig. I tried not to feel his disapproval rolling over me in heavy waves. I was never his favorite son; he had always made that clear. That honor had gone to Jacob, a demon he created in his image, then to Marco, the middle child who got himself exiled from Verona years ago, thanks to his tendency to lash out with violence first, talk never.

I'd been my mother's favorite. I'd been born premature and she'd almost lost me. I had been the smallest of her three sons. Because of that, she had treated me with kid gloves, to the disgust of my father. She'd made me soft in his eyes.

We drove for a few minutes in silence. My phone pinged.

Mercutio: WTF? Where r u going? Want me to follow u?

I quickly texted back.

Me: No. I'll get him to drop me off at the airport.

Mercutio: Your passport's in the duffel.

Shit. I didn't think about that.

Me: Meet me at the airport?

Mercutio: K.

Me: Thanks, Merc. I owe u.

Mercutio: Just don't get killed.

It would have been funny if it wasn't a real possibility. I slipped my phone back into my pocket.

"Have you enjoyed your time in Europe?" my father asked, irritation clear in his voice. Before I could answer, he added, "Wasting my fucking money?"

I gritted my teeth. "I've been studying, learning about—"

"I know about all the fucking things you've been learning. How many parties you can attend, how many fights you can get into, how many European heiresses you can fuck."

I bit my tongue. My blood turned bitter at his disapproval, harsh but accurate.

My father smoothed down his jacket, composing himself. "I've withdrawn you from your legal studies at Notre Dame. Your time in Europe is over."

No! I was supposed to go back to London, away from all this shit again. "You can't—"

"I can and I have."

"I have one more semester to go." I could buy some time. One semester. I could save money in one semester, get a job in Europe after I'd finished my degree. Then I wouldn't be financially reliant on him. Fuck, why hadn't I thought of doing this sooner? Because I didn't plan on Jacob dying. I thought monsters were invincible like my father seemed to be. Only the innocents around them died, like my mother. "I can't quit right before I finish. Send me back for one last semester."

My father sneered. "You've been one semester from finishing for the last two fucking years. You had your chance to finish your degree. You wasted it."

I sank back into the seat, feeling like it was going to swallow me up, my throat tightening around the realization of my fate. "You can't do this."

"You listen to me," he leaned forward and thrust his finger into my face, hatred glittering in his eyes. "I have let you drink and fuck your way around Europe for the last eight years," my father barked out. "What do you have to show for it? *Nothing.*"

Rebellion swirled around in my gut. I wanted to slap his hand aside. I knew better than to actually do it. I knew better than to fuck with Giovanni Tyrell when he was like this.

"I have a life back there," I said, through my teeth. "Friends. An apartment. I have to go back and say goodb—"

"Your life is here. I have let you carry on like a spoiled brat for too long. This ends now."

"This isn't f—"

"Jacob, God rest his soul, is gone. And Marco, exiled, thanks to his stupidity. He can't run the family business from Colombia. As much as it pains me, you are now the heir to my throne. You are a Tyrell and you're goddamn going to start acting like a fucking Tyrell, you understand me?"

That was the end of that discussion. I swallowed down every single raging, defiant reply. They swirled hot in my gut like heartburn. I had no choice. I was the last heir to the Tyrell empire. My father was never letting me get away now.

A single ray of light pierced through the darkness. If I was forced to stay here, then Julianna and I...

Until she found out who I was. Until she ran far, *far* the fuck away from me.

"Roman, have I made myself clear?" My father's gravelly voice broke through my thoughts.

"Yes, father," I ground out. *Welcome home, Roman.*

"You will stay at one of our apartments here in the city. I've already organized for the current tenants to move out. I'll arrange for the stuff in your London apartment to be packed up and shipped back."

"I don't give a shit what you do with my stuff," I muttered.

He snorted. "Wasteful, ungrateful son of a bitch. If your mother were alive—"

I saw red. "You think she'd approve of what you've turned this family into, huh? Mama would turn over in her fucking grave if she knew what you did to our family, that you killed her eldest son with your—"

My father's fist lashed out faster than I could react. It slammed against my cheek, knocking my face aside, a burst of pain exploding through my cheekbone. Before I could react, he grabbed my chin with his meaty hand and yanked me forward. He leaned in, his eyes like coals burning into me. Suddenly I was twelve again. "If you *ever* talk to me like that again I will shred you down to your worthless bones with my bare hands. I brought you into this world, I will fucking take you out of it if I have to."

He shoved me back, a snarl of disgust on his face. I turned my face away from him, my hands fisted by my sides, my face throbbing on the left side. I could feel a small trickle of blood running down to my jaw, probably from where one of his fat gold rings broke open my skin, but I didn't wipe it away. Fury whirled around my body like a tornado.

I had a looming sense, a premonition, that this would end with my father and me facing off. Only one of us would walk away.

The limo rolled to a stop and I flinched. I hadn't been paying attention to our surroundings.

"Get out."

Thank fuck this conversation was over.

"Always a pleasure, *Dad*." I didn't wait for the driver. I kept my fury tightly packed into my veins and threw the door open myself. I stepped out. And froze.

We weren't at my new apartment.

We were at the docks, the smell of salt in the air, parked in front of a dark-looking warehouse, several men with large guns —AK-47s to be precise, judging from the shape and size of them —standing guard at a door, a single floodlight illuminating the entrance, corrugated iron surrounding it. The limo doors opened behind me. Abel and my father got out of the car.

"What are we doing here?" I asked, trying not to let any fear leak into my voice.

Abel sneered at me. I recognized the same smug satisfaction in his face as earlier. I should have picked up on it before. I should have known something was up.

My father merely leveled a cool stare at me. "We're turning you into a man, my son."

ROMAN

Inside the warehouse, I walked down a dark corridor, my father and two of his men in front of me, Abel behind me, herding me like an animal. The only sound was the echoing of our footsteps and the thud of my heart in my chest. No one would tell me what we were doing here. I knew better than to ask again.

I ignored the apprehension swirling around me and strode onwards with my chin held high. My father and his men were like dogs. If you showed them fear, they would smell it, sense it, and they would tear you to shreds.

We came to a locked door up ahead. One of the guards pushed in a pin code and a beeping noise sounded. The door ahead clicked open. We gathered into a small security chamber, an iron coffin with yet another door ahead locked by yet another pin code. Abel closed the door behind us, trapping us, the lock clicking into place. I could already feel the oxygen running out in this tiny room, filling instead with the stench of sweat and stale cigarettes. In the top corner of the chamber, the black eye of a camera stared down at us.

The next door beeped, unlocked and opened, a rush of air

flooding the cramped space as I moved forward. The room I stepped into was dark around the edges so I couldn't quite make out how large it was. I could sense the watchful eyes like hungry beasts around the edges of firelight. I could make out the shadow of pointed guns. The scent of acrid vomit filled my lungs. I repressed a gag. Underneath it, was the smell of piss and the metallic scent of blood.

A single spotlight cut through the darkness, falling on a man tied to a chair. Jesus Christ. His face had been beaten beyond recognition. All that remained was a swollen mass like a bunch of overripe grapes about to burst. Slits were all that were left of his eyes and mouth. He was covered in blood, drenched in it as if someone had showered him with it, now clumped and coagulating in places.

By his chair was a small silver trolley. Various knives, a large needle and other sharp metal implements were laid out on it, along with vials of liquid, everything smeared with blood.

My stomach curdled. I fought to keep the horror from my face. I spun around to my father, standing by my side, his face impassive, merely studying me. I'd always known that he did these kinds of things. Until now I'd been spared the morbid exhibition. I was no stranger to violence; I had inherited the Tyrell temper and had started more than my share of fights, but this was different. This was joyful pleasure in the prolonged pain of another. I didn't think I'd ever hated my father more in my entire life.

"What the hell is this?" I demanded. Was this a demonstration of what he'd do to me if I disobeyed him? Some fucked up way of warning me to keep in line?

"He's one of Veronesi's men," my father said.

I stiffened. The Veronesis were the rival family blamed for the massacre that had killed Jacob. I turned back to the Veronesi man, my head spinning. I hated whoever killed Jacob. But every slice of me was crying out that this display of torture was wrong. "Did he actually pull the trigger?" I bit out.

I heard a voice inside of me, laughing. *Your father's right. You are soft.*

"He sides with the Veronesis, which means he as good as pulled the trigger."

That was my father's brand of justice. He was the judge, jury, and executioner.

The accused didn't move. I could see several of his fingers were missing on each hand. I felt sick when I imagined the pain he must be in. I couldn't let myself feel anything. Any show of sympathy could be the end of both of us. I steeled any emotion away, crossed my arms, trying to look bored and unaffected. "Is he dead?" I asked, hearing how cold and hollow my voice had become. For his sake, I hoped so.

"He's told us that the Veronesis were not the ones who organized the hit on your brother," my father said, ignoring my question.

"He's lying," Abel snarled as he snapped on rubber gloves. "All Veronesis are liars."

"He eventually broke," my father continued. "He admitted everything."

Did he? Could any man withstand this kind of torture and not say whatever they wanted him to?

"As always, Abel got him to talk." The pride in my father's voice was clear.

I made the mistake of looking over to Abel. His eyes were fixed on me, glittering with amusement and...pride. The monster was proud of what he did.

"It's an art," Abel said, as he brushed tender gloved fingers across the bloody tools on the trolley. "To be able to inflict the maximum amount of pain on a human being without killing him."

"You're a regular Monet," I spat out.

To my horror, the man moved, his head lolling back. Within the mass of purple, one of his black slits opened slightly. He was looking at me. "Please," he whispered. Even through the unidentifiable mess of flesh and blood, his voice made him human.

Dear God. I swallowed down the bile lurching up from my stomach and bit back the sting at my jaw. This couldn't be happening.

"How the fuck is he still awake?" I blurted out. This man should have passed out from the pain already.

I caught the proud smile on Abel's face. "I always make sure that I have a ready supply of adrenaline. To make sure he won't miss a thing."

The needle and vials on the tray. The sick fucker. I turned away from Abel, unable to look at him anymore.

"What do you think, Roman? What should be his sentence?" my father asked. "For lying to us. For his part in your brother's death."

I knew my father only wanted one answer.

I regretted it the second I looked at the disfigured man in the chair.

"Please," he whispered again.

Something good. I needed to hang on to something good.

From the darkness, Julianna's face rose into my mind. I could see her clearly, the lovely sweet lines of her face, the sadness and love that shone in her eyes when she spoke about her mother. See, there was still love in this world. Still beauty. There was still goodness.

"Roman," my father barked out. "What say you?"

I stood there, cold and uncaring, an actor playing a part on a stage, a part that I had been born and raised to play, Roman Tyrell, son of Giovanni Tyrell. In my mind, I was elsewhere, wrapped around Julianna with my nose in her hair and her laughter in my ears. I spoke my next line as if I had rehearsed it. "He deserves to die."

My father's face split into a real smile, a horrifying smile, thin and cruel. For the first time in my life, my father stared at me with approval, with pride in his eyes. I had finally gotten what I had wanted from him since I was a boy. And it only took giving up my soul. I could feel darkness seeping into my pores.

My father reached into his jacket and pulled out a gun. He held it out to me. "You do the honors."

Fuck. No.

Twenty-six years I'd managed to keep my hands clean. Twenty-six years I had managed to keep some of my goodness intact, some of my mother in me. I had hidden her in the cracks of me. I'd managed to protect her memory. Until now. If I pulled the trigger, if I took a life, the last of her would die. I would be reborn, remade completely in my father's image.

The memory of Julianna thinned into a ghost and disappeared. I stood in this dark warehouse, the stench of shit and clotting blood clogging my lungs. Julianna wasn't real. But the darkness was waiting as it had been all these years, like a hungry beast, to pull me into it.

I couldn't do it. I couldn't pull the trigger. I couldn't let my father turn me into him.

I sneered and pointed to my shirt. "Do you know how expensive this outfit is? I'll get blood on it. Make your dog do it."

I could see Abel smiling from over my father's shoulder. He knew I was stalling, fighting for some way *not* to do this.

"You know," my father said, "Abel is not convinced that you're the right one to lead this family after I die. As are most of my men." He nodded to the silent figures watching us from around the room. "I know you could be. You have your mother's nature, but you also have my blood running in your veins. You are a Tyrell, son. That means that you bow down to no man. You bend to no one else's rules. You just need some…encouragement to earn your crown." He grabbed my hand and shoved the gun in it, the barrel as cold as death in my palm. "Kill him. Or I have no son. And the first bullet in this chamber will be for *you*."

I stared back into the face of my father, inches from me, both of us breathing the same acrid breath. In his eyes I saw the twisted, soulless gargoyle he'd become. I saw my future.

The life of a stranger...or mine.

An honorable man would lay down his own life for what was good, for what was right. A good man would take this gun in my hand and press it to his own skull. He would give himself up instead of taking away a life that wasn't his to take. He would choose to keep his soul even if it meant he'd lose his life.

I wasn't honorable. I wasn't *good* enough. The emptiness of death, the eternal blackness stretched open in front of me, and I lurched away from it. I wanted to live. Him or me. And I wanted to live. My stomach knotted. I was a coward because I wanted to live. *Forgive me, Mama.*

"Fine. I'll do it." With those words, I signed my soul to the devil.

I turned towards the man in the chair, forcing my eyes to look past him, making his figure into a blur. It was the only way I could do this. *He's not real. This isn't real. I'm not really here.* I lifted the gun, my barrel pointed towards him.

I didn't even know his name. I was going to take his life and I didn't even know his fucking name.

The man sucked in air audibly into his lungs, startling me. I made the mistake of seeing him, really seeing him. My gaze locked onto his one eye that wasn't quite swollen shut. "Please," he whispered, his voice cracking on every word. "I have a wife..."

My hand shook, even as I tried to hold it steady. *Fuck you,* I screamed inside me. *Don't make this any harder than it has to be.* I fought to hang on to any sense of justification, some sense of righteousness. He killed my brother. He deserved to die. I found myself hating this man for begging for his pathetic life as I hated myself for having to take it. Fuck him for begging. Why couldn't he just shut up and die?

I needed something good. Where was something good to hang on to? Where was the beauty? Where was the goodness? Even Julianna had left me now.

"I have children."

Children. He was a father. I was taking the life of a parent. The pain of losing my mother ripped through me. Could I do that to another child?

My gaze landed on his colorful socks peeking out from under the hem of his trousers. Bright blue with a cartoon dog on it. The kind of socks a child buys for his daddy.

I couldn't. My hand holding the gun dropped.

I felt a barrel in the small of my back as my father stepped up behind me.

"Do it," he commanded into my ear. "Do it. Or I swear to fucking God, I'll kill you myself."

I squeezed my eyes shut. My life or his.

You have no choice, Roman. It's self-defense.

"Roman," my father's voice softened, the anger slipping away and the cursed poisonous slither of disappointment slid into my ear. "Don't fail me, son."

My heart crushed in my chest. My finger slid into the trigger. All I had to do was squeeze. One tiny movement, that was all. That was all. I aimed the gun at the man in the chair. No, not a man. Not a human. Not a soul, not a beating heart. It was a thing.

"Please…"

My veins filled with ice. I let the darkness wrap her hands around me, soothing my ragged guilt with her numbness. And I pulled the trigger.

JULIANNA

I sat alone at my dining table drinking a cup of tea, and listening to my mother's voice fill the room, wrapping myself in her voice.

Abigail: "You don't have to tell me your name. Let's call you...Joan. After Joan of Arc. She was a strong woman, just like you."

Joan: "I'm scared."

Abigail: "I know. I'd be scared too. Take a deep breath. And remember why you want to do this."

My chest filled with pride. That was my mother, so patient, so filled with compassion. She always knew what to say. I wished I had inherited that trait from her.

There was a pause on the tape and the sound of someone

breathing hard.

Joan: "Are you a mother?"

Abigail: "I am. I have a beautiful little girl. She's eleven. And I would do anything for her. Anything. *Be strong for your children, Joan. Be strong for them."*

Joan: "Okay..."

It had been a phone conversation she'd taped a few weeks before her death. When I made detective six months ago, I had snuck into the records room and copied every piece of evidence from that file. My father would hate it if he knew I had this tape, that I played it over and over again on nights alone, listening to her voice and pretending she was in the same room as me. *"I have a beautiful little girl. She's eleven. And I would do anything for her."*

The recording ran to its end. I sat in the preceding silence. My apartment seemed cold and empty. Quiet. Too quiet.

I used to love the silence of my apartment, the way the things I left remained where they were exactly how I left them, no one else's invading touch. Everything right where it belonged. Every bit of space mine.

Tonight, I stared around the apartment as if it was my first time in here. The furniture I liked enough but it was all so generic and far from personalized. There were no pictures on my walls. No artwork. Nothing to reflect my tastes. I'd been waiting, it seemed, expecting that one day I would leave. That my real life would then begin.

That chance had come with Roman. That possibility had

stretched out its hand to me. I did not have the guts to take it. Why didn't I have the guts to leave with him? Why didn't I say yes?

I felt his warmth and his body pouring into me, filling me up. Our cries echoing throughout the room.

I shook my head, closed the box containing my mother's case file, before dumping my cold tea down the sink drain. I was being silly. I barely knew the guy. I was reeling from the insane amount of orgasms he'd given me. That was all.

Tomorrow, I'd feel better. Tomorrow things would go back to normal.

I lay in bed, staring at my ceiling, the moonlight painting squares of pale light across it, chewing on my lip. My eyes kept drifting over to my phone, the only link I had left with him.

Nora had long since gone home but her words had stayed behind with me. *"When you get to my age you realize that life is short. Sometimes you don't need to know the 'point' of it before you jump in."*

I snatched up my phone from the bedside table and opened a new message, the blank screen waiting for me to say all the things I wanted to say.

Is it strange that I miss you?

Is it crazy that I can't stop thinking about you?

I wish I had said yes to Paris.

I didn't write any of these things.

Me: I wish we hadn't left things the way we did. Let me know you've arrived in London safely.

I turned over, my back to the phone on the bedside table, and tried to find peace in the darkness. The image of his eyes haunted me, chasing me into a restless sleep.

ROMAN

I killed a man.

Back in my father's limo, I stared into nothing as this single thought looped over and over in my brain. The repeat of the gun booming throughout the warehouse room, the gun jerking my hand back, the small black hole that appeared on his forehead, the slim river of blood that dribbled from it. And those stupid cartoon socks.

The gun became so heavy that I let it hang at my side. My father's hand clasped my shoulder and his voice echoed in my skull. "Well done, son."

I had killed a man and he had been proud of me.

My hearing had gone fuzzy after that.

Someone had pulled the gun out of my hands. I knew it'd be wiped down, the barrel scratched with a wire plunger designed to change the internal grooves so that the next bullet's striations were different. No one would ever trace the bullet in that man's brain to me. That was how my *family* worked. They were professionals at this, too well-oiled and rehearsed to be taken down by the law. Soon I would be adding to them, bringing my knowledge of the criminal law system so we could bend it further to my father's will. It had been the only reason my father had agreed to let me move to Europe to commence my legal studies.

I would soon help this monstrous empire grow stronger. I would help feed it with my life and my soul. It didn't matter how hard I fought against it, I could not escape what I was destined to become.

I was alone again in the limo with my father, barely paying attention to what he was saying. "Things have changed in Verona since you left. The political landscape is not so...friendly. We have a new chief of police elected nine months ago. They call him the incorruptible." My father let out a snort. "So far he seems good to his word. He's made us public enemy number one. Vowed to clean up the streets."

I nodded, my body cold.

"I'll have a dossier sent to you with everything you need to know about who's who. Read it, memorize it, learn it."

"Yes, sir," I said, automatically.

The limo stopped. Moments later someone opened the door for me. The cool night air did little to cut in through the fuzz around my head.

"Go drink," my father said. "Have fun with your friends. You've earned it."

Go drink, have fun, while a man who you sentenced to death is being dumped somewhere like trash. Go have fun, you've earned it. I choked on these thoughts.

I don't know how I managed to get out of the limo. I stood in a smelly back alleyway, the walls of the buildings around me seeming to cut out all the light of the stars. Someone opened the back door of the bar for me, their body silhouetted in the dim light that misted out of the doorway. The thudding of the music coming from inside sounded like someone's violent heartbeat. Before I could take a step forward, Abel stepped in front of me, blocking my path.

The sight of him was like a splash of cold water on my face, cutting through my fog. I growled and bared my teeth. "Get out of my way, dog."

He smirked at me. "Relax, Roman. I just wanted to congratulate you. We're all surprised at how you...stepped up tonight."

A feeling of nausea bubbled up again like clotting blood. "Fuck off."

His grin widened. He shoved something in my hand before I could stop him. "I thought you'd like to keep a souvenir." He cackled, his laughter echoing off the insides of my skull. He disappeared back into the limo.

I looked down into my hand. He had pushed a single thin gold ring into my palm. The man's wedding ring, dried blood still clinging to the skinny gold band.

"I have a wife..."

It fell from my fingers into the muck.

I stumbled into the bar through the back entrance, searching, looking for... a drink, I needed a drink. I probably looked like I was already drunk, even though I was sober as fuck, everything blurry, my movements clumsy.

I had to get my shit together. My mother had been a Lettiere before she was married. I was a Lettiere. Lettieres didn't fall apart.

You're not a Lettiere. You're a Tyrell, a voice inside me taunted.

I was in a nondescript bar off the main strip, old wood and creaky leather, dim lighting casting the place in a dull brown light. It was where Mercutio and I used to meet after bad shit happened at home. None of my "family" or other "friends" came here. I was anonymous here.

Mercutio was already waiting for me inside, his eyes on the back entrance, leaning against the old wooden bar, chipped and lacquer peeling from years of spilled drinks. He'd driven all the way to the airport and rang my cell six times before I was capable of texting him back, asking him to meet me here.

He took one look at my face and his fell.

I almost turned around and left, not sure if I could take his judgment, his piteous look. I had nowhere else to go. I pushed my way through to the bar and leaned against it, just trying to breathe.

"You're not leaving Verona," he said.

It didn't sound like a question. I shook my head anyway. *No, I will never be able to leave now. I will die here.*

"Jesus, what did he do to you?" he asked quietly. I could hear the hesitation in his voice. He didn't really want to know.

I shook my head again, words failing me. *It's better you don't know.*

He cursed under his breath. I didn't have to say anything to Mercutio. He just…knew.

I closed my eyes, the gunshot echoing over and over, the backs of my eyes splattering with crimson. It had been the thing I had feared most since I watched my brother turn into a monster by my father's hand. I could feel the stains on my body, the darkness leaking into my veins and mixing with my blood.

"Here." Mercutio pushed a drink into my hand, snapping me partly out of my thoughts. I could feel the pity exuding from him. I could hear it in his voice. I hated him for pitying me. But I understood. Even I pitied me.

I downed the drink without even asking what it was, letting the alcohol burn all the way down in my throat. If only it could burn away my sins.

What I wanted was Julianna. I wanted to bury my face in her hair and lose myself in her body, letting her pure light absolve me of my sins. When I had been with her I'd forgotten about my cross to bear. I had been filled with a lightness I had long forgotten I could feel. Joking and laughing with her, and worshiping her beautiful body, had all felt so natural. I was no longer a Tyrell. She looked at me, really looked at me, and reminded me of the man I was underneath.

My phone beeped with a text.

. . .

Jules: I wish we hadn't left things the way we did. Let me know you've arrived in London safely.

It was like she could sense that I was thinking of her. That I needed her. Even though I had been such an asshole to her when I had left, here she was showing me the concern I didn't deserve.

I could go to her. Tell her I wasn't leaving Verona. Ask her to be mine. I stabbed my thumb on the screen to reply. I caught the sight of dried blood like a dark crescent moon under my nail. I froze. My hearing went all fuzzy. I thought I had washed off all the evidence from my hands. Here I was, still stained.

How could I touch her with these bloody, poisonous hands?

I had to let her go. I couldn't drag her into the darkness of my life. Things would only get worse from here.

I deleted her message before shoving my phone back into my pocket. I looked up and my breath stuck in my throat. There she was. Julianna, staring at me from across the bar. My heart slammed against my ribs. I didn't deserve her, but she'd found me anyway.

I blinked. Julianna faded from her face, revealing a pretty blonde stranger. She smiled at me and her sticky pink lip gloss caught the light, her thick fake eyelashes fluttering like moths.

I had a new mission. Drink. Get wasted. Let this stranger help me forget the shit my life had turned into.

Usually picking up girls was no problem for me. Tonight... everything felt off. I wrapped my hands around my glass and drank, before slamming it on the counter. My head felt like cotton wool and my body was numb. Not numb enough. I waved at the bartender for another one.

I felt a light touch on my arm and an overpowering floral

perfume pierced through the smell of spilled beer and sweat. Oh, right. The blonde. Rachel or whatever.

"Is your name, like, actually Roman?" she said with a giggle. Her voice was high-pitched and she spoke like she was scattering her words. I missed Julianna's husky warm voice.

"Yup." I stared at my glass as the bartender refilled it with amber liquid, the color of Julianna's eyes.

"Like the city, right?"

I downed the fresh glass of whiskey and hissed as it burned my throat. "That's Rome, not Roman."

"What?"

I turned to her. "I like to fuck rough."

Her mouth dropped open. "W-what?"

I leaned in, her face blurring through my alcohol-soaked vision. I hated her because she wasn't Julianna. "I fuck rough and I fuck hard. If you come home with me tonight you'll probably get hurt, but I can guarantee you'll like it."

Her cheeks flushed and she licked her lips, swiping some of her glossy lip shit off. "I don't usually do this."

"I don't give a shit about whether you do or don't. You have three seconds to make up your mind. Are you in or are you out?"

She inhaled, then let out a breath. "In." She pressed up to me for a kiss. I turned my head and her sticky mouth landed on my cheek.

I wiped the goop off with the back of my hand and leaned across the bar, swiping a bottle of Jack from behind the counter. "How about we stop talking and get the fuck out of here?"

"Let's get out of here." Julianna's voice rang in my mind, tinkling like silver bells.

The blonde beside me giggled, breaking through my thoughts. I grabbed her hand, bottle of Jack in the other, and led her to the exit, ignoring the yells of the bartender behind me and Mercutio trying to calm him down.

Anger swirled inside me. I hated this girl trailing after me. I hated my father for what he'd done. I hated Julianna for being the one woman I wanted and couldn't have. Most of all, I hated the monster I'd become.

JULIANNA

I hadn't slept well last night, tossing and turning, thinking of a certain dark-eyed man, missing his hands on me, wishing I could hear his voice. I still hadn't heard back from him. He would have landed in London hours ago. He should have seen my text by now.

He was ignoring me. Deliberately. I felt a stab in my gut. Was he really that bitter about how we left things? Did I really deserve the silent treatment?

Or he'd already forgotten about me, I thought bitterly. I was just another notch on his belt. Just something to pass the time...

Don't be ridiculous, Julianna. You were the one who rejected him. He had every right to ignore my painful reminder. I would have to accept that he didn't want to speak to me again.

It would be almost three p.m. in London now. Perhaps we'd be walking arm in arm along the Reine, or licking croissant flakes from each other's fingers or lying on a blanket on the grass at Tuileries Garden. If I had said yes.

When I was little, my mother told me that if I was lucky, one day I'd meet a soulmate. I had asked her what a soulmate was. A soulmate was the truth, she said. A mirror. They reflected yourself back to you, exactly as you *were*. All of you, even the pieces you hated or the ones you hid well. At first, it would hurt. And it should hurt. No tree broke through the canopy without stretching for it. No flower ever saw the sun without opening up.

The wake of Roman's presence had left me reeling, viewing my life from a perspective I'd never seen before. He left me turning over each piece in my hands.

Roman had been a soulmate. Undoubtedly.

A soulmate I'd stupidly let walk away.

The saddest part was that he'd never know how much he'd affected me. I'd never be able to tell him thank you. I'd just be a memory he'd sometimes pull out and dust off.

I shook myself. No point in feeling sorry for myself. I would be glad I had a chance to meet him.

Next time, *if* a soulmate came along again, I would hold on to him and never let him go.

"Rough weekend?" my partner Espinoza asked as I jumped into his dark blue work sedan the next morning.

I thought I'd done a good enough job of covering up my bags with concealer. Obviously not. I should have known he'd pick up on it. Even though Espinoza had only been my partner for six months, he seemed to notice this stuff.

"You could say that," I said.

Espinoza's thick, dark brows furrowed as he studied me. He wore his smooth brown baby face with the rugged air of a confident man, which always meant there were at least a few women hanging around wanting more. He was a confirmed bachelor in his mid-thirties, dating regularly but never with a serious girlfriend, at least not for the time I'd known him.

I avoided his eyes and nodded to the road. "We gonna park here all day or are we going to work? Murders aren't going to solve themselves."

Espo let out a snort. "Oh, I see."

"What do you see?"

"You're losing sleep over a guy."

I flinched. Dammit.

"Hah!" He nudged my arm with his elbow. "Come on. Who is he?"

"He's no one."

"Ooooo," he sang, "Capi's got a boyfriend."

I rolled my eyes. "Shut up and drive, Espo."

"Am I gonna get a name?"

"Drive."

"Not even a name?"

"Espo," I warned.

"Alright, already. Jeez, I tell you about my women." Espo pulled out into traffic.

I made a face. "And I'm still in therapy because of it."

Espo tapped his fingers on his chest. "Here. You hurt me right here."

I let out a laugh. I caught the flash of his grin out of the corner of my eye. "What's on the menu this morning?" I asked, changing the subject.

"A body dump off Brunswick Street. Hope you skipped breakfast."

Finally. I was being assigned a real case. Looks like my father had taken what I'd said to heart. My stomach fluttered with nerves. This was my chance to prove myself. I could not screw up. I grabbed the handle above the door as Espinoza took the corner hard.

Ten minutes later we had parked and were walking down an alleyway in Little Italy. The smell of rotting cabbage and sour fish hit my nostrils, making me scrunch up my nose. This alley backed up a large Italian restaurant called La Cucina that specialized in wood-fired pizzas. Best pizza in the city, in my opinion.

We signed in with the officer manning the crime scene perimeter, pulled on shoe booties and snapped on rubber gloves.

"After you," Espinoza hiked up the yellow crime scene tape for me that had been strung across the alley.

"Nice to see chivalry isn't dead," I teased.

Lacey, our newest and youngest medical examiner, was already at the scene. Young, only in her early thirties, she had moved in from out of state. Rumor had it she had graduated with a doctorate in forensic pathology from Harvard Medical School. From my dealings with her, she was thorough, sharp and professional. Best of all, she didn't take any shit from anybody, most of all because she was a woman of color. She was bent over a body, her thick dark hair tied back from her pretty chocolate-skinned face.

Espo let out a low whistle. He was staring at Lacey's ass.

I slapped his arm. "Are you really ogling her at a crime scene?"

"What?" Espo gave me one of his trademark "I'm so innocent and even if I weren't you still love me" grins.

I rolled my eyes. "You are hopeless."

"Hopelessly in love."

"You're hopelessly in love at least once a week."

"Nu-uh. Put in a good word for me?"

I shook my head firmly and gave him what I hoped was a "leave her alone" glare. I sidled up to Lacey and said a quick hello. From what I could see, the body was male, laying on his back, wearing dark slacks and a dark shirt, soaked with blood. His face was turned away, his clothes torn and he'd been beaten up before he died.

"Morning, beautiful," Espinoza said, flashing Lacey a grin. Obviously, my glare wasn't scary enough. "What do you have for us?"

Lacey shook her head, the hint of a blush playing at her

cheeks. "This man was tortured, brutally, before he died. Cause of death was the gunshot wound to the head." She pointed to his forehead. I moved around the body to get a better look. His face was like an overripe grape, purple and engorged, eyes almost completely swollen shut, lips busted up, a small dark bullet wound on his forehead.

"There's no blood pooling around the body, indicating he was shot somewhere else and dumped here," continued Lacey. "Lividity also confirms he was moved."

I nodded. There were dirt and smears of something oily around him but no blood. "Time of death?"

"I won't know for certain until I get him back to the lab. Based on liver temp and the ambient temperature of this alley-way, I'm estimating sometime on Sunday night."

I leaned down to feel in his pockets. They were totally empty. "No wallet. No I.D. No phone."

"No eyes on the alleyway," Espo said, indicating the lack of security cameras. "Maybe one of the nearby traffic cams caught something. I'll get uniforms to start canvassing the area for witnesses."

"You won't get anything," I said, a heavy feeling in my chest. Verona's Little Italy was filled with undocumented workers and people hiding from authorities. The locals were notorious for turning a blind eye and keeping their mouths shut. This body dump was a pro job, cold and calculated.

"I know," said Espo. "But we have to try."

I nodded. "We have to try."

"Ligature marks around his wrists and ankles suggested he was tied up for a while," Lacey pushed up the sleeves to reveal the bruising around his wrists. "And he's missing fingers..."

I shuddered as I counted three, four, five missing digits. "Have we found the fingers?"

"Not yet. The techies are still looking."

Around the alley, three crime scene techs scoured the area, one of them with a camera in her hand, snapping pictures.

"So...he was tied up, beaten, tortured, then killed with a single gunshot to the forehead, execution-style, then dumped. This was a professional hit. They wanted something from him before they killed him." I spotted something. "He has a tan line on his left ring finger. A ring was there. He was married."

Lacey let out a whispered curse. "I hope he doesn't have kids."

"Let's hope not." A heaviness descended on me. I knew what it was like to lose a parent like this. "Hey, Espo," I called over to him. He was standing over at a dumpster talking to a crime scene tech who was digging around inside. "Any luck with I.D. in the dumpster?"

"No." Espo jogged back over and walked around the body so he could see the victim's face. He scrunched up his nose and tilted his head. "This badly beaten, it's going to be a bust trying to do facial recognition against the missing person database. I doubt his own mother could recognize him now."

"I had his fingerprints scanned," Lacey said. "Or at least, what fingerprints he had left. One of the techs is running them now."

"So far no gun in the dumpsters either," said Espo. "Though I doubt the boys will find anything there."

I nodded. "This killer was too smart to throw the weapon away near where the body was dumped."

"No casings have turned up either."

"And there's about a million pieces of trace evidence around him," I said, pointing to the grit, oil, and food waste around him. "Maybe forensics will find something on the body."

My phone beeped in my pocket, so I pulled it out.

Dad: Don't let me down.

. . .

He'd specifically assigned me to this case. Determination knotted in my throat as I tucked my phone away. I would not let him down.

"We've got a hit off the database," someone called. A crime scene tech, a young man, came jogging over with a palm-sized machine. "He's in the system."

"Vincent Torrito, or Vinnie to his friends," Espo read off the screen. Above the text was a small arrest photograph showing a rough-looking man, mid-thirties, with hair cropped close to his skull, a disfigured nose from being broken several times, and a stud showing in his ear. "And boy, does he have some bad, bad friends."

"Now I recognize him," I said. "He's one of Veronesi's men, a known mid-level dealer. Vice picked him up a week ago on drug charges and captain got a chance to interrogate him about the murder of Tyrell's son."

"Oh, yeah," said Espo. "The massacre down at the docks at the Tyrell's warehouse? Vinnie didn't say shit as far as I remember."

"Of course, the Veronesis are denying any involvement." None of the mob members would talk to the police, not even about a rival family. They had their own style of justice and judgment. I stared down at the dead man. Whatever he knew, he was truly silent now. "Vinnie didn't talk to us, but...somebody thought he knew something."

Espo cursed. "Two weeks ago the Veronesis supposedly gun down Jacob Tyrell. Now a Veronesi body turns up. This fucking thing is going to blow up into an all-out war."

The canvas of the neighborhood turned up nothing, as expected. Nobody heard or saw anything Sunday night.

Once the body was back in the morgue, Lacey narrowed time of death down to between seven thirty and ten o'clock Sunday night. The body hadn't been there when a restaurant worker had gone out for a cigarette at eleven p.m. Sunday night. When another worker had taken out the trash first thing Monday morning at seven minutes after five, he'd found the body, so it'd been dumped between those hours.

During a tearful interview with Mrs. Torrito at her home, a one-bedroom apartment in a rough Verona neighborhood, we'd found out that Vinnie had left the apartment on Friday night without telling her where he was going. He hadn't come back.

When I asked her why she hadn't reported him missing, she shook her head. "He goes off sometimes. Comes back a few nights later, sometimes banged up, but he always comes back. He wouldn't just leave Jimmy and Jake."

His kids.

Jimmy and Jake clung to their mother's side as she cried, both watching me with solemn round eyes. The boys were seven and nine, and I prayed to hell they didn't know what their father *was* when he had been alive.

Vinnie's car, a black sedan, was also missing and currently unaccounted for.

I came into the station early Tuesday morning to find the place a hive. A canvas of the nearby traffic cameras turned up footage of several vehicles driving around the area between eleven p.m. and five-oh-seven a.m. We ran the license plates on the vehicles. Only one name stood out. A black Escalade was seen driving into the area in the body drop window, at around two a.m. The Escalade's windows were tinted and the security footage was grainy, so we couldn't get a visual on the driver and passenger. It was registered to none other than Tyrell Industries, a company owned by the Tyrell family, one of the ruling mob empires this side of the country.

"Let's round up Giovanni Tyrell," I said as I stared at the still of the black Escalade on the large screen in the tech room.

"And his son," said Espinoza, standing beside me and chewing on a lollipop stick.

"His son?"

"Word on the street is, since Jacob died, the youngest son has been recalled back into the fold. The prodigal son has returned and there's a new heir to the throne. The new Prince of Darkness has come home."

ROMAN

I woke up with rough hands shaking me, then a slap on the face.

"Fuck you," I muttered to my assaulter. "When I wake up properly, you're dead." Fuck, my head hurt. What time was it? Hell, what day was it?

I attempted to open my bleary eyes. My cousin, Benvolio, was glaring at me like I was a petulant child late for school. He looked like the rest of us Tyrells, a generous crop of dark hair, strong jaw, dark hooded eyes and a permanent snarl to his lips. "Wake up, fucker," Benvolio slapped my face again. "Have a shower and get dressed."

I shoved him back so he couldn't hit me again and sat up, rubbing my face. Sometime last night I had passed out on the couch in the living room of my new apartment, all three bedrooms of opulence, cold and impersonal like a hotel. My foot kicked at an empty bottle of Jack across the plush cream rug. "Where's the fire?" I grumbled.

"The cops are coming to take you to the station."

Cops? A shot of adrenaline rushed through me. Now I was awake. "What?"

Benvolio rolled his eyes. "Shower. Now. A Tyrell never goes in public without wearing suitable attire. Reputation is everything." He pointed to the fresh suit still in its dry-cleaning plastic, hung across the back of a straight-backed dining room chair.

Reputation is everything. I snorted. "You're sounding more and more like my old man every day."

Benvolio's eyes narrowed. "And you're not sounding enough like him."

I gritted my teeth. For a long moment, we glared at each other, Benvolio hating me because I was next in line to the Tyrell throne, me hating him because he wasn't.

Benvolio pointed towards my bathroom. "Shower. Go."

"What? You're not going to wash my ass for me?"

"I don't get paid enough to wash your fucking ass. Why don't you get one of your groupies to do it for you? Speaking of groupies, why are you alone? Shouldn't you have a naked girl or three draped over your dick?"

I snorted. "What the fuck do you know?"

"Please. Your sordid reputation in Europe even reached us in Verona."

I didn't answer him. I got up, walked to the bathroom, and tried not to barf all over the pristine cream marble tiles. In the shower, I let the hot water run over me. I felt like someone had taken a baseball bat to my body. My muscles ached. My head throbbed.

What hurt worst wasn't physical. I felt raw and torn, a mere cavity inside me where my soul had been, where hope had once lain. Not even that pretty and willing blonde from the other night could soothe me.

After I got her back to this apartment, Rachel, or whatever her name was, had begun to undress. I'd stood there drinking straight from the bottle. I kept comparing her to Julianna. Her tan was fake, not like Julianna's smooth, natural glow. Her body was too skinny and I could feel her ribs when she pressed up against me, not like Julianna's soft, warm flesh and perfect natural curves.

I reached for the blonde's lips anyway, praying that they would quiet the noise in my head like Julianna's had.

They hadn't. The world still whirled around me, the voices—mine, my mother's, my father's—all yelling at me in my head. I needed peace and peace was in Julianna's touch.

But I couldn't have her. Not now. Not anymore.

I tore my mouth away from the blonde and let out a growl of frustration as I pushed her off me. She let out a whine of disapproval.

"I can't do this," I told her.

She stared at me, wide eyes looking pained, then she glanced down. I was totally flaccid. "You drank too much?"

"Yeah," I muttered. Let her think that. I hoped it would make her feel better when I kicked her out.

She wouldn't take the hint. "I can fix that for you." She pressed up against me, her hand shoving down into the front of my pants. Even in her palm, my dick was limp.

Julianna.

Julianna Julianna Julianna. That's all my fucking body was crying out for. She was a drug that I'd somehow become addicted too. Nothing else would satisfy me. The gorgeous woman with the whiskey-colored eyes had ruined me.

"You should go," I said to the blonde.

She left in a huff, refusing the wad of cash I handed out to her. "I am not a fucking hooker," she yelled at me.

"It's for your cab."

She slammed the door behind her and it rattled in its frame.

I took my bottle of Jack and sank into the deck chair out on the main balcony and stared up at the stars.

When I was a boy, when my mother was alive, she used to lie out under the stars on a blanket with me, and we'd pick out constellations. She'd pick out one, a real one, then I'd pick out one. I used to make mine up, but she never let on, pretending that she saw them too.

Julianna had shone brighter than the stars to me. A perfect constellation. I had to let her go. Because I didn't deserve her. She didn't deserve me.

I shut my eyes, wishing I was somewhere else. I drank until it all went black.

I turned off my shower, forcing myself back to the present.

When the police knocked on my door, I answered it, pressed and polished in a tailored Armani suit. It had been Jacob's and now it was mine. Apparently, I had grown to fill it out in the eight years I'd been gone.

I greeted the uniforms at my door with cold civility. They seemed surprised to see that I was ready and waiting for them. They should know by now that nothing went on in Verona without the Tyrells knowing about it. My father had friends and little birdies in all sorts of places.

I traveled to the police station with Benvolio driving his Escalade, the police car behind us, with another black SUV following us at a distance with two other hired men. No Tyrell would be caught dead in the back of a police car like a common criminal.

In the car, Benvolio spoke only to tell me, "Your father has already been summoned to the station too."

"Great. A father and son excursion."

I ignored Benvolio's look.

Verona's main police station was a solid five-level building that took up half of a block, a parking lot located out the back. After I exited the car, I was escorted by two officers to the third floor where, apparently, I would be interrogated. Benvolio and the hired men remained outside.

As I strode down the corridors of the police station to the interrogation room, the other police officers flinched away from me. I could sense their fear; I could almost smell it. Fear because of who my family was. Who they thought I was. The addictive rush of power swirled in my veins before I could stop it. I lifted my chin and glared back at these officers of the law, looking my natural enemies straight in the eyes.

I was a Tyrell. I had learned how to lie to the world. It was lie or die.

I was shown into a tiny interrogation room where I folded my body into a plastic chair at a table, two chairs opposite me. The room smelled musty and slightly of sweat. How many criminals had they broken in this very chair? They would not break me. They would not break a Tyrell.

I faced a large mirror that took up almost the entire wall and wondered how many of them would be watching through the one-way glass. I smirked into the mirror and spent some time rearranging my hair that was still perfectly in place. I noted a small video camera in the top right-hand corner of the room, also trained on me.

They made me wait a whole forty minutes before the door opened and a male Hispanic detective walked in. It was an interrogation technique, making the interviewee sweat. It wasn't going to work on me. If they had anything on me, I'd have been arrested. I repressed the emotions and questions swirling around inside me.

He sat opposite me and placed a manila file on the table top. I hid my curiosity as to what was contained within. I suspected enough.

"I'm Detective Espinoza," he said, folding his hands and placing them over the folder. He was a baby-faced guy, olive-skinned, round cheeks softening the hardness to his eyes. I suspected this detective wasn't one to be fucked with.

I stared at him for a few seconds, refusing to blink or show any emotion. *A Tyrell never shows fear.*

"You want to tell me what this is about, detective?"

"Just some questions."

I lifted my ankle onto my other knee and leaned back in the chair, placing my arm along the back of the chair beside me, acting as comfortable as if this place was my own personal living room. Like he was my guest. "By all means. Ask away."

"We're waiting for my partner."

The door opened to the right of me. This must be the partner. I turned in my chair to get a glimpse of the poor schmuck. My heart slammed against my chest at the sight of the woman in the doorway. Whiskey-colored eyes of my dreams. Perfect honey-gold hair pulled back into a no-nonsense ponytail, a conservative gray pantsuit covering the most incredible body that I'd ever laid my hands on.

The blood drained from my head.

Julianna was a detective.

Her gaze locked with mine and recognition filled up her widening eyes. Then came the realization.

Even though I had decided to let her go, even though I knew she deserved better than me, I had prayed that somehow, some way, in this city of four million people, that fate would somehow manage to drag her back into my life. But not like this. Not like this.

Julianna was the detective who was about to interrogate me.

Life could not get any fucking worse.

I forced my face into a calm mask. I felt the surface of me crack over as it froze. Underneath I was a whirling, furious current.

Detective Julianna Capulet.

Something in the newspaper clippings my father had sent over for me to read yesterday caught my attention. I hadn't fucking put it together until now.

Montgomery Capulet was the new chief of police. My family's enemy number one.

And the woman I couldn't forget was his only daughter.

JULIANNA

I hurried down the station corridor to the interrogation room. Espinoza was already in there with our suspect, Roman Tyrell. Espo had given me a rundown of what we knew about him. At twenty-six, he was the youngest son of Giovanni Tyrell. He didn't have a record. Yet. At least not in this country. He'd been out of the country for the last eight years, no doubt breaking laws somewhere else. Which also meant we didn't have any recent pictures on file for him. Wasn't it funny that he had the same first name as my Roman?

I slapped myself internally. Roman Lettiere was not *my* Roman. I couldn't think of him as *my* Roman. I had my chance to run off to Paris with him and I turned him down. He still hadn't replied to my text. He'd probably hated me. I tried to bat away the sting in my heart.

I had to stop thinking about him. I could barely concentrate on this case. I had to stop replaying our night together at inappropriate times. Like right now. Right now, I was supposed to be in the interrogation room where Espinoza was already waiting alone with the dangerous Roman Tyrell.

I pushed open the door to the interrogation room, ready to

break this new Tyrell heir. *This is my town, Mr. Tyrell. You're in for one hell of a wake-up call.* I got my first look at Verona's new Prince of Darkness.

Oh my fucking God.

Sitting in the chair opposite Espo, was Roman. *My* Roman.

My stupid heart began to beat in my throat at the sight of him. He looked incredible, like a GQ model. The strong body I had memorized with my hands filled out a tailored dark gray Armani suit. His thick dark hair, the hair I yearned to run my hands through again, was slicked back and curling at the collar.

I thought I'd never see him again. Here was the man I'd spent the most incredible twenty-four hours with, the man who I had been mooning over since he'd gone. He was the son of darkness, the heir to the Tyrell throne.

Anger spilled out over the lust rushing through my body. Did he know who I was? Did he screw me for information?

He never asked about my work, not once.

Was this supposed to be some sort of sick joke, then? Did he fuck me as some sort of bet, a prize, something to be bragged about later?

I knew some of the cruder cops had made such wagers when I had first joined the force—who would fuck me first. I wasn't an idiot. I kept my nose clean and the stupid players soon got bored when they realized I was not here to fuck around, just to do a job and to do it well.

Had Roman played me?

Playboy Mafia prince, Roman Tyrell, fucked the police chief's daughter and fucked her good.

Our connection had felt real to me. It had all felt real. And his invitation to Paris. Was that a lie as well?

Roman Lettiere was Roman Tyrell. Son of Giovanni Tyrell. The new Prince of Darkness. A criminal.

A monster.

I couldn't reconcile *my* Roman to this idea. *My* Roman could not be a monster.

But here he was, in the god-like flesh. Prime suspect for our murder investigation.

His head turned towards me. Our eyes met. I saw the recognition in his eyes and watched shock slacken his jaw. He hadn't been expecting me. I wasn't the only one side-swiped by fate's cruel joke.

Just as quickly, his face drew back into a mask of cool detachment that hit me like a fist to my gut. What did I expect he would do? Run over and take me in his arms? Kiss me in the middle of a police station? Did I think he'd be *happy* to see me?

I turned and shut the door behind me, using this moment with my back to him to force my face into an emotionless mask. Even though my brain was screaming, *what the fuck is happening?*

Espinoza hadn't seen my surprise. He'd been watching Roman this whole time. Did he notice Roman's flare of recognition? Or did Espo pass it off as a man checking out a young woman detective?

I wasn't sure how I managed to walk over to the spare seat next to Espinoza. Every step closer to Roman made my world feel more unbalanced, like I was rocking around on a boat lost at sea. I could feel Roman's dark stare on me as if it could burn the clothes off me. I had let him put his hands on my body. His tongue. He had been inside me. Watched me come. I sat down and folded my hands in front of me before I dared look up. He watched me impassively.

He was as beautiful as I remembered him, sharp cheekbones and perfect lips. Today his face was clean-shaven and free of the stubble that had scratched at the insides of my thighs. I pressed my knees together, my whole body buzzing at his nearness. I suddenly felt too hot in this suit that was too tight around my body. It had become a boa constrictor, wrapping around me so I couldn't breathe. How the fuck could I conduct this investigation when he affected me like this?

"This is Detective Capulet," Espinoza said, a slight edge to his tone.

Right, I was supposed to have introduced myself to this suspect, to this man that I was supposed to have never met before.

Jesus Christ. I had to get it together. Roman was a suspect. I had to interrogate him like one.

I had a duty to report a relationship with any suspect. It'd be deemed as a conflict of interest. What the hell was I supposed to say to my superiors? To the chief? To *my father*? I'd spent the night being intimate with Roman fucking Tyrell without realizing who he was.

First things first, Julianna. Just get through this interview. Then figure out later what the fuck you should be doing next.

Espinoza cleared his throat. I was the one who was supposed to be taking the lead on this interrogation. We had both decided this. Roman Tyrell was a reported playboy and Espo had thought it might work in our favor if I, a woman, interrogated him. That's why I had worn my most flattering suit today with the jacket that nipped in at my waist, a waist that Roman could encircle with both his hands. I almost choked on my own tongue. Roman Tyrell was a reported playboy. How stupid was I to think that I had been something more to him?

Later, I would shoot the shit out of a target. Right now, I had to bury all this... *this* and get through this damn interview.

"Mr. Tyrell," I began.

"Please, Detective Capulet, call me Roman." His voice was exactly as I remembered from my fantasies of him: rich, deep and crooning like a blues singer.

Our eyes met. My throat went dry. My heart hammered in my chest. I ignored my stupid body and forced a smile as I cleared my throat. "We understand that you were only supposed to be back in town for a few days. But you're still here?"

"I came into town for my brother's funeral."

Jacob Tyrell. The massacre at the Tyrell warehouse at the docks. That had been his brother. I couldn't help the thread of pity I felt in my chest. "I'm sorry for your loss."

"Don't be. It wasn't much of a loss."

I flinched. Was this the real Roman I was staring at now? Cool, cold and callous about his older brother's death? It was like I was looking at a man other than the one I'd met only days ago, the one who seemed so tortured by his brother's demise. Had he...somehow been a part of that death?

"You seem very blasé about your brother's death. Are you this careless about murder in general?"

His eyes narrowed. "My brother wasn't a very nice man."

"And you...would you consider *yourself* a nice man?"

I could feel Espo's eyes on me. I was totally going off script. I ignored him. As far as I was concerned it was just Roman and me in this interrogation room. Him and me and all the things unsaid, sticky and hot between us.

Roman leaned forward in his seat. I fought the urge to lean forward. I caught the whiff of his cologne; that dark masculine scent that had surrounded me as he'd fucked me long into the night.

"You seem very young to be a detective," he said.

I snapped out of my reverie. "My age is irrelevant. I'm good at my job."

"I bet you're good at anything you put your...*hands* to." He gave me the hint of a smile.

I felt my cheeks heat at the suggestiveness of his words. An image of my hands wrapped around his shaft assaulted my senses before I slammed it back away into a corner of my mind.

Focus, Julianna.

"You never answered my question earlier. You were supposed to have left Verona. Sunday night, if I'm correct. Why didn't you?"

Now Espo's eyes were burning into the side of my head. How

did I know Roman was supposed to have left? This information wasn't on his file. I would have to figure out some excuse for my information. But not right now.

"Plans changed. Trust me, it was not my intention to stay. My father can be very persuasive."

Espo pulled a photo out of the file, shooting me a look, before turning back to Roman. "Do you know this man?"

Roman's eyes flicked down to the photo that Espo had pulled out of his file. It was Vinnie's arrest photo blown up to A4 size. I didn't take my eyes off Roman, holding my breath, as he pulled the photo towards him. I searched his face for any sign of recognition. I didn't see any.

"No. Who is he?" Roman asked.

"His name is Vincent Torrito. Otherwise known as Vinnie."

"Vincent Torrito," he repeated. I swore I heard a slip of sadness in his voice.

"He's a known associate of the Veronesi family. The same family who is rumored to have murdered your brother."

There was something unsaid in Roman's eyes. I couldn't decipher it. He pushed the photo back towards me. "I don't know him."

"Are you sure?" I asked. "Take another look."

"I assure you, Detective Capulet, I don't know this man."

"You haven't asked why we're so interested in this man," Espo said.

Roman leveled his stare at my partner. "I assume because you fine detectives are asking me about him that a misfortune has happened to this... Mr. Torrito, did you say his name was?"

"Where were you Sunday night?" I asked.

His eyebrow lifted, a questioning look. "Do you have a specific time in mind?"

Yes, you fucker. What were you doing after you left me at your hotel room? "How about you tell me everything you did from, say, seven o'clock."

"You think I was involved?"

"Just answer the question."

"In fact," inserted Espinoza, "start with where you were Friday night, then go through step by step what you did that weekend, ending with Sunday night."

Shit. Fuck. Shit.

Espinoza was trying to establish Roman's whereabouts not only for the murder but for during the time frame when Vinnie could had been kidnapped. I was going to be sick. Roman had been with me.

"You want my exact whereabouts...from Friday afternoon," repeated Roman, "until Sunday."

"Exactly," said Espinoza.

Roman stared at me. "You want *every* detail?"

My body, already taut as a drum, tightened further. This was where it was going to come out, our time together. I was his fucking alibi for the abduction.

I was so fucked. I should speak up now, pull Espo out into the hallway and explain before Roman spilled everything, in detail, right here on record.

I couldn't move. I could barely breathe.

"I was at my brother's funeral Friday afternoon. Then I met up with my best friend Mercutio, afterward."

"This Mercutio have a last name?"

"Brevio."

Espo wrote this down on his pad. "What did you guys do?"

"We caught up at his grandmother's house. Had dinner. Got ready, had a few drinks. Then we went out to Club Luxe around nine thirty."

"We'll need the phone number and address of Mercutio and his grandmother. I assume they can corroborate your story."

"Of course."

"What happened after that?"

136

"Like I said, I went to Club Luxe where about a dozen people saw me."

"And you stayed all night? Until when?"

"I left at about eleven p.m." He cleared his throat. "With a lady friend."

I swallowed hard, my throat developing a lump. He'd have to produce the name of this "lady friend" for us to corroborate his whereabouts. My name. The irony.

"Where did you and this lady friend go?"

"We spent the rest of the night together in my hotel room."

"Which hotel?"

Oh shit. The hotel would have security cameras in the lobby. I was doubly screwed. The security cameras would be confiscated. I would be seen with Roman Tyrell. Irrefutable evidence, right there. My head spun.

"The Marriott, off Broadway."

"And when did you leave your lady friend?"

"I left at around seven o'clock on Sunday."

"You spent an entire day with this friend?"

"She was...special."

I froze. My eyes caught his across the interrogation table. Did he just call me special? I searched Roman's face. I couldn't see anything under his impassionate mask.

Roman looked over to Espinoza, but his words were for me. "I don't know if you ever met a woman who made you crave her, who...was like a drug. That you couldn't get enough of. A woman you wanted to protect and worship. Always."

As he spoke my stomach twisted into heated knots. My nipples turned hard, pressing painfully against my bra ...*a woman who made you crave her, who was like a drug. That you couldn't get enough of.* He felt those things about me.

Liar! He was fucking with me. He wasn't even touching me and he was still fucking me. He was trying to manipulate me. He wanted me to think he was innocent.

What if he was innocent?

Was the Roman I met someone I could imagine torturing and killing Vinnie in such a cold, heartless manner? Someone who could dispose of the body and murder weapon with such a practiced manner? He didn't feel like a heartless killer to me.

What did I really know about Roman Tyrell?

Espinoza smirked. "I can't say I've ever felt that for a woman."

"It's a rare thing to find, indeed," Roman said.

"And does this special friend have—"

"Where did you go after you left her?" I interrupted Espo. I wasn't ready for Roman to spill our dirty little secret. I could feel Espo glaring at me for interrupting him. We never did that in interviews. It was one of our rules to maintain a singular front. No disrespecting the other person. No arguing. No interruptions. Unless, of course, we were trying for an interrogation play.

Roman looked over to me, folding his large masculine hands in front of him, hands that fit perfectly around my neck as he fucked me from behind. Wetness pooled in between my legs as the memory flashed through me.

"I went to meet my father," Roman's voice cut through my thoughts. "For dinner."

"Where did you have dinner?" Espo asked.

A restaurant with wait staff could corroborate his story. Roman could be innocent of this horrendous crime after all.

"We had dinner at his house. You can ask my father, his staff…"

His father's house, where only the people his father paid were alibis.

Espo pursed his lips, and I knew this was what he was thinking too. "What was for dinner?"

"Rib-eye steak with steamed green beans and roasted potatoes. I had mine medium rare, my father had his rare. Did you want to hear what we had for dessert as well? Perhaps the wine list?"

He was mocking us. He recited the menu as if it were a list he'd memorized. I was sure Giovanni would tell us the exact same thing. The Tyrells were too smart. If they had planned their alibis, we wouldn't find a hole in them. This was why Giovanni Tyrell had managed to evade justice for so damn long.

"When did you leave your father's?" Espo asked, giving up that line of questioning.

"I stayed until about ten thirty p.m., after which he dropped me off at Copan Bar. Mercutio can vouch for me again."

"A good friend, is he?" I asked.

Roman's eyes flicked to mine. He hesitated for a second. Then said, "Yes, a good friend." I realized Mercutio was a weak spot for him.

"Good enough that he would lie for you?" I asked.

Roman's eyes narrowed. "I'm insulted at your question."

I leaned forward on my elbows. "You still haven't answered it."

Roman leaned in too, matching my posture. "Mercutio doesn't need to lie for me, detective."

We were practically breathing the same air. Our faces only inches apart. We were so close that I could see his irises dilate so that his chocolate eyes now looked as black as night. Was he angry or...turned on? His eyes dropped to my lips. Oh God. He was turned on.

Fuck, so was I. Heat pooled in the base of my belly as my gaze drew to his mouth. I could remember how soft yet firm his lips were when he kissed me, claiming me, sucking my bottom lip into his mouth.

Our lips were so close. If I leaned in further I could—

Espo cleared his throat. I threw myself back into my chair. What the fuck was I doing? I was about to kiss the prime suspect in the interrogation room. Espo gave me a strange look which I ignored while I tried to calm my racing heart.

"How long did you stay?" I continued like nothing had

happened.

Cool as anything, Roman leaned back in his chair and adjusted his jacket. "Not long. I left at elevenish."

"Alone?" Espo asked.

"With a girl," Roman said.

"This mysterious special friend again?"

Roman flinched. My stomach hardened. He glanced at me, hesitation clear in his eyes.

"Mr. Tyrell," Espo warned.

"No. I left with another girl," he admitted, his voice heavy.

The fucker. The fucking fucker. He was exactly the playboy that his reputation afforded him. I can't believe I fell for it. Less than four hours after he left me he was taking another woman back to his bed. I wanted to punch him in the face. I leaned back in my chair and fisted my itching hands across my chest.

"*Another* woman?" I said. "Where did you two go?"

"To my apartment." His words stabbed me.

"And was this one *special* as well?" I fought and failed to hide the bitterness in my voice.

"No. I…I thought the special woman was lost to me. I…" For the first time during this whole interview, Roman seemed unsure.

"This other woman have a name?" Espo asked.

He shrugged. "I'm sure she did, but I didn't catch it. Rachel or something."

"And did she stay at your place until seven the next day too?" I asked.

"No… she only lasted ten minutes or so before she left."

"That was quick."

"I changed my mind about her company."

I stared at Roman, wondering if this was at all true.

"Leaving you alone?" Espo asked.

"Just me and a bottle of Jack."

"And you have no idea who this mystery woman was?"

Espinoza's voice bordered on sarcastic, betraying his doubt in Roman's story.

"No."

"So you have no alibi for Sunday night after you left the club at around ten." Barely enough time to kill Vinnie and dump the body somewhere.

Roman's eyes hardened. Once more the Roman I knew felt lost to me. "My building has security cameras. I'm sure you could get a hold of them."

"We'll have to check your story. We have your father in the next room."

If Roman was guilty he may have flinched. Instead, he smiled without humor. "Say hello to dear old Dad for me."

"And this special girl," Espo said. "The *first* one. What was her name?"

Roman caught my gaze. This was it. The moment I become a fucking laughing stock of the entire precinct. I braced myself.

"Rosaline."

What? I stared at Roman. His face gave away nothing. He was lying. The fucker was lying. "Rosaline who?" I demanded.

"Rosaline le Monde."

"Pearce le Monde's daughter?" Espo asked. Mr. Le Monde was a prominent Verona businessman with a vast property portfolio.

"One and the same."

"Who is she to you?" I demanded, trying to sound like a cop and not a jealous girlfriend.

I caught a slight quirk of the corner of Roman's lip. He knew I was jealous and the bastard was amused by it. "She's an old flame."

My blood flared hot as a possessiveness I've never felt thundered through me. It took all my willpower not to growl. What in the ever-loving fuck was wrong with me? I could not be getting possessive over a man I slept with once. Correction: I had the best sex of my life with, multiple times over twenty-four hours.

I shoved a pad of paper and a pen in front of Roman. "Write down her number and address. We'll be checking her story too."

"Of course, Ms. Capulet, or is it Mrs. Capulet? Is there a lucky *Mr.* Capulet? I didn't quite pick that up when we first met." Roman wrote in neat scrawl on the pad.

"*Detective* Capulet."

"I see. Well, *Detective* Capulet," he placed the pen down on the pad, "you seem like a woman with a lot of *hidden* talents. Do you think I killed poor Mr. Torrito?"

"I prefer to reserve judgment until I have all the evidence."

"A perfectly valid statement. Good to see that you're not the kind of woman to make judgments without *all* the evidence in place." There it was, the flash of anger behind his cold eyes. Was he angry at me? For thinking that he might have done it? He was a Tyrell, for fuck sake.

"Now, if you don't have any more questions, I'm leaving." Roman pushed himself up to standing, his wide frame feeling like he was crowding out this tiny room. I found myself eye level with his crotch. The image of his thick shaft flashed into my mind, my lips around it, licking it until it was wet enough to slide smoothly inside me. The wave of desire that hit me was so hard that I almost groaned, my clit turning into a pulsating button. I stood suddenly, so harshly that I almost toppled the chair behind me, trying to shake off the shudder running down my spine. All the air seemed to have been sucked out of the room and I was having trouble breathing.

"It was so lovely to meet you, Detective Capulet." His eyes burned into mine. "I'm sure I'll be seeing you around."

"Don't leave town," I called after him as Espinoza escorted him from the room.

He paused at the door, giving me one last burning stare. "I wouldn't dream of it."

JULIANNA

I sank into my chair as Roman slipped out of sight. For the first time since I'd stepped into this interrogation room, I felt like I could breathe properly.

Jesus Christ. My head was throbbing as the beginnings of a headache pierced my skull. I ran my mind over the entire interview. What the fuck just happened?

"Capi," Espinoza said, startling me. At some point he'd reentered the interrogation room. I could hear the question in his tone. I couldn't deal with him just yet. I had to process all of this. I had to decide what the hell I was going to do.

"I have to go to the bathroom," I blurted, as I pushed my chair back and raced out of the room. I ran for the ladies' room at the end of the hall, ignoring the strange looks of the other officers as I shoved past. In the bathroom, I locked myself into a stall. I collapsed on the closed toilet lid and let my face fall into my hands.

Roman fucking Tyrell was *my* Roman.

The man I had almost run away to Paris with was a criminal. Not just any criminal, but the new heir to the Tyrells' bloody empire. Jesus Christ. How could I have gone home with a man like that? How could I have given myself, my body, to a Tyrell? I shuddered. I'd seen the crime scene photos of the many alleged victims of the Tyrell family and their mob infighting. Like the massacre at the warehouse when his brother, Jacob Tyrell, had died along with dozens of his men. And of Michelle Rossi, a mob-bunny turned informant. They had raped her and beaten her to a purple mess before someone had mercifully put a bullet into her head.

I tried to imagine Roman standing over someone with a gun. Or even hitting a woman.

I couldn't.

Roman had come to my defense at the club when that jackass started manhandling me. *"I was just coming over to save you..."*

"Why? Because I'm a girl and all I need is a big strong man to come save me?"

"No, because you're a human being. I don't like it when I see other human beings being treated without respect. Not when I can do something about it."

Could that have been an act? Why act in front of me?

I tried to fit these two pieces of the same man together. I tried to reconcile Roman Tyrell with the man who I'd bared my body and my soul to.

I couldn't.

What should I do now?

I had a conflict of interest in this investigation. I shouldn't be on this case. I had slept with the prime suspect. I had to report my involvement with Roman. I cringed as I imagined how that conversation would go down with the captain. Oh shit. My father, the chief... he'd specifically given me this case. And Espo... what would I tell him?

I couldn't do it. I couldn't tell anyone. It'd ruin my career. Any respect or reputation I'd worked so hard to create would be shattered. I'd never be taken seriously as a woman detective again.

Could I work this case? With my body still reacting to him the way it did?

I had to. I had to do my job, no matter what it was that I felt. I could work the case. I could be unbiased. Just because I had slept with him—had the most amazing night of my life with him—I could still work the case like he was any other suspect. Right? Just because my body reacted like a live wire whenever he was around—stupid mutinous body—I could still rationalize the evidence. I could arrest him and put him away if he was guilty. Right?

I had to put all my feelings for Roman aside and work the case. Treat him like any other suspect. And hope that he'd keep his mouth shut about us.

ROMAN

What the fuck just happened?

I stole one last glance at Julianna before I strode out of the interrogation room, my body still alive with the current that flowed under my skin when she was near. My pull towards her hadn't gotten any weaker. If anything, the chemistry between us had magnified in that tiny room. Fuck, I had almost grabbed her and kissed her. I almost kissed a detective in the middle of a fucking police station. I would have laughed at myself if it wasn't so fucking serious. She was making me lose my mind.

I had dreamed about seeing her again. Not like that.

For a second I had thought that our meeting had been a police sting. But the look of shock on her face when she walked into the interrogation room had been genuine. She hadn't expected me to be sitting there. She hadn't expected to see me again at all.

What would she do now?

She had a conflict of interest. She would have to report our relationship.

Shit. My father would find out.

I cursed under my breath. My father, I could handle. He wouldn't hurt me. Would he harm Julianna if he knew how close she'd gotten to me?

My gut tightened. Of course, he would. *No weapon. No evidence. No witnesses.* Those were his mottos, the reason he'd been able to stay one step outside the law.

Julianna was a liability.

I spotted Abel and another one of my father's goons standing by the door of another interrogation room. My father must be in there.

I couldn't face him right now.

I strode towards the elevator. Abel stepped out in front of me, blocking my path. "Your father isn't done yet."

I glared at him. "Get out of my way."

"You're to return home with your father when he's done."

"I don't take orders from you, dog."

Abel's lip pulled up. The skin around his eyes and jaw tightened.

"Is there a problem here?" A male voice spoke from behind me.

It was the male detective, Espinoza, Julianna's partner.

"No, problem, Detective Espinoza," I said, trying to relax my face and attempting to smile. "I was just leaving."

Abel scowled but he stepped aside, unable to stop me under the wary stare of the detective.

I had to figure out a way to talk to Julianna. I had to get her alone somehow. I had to warn her not to tell anyone about us. Would she even want to see me again? Would she even listen to me? Despite the way her body still reacted to mine in the interrogation room, I could see the shock-turned-anger in her when she found out my last name was Tyrell.

It didn't matter. I had to get her alone and make her listen to me. Then after that, I had to stay the hell away from her.

JULIANNA

After washing my face, I walked out of the bathroom and almost ran into someone in the hallway. I swallowed as the imposing figure of Giovanni Tyrell took up my vision, two men in suits flanking him. I could see the resemblance to Roman in his thick dark hair, the same strong jaw and hooded eyes, except there was a glittering menace in Giovanni's stare. I felt like I was looking into the future. Would this be who Roman turned into?

"Mr. Tyrell," I said courteously, with a small nod.

He stared me over and I felt like I was being inspected. "So," he said, his voice like gravel, "you're Montgomery's only daughter. Pretty young thing. You look like your mother."

My blood turned to ice. "How did you know my mother?"

He smiled and it was cruel and hard. "I watch the news. The senseless death of a state prosecutor was a tragedy. I heard you were going to follow in her footsteps until she died. Instead, you became a cop, like your father."

He knew so much about me. Too much. Giovanni Tyrell was a snake. He was trying to shake me. I would not let him.

"Do you need an escort out of the building?" I asked with a firm voice, indicating that this conversation was over.

He didn't move. He didn't even blink. "It's a dangerous job, being a homicide detective. You never know what lies in wait for you."

I lifted my chin. "Are you threatening me?"

He laughed, but the sound was hollow. "I don't threaten. Merely an observation from a concerned citizen. You wouldn't want to wreck that pretty face of yours in, say, an accident. Or a tangle with the wrong end of a knife."

I gritted my teeth. "Excuse me. I must get back to work."

"You people haven't discovered yet who killed my son. I *doubt* you'll find out who killed this Torrito fellow." Before I could answer he turned, his two bodyguards flanking him. I remained frozen for a moment as I watched him walk towards the elevator.

"Are you, okay?" Espinoza stepped to my side. I hadn't noticed him approaching.

"Fine," I said automatically.

Espinoza stared after Mr. Tyrell as the elevator doors closed in front of him. "Don't let him rattle you."

I shook my head. "I'm not rattled."

"Like a desert snake." Espo turned to face me, concern on his brows.

I looked away. I didn't know if I could stand any more scrutiny. "How did the interview go with Tyrell Senior?" I asked, changing the subject.

"He backed his son's claim, of course. As did his two goons, but…"

"They're paid to do whatever their boss tells them to."

"Have you…" Espo paused, the hitch in his voice making me flinch. "Have you ever met Roman Tyrell before?"

Keep a straight face, Julianna. "No. Why?"

"When you walked in, for a second he looked like he'd seen a ghost."

I shrugged, hoping that Espinoza couldn't hear how loud my heart was banging in my chest. "I don't know." It was the first time I'd lied to my partner. The ground had turned into a slope and I was starting to skid.

I had no choice but to lie. If it got out that I had spent a night with Roman Tyrell, my career would be ruined. I'd be forever tainted. No cop would ever trust me again. And my father... my heart squeezed. The new police chief would be publicly humiliated. He'd be so disappointed in me... I couldn't bear it. I could not let him find out.

"You seemed rattled in the interview." Espo wasn't letting it go just yet.

I shook my head, trying to remain calm. "Just...very little sleep. I need a large coffee."

Espo made a small noncommittal noise in his throat. "How did you know about his plane ticket?"

"I...er, I checked the flight registers for his name. Found one leaving direct to London at ten p.m. Sunday," I said. More lies.

"What made you do that?"

"Just a hunch." I hated lying to him. What choice did I have?

"We've got Alberto Veronesi coming in later this afternoon. You want me to take point during the interrogation?"

"I'm fine, Espo."

He gave me a look which I read as concerned disbelief. "I'll take point on this one."

I didn't have the heart to argue with him.

ROMAN

I didn't make it two steps outside the police station before I was flanked by two guys in suits. Two of my father's men. One of them waved his hand to the side indicating the police station parking lot located around the side of the building. "The limo is parked over there."

I glared at the hired muscle. "I'm not coming with you. Benvolio is—"

"Benvolio has been sent away on other duties. You are to ride with your father."

"I can get a ride with someone else."

"Sir." One of them reached for my arm.

I yanked myself out of reach. "You fucking touch me and I will end you."

The two men glanced at each other, wariness clear even behind their dark sunglasses. They remained close as if guarding me. Neither of them tried to touch me again.

I pulled out my phone and called Mercutio. "Merc, you free? I seem to have found myself at the police station without a ride." I needed to buy myself a car if I was forced to stay in Verona.

Mercutio spat out a string of curses. "What the hell are you doing at the police station?"

"It's just a misunderstanding."

"I can't, man. I'm at work."

"I'll figure something out. Catch up later, k?"

"We better."

I shut my cell. I'd grab a cab instead. I searched the street, filled with weekday traffic, for a free one.

"Roman!" My father's voice boomed out from behind me. Too late. I wasn't getting away now. He strode up to my side and clasped my shoulder. His hand felt heavy like a shackle. The limo pulled up in front of us. "Get in."

I decided it would be better if I went along with him for now. I got inside the limo. My father and Abel climbed in after me. One fucked up family. The other men got into a black SUV behind us.

"Did your interview go as planned?" my father asked as the limo pulled away from the curb. "Any surprises?"

I almost choked. Only the biggest surprise of my life. "It went fine."

"Good. Everything with Rosaline has been arranged."

I stiffened. "You didn't have to do that."

"If you could remember the names and faces of the women you fuck, then you wouldn't need me to pull strings," my father said.

"I didn't realize when I took her home that I would need to use her as an alibi," I muttered.

My father pointed a thick finger at me, his gold ring flashing. "Your *life* in Europe is over. So is the disgusting way you carry on with your whores."

I gritted my teeth together, trying to bat away the sting of his disapproval. "They're not whores."

My father continued, "Tyrell men are family men. You are my last heir. You will choose a wife and continue the Tyrell name."

"What?" I snapped my face towards him, stunned at what he was saying.

"You're almost thirty. It's time to settle down."

"I'm twenty-six."

"You're old enough," my father bellowed. "Time to start taking on your responsibilities."

I stared out the tinted window at the city passing us, crossing my arms over my chest.

"Rosaline's father is a friend of the family," my father continued, "as is Rosaline." His voice weighed heavily on her name. My father never hid that he liked the idea of Rosaline and me together. Rosaline's father was a powerful business man in this city, his reach stretching out farther than the city limits, and if rumor were to be believed, he wasn't above crossing the line to ensure his empire expanded; all things my father respected. "She likes you, as far as I hear. It would be an advantageous match."

What about love? I thought but didn't say.

My father married for love, and she died because of who he was. Anybody I married was signing up for a short life. Marriage to me would be a death sentence. Rosaline didn't deserve that. No one did.

"Did you see that hot lady detective?" Abel asked with a dark gleam in his eye.

Julianna. He was talking about my Jules. Anger boiled underneath my skin. I wanted to rip his head off. I didn't. If I showed any affection towards her, it would be dangerous for her. I shrugged. "I've seen hotter in Europe."

Abel let out a snort. "They don't get much hotter than that."

I glared at him. "Don't waste your time. She'd never go for someone like you."

"Or you." Abel said with a smile, his words stabbing me through the chest.

"She's the daughter of the new police chief," said my father, a tight smile on his face. "A very...interesting girl."

153

My blood froze in my veins. Did he know about us? Had he been following me? "She doesn't seem that interesting," I said, as casually as I could.

"Her father is a righteous man, hard line, and he's stubborn enough to believe that he can clean up this city. Incorruptible, they call him. I think I just found what he'd be willing to bargain for."

I stared at my father. I wasn't sure what he was saying. Something in his smug tone began a growing unease in me. "What are you talking about?"

My father shared a look with Abel. He turned back to face me, a cruel smile stretching across his face. "No one is incorruptible. Everyone has his price. You need to find their weak spot and know when to push."

My stomach turned as I imagined Julianna being used as a pawn in my father's hands. "What are you going to do to her?"

My father appraised me. "Nothing. Yet. We have more urgent things to take care of."

"Like?"

My father said nothing. I realized from the flash of industrial buildings out the window that we weren't headed back to his house. The tension grew in my shoulders. "Where are we going?" I demanded.

"To the docks."

My gut tightened. Images of the man I was forced to kill the last time I was at the docks flashed through my head. Vincent Torrito. I knew his name now. *I have a wife...children..."*

I swallowed down my guilt. "Need me to clean up your dirty work for you, again?" I said, bitterness squeezing out in my words.

My father sent me a stern look. "If you're going to take over one day, then you have to understand the business side of things. Time for you to learn the ropes."

I leaned back into the leather seat and shut my eyes. It was inevitable. I could feel the abyss like a black hole tugging on me. I wasn't sure how much longer I could fight it. "We're meeting with the Veronesis."

My blood ran cold. "With the men who killed Jacob?"

"Yes."

"And what do you plan to do at this meeting?"

My father gave me a look. "I hope you wore your vest under your suit."

I swallowed. Of course, I didn't wear a fucking bullet-proof vest under my suit. I thought I was just going to an interview at the police station. Not into a goddamn gun fight. "I don't have a gun."

My father nudged his head towards Abel, then me.

With a snarl aimed at me, Abel pulled out a black Glock and handed it over. "Don't shoot yourself."

"I know how to handle a gun." I took it from him, released the canister, checked it was loaded then clicked it back into place in one swift move. My father had bought me my first gun on my thirteenth birthday and taught me how to shoot. I still held on to those long summer afternoons he spent crouched by my side, teaching me to shoot. They had been some of the rare times I had cherished with my father.

"Do you remember how to aim?" my father said. He shared a look with Abel as if this was a joke they shared between them.

I pressed my lips together and said nothing. Of course, I maintained my shooting skills. Even in Europe, I was at a range every other week. I may not have wanted to be a Tyrell but I wasn't stupid. I knew my surname was a target on my back.

The limo pulled up to a stop in front of an abandoned warehouse, owned by neither of our families. Neutral property. We sat in the limo, sweat collecting at the base of my spine as we waited for my father's men to check the area for an ambush. All clear. For now.

We exited the limo and entered the warehouse, my father and

me in the center, Abel and four other men flanked around us like a walking shield. My ears were pricked, my eyes darting about me, peering through the shadows and the scattered machinery hanging like rusty skeletons.

Already waiting for us was Alberto Veronesi in the center of four suited men. He was my father's age, although he didn't wear his age as well. His belly bulged over his tailored pin-stripe pants, his matching jacket hanging open, and his wrinkles were deeply lined in a pale, puffy face. His once dark hair was now gray.

I scanned the faces of the other men there. I didn't recognize any of them from the dossiers my father had sent over to me. A prickle scattered over my skin. Alberto's four sons were missing from this meeting.

I had only met Alberto in person once, at the funeral of my mother. He had been a childhood sweetheart of hers and a friend to my father. She left him to be with my father. This, as well as territorial disputes, caused a bitterness between these two men extending back several decades. My mother had been the prize my father had won. Alberto had never forgiven him.

"I thought we agreed to limit our associates who were to attend this meeting," Alberto said, eyeing our seven to his five.

"I'm surprised you had the nerve to call this meeting," my father said.

Alberto's eyes met mine and a smile crept across his face. "So, this is the new heir to Tyrell's empire. You've been away for several years, my boy. You ready for the games that real men play?"

Before I could answer, my father interrupted. "You do not get to speak to him. You called this meeting with me. You shall address me."

Alberto stiffened and turned to stare at my father. "We did not order the attack on your son. We would not break the code like that."

Even as a child my father was always talking about the code. No Made Man was to be killed without consent from the Commission, being the head of the five biggest families in the country. The Tyrell family, however powerful, still bowed to the de Lucas. Sonny de Luca, the current capo, would not have sentenced Jacob to die. Sonny and my father had a long, close history.

Four years ago, Jacob had been wanted for the murder of an informant after his ex-girlfriend turned against him to testify that she'd seen him shoot the poor woman in cold blood. He had escaped and gone underground. There was no reason to order his execution. Not now.

Or was there?

"Why should we believe you?" my father said. "It's common knowledge that your family has been making plays for more power in this district for years."

"Do you think I want a full-scale war?" Alberto bristled. "Do you think I am stupid enough to incite one? With you? I do not want a war. It's not good for anyone's business."

"If there is a war, I did not start it."

"You think I'd be reckless enough to carve a V on your boy's chest? If you think that, then you're as stupid as the man who ordered your son's death." Alberto growled.

The tension in the room shot up by several degrees, our men and his men eyeing each other, their hands floating ever so closely to their hips where an arsenal of guns waited.

"If you didn't do it," my father spat out, "then who did? One of the other families? I don't think so. They wouldn't dare. Only you would."

"You're forgetting the third option."

My father stiffened. "Which is?"

"The fleur-de-lis," Alberto said with a hiss.

The fleur-de-lis? "They're a myth," I said. A group of faceless vigilantes hell-bent on taking the law into their own hands.

"Quiet, boy," my father snapped at me.

"My man, Vinnie Torrito, turned up dead a few days ago. Tortured, shot in the head, and dumped in our territory. Do you deny you killed him?"

"Of course I do," my father said.

He just lied. No doubt, Veronesi was lying too.

Both sides glared at the other, eyes watching twitchy fingers. Two men, two fathers, two sides filled with bitter hate. This was a combustible situation, mistrust leaking into the air like gas. Any minute the spark would ignite the whole damn place. We'd all be consumed along with it.

"What about you, boy?" Alberto turned towards me. "Do you know who killed my man?"

"He'll tell you the same thing," my father said.

"I want to hear it from him."

I felt all eyes turn towards me. I couldn't let myself flinch. "We didn't have anything to do with your man's death," I lied, keeping my face passive and cold like I'd learned from my father.

"I guess the fleur-de-lis also killed your man," my father sneered at the boss of the Veronesi family.

"Don't mock me," he replied.

My father glared back at him. "I'm not your only enemy, Alberto."

"And I'm not yours. You expect me to believe you had nothing to do with Vinnie's death?"

"You expect me to believe you had nothing to do with the death of my son?" retorted my father, anger coloring his voice. He snatched out his gun and pointed it at Alberto.

Fuck! I snatched out my gun and the sound of drawing weapons filled the warehouse. My nerves were wires about to snap. I counted three weapons aimed at my father, the remaining two were on me. If my father fired, he and I would both be dead.

The only one who remained weaponless was Alberto, his face a steely mask, despite the guns trained on him.

"I could kill you right now," my father snarled.

Alberto stared at my father. "You pull the trigger and you and your son die."

"But I will take you down with me," my father said, his words filled with pleasure. "My eldest son deserves justice."

"You'd lose your life and you'd lose a chance at justice because I didn't kill your son. Do you really think I'd take out an entire slew of your men and carve a V on their chests? You might not like me, Giovanni, but you know I am not reckless nor am I stupid enough to incite a war like that."

"I know that I will enjoy killing you."

"If you kill me, I have four boys ready and waiting in the wings to take over my business. You brought your only remaining heir. Who would carry on your name if you were both to die today?"

Out of the corner of my eye, I saw my father flinch. Alberto Veronesi had found his weak spot and had just pushed. I almost felt impressed.

"You son of a bitch," my father spat out.

Alberto sighed. "This doesn't have to end in bloodshed. I called this meeting to offer you a truce."

"What truce?"

"Put down your weapons and let's talk like men."

There was a long pause. The air in the room became hot and sticky, sweat beading on my forehead. We would all die here today if my father didn't back down. Our lives were in his hands, balancing on a blade's edge. I could feel the hatred rolling off my father. He would have to put away his pride if we were all to live. Lord knows, how hard he'd have to fight himself to set aside his pride.

Don't be reckless, Father. Back down.

I shifted my weight slowly from one foot to the other. Any sudden movements and everything would erupt in a storm of bullets and blood. This next breath could be my last. Julianna's face flashed in my mind and my stomach twisted with regret.

"Fine," my father said. He withdrew his gun.

I let out the breath I'd been holding and lowered my own weapon. My blood pounded in my ears as a rush of relief flowed over me. I would not die today. Not today.

Slowly the men around us withdrew their weapons.

Alberto nodded. "Thank you, Gio. I stand by my statement that not I nor any of my family had anything to do with the death of your son. The people who did this, cut a V across his chest to make it look like we did. I propose that we call a truce while we search for the real murderer because they are targeting my family as much as yours."

"These mysterious murderers haven't killed *your* son, have they?"

"No, but they might." Alberto lifted his hands, palms open, in a gesture of surrender. "Think about it. You can call me when you have an answer." He turned and the men closed ranks around him, creating a wall as he strolled out of the warehouse.

I could hear father growling, his fingers twitching at his side, as he watched Alberto walk away.

"Do you believe him?" I asked my father once we were back inside the bulletproof limo.

He snorted. "Of course not. The Veronesis are liars."

"Is he really that stupid to start a war between our families? Why? And why now?"

My father sighed. "I am getting old, Roman. In murdering Jacob, he weakened our family. I don't think Alberto ordered the hit, it was too brash, too messy to be his style. I do think he knows who did it. Someone in his family maybe, one of his sons trying to impress him or to make a play for power."

"Dante, the second brother, is reckless enough," said Abel. "It's common knowledge he's been making power plays as to who will rule the family once Alberto is gone. The power struggle between the brothers could be their downfall."

"Are you going to accept the truce?" I asked.

"Of course. It's to our advantage to play along." There was a glint in his eyes. "Mark my words, son, we are going to get our revenge."

JULIANNA

I t was late by the time I left the station. Almost nine o clock. I'd buried myself in my work all day to avoid thinking about Roman and the revelation that he was a Tyrell. A Tyrell and my prime suspect. As I walked out the back exit into the parking lot, the heels of my boots clacking against the concrete, echoing between the dark locked cars, I had nothing left but my thoughts.

Why had he lied to me about his last name? How could he be so callous as to trick me? And why?

A thought struck me with such force that I gasped. I had heard of the creative ways that criminals used to blackmail people. He had insisted that we go to his hotel room. I had...I had let him do whatever he wanted to me. Dear God. What if he had photos of me? Footage? I felt sick.

I was so absorbed in my thoughts I didn't register that I wasn't alone. Something shifted in the dark before me. A wide figure detached itself from the shadows. I halted, my heart slamming to my throat and my fingers going to my gun at my hip.

He stepped into the light, his familiar features made harsh by the shadows. A jolt of pain and confusion slammed through me.

It was Roman.

What was he doing here?

His stare was pinned to me, his eyebrows drawn together in a look that, if I didn't know any better, I'd almost call desperate. He was here for me.

He shouldn't be here. We were meters from the entrance to the police station. If he were caught…

Roman started forward, his mouth opening as if to call for me—

"Julianna!" My father's voice cut through the air from behind me.

Roman gave me one last piercing look before he melted back into the shadows. I felt a tug inside my gut as he disappeared.

I spun, my heartbeat so erratic against my ribs I was sure my father would hear it. He cut across the parking lot towards me with his familiar long stride. From the calm look on his face I knew that he hadn't seen Roman.

Roman… What had he wanted? Had he come to gloat? To taunt me? Had he come to blackmail me? To name his terms for his silence?

Roman's not like that, a voice inside me said. *Give him a chance to explain…*

Don't be stupid, Julianna. He lied about who he was to get you in bed. Don't fall for his lies again.

I realized my father, now standing before me, had said something. I shook myself. "Sorry. What?"

"I asked if you brought your car into work. Do you need a lift home?"

I blinked. My car. I had my… No. Wait. Espo had picked me up today. My mind had been so much elsewhere that I had walked out of the station thinking I had my car here. Idiot.

"Julu," my father frowned at me, "are you okay?"

I glanced to the shadows that had swallowed Roman Tyrell. I couldn't see him anymore, but I could feel him. I could sense him watching us. Watching *me*. The hairs on my skin stood on end. I wasn't sure if it was from fear or…something else.

"I'm fine," I lied.

JULIANNA

"Capi," Espinoza's voice made my head snap towards him. I hadn't realized he was standing at my desk at work, waving at me as I stared into space like a zombie.

I shook myself. *Get yourself together, Julianna.* I had to get my head back in the game. I had to stop Roman Tyrell from getting under my skin.

Too late.

"Sorry, what?" I asked.

Espo frowned. "Lacey just messaged. She's finished Vinnie's autopsy report. You coming?"

I followed Espinoza through the corridor. As we waited for the elevator, I could see him looking at me out of the corner of his eye. "You got something to say, just say it," I snapped.

His frown deepened. "Are you okay?"

Why was everyone asking me this? "Fine," I muttered.

"Uh-huh." The tone of his voice told me he wasn't at all convinced. "You seem off lately." We entered the elevator and Espo pressed the button to the basement where the morgue was located. "Like in the interrogation with Roman Tyrell."

I stiffened and tried not to sound so defensive. "What are you talking about?"

"You went off script with him. You got emotional. I mean, Jesus, at one point I thought you two were going to jump across the table and start hitting each other."

Or ripping each other's clothes off. I flushed at the memory and turned my head to hide my face.

"I don't like him," I admitted. "Something about him just... gets under my skin."

I wasn't lying. He lied to me about his surname. I had been tricked into my feelings for him. I hated the way I couldn't seem to switch them off, even now that I knew who he really was. I hated that I was lying for him. I hated that I wanted so badly to believe him. He was an infuriating, confusing mess that I didn't need in my life.

Espo made a noise in his throat. "He *is* a Tyrell. Your instincts are correct about him. It's not like you to take these things so personally."

If only he knew how *personally* things between Roman and me went. "I'll do better. I'll try not to get so worked up about the case."

Espo clasped a hand on my shoulder. "Don't worry, Capi. We're going to nail him."

That's what a fucked-up part of me was worried about. "We don't have the evidence to back up our case."

"Hopefully Lacey will have something for us," Espo said as the elevator doors dinged. We stepped out into the cold, eerie light of the basement corridor and walked through the double doors into the morgue. The sharp air of disinfectant and death hit my nose. I didn't think I'd ever get used to it.

Lacey was standing in her scrubs by a metal slab, Vinnie's body lying on top of it. The body was naked, cleaned of blood, a Y incision made into his chest, now sewn back using thick Frankenstein-like stitches.

"Have you got something good for me, baby?" Espo grinned at her.

Lacey shot him a coy smile, her long dark eyelashes fluttering. "I always have the goods, Espo."

Espo made an appreciative noise in his throat as his eyes roamed over her. "Don't I know it."

I rolled my eyes. "Are you two actually *flirting* over a dead body?"

Espo and Lacey shot each other another weighted smile before Lacey turned towards Vinnie's body. Her face grew serious. "Now that I've washed off all the blood, I can see the extent of his injuries." She shook her head, a heaviness pulling down the corners of her lips. "They did him over real good. I hope you catch the bastards." Using the closed tip of a pen she pointed to the body as she spoke. "Premortem bruising all over his torso. I count at least six cracked ribs. Five phalanges were cut off at the proximal phalanx."

"That's the fingers cut off at the closest bone to the palm," I translated to Espo.

He smacked my shoulder. "I understand geek-speak. Sort of."

"The remaining fingers were all broken," Lacey continued, her voice growing quieter. "Shallow cuts, at least two dozen, made all over his body. His kneecaps were shattered; blunt force trauma, so I'm assuming they used a bat or something like that."

I stared at the man on the table. Vinnie Torrito had an arrest record as long as my arm. He had not been a good man, but nobody deserved to die like this.

"Whoever shot him used a .22 caliber. Right in between the eyes. I recovered the bullet, already sent it to ballistics. Without a gun to match the striations to it's pretty useless."

"Could this all have been done by one person?" Espo asked.

Lacey's lips whitened as they pressed together. "Could be. Could be more than one. It's hard to tell. It's horrifying to think that a single human being could do this to another person."

"These Mafia families are all bred to be monsters from birth," Espo said, his voice hard and unflinching. Roman Tyrell flashed through my mind. I hated that Espo was right.

"He would have been in so much pain." Lacey stared at me with big brown eyes. "I hate to say this but... I'm glad they finally killed him. At least they put him out of his misery."

~

Mercutio Brevio sat across from me in the interrogation room in a closed-off silence until spoken to, a very different demeanor than Roman Tyrell when he was sitting in that very chair. They could have been brothers, I noted. They had the same dark features, except Mercutio's build was long and lean while Roman's was thick and intimidating. Mercutio didn't seem scared or worried. He was alert, his dark eyes darting around him as if he was memorizing everything. So far he had corroborated Roman's timeline for Saturday afternoon leading up to Club Luxe.

"How long have you known Roman Tyrell?" I asked as I leaned forward in my chair.

"Practically my whole life. We were pretty much raised together." Mercutio had a steady, calm voice. His diction was smooth, letting me know that he was better educated than the various men associated with the Tyrells.

"You're good friends," I clarified. Roman had indicated as such.

"Like brothers."

"You were there for him when his mother died."

"Yes."

"Like he was there for you when your father left."

Mercutio weighed this question up. "Of course."

"Would you lie for him?"

Mercutio's eyes cut to me, a hard anger glittering in his irises.

He didn't make any other indication that he thought my insinuation was an insulting one. This man had incredible control over his emotions.

"I'd do anything for him," Mercutio replied, his voice even, "even lie if he asked me to. But he didn't ask me to lie about anything."

"He was supposed to leave Verona Sunday night. Why didn't he?"

"Why don't you ask Roman?"

"He said his father convinced him to stay."

Mercutio stared at me, his head shaking slightly. "Mr. Tyrell Senior is a persuasive man. No doubt he made Roman an offer he couldn't refuse."

"You're Tito Brevio's son," I said, changing tactic.

Mercutio stiffened. "You can do research. Good for you, detective."

"He was the Tyrell's accountant for many years until he pulled that stunt in court, then disappeared."

"Are you here to rehash my family history or do you have a question?"

"You have a clean record, Mercutio. Not even so much as a parking ticket."

I could feel Espo's eyes on me. Where was I going with this? I was going off script again.

"What's that got to do with anything?" Mercutio crossed his arms over his chest and met my stare with a cold look. His jaw twitched. I was getting to him, although he was trying hard not to show it.

I just had to push a little further. I had to make him angry. "Why are you friends with someone like Roman Tyrell?"

"What is that supposed to mean?"

"We all know his reputation. Violent, aggressive, heir to a Mafia empire... Why do you hang around him? Do you get his protection? Do you work for him? Does he pay you to stick around?"

"It's not like that," Mercutio said through gritted teeth.

I kept going. "Or maybe you can't come to grips with the monster he's become? Maybe childhood sentimentality keeps you by his side?"

Mercutio's nostrils flared. His hands flew out from their constricted place across his chest and slammed on the table. He glared at me as if he might leap across at me at any second. "Roman's a good guy. He's not like his family. He's not what everyone thinks he is. He wouldn't kill anybody."

I leaned back in my chair, letting Mercutio's words soak into my bones. I had gotten what I wanted. A passionate, truthful outburst. I wanted to believe Mercutio. I wanted to believe my gut feeling about Roman. But...

Mercutio inhaled loudly, then let out a breath. He sank back into his chair, an uncomfortable look on his face. He'd come into this room determined not to say a bad word about anyone. I had managed to get him to admit how he really felt.

"If you don't have any more questions for me, detective," Mercutio's eyes landed on me. For a second I wondered if Roman had confessed to him about our night together. "We're done here."

"Do you actually believe that guy?" Espo said with a snort. "He actually thinks Roman Tyrell is innocent."

"Roman's a good guy."

I let out an absentminded laugh. Roman, innocent. How funny.

"Either Roman has him fooled or he's the world's best actor. I mean, for a second there *you* looked like you believed him."

"He's not like his family. He's not what everyone thinks he is."

"You okay, Jules?"

My thoughts were rattling around my head like pans as I entered the interrogation room. Espinoza closed the door behind us.

"About time," said Rosaline, her voice thick with annoyance.

Rosaline le Monde, socialite daughter of Pearce le Monde, and Roman's alibi. She sat at the interrogation table, legs crossed, thick waves of perfectly highlighted caramel hair falling over her shoulders, her huge breasts wrapped in an expensive-looking blue dress. Her manicured nails, a garish red, were clicking on the tabletop along with her gold bracelets. Her dark eyes were heavily made up, dark eyeshadow, dark eyeliner, and false eyelashes.

We could have passed for sisters except that Rosaline's features were sharper, she wore more makeup than I'd ever dream of doing, and her arms were bony while mine were defined.

Roman had a type, it appeared. I fit into it perfectly. Along with how many other women? My fingers tightened on my notepad. My heels struck the floor harder, sounding louder than usual as I stormed across the room and took my seat in front of her. I ignored the curious glance that Espinoza gave me as he sat next to me.

"Thank you for coming in Ms. le Monde," I said, trying to keep my face and voice passive. Espo and I had decided that it would be better for me to take point on this interview, as my being a woman might make Rosaline feel more at ease. I was not counting on this irrational desire I had to lunge across the table and punch her right in her stupid face.

Rosaline crossed her arms over her obviously fake breasts. "Anything for Romy."

Romy. What a stupid nickname.

"I assume when you say Romy you mean Roman Tyrell," I clarified for the interview recording.

"Obviously."

Obviously, you're a twit. "And how would you define your relationship with Mr. Tyrell?"

She broke out into a sticky red smile. "Me and Romy go way back, if you know what I mean."

"No, I *don't* know what you mean, that's why I asked," I said through gritted teeth.

"Romy and I are childhood sweethearts."

I opened the file in front of me, pretending to find the information I was looking for. I didn't need to. I knew the details of Roman's file by heart. Every piece of information I came across about Roman had been studied, analyzed and carefully stored away. "I understand he's been in Europe for…the last eight years. If you were *so* close, why didn't you go with him?" I knew I sounded bitchy. I couldn't help it.

"Romy," she fluttered her hands about her, "is like a wild stallion. I knew he needed a few years to go and do whatever he needed to do. At the end of the day, he will *always* come back to me. He loves me."

Her words stabbed me in the heart. Was it true? Did Roman love her? Had I just been a *whatever* he needed to do?

"We're you with him on Saturday the eleventh? Last Saturday."

"I was with him all night," she smirked at me.

She was lying. I knew she was lying. Roman had been with me. But I couldn't contradict her without ruining myself. I studied her face. Did she know she was sitting across from the woman Roman was *actually* with that night? "Why don't you take us through your evening with Mr. Tyrell. Start with what time you met and where."

"We met about ten thirty p.m. at Club Luxe…" She proceeded to outline Roman's night with *me*, starting with leaving Club Luxe and going to his hotel room, how we stayed in the next day, ordered room service, ending with our goodbye around seven p.m. Sunday night. As she spoke the blood drained from my limbs. She knew exactly what Roman and I had been doing. Which meant that Roman told her about our night together, *details* about our night together.

All I could do was stare at her, even after she finished talking, my mind going at a million miles per hour. Roman had told her *everything* about our time together. They must be close. Did she know she was talking about Roman and *me*? Was she mocking me?

Had I just been a fling? A substitute for her? Had he been fucking me and thinking of her that night? My heart burned as all these questions piled one on top of the other.

Espinoza cleared his throat. I could see him staring at me out of the corner of my eye. He was waiting for my next question. I couldn't get anything coherent to come out of my mouth.

"Ms. le Monde," Espo said.

"Please," she said, sending Espinoza a sticky smile, "call me Rosaline."

"Okay, Rosaline. Do you remember what you were wearing that night?"

"An LBD. Chanel."

"LBD?"

"Little black dress."

"Right." Espinoza paused as he wrote a small note on his notepad.

"How do we know you're telling the truth about your relationship with *Romy?*" I spat out before I could stop myself.

Rosaline stared at me, the smirk on her face never faltering. "Romy has a small birthmark on his lower left hip, shaped like Italy." Her grin widened. "Have fun checking it out. It's as close as you'll ever get."

His birthmark. I forced myself to take a deep breath and leaned back in my chair. She knew about his birthmark. How many other women knew about his birthmark? Why did I think I had been special?

"We'll, um, check that out," said Espinoza. "That's all, Ms. le Monde."

Rosaline sent me one more smug look before she let Espinoza escort her out. I was left alone in the interrogation room with my thoughts.

I felt violated. She had known every detail about my time with Roman. He had told her everything. Had it not been sacred to him? Had they laid in bed together and discussed me? Did Rosaline know that the woman Roman had been with was me?

I was totally wrecked by the time I left the station that evening. My stomach was empty and in knots. I hadn't been hungry all day. I had driven my car into work today and had *remembered* that I had driven it in. I found myself searching the parking lot shadows. I chastised myself. I didn't want to see Roman Tyrell again. I didn't want an explanation from him. I just wanted to get enough evidence on him to put him away. Then to forget about him and his stupid beautiful face and his stupid beautiful body.

I closed my apartment door behind me, dropping my keys and bag automatically on the side table. Before I could reach for the light, I saw the shadow moving in front of me. Someone was in my apartment.

JULIANNA

My training kicked in. I slammed my back up against the front door and grabbed for my gun, my veins flooding with adrenaline.

A firm hand on my forearm stopped me. "Relax, Jules." I heard Roman's voice. A strange sense of relief washed over me.

It took me a second for my mind to catch up. Roman Tyrell had broken into my apartment. I should *not* be feeling relief. In the dim moonlight streaming in through my living room windows, I could see his wide frame taking up almost my entire vision. Where he was touching me, felt like it was burning.

I found my voice. "Let go of me."

"Only if you promise not to shoot me," he said, his tone light.

"I'm not promising anything." I could smell his familiar masculine cologne of wood and citrus. I hated that I wanted to press my nose into his chest and fist my hands into his shirt. He was a criminal for God sakes.

He chuckled softly into the dark, the noise sending shivers down my spine. "I guess I'll have to take a chance that I'll survive you."

What the hell was *that* supposed to mean?

He let go of me but he didn't step back, leaving me no room to breathe. I was suddenly all too aware that I was standing alone in the dark with Roman Tyrell. My nerve ends felt electrified, as if we were two live wires that would spark if we got any closer. I couldn't be in the dark with him. It was too intimate. Too intense.

I reached out to the side and flicked on the closest light switch. It turned on the living room light, which fell partly into the entryway through the kitchen. Now his handsome features were bathed in light and shadows. Dear God, he was beautiful. And too close. Much too close.

I sank back against the door and realized too late that I had cornered myself. "What are you doing in my apartment?" I asked, trying to keep my voice steady.

He stared at me with those intense eyes of midnight fire. "We need to talk."

No, we needed to stay as far away from each other as possible. I swallowed. "How do you even know where I live?"

His perfect lips twitched. "I'm a Tyrell. I have…resources."

Don't forget that this man is a Tyrell. He is dangerous. I should be terrified that he'd found out where I lived and broke into my apartment. For some reason, I wasn't.

I thought back to my lock. I hadn't noticed any pick marks. I couldn't imagine Roman Tyrell bothering to pick a lock. He'd more likely kick the door down. "How did you get in? This is a secure building."

He frowned. "You should get an alarm system. You never know who might be lying in wait for you in your apartment. It's not safe."

I snorted. "This coming from you. You never answered me; how did you get in?"

"You left your bedroom window unlocked."

I blinked at him. "You scaled my building?"

He shrugged. "There's a fire escape out there. It wasn't hard to jump from the fire escape to your window."

I ran my mind over the structure of the side of the building, of the fire escape and my window. I gasped. "You idiot. You could've been killed."

"So you do care about me," he said, his voice softened.

I glared at him. "I don't *care* about you. I care about how the hell I would explain the body of Roman Tyrell splattered all over my sidewalk. Never mind the paperwork."

He grabbed his chest as if I shot him through the heart. "Ouch. You really know how to wound a guy."

"What the fuck happened at the interview?" I hissed at him. "Was that your idea of a joke?"

"I was as surprised as you were."

"How could you possibly expect me to believe you didn't know who I was?"

"How could I? I haven't been in this damn country for the last eight years. I take it meeting you wasn't some kind of police organized shakedown."

"No. Just a crazy coincidence."

"Fate."

I snorted. "I don't believe in fate."

"How do you explain us?"

Us. Memories slammed through me. His naked body, hard and unyielding, his hands searing into my skin as he gave to me as much as he took.

I shoved these images away. I would not allow myself to lose my head around him. I could not.

My body betrayed me. My nipples were painful pebbles against the material of my shirt. I was sure my cheeks were flushed and my pupils dilated. All of these things I hoped he couldn't see.

"There is no *us*," I hissed at him.

"Don't tell me you don't feel—"

177

"I feel nothing."

"You're lying," he said, his dark eyes probing my face. "Don't tell me that if I pressed you up against your door and kissed you right now, you could push me away."

I sucked in a breath as my panties flooded with wet heat. "You…you wouldn't."

His gaze burned into me and aggression rolled off him. He inched forward, his muscles tensing as if he was fighting to hold back from making good on his threat.

My own body tensed as my mind warred with my body. I wanted him. Even though I knew who he was, my body begged for his touch. I hungered for him to slam me against this door and to do his worst.

He might have killed someone, Julianna! a voice inside me screamed.

I had known from the minute I'd met him there was something dangerous about him. But he wasn't a killer. Right?

"Did you do it?" I blurted out.

"Do what?"

"Kidnap Vinnie. Torture him."

"I already told you, no."

"Off the record." I swallowed, hard. "*I* need to know… Did you?"

He didn't so much as flinch. "I never touched him," he said, his voice flat.

I didn't think he was lying but there was something off about his response. "Tell me you didn't press a gun to his temple and pull the trigger."

His eyes narrowed. "Like I said, I never touched him."

Why did I want to believe him?

"Julianna," he said, his voice rolling around my name as if he was caressing it. "I'm not—"

"You lied to me. You told me your name was Roman Lettiere."

His shoulders fell. "Lettiere was my mother's maiden name. I always felt more like a Lettiere than a Tyrell."

"You still lied to me. Why should I believe anything you say?" I wasn't ready to believe him. Even though, deep down I wanted to.

"Because you *know* me, Jules." He grabbed my arm, his grip so tight that it bordered on painful. "Look past the last name I was given."

I yanked against him but he wouldn't release me. "Let go of me."

"You *know* me."

I scowled at him. "You're a prime suspect in my active murder investigation. As far as anyone else is concerned, I don't know you."

"You didn't tell them about us?" The word *us* came out like a breathy whisper and the word slithered down my spine, unleashing a series of unwanted images through my mind: his hands on my hips, his mouth claiming mine, his beautiful cock sliding into my aching core. My clit throbbed.

I swallowed and tried to wrestle control back from my mutinous body. "No. I didn't tell anyone."

"Good." He let out a huge breath. He was relieved.

"Don't worry, I don't want to be associated with you either," I snapped, a stab of hurt embedding in my stomach. "My career is not worth ruining for you."

He frowned. "I'm not worried about me, I'm worried about... If my father found out that you and I..." His mouth snapped shut. What was he about to say? "You're better off not telling anyone about us."

Us? That word was like a taunt. *There is no us*, I wanted to yell. "Why didn't you tell me who you were?" I demanded, pent up betrayal finally surfacing. "Why did you lie to me and tell me your last name was Lettiere?"

"I didn't want you to look at me the way you're looking at me now."

"How am I looking at you?"

"Like I'm a criminal. Like someone to avoid." He sounded almost sad. "Some girls… it turns them on. They like the danger of being with a Tyrell. I knew you weren't like that."

Wasn't I? Being here with him right now was pretty damn dangerous but I was still, for some screwed up reason, turned the hell on.

He stepped closer. "Don't tell me you would have come with me if you knew I was a Tyrell."

"Of course I wouldn't have gone with you. Do you think I like being in this position? Having to lie to my partner, to my superiors, to my father?"

"No, I don't suppose you do," he said, his voice turning hard.

"It was a mistake," I blurted out. "It shouldn't have happened."

"A mistake," he said, his voice laced with anger. "Yes, I suppose it was."

"You also shouldn't have lied about not having a girlfriend."

His eyes narrowed. "I don't have a girlfriend."

"Rosaline came to the station today to corroborate your alibi, or should I say, to lie for you. She seemed to think differently about your relationship."

Something dark crossed his face. "Rosaline has this idea of us that doesn't match reality."

"And yet you still called on her when you needed help," I spat out. "Did you tell her it was me?"

"Of course not."

"I questioned her. She *knew* everything we did when we were together. You told her everything."

"Are you mad because she lied," he spoke in a low voice, "or are you angry because I shared what was ours with her?"

My heart stabbed. "I'm angry that you put me in this position.

I know that a witness is lying to me but I can do nothing about it."

He pursed his lips, then a look of amusement lightened his face. "You're jealous."

I stiffened. "I am not."

He leaned his hands on either side of me, trapping me against the door. His nose brushed alongside my neck. "I can smell it rolling off you."

I gulped at the air, trying to get enough breath into my lungs. My mind was short-circuiting with him so close.

"Why are you jealous, Jules? Tell me."

I had to make him stop. I could feel my willpower wavering as his heat rolled off him. Any second now I'd give in and lift my mouth to his lips, now running along my cheekbone, causing shivers to cascade through my body.

I shoved him back and he stepped out of my space. "Leave. Now."

"I'm not done talking."

"I am." I snatched my gun from my hip holster and raised it to point at him. "Get out."

He raised his hands in surrender, his face smoothing out into that mask I'd first seen in the interrogation room. He took a step towards me. I sidestepped around giving him the space he needed, keeping my gun trained on him. I didn't trust *myself* without it.

He opened the door and paused in the doorway, turning to face me once more. "Thank you," he said, his voice hard as steel.

"What for?"

He stared at the barrel of my gun, then up at me. "For reminding me which side I'm on."

His words were like bullets in my chest. Before I could speak, he was gone.

ROMAN

I pulled my collar up, keeping my face turned away from the security camera I knew was mounted over the lobby door, as I exited Julianna's building. I eased down a side street and slunk into the shadows, becoming one with the night.

She had pulled a gun on me. She had pointed the black barrel at my heart and fear flashed across her beautiful face as she yelled at me to "get out".

She was scared of me.

A surge of rage went through me. I lashed out, kicking a garbage can, causing it to fly across the alley and smash against the slimy brick wall. It exploded, the trash contained within spilling out all over the ground. The stench of rotting fruit reached my nose. I stood, chest heaving, staring at the destruction before me. The destruction I had caused.

Look at me. She was right to be scared. I was a Tyrell, a blackened heart, a thing to be feared. A destroyer of everything he touched. Why did I ever think I could be anything different?

Because she had made me feel like I could be different. Because when she had gazed up at me, her honeyed hair spread across the pillow, her soft body naked and open, she gave me a reason to be different.

Knowing who I was had chased that look away. She was lost to me. The man I could have been was lost to me too.

A door banged open farther up the alleyway, fluorescent light spilling out from the fast food joint. A short fat man stepped out yelling obscenities at me for kicking over his garbage can. I turned towards him and watched fear flash in his eyes. He retreated without another word and slammed the door shut behind him, the lock clicking.

I stood alone in the dark once more.

I had done my duty. I had warned Julianna. I was sure she wouldn't tell anyone about the night we'd spent together. Now I just had to keep away from her.

JULIANNA

" T hank you." Roman stared at the barrel of the gun I pointed at him, then up at me. "For reminding me which side I'm on."

I didn't put him on the other side. He did. He did by... by...

By having the wrong surname.

The knot in my stomach grew. I kicked off my bed sheets. Damn you, Roman Tyrell. Another sleepless night thinking about you. It was too damn hot. I felt like I had a fever.

I got up out of bed and threw open my window, the cool night air like a balm against my burning skin. My fingers traced the window sill. He slipped inside through this very window earlier. My skin prickled as I gazed down the fire escape that Roman had climbed earlier to get to me. Was he down there? Watching me? Was he in the shadows staring back up at me?

I tore myself away from the window and fell back into bed, squeezing my eyes shut and demanding that I sleep.

"My father is a difficult man. My family is...complicated. We have a family business and the politics... The politics are killer. I didn't want to be a part of it. I wanted to be my own person."

"That's very brave of you."

"Or desperate."

Could it be true? Did Roman Tyrell have nothing to do with Vinnie's death? Or was this just what he wanted me to think? Was Roman Tyrell trying to manipulate me?

I recalled the desperation in his voice as he begged me to believe him. *"Look past the last name I was given. You* know *me."*

I sat up in bed, my head spinning. What if... What if the world was wrong? What if the Roman I had met *was* the real Roman Tyrell? What if he wasn't the monster everyone thought him to be?

"Thank you... For reminding me which side I'm on."

Guilt stabbed at my gut. I had made him feel like a criminal tonight. I had to apologize.

Apologize, Julianna, are you nuts? He was still the prime suspect in Vinnie's murder.

If he's cleared of Vinnie's murder, then you can apologize.

I couldn't apologize. Even if he was cleared. I was a detective, the police chief's daughter. He was the son of Giovanni Tyrell. I couldn't apologize to him.

At least not publicly.

Roman and I could never be seen together, even if he were deemed innocent. We could never be friends.

Friends. As if Roman and I could ever just be friends. The ghost of the electricity I felt when he was near me coursed through my veins. Every time we'd gotten near each other we'd almost torn each other's clothes off.

I shook my head. Things were too complicated. My body had a mind of its own when it came to him. I couldn't trust myself around him. Roman and I had to stay the hell away from each other.

JULIANNA

"**D**etective Capulet." The familiar deep voice called me.

I glanced up from my work desk. Police Captain Foster was standing at the doorway to the stairs, his thick eyebrows furrowed over his sharp gray eyes. He was only late forties, but the stress of the job had cut deep grooves into his forehead and dusted his hair with salt and pepper. Captain Foster had been almost like an uncle to me. He and my father had attended the Academy together. They had even been partners at one time.

"Yes, captain?"

"The chief's office, now."

Oh my God. My stomach dropped like a stone. Had someone seen Roman leaving my place last night? Had one of the witnesses from Club Luxe recognized me?

This was it. I was caught. What the hell was I going to say to the captain? To my father?

"Capulet?"

"Coming," I called out automatically.

I pushed away from my desk, my breathing going erratic.

Somehow I managed to follow him up the stairs. I felt like I was being led to the principal's office, everyone turning to stare at me as I walked past, wondering what I did wrong.

I could turn around and run. Disappear. I wouldn't have to face the consequences of my fated actions. Nor would I have to explain the intimacies I shared with Roman Tyrell.

The captain entered my father's office and held the door open for me. This was it. Last chance to run.

A Capulet never runs from danger. A Capulet does their duty.

Running would only make things worse. And where would I go? All I could do was beg for forgiveness and hope I wasn't fired.

I entered the office and stood just inside the room, flinching as the door clicked shut behind me. The captain sat in one of the chairs in front of the desk. My father, Chief Montgomery Capulet, sat behind his large desk, his palms flat on the surface amidst small neat piles of paper, a computer and a single photo frame. The frame faced away from me but I knew what it contained: a photo of me and my mother taken two weeks before she died.

My father's narrowed eyes caught mine, the dark look on his face growing darker. A knot developed in my throat. How many times in my life had I seen that look on his face, that heavy disapproval, that bitter disappointment, that tightly controlled anger? It took every ounce of effort not to throw myself on his desk and beg for his forgiveness. *Please still love me.*

A figure I only just noticed, sat in one of the chairs facing my father's desk, turned to look at me. It was Espinoza, a similar grim look on his face. Oh God. They were all here. The only people whose professional opinion mattered to me.

I walked like I was facing the firing squad to the only spare chair, right between the captain and Espinoza. I could feel all three pairs of eyes staring at me, burning holes through my lies like fire through paper. I fell into the chair, gripping my hands together in my lap and stared at the desk. I couldn't meet anyone's eye. I couldn't bear to see the disappointment. The air was heavy and hot, my neck prickling under my collar as I waited.

My father leaned forward in his large brown chair, the leather creaking mournfully under his solid build. I swallowed hard, hoping that I would somehow find the right words. Time to bite the bullet. I looked up and opened my mouth to apologize. "Dad—"

"Where are we with Vinnie Torrito's murder?" my father interrupted, shooting me a glare. He had a rule that I was never to call him dad or show any sign of affection at work.

I blinked. Was this what this meeting was about? Had my guilt forced me to jump to the wrong conclusions?

I realized I was still sitting in stunned silence when Espinoza spoke instead of me. "We questioned Giovanni and Roman Tyrell, as well as a few of their men. They all alibied each other out. So far we can't find any holes in their alibis. The only thing we have is the traffic cam video showing one of their SUVs in the area during the time."

"That's purely circumstantial. It's not enough." My father growled and leaned back in his chair, the hinges protesting. "What about witnesses?"

I couldn't believe my luck. No one had found out about Roman and me. *Yet,* a small voice in me whispered.

I cleared my throat and spoke up. "We've canvassed the area around the body dump but no one saw anything. Or at least if they did, they're not speaking to us."

"Any trace on the body?"

I let out an easier breath. "No trace. Whoever committed the crime was a pro and knew to clean up and wear gloves."

"And the slug?"

"It's not a match to anything in the system. We haven't found the gun. Uniforms have searched all the dumpsters in a three mile radius to the body dump."

"We won't find the gun. Even if we do these bastards are too smart to have it lead back to anyone." My father swore. He rarely swore in front of me. He leaned forward, his elbows on the desk, and rubbed his face with his hands. "I'm getting pressure from upstairs to stamp out gang activity, which means putting Giovanni and Roman Tyrell away. We haven't been able to pin anything else on them. This murder is our best chance."

"What if," I spoke up, "what if it wasn't the Tyrells?"

I felt all three sets of eyes focus on me, burning holes in me. I regretted my words immediately.

My father's lips pressed together. "Don't be stupid, Julianna. Jacob Tyrell was killed two weeks ago by the Veronesis. Now one of Veronesi's men has turned up dead. Of course, the Tyrells were behind this kill. If they didn't pull the trigger, then they hired the man who did. This has the potential to lead to a full-scale war. When that happens, too many innocents will get pulled into it, they always do. We cannot let this escalate. We need to find some way of pinning the Tyrells for this murder."

I frowned. "What about Jacob Tyrell's murder? Shouldn't we be focusing on that case as well?"

My father stared at me. "That is not your case."

I bit down a rise of annoyance. "If these two cases are related, it might help us to have a look at the case file for Jacob Tyrell's murderer."

My father shook his head. "I already have people sifting through that evidence. There's a hell of a lot of it. Your job is to focus on putting Giovanni and Roman Tyrell away. Is that understood?"

"Yes, sir," Espinoza and I said together.

My father directed his next comment straight at me. "Don't disappoint me."

My stomach tightened. "I won't, sir."

"Good. Now get out of here and find me something to pin on those Tyrell bastards."

I was silent as Espo and I walked out of my father's office. Why was my father so determined to pin the Tyrells for Vinnie's murder? We had no evidence they'd done it. My father was instigating a witch-hunt to try to bring down all the Tyrells.

What if Roman wasn't like the rest of them?

"Look past the last name I was given. You know *me."*

~

Later that night, I tossed the empty Chinese takeout box into the trash can by my desk and stood up, stretching, nodding goodnight to a fellow officer as he walked past me towards the elevator. I scanned the empty workstations and darkened offices. Perfect. I was the last one on the floor. What I wanted to do, I didn't want to do while worrying that someone might be looking over my shoulder.

I pulled my chair under the desk and opened an internet browser. Glancing around myself one more time, I typed in "Roman Giovanni Tyrell" and clicked *search* before I could change my mind.

The search results came up in an instant. There were articles from various social magazines about the European heiresses and trust fund babes he'd been connected with. I cast my eyes over the various photos of him at parties, in clubs, on yachts, a bottle in one hand, the other slung around a bevy of beautiful girls. My heart squeezed. Was I just another one of his revolving door of girls? How many more of them had he invited to Paris with him? And if he was used to dating heiresses, what had he been doing with me?

I closed the browser, a growing sick feeling in my stomach. I opened an email I'd received from an old colleague who was working for Interpol in Lyon, France.

. . .

Good to hear from you, Julianna.
Here's everything we have on Roman Tyrell.
Jerome.

I opened the attachments. While Roman Tyrell had been in Europe he hadn't been linked to any of the European Mafia families. He had been picked up no less than five times for drunk and disorderly behavior, and disturbing the peace, all of them from bar fights. He had a string of speeding tickets. Nothing more serious than that. Drinking, speeding and fighting. How had he graduated from drunken fist fights to torture and cold-blooded murder?

I found the witness statements to the fights and read through them. I frowned. They had all claimed that Roman had been defending himself or someone else. According to the gossip columns, Roman was the one who was supposed to have started the fights. He even bragged about it in an interview. Why would he do that? Why would he make himself appear worse than he was?

He'd been enrolled in a Criminal Law Degree at the Regent University, located in the green heart of Regent's Park in London.

Criminal law. How ironic.

He'd pulled out of his degree the day of his return to Verona with only one semester to go. As far as I could see, he hadn't transferred to another university closer to home. Why did he just quit like that?

I searched back through public records from before he left for Europe. He had attended St. Andrews Private School, Verona's most prestigious high school. I had gone to the local public school and was a grade below him. Our circles would never have crossed paths, not until last Saturday.

I couldn't get access to Roman's school records without a

court order, but I did have access to the files kept by the school police. He had a few reprimands in his record: truancy, fighting, problems with authority figures.

I sank back into my chair. To the world, Roman Tyrell looked like a violent, irresponsible playboy. I remembered the man I had spent the night with: charming, funny, insightful. The Roman that the world seemed to think existed wasn't the Roman that I had experienced. How could it be possible that the world got it so wrong?

"My father is a difficult man."

I pulled up the file on Roman's father. Giovanni Tyrell, known Mafia boss, controller of the Tyrell empire, suspected of running drugs and guns from Colombia, his illegal activities covered up by his legitimate interests: property investments, clubs, restaurants and transportation companies. There was a suspected string of dead bodies in his wake, but with no convictions.

I chewed on my lip. Roman's mother's murder case file would be in our system. It would have been before our files were digitized so it'd be stored in the file room down in the basement. I wasn't about to check out the files from the file room. I searched for newspaper articles online instead.

Maria Tyrell, Wife of Mobster, Murdered.

She'd been discovered by their housekeeper in her garage with her throat slit. No weapon was found at the scene.

My heart skipped a beat when I read the next few lines. Roman Tyrell, her youngest son, was discovered hiding in the corner of the garage covered in her blood. He may have been the only witness. He'd been treated for shock but was otherwise unharmed. He had been twelve.

Jesus Christ. I imagined a young Roman finding his mother dead in the garage. My heart cried for him. That was something no child, no human, should ever have to go through.

I would have been eleven. Old enough to remember. How did I not remember this? This was huge news.

I looked at the date of the newspaper articles. Of course. This was the same time as my mother had died so I'd fallen into a deep grief-hole where nothing else had penetrated. Fourteen years ago, Roman Tyrell and I were on opposite sides of the city, living in two different worlds, yet struggling with the same grief.

I kept reading further, my stomach twisting into knots. Roman Tyrell hadn't told the police anything. He'd refused to speak to them even after the case went cold.

It had been a gang-related hit, the newspapers mused. Others, were more sensational.

Did Roman Tyrell Kill His Own Mother?

My stomach turned as I read, unable to stop. Police believed that Roman Tyrell held the key to solving his mother's murder. Why wouldn't Roman speak up? Was he protecting someone? Or was *he* the one hiding the violent secret? Like father, like son.

I swallowed my anger down. How could the papers even speculate that a twelve-year-old boy could do something like this? Roman Tyrell had not even been a teenager before this city began to persecute him, all because of who his father was.

What about Maria Tyrell? Roman spoke of a gentle, kind woman when he spoke about her. I stared at a black and white photo of Maria. Her thick dark hair was a wave that tumbled over her shoulders, framing a sweetheart face. She had been a beautiful lady with a wide warm smile; the same smile as Roman's. My heart clenched.

I dug through the digital records and found the file on the massacre at the docks where Jacob Tyrell, Roman's brother, had been slain. The "dirty docks massacre", the newspapers had called it. I glanced around, making sure I was still alone before I began to click through the crime scene photographs. A single gunshot wound on each body, a V slashed into each of their chests. It had been without a doubt a professional hit.

Except for Jacob.

Jacob Tyrell, wanted for murder and gone underground for four years, had been found dead in a converted apartment on the top floor of one of the buildings. There was a V on his chest like the others, but he'd also taken a beating before he had died. An entire clip of bullets had been released into his torso and he had a stab wound to his leg. It had been personal. It left no doubt that the massacre had occurred to target Jacob.

So much violence. How much blood could a man's life be bathed in before the darkness began to soak into his soul?

Roman's words to me kept echoing in my brain. *"My family is...complicated. I didn't want to be a part of it. I wanted to be my own person."*

This was why Roman had left Verona all those years ago. This was why he wanted to return to London after his brother's funeral. But he hadn't returned to Europe. He stayed in Verona. Why had he changed his mind? Had he given up trying to fight his family legacy?

Or was there some other reason?

Maybe we were looking at this wrong. Maybe, it wasn't his father who was lying for Roman, but Roman who was lying for his father.

I slipped into the empty tech room. One side of the room was covered in large monitors, a curved control station with more buttons, panels and keyboards than a spaceship command center. I had spent hours in here beside the techies, scouring through traffic cameras around Vinnie's dump site. I knew how to handle the controls, at least enough to be able to access the city's traffic camera footage. If I could somehow trace Roman's steps from the hotel to wherever he went that night, maybe I could prove that he hadn't been with his father. Maybe I could tear his father's alibi apart.

In the interview, Roman had said that his friend Mercutio had picked him up and dropped him off at his father's. From a DMV search of Mercutio Brevio, I knew that he had a black Ford Taurus registered to him. I wrote his license plate number on a piece of paper beside me.

I couldn't see which way Roman had left the hotel. We hadn't gotten the security tapes from the Marriott Hotel yet as we were still waiting on a court order. Assuming Roman had been headed to the airport, they would have turned right out of the hotel. I pulled up a map on the city's traffic cameras on one monitor and then located one that I suspected might have caught a glimpse of him.

I lined up the time to seven ten p.m. that Sunday, just as Roman would have been saying goodbye to me. And hit play. The seconds ticked over as I stared at the grainy screen, eyeing the various cars that passed the intersection. I spotted what looked like a Ford Taurus and hit pause. I leaned in towards the screen. I could see two figures in the front seats. When I zoomed in I could make out their faces. I recognized Roman's wide shoulders in the passenger seat. I pressed play again and watched as they drove off-screen. I turned back to the map of traffic cameras, picked out the next camera that they might pass and lined that footage up.

The work was painstaking, but I was able to follow the Ford Taurus towards the outskirts of Verona. I frowned. They really were headed to the airport. So why didn't Roman catch his flight?

In the footage from a freeway camera mounted high on an overpass, I spotted several SUVs converging around the Ford.

My skin began to prickle. One of the SUVs sped up beside Mercutio's vehicle, then veered in front of the car to block it. The Taurus braked and skidded to a halt. A second SUV blocked the back of it. The few other cars on the road braked before merging into the left lane to get around the road blockage.

"What the hell?" I muttered.

A man got out of the front SUV. I paused it and zoomed in, squinting at his face. My eyes widened when I saw the scar cutting across his left side. Scarface. The man from the cemetery.

He had a gun in his hand.

I zoomed out and hit play. The passenger door of the Taurus opened and Roman stepped out of the car. Seeing him, even in black and white, caused something to tug in my chest. A limo drove up in the left lane and stopped beside them. Scarface pointed his gun towards Roman. I watched in disbelief as Roman got into the back of the limo. Scarface got into the front. The convoy drove off.

Roman had been kidnapped. By whom? Who were these men? Who was Scarface?

Did something happen to Roman to get him involved with Vinnie? Why did his father claim that they were having dinner?

I ran the license plate of the black limo. The hairs on my arms rose when I read the registration details.

Tyrell Industries.

Giovanni Tyrell had kidnapped Roman on the way to the airport. But why?

I followed the convoy through the traffic cameras. I lost them soon after they turned off the highway. I sank back into my chair.

"I'm running away from my father."

What if Roman didn't want to live the life his family did? What if that's why he left Verona? What if Vinnie's murder was something Roman got pulled into?

"Julianna, you're still here?" Captain Foster poked his head through the partially open door. I jumped and clicked the minimize button on the screen. The traffic camera footage disappeared.

I turned to face him. I hoped from his angle at the door he hadn't been able to see what was on the screen properly. "Yes, captain. I was just running through a hunch."

He stepped farther into the room. "Did you find anything?"

I shook my head. "Nothing interesting," I lied. I couldn't tell the captain about my theory on Roman Tyrell. Not yet.

He glanced at the blank screen, then looked back at me, his face unreadable. "Are you leaving soon?"

"In a bit."

He shook his head and gave me an affectionate smile. "You're like your father. You work too hard."

I let out a nervous laugh. "Thanks. I think."

"It is a compliment. I'm waiting for the day that you surpass me in rank. Anyway, good night. Make sure you get some sleep."

As soon as the captain left, I sagged with relief. I had to be more careful. I opened up the traffic camera footage again and stared at the screen.

What should I do with this footage? All that it proved was that Roman got into a limo owned by his father. They already claimed that they had had dinner together that night. Unfortunately, this new footage didn't disprove that. Why would Giovanni Tyrell force his own son into his car?

What was going on? Who are you really, Roman Tyrell? What happened with your father?

"My father is a difficult man. My family is...complicated. We have a family business and the politics... The politics are killer. I didn't want to be a part of it."

What if Giovanni *did* kill Vinnie, or at the very least, had Vinnie killed? Perhaps all Roman was guilty of was lying about being his father's alibi. How would I prove this?

Roman.

Roman was my proof.

~

The next evening, I stood in front of my closet looking across the items in my wardrobe. I needed to be sexy without being obvious. My eyes were drawn to a dress in a deep red.

He let out a groan. "You're wearing red lacy underwear?" His voice came out tight, almost pained. "Please tell me the bra matches."

My cheeks heated. Red. Roman liked me in red. I pulled the dress out and slipped it on, a red fitted dress with buttons running the whole way up the front. I slipped on a pair of nude heels and stepped in front of the mirror. It held on to the lines of my curves without being too clingy, and if I left the top button undone, you could see the peak of the top of my cleavage. It was perfect.

Except there was no place to hide a gun.

The thought of walking into enemy camp without a gun made me feel...naked. A shiver slipped down my spine like a melting ice cube. Did I really think that Roman could be dangerous to me?

No.

At least, not physically. My heart skipped a beat as if to make a point. A point which I summarily ignored. I grabbed my keys, Roman's address which I had copied from his file, and left before I could change my mind.

Less than thirty minutes later I walked out of the elevator to the top floor of an inner West Verona apartment block, all creamy walls, warm cherry wood and silver finishes. It appeared there was only one apartment on this penthouse level. I walked down the short corridor, my heels muffled on the cream carpet, stopping in front of a painted midnight blue door, a silver number "70" and a matching silver knocker centered at eye height. I smoothed down my dress and took a deep, steadying breath. It didn't work. I knocked on the door, my rapping echoing down the empty corridor.

I heard footsteps approaching the door from inside. The sound turned my heart into a tribal drumbeat inside my body. I shook my clammy hands by my sides and forced what I hoped was a sexy smile on my face. I had a touch of eye makeup to darken my eyes and a natural-colored gloss on my mouth.

The small peephole darkened. My skin broke out into goosebumps, the way it did when Roman looked at me. There was a pause. I could almost feel him stop breathing. Or perhaps I was projecting because I certainly had.

Here we were. After...everything. Less than two inches of wood separating us.

I heard the lock click. The door opened a few inches, stopping against the strain of the chain still hooked on. Through the gap, one of Roman's dark hooded eyes stared out at me. "What are you doing here?" His deep voice, like honey and gravel all at once, rolled like a wave over me.

"I...I want to talk to you."

"As who?"

I blinked, wondering if I misheard. "Sorry?"

"Are you here as Detective Capulet, or as my Jules?"

My Jules? "Jules," I blurted out. "I'm here as Jules."

As he stared at me, nothing seemed to pass across his eyes. The door shut in my face.

My shoulders sagged. He wasn't even going to speak to me.

I heard the chain being unhooked. The door opened wide and Roman Tyrell stood in front of me. I choked on my tongue. He was standing in front of me wearing only a towel wrapped around his waist, his glorious torso on display, damp chest hair coiled on his firm chest, droplets of water scattered across his golden skin. My eyes slid down over his six-pack and those damn sexy V muscles. The V disappeared under his towel that sat low—too low, *way* too low—just above his pubic bone. My body flooded with desire from the top of my head to my toes, making me feel like I was melting into the ground. This was a bad idea. A very, very, bad idea. I should walk away, right now. If I could even walk. Nope, legs don't seem to want to function right now.

I was staring. I was staring at the bulge in his towel. Shit. I lifted my eyes, cheeks burning, hoping he hadn't caught me.

He was watching me, a slight smile pulling at the corner of his lip.

Fuck. He had so caught me.

"Come in, Jules." He stepped aside, revealing the interior of a stylish modern bachelor pad. I could hear the strains of an instrumental guitar coming from deep inside his lair. It felt like a trap. A beautiful trap.

"You… I… You…" I stuttered, unable to move from the spot.

His look was unapologetic. "I just got out of the shower. You didn't exactly warn me before you came over."

I found my voice. "Why would that have made any difference?"

His grin widened. "If I knew you were coming, I wouldn't have bothered with the towel."

My mouth dropped open. I was hit with another wave of lust, wetness trickling into my panties.

He laughed. "You're so easy to tease. Come inside."

I stepped inside his apartment before I could change my mind. I stopped at the edge of a formal living room decorated in black leather, chrome and mahogany. There were no photo frames, no books, no personal touches. It could have been a luxury hotel suite, cold and detached.

The door shut and locked behind me with a loud click. I spun. Our gazes fused together and I was stunned into blankness. He was so lovely. A perfect Roman statue come to life. I felt under-dressed in my cotton dress and heels. Next to this god of a man I would probably feel under-dressed in a ball gown designed for a princess.

For a moment, we watched each other. His gaze drifted across my face and the longing that flashed in his deep-set eyes caused my stomach to twist into knots. It took everything I had not to close the distance between us and press myself against him. Too much. It was too much. *He* was too much.

This time, there was something different about the hunger in his eyes. It was...tainted with regret. Sadness. Reduced to "what if's" and "if only's" whispered into the dark.

I watched as his features hardened into that cold mask I'd first seen in the interrogation room. This saddened me more than anything. He was a master at tucking all his emotions away on command. I hated it. It made me feel so unbalanced. I wasn't as good as he was at pretending I was okay with all of this.

I schooled my own features into what I hoped was cool detachment and tried to ignore the fissures of heat running through me at the sight of his beautiful body. "You should put some clothes on."

"I'm quite comfortable the way I am."

"I would be more comfortable—"

"Why did you come here, Julianna?" he interrupted, his voice an icy crisp version of the baritone that could reduce me to liquid heat. "What do you want?"

I cleared my throat. If he was fine being questioned half naked, then I would be too. "I traced your route after you left me at the hotel using the city traffic cameras."

He made a noise in his throat, his dark eyes appraising me. "No wonder you made detective so young." If I didn't know any better, I would have said that his voice held a hint of pride.

"I saw the SUVs creating a blockade. I saw the man with a gun."

His mouth pinched but he didn't respond. That was the only sign that I had surprised him. I moved slowly towards him, like I was approaching a wild horse that I wanted to tame. "It was your father in that limo, wasn't it?"

"You're the detective. You tell me." He shifted back, moving away from me.

I kept approaching, my voice low and steady, trying to tell him that he had nothing to fear from me. I was on his side. "He forced you into his limo. You didn't want to go with him."

"Nobody forces me to do anything." His back hit the door.

I only stopped when we were toe to toe. He didn't move, he just let me cage him. God, he smelled divine; fresh and clean. We weren't touching but I could feel the heat radiating off his body. I wanted to fall against him, to melt against his hardness, to run my hands down his body and lose myself in him again.

I couldn't lose focus now. "Where did he really take you, Roman?"

"I told you, we had dinner together."

"Don't lie to me. Where did he take you?"

He flinched. "This is poor form, Julianna. Using our *history* to try to trick evidence out of me."

"I didn't come here to get evidence on you."

He snorted. "Then why are you here?"

"I...I want to help you."

"Nobody can help me," he said quietly. The tone of his voice was hopeless and resigned. It stabbed me in the heart.

I wanted to reach up to touch his face, to comfort him. I was afraid that if I touched him I'd forget why I was here. "It's just you and me here, Roman," I whispered. "You can tell me."

"You, me, and the wire you're wearing."

"I'm not wearing a wire."

"Now who's lying."

He didn't believe me. He didn't trust me. He shouldn't. For some reason, it hurt that he didn't. A part of me had hoped he would look past my badge to the woman who had shared so much of herself with him that night. Roman Tyrell had learned to trust no one. I wanted him to trust *me*.

Before I could change my mind, I lifted my hands to my chest and found the top of my dress. I fumbled with the button for a moment before I got it open. My dress popped open, revealing my cleavage and the red lacy bra underneath, the same bra that he had pulled off me that night.

Roman's eyes dropped to my hands, then widened. "What are you doing?" His voice sounded shaky. Just like my fingers.

I dropped to the next button and kept going. He didn't stop me. He didn't say another word. He stared, his breathing growing labored, his hungry eyes becoming almost demonic-looking. I heard the sound of fingernails scraping wood and realized he was gripping at the door behind him. I grew lightheaded, the wobbling in my heels becoming worse with each button I released. One at a time I popped my buttons until I reached the button at my navel. The dress gaped open to reveal my torso.

"See," I said trying to keep my voice from shaking. "No wire."

He sucked in a breath. Without warning his hands grabbed my shoulders and spun us around so my back slammed against the door. The air was knocked out of me.

"Don't move," he commanded before his hands dropped from me, leaving scorching handprints. I wasn't sure I could move even if I wanted to.

He slipped both hands inside my dress, his fingertips brushing against my stomach. I inhaled sharply. He trailed his fingers up my front, sliding my dress open further until he'd pushed it off my shoulders and it hung from my hips.

His gaze fell to my half-naked body. My thighs shaking, I clung to the door hoping it would keep me upright. He made a low growling noise in the back of his throat. "No wire," he repeated.

I swallowed, hard. Suddenly it seemed like a stupid idea to have come here.

His head snapped up. His gaze bore into mine, his lip curling up. He was angry about something. I wasn't sure what. "You're playing with fire, little girl."

"I like the flames," I admitted in a tiny voice.

He let out a growl and glared at me. "You're going to get burned."

"I...I don't mind."

"Does anyone know you're here?"

"Yes," I lied.

"Liar," he said, his face and voice hard as stone. "You're here alone without a weapon or backup with a known criminal."

"You're not a—"

"I'm a Tyrell. Don't forget that."

"That doesn't mean—"

"I could fuck you against this door then gut you like a fish and nobody would ever find your body. These walls are soundproof."

"You...wouldn't." My Roman wouldn't hurt me. Right?

He's not your Roman, stupid!

His nostrils flared. "Some women want me because the danger turns them on. You *are* one of those women, aren't you, Jules?"

"I'm not," I protested weakly.

His gaze dragged lazily across my breasts. If I wasn't so busy holding on to the door, I'd have covered my chest with my hands. "Didn't you come here to walk on the wild side? To relive our night together?"

"No."

His eyes snapped to mine before narrowing. "Then what are you doing here?"

"Tell me what really happened that night."

He shook his head slightly. The motion made the strands of his hair fall over his forehead. I wanted to brush them out of the way, to touch his soft hair. "I already made a statement."

"I don't want your statement. I want *you* to tell *me*." I couldn't take it anymore. I couldn't be this near to him and *not* touch him. I lifted my hand towards his face.

He grabbed my wrist before I could reach his cheek. "You need to stay away from me. Do you hear me?"

I wasn't sure I could. "I can help you. You just need to trust me."

"You can't help me. No one can."

"Please..." I begged, although I had stopped knowing what I was begging for. His proximity and his smell and his heat, all of it were drawing me in like a moth to an open flame.

Something banged behind me and we both jumped.

"Roman!" A deep male voice came muffled through the door. "Open the hell up. It's Abel."

My blood turned to ice at the name. Abel "The Butcher" Montero was Giovanni Tyrell's right-hand man, linked to over two dozen murders, a convicted rapist and ex-surgeon so he knew how to wield a knife. I found his thick file amongst our list of Tyrell's known associates and recognized him as Scarface from the cemetery. There had been something in Abel's eyes that chilled me to the bone as I stared at his grainy black and white arrest photo; they were dead. No soul left.

Now, I was trapped in Roman's apartment without a weapon, a violent man on the other side of the door. The only thing between us was Roman Tyrell. He was my only hope of getting out of here unharmed.

I watched as an emotion flashed across Roman's face too quick for me to discern what it was. He was a Tyrell. On their side, not mine. Once he opened the door, who knew what Abel and Roman would do to me. His earlier bluff to rape me, kill me and make my body disappear flashed through my mind.

I was so screwed.

JULIANNA

I n all my nightmares of how my life would end, I never expected it would end like this. Trapped in the apartment of my mortal enemy, an apartment I walked myself into. Weaponless. And wearing a stupid red dress.

Why did I ever come here?

Abel banged on Roman's apartment door again, making it thunder against my back and into my body. "Roman, open up!"

Roman's fingers tightened on me. Any second now he would open the door and feed me to the monster. It's what he *should* do.

In my mind's eye, Abel's face glared back at me from his arrest photo I'd found among the files of the Tyrells' known associates. I'd recognized him instantly as Scarface from the graveyard. The one chasing Roman, the one I had mistaken for Roman's father. I knew Roman must hate Abel, or at least dislike him. But not enough to help me.

Stolen glimpses of crime scene photos of women who had crossed the Tyrells flashed in my mind. Dresses torn, skin slashed into ribbons, bodies violated over and over again before they likely begged for death. I doubted anyone would ever solve my murder.

Roman lifted his hand towards the door. This was it...

Instead Roman pressed a finger to my lips, making me flinch. I stared at him, my mind a tumble. He wanted me to stay quiet. Was he...*helping* me? His features were impassive except for the pinch of his mouth and a hint of wildness in his eyes. He was afraid. For me?

Of course it wasn't for me. He feared for himself. It wouldn't look good for him if he was caught alone and half-naked with a lady cop in his apartment. His loyalty to his family would be immediately put into question. With these kinds of families, loyalty and trust meant everything.

"I know you're in there," Abel yelled again. "You little shit," he added in a lower voice. There was the sound of a keys jangling. Roman's eyes widened. He grabbed me around the waist, picking me up as if I weighed nothing, and strode across the living room, his feet barely making a sound against the tiles. I could barely breathe. I didn't dare protest or make a sound; I just had to trust that whatever he was doing was going to save my ass because it meant saving his own.

The key sliding into the lock sounded like a saw going through wood. The lock clicking open sounded like the cock of a gun.

Roman dropped me on the bed in his room and flipped me over to my stomach. He grabbed a hand around my hips and yanked me back so I was on my knees at the edge of the bed, my hips in the air. He growled in a low voice. "Play along if you want to live."

What?

The front door banged open. I heard Roman's towel drop to the carpet. He shoved my dress up to my waist and pressed against me, the backs of my thighs were flush against him. Holy shit. He was naked. And *hard*.

My cheeks flushed as I remembered the last time Roman and I were in this position.

"Roman?" The bedroom door creaked open. I muffled a small scream into the mattress. "Jesus Christ," Abel muttered.

My cheeks flared when I realized what he would be seeing. Roman naked and my ass in the air. At least he couldn't see my face. *Just play along, Jules. You might get out of here alive.*

Roman let out a small snort. "Get out, dog. I'm busy." As he spoke he ground his hips against my ass in a slow, lazy way as if he were fucking me. His hard cock slid along the front of my panties, rubbing at my clit. I let out a moan. There was no need to "play along" there. Despite myself, I lifted my ass and pushed back against him. I wanted more of that delicious friction. I heard a low curse coming from Roman as his cock pulsed between my thighs. He wanted this as much as I did.

"Your father wants you," Abel said, cutting into my thoughts. What the fuck was I thinking? Had I completely lost my mind? Abel, Giovanni's "butcher," was still here. I was still in danger, and all I could do was wriggle around on Roman's dick like a horny teenager?

"I'll come after I'm finished," Roman said.

"I'm to bring you to—"

"Get the fuck out, dog. You're killing the mood."

"Maybe your lady friend would—?"

"She is *not* for you." Roman's fingers dug into my hips and I let out a small squeal. "Now get out before I fucking throw you out."

I could feel the tension heating up the room like a suffocating steam.

"Fine," Abel finally acquiesced. "But you are to go to your father's as soon as you're done." The door to the bedroom creaked behind him.

"Yes, father dear," Roman muttered.

The front door slammed shut. I let go of the breath I'd been holding. That was so close. Too close.

Now I was alone again. With a naked Roman. In his bed. I

could feel his cock along my aching core—God only knows how he managed to stay hard this entire time: his hips still pressing up against my ass, making all those delicious feelings from *that night* slam through my body. Just one thin strip of lace separated us from total bliss. I pushed back against him.

Roman launched off me as if my skin was suddenly burning him. I spun to face him, sitting on the mattress, clutching my dress, still unbuttoned from earlier, to my chest. "Roman?"

He glared at me, then strode out of sight. I yanked my dress back down over my legs and buttoned up the front as I followed Roman out of his bedroom. He was standing in front of his large TV, remote in his hand, still gloriously buck naked, although his erection had softened.

"What are you doing?" I asked, coming up behind him.

He didn't answer. His shoulders seemed to tense as I drew to his side. He turned the TV on, flicking through the channels until a black and white view of a stylish lobby showed onscreen. That lobby belonged to this building. I flinched as Abel strode out of the elevator. It must be the security live feed. Roman flicked the channel again, this time showing the front of the building, another live feed. We were both silent as we watched Abel get into a black SUV passenger seat; it then peeled away from the curb.

Roman turned off the TV and threw the remote onto one of the cream leather couches. I instinctively took a step back as he slowly turned to face me, fury rolling off him like hot waves, his beautiful features twisted. For a moment, I felt a shiver of real fear zapping down my spine. "Leave."

"I haven't—"

"Leave now. Don't *ever* come back here again."

I blinked back a sting at the back of my eyes. He blamed me for almost getting caught.

You were the one who decided to waltz right into enemy territory unannounced.

"It's not my fault he showed up," I said limply.

Roman strode right up to me until our noses were only inches apart. "Leave before I call the *police*."

The irony of his threat wasn't lost on me. I gritted my teeth at the surge of bitter rejection that flowed through my veins. "This conversation isn't over."

His eyes narrowed. "Yes, it is. If you want to talk to me from now on, call my lawyer. Now. Get. Out."

I couldn't bear his glaring at me, his eyes now glistening with fury instead of desire. I turned before the tears could betray me and ran for his door. My heels clacked heavily against the marble. I came here to help him. Instead I screwed it all up. Why did I even think I could change anything? Why did I think I could convince him that I could help him?

"Julianna," I thought I heard him calling, his voice softer and pained. I didn't stop to find out whether it was real or just my imagination.

ROMAN

S he had some balls, I'd give her that. Coming into my apartment dressed like that, wanting...hell if I knew what she wanted.

She wanted you.

No, she wanted to play on my connection to her. She wanted to use me against my family, against my father. Don't forget who she is—a cop. Don't forget who she thinks you are—the criminal. She had a job to do. She came to my apartment to do it.

Why did she flush when you got near her? Why did her pupils dilate? Her breath deepen? Her nipples harden?

She was a good actress. That was all. Besides, she could *want* me and still want to put me away.

Sitting down on the park bench, I stretched my long legs in front of me and leaned an elbow casually across the back of the bench. On the other side of the bench sat my cousin Benvolio, but I didn't turn to him. I didn't even look at him. To anyone who might be looking we were two strangers enjoying the sunny weather. I stared at the ducks across the pond as they fought over bread being thrown to them by an overenthusiastic boy, his mother clinging to his elbows to keep him from falling in. My mother used to take me to this park. We used to feed the ducks together. Happiness used to be that simple.

"What have you got for me?" I said in a low voice.

"Julianna Capulet," Benvolio began in a matching low voice. "The only daughter of the current Chief of Police Montgomery Capulet and deceased Prosecutor Abigail Capulet. Awarded top marks at her police training academy, including an award for marksmanship. One of the youngest to ever make detective, six months ago. Her and her partner, Luiz Espinoza, have been working together since then at the twelfth precinct. Her partner is loyal to her father; they worked together at one point. Rumor has it that Daddy hand-picked Espinoza as her partner to keep her out of trouble and to report back on what she's up to."

I flinched. "Her father's spying on her?" I thought I had problems.

"Not spying exactly...but keeping an eye on her."

I doubted Julianna knew about this. If she did, she wouldn't stand for it.

Look at you, thinking you know the lady cop so well.

"She's well liked, well respected," Benvolio continued, "has a reputation for keeping her nose clean. I suppose with who her daddy is, that's not a surprise."

"Tell me more about this partner, this Espinoza guy?"

"He's in his mid-thirties, never married, no kids. Also a spotless record. Him and Julianna are close, if you know what I mean."

Only then did I glance over and catch the smirk on his face. My stomach tightened. "No," I said through gritted teeth, "I *don't* know what you mean."

"They're fucking, man."

The idea of her being with anyone else, the idea of anyone else touching her, was enough to make me vibrate with fury. I wanted to rip this bench out of the ground and beat the shit out of Benvolio for daring to suggest that she was fucking someone else. "How do you know that?"

"That's the word on the street. And you know what they say, where there's smoke, there's fire."

Julianna and Espinoza. My mind flashed to them sitting across from me at the interrogation table. Had they been sitting closer than they should? Where were his hands? Could they have been on her leg?

Why the fuck did I care?

I studied this unfamiliar biting feeling coursing through my veins. The answer smacked me in the face. I was jealous. I didn't get jealous. I heard a growl and realized it was coming from me.

"You okay, bro?" Benvolio asked.

I shoved my emotions down and forced my face into a cold mask. Later I'd go bash the shit out of a bag in my private gym. For now, I had to keep my shit together. I couldn't let Benvolio get even a whiff that I cared about who Julianna was fucking. "What about her friends?" I barreled on like nothing was wrong. "What does she do outside work?"

"As far I can see, her work is her life." Benvolio was staring at me out of the corner of his eye. "If you're thinking of approaching her with a bribe, it won't work. It'll cause you more trouble than it's worth. Besides, they don't have anything to pin Vinny's murder on you."

I snapped my head towards him. What the hell was he doing? He should know better than to say anything incriminating out loud, especially in a public place like this. I narrowed my eyes at him. "I don't know what you're talking about. I don't know anything about Vinny's murder. Neither do you."

Benvolio's eyes widened, then he nodded. He stared around us, as if looking for anyone who might be listening. "Yeah, right. We know nothing about nothing."

I almost rolled my eyes. Benvolio was like a squirrel, great at ferreting out hidden nuts of information, but he had a brain the size of a nut.

"If that's all you've got, then I have somewhere to be." I got up and left him sitting on the bench, my head a fucking mess.

What the hell was wrong with me? I was getting jealous over a woman. Not just any woman, but Julianna fucking Capulet.

My enemy.

JULIANNA

S tupid stupid stupid.

I shouldn't have gone over to Roman's apartment unannounced, dressed in his favorite color, wearing matching underwear. What did I think he was going to do? Pull me into his arms and confess his feelings for me? Beg me to run away with him again?

I was so stupid. He'd made it clear; he didn't want anything to do with me. Once he made sure I wasn't going to tell anyone about our clandestine affair, he was done with me. Our connection was all in my head.

"Capi," Espo's voice called. I straightened at my desk and whipped my head around towards the direction of his voice. Espo was ambling towards me with a smirk on his face and a long white box in his hand. "Got something delivered for you."

He slid the box on my desk. I stared at it and frowned. There was no card. No note. No indication what it was or who it was from. "What is it?"

"Beats me. Courier delivered it. No return address."

Our station's policy was to scan every parcel that was delivered here, which meant that at least it couldn't be a bomb or anthrax. Still, you could never be too careful. There were some weirdos out there. I picked up a pen and used it to flip open the lid. I was not expecting what I saw.

In among the delicate white tissue paper was a single long-stemmed rose.

Who could have sent this to me?

I extracted the rose from the box, careful not to pierce myself with its thorns. It was a deep blood-red, silky and perfect.

Espo sniffed, reminding me he was standing at my side. "You got a boyfriend I don't know about?"

Roman.

I shook my head as I shoved that cursed name aside. He kicked me out of his apartment. He told me never to speak to him again. Why the hell would he send me a rose?

Maybe it was some kind of warning? A threat?

If it were a threat, shouldn't the rose be destroyed? At the very least there would be a threatening note.

"Come on, Capi. Don't hold out on me."

I fingered a silky petal before lifting the rose to inhale its full sweet scent. "I don't know who sent it, I swear."

Espo let out a whistle. "Capi's got a secret admirer."

A secret admirer? But who?

That night, with my room smelling like the rose I'd set in a vase upon my bedside table, I found myself standing at my open window, my eyes instinctively searching the shadows below for any sign of Roman Tyrell. He'd entered my apartment through the window before. Maybe tonight...

Don't be so stupid, Julianna. I slammed the window down even though the night was warm, turned off the light and slipped into bed. I had to get him out of my head. I had to stop believing that I could help him. I had to stop imagining he wanted me to.

A small beep alerted me to a new text. I grabbed my phone and frowned. It was almost midnight. Who would be texting me now?

Unknown: Are you awake?

I stared at the phone number attached to the message. I didn't recognize it. Perhaps Christian got a new number? I texted back.

Me: Who is this?

There was a pause before my phone beeped again.

Unknown: Somebody who shouldn't be talking to you.

My stomach clenched as the image of a certain dark-eyed man rose in my mind.

Me: Roman?

Unknown: So we agree. We shouldn't be talking.

It was Roman. He messaged me to tell me we shouldn't be talking?

. . .

Me: What do you want?

Roman: Did you receive my gift?

I blinked hard. It was *Roman* who sent me the rose? I stared at my phone. I wasn't sure what I supposed to say. Thank him. Swoon. Demand an explanation. All the above.

Me: If you're talking about the rose, then yes.

Thank you, I added after a moment's deliberation and hit send. I wasn't sure what I was feeling. Startled. Happy. Angry. Confused was the only sure thing.

Roman: It's an apology.

Me: For what, exactly?

Roman: I was rude earlier. I'm sorry. But it's better this way.

Me: I don't understand.

Roman: You have to stay away from me. And my family.

. . .

I gritted my teeth. He was trying to scare me off the investigation.

Me: Don't you dare threaten me! I'm not dropping the investigation.

Roman: I'm not threatening you.

Me: Sounded like a threat to me.

Roman: I'm trying to warn you. You don't want to get involved with us.

I stared at his message. He wanted to warn me? Why would he do that?

Me: Why do you care anyway?

There was a long pause before I received his answer.

Roman: I don't know.

Me: What the hell is that supposed to mean?

. . .

He didn't reply. I stared at my silent phone for what felt like hours before I gave up willing him to respond. Infuriating man. I threw the cell phone on my bedside table and turned my back on it, gripping the sheets with my fingers. It was a long time before I could fall asleep.

The next day at work I looked up the cell phone number Roman had texted me from. It was unregistered, a prepaid burner phone activated yesterday. The only number he had contacted using the phone was mine. Roman got a burner phone just to message me.

Arrogant girl. Why would he get a burner phone just to message you?

Maybe I'd hear from him again? My stomach fluttered at the mere thought.

Stupid girl. You don't want to hear from him again. Block the number.

But I couldn't, for some reason, bring myself to.

~

Over the next few days I jumped every time my phone beeped, thinking it might be Roman. I grew more and more frustrated at myself when it wasn't. I hoped that he'd change his mind about my help. I figured that I just had to be patient.

But just as the rose faded, the blood-red draining from its velvet tips, the petals falling and drying up without any sign from Roman, so did those hopes. Damn him. What game was he playing? Why did he go from appearing to care about me to pushing me away? Why did he send me a beautiful perfect rose only to ignore me?

I'd seen this kind of push-pull behavior before in victims of domestic abuse or children from broken homes, torn between familial loyalty and self-preservation. Roman wanted help—my help—but he didn't know how to ask for it. He wanted a way out but didn't know how to make one. I had to be persistent. I had to prove that I wouldn't back away. I had to make him see that he could trust me.

The next Saturday morning, I found myself standing in front of a faded blue door of a single-story brick cottage in a leafy suburb in eastern Verona. Behind this door lived Roman's good friend, Mercutio Brevio. Mercutio seemed to really care about Roman. He was the only one of Roman's friends who wasn't associated with the Tyrell family. He was the only one who might be able to help.

I chewed my lip. I still wasn't sure that this was at all a good idea. But I was here.

I raised my fist and knocked before I could change my mind. I glanced around as I waited. The curtains of the neighboring house shifted as my gaze rested upon it. I was being watched.

A thought crept into my head. What if I was wrong? What if I was walking into the lion's den just like I had when I strode into Roman's apartment? Espo had no idea I was here. No one did.

Before I could back away the door clicked and opened. A tiny old woman with white hair appeared in the doorway.

I started in surprise. "Oh. Hi."

This must be Mercutio's grandmother. Given Mercutio's age, she must be at least in her sixties, but her warm brown skin was carrying it well, her cheeks still plump and the whites of her eyes still clear. A warmth radiated off her, making me feel instantly calmer.

"Can I help you?" she asked, her melodic voice curious rather than suspicious.

"Um, is Mercutio here?"

She smiled, her brown eyes sparkling as she appraised me again. She must think I was here *for* Mercutio. "No, he's just run out to do some things for me. He's such a good boy. Always helping his Nonna out. Do you want to wait inside for him?" She stepped aside and held open the door for me.

"Sure. Thanks." I walked inside before I could change my mind.

The cottage was small but cozy. The furniture was well worn yet everything looked comfortable and welcoming. Mercutio admitted in his interview that Roman had spent a lot of his childhood here. I suddenly got an image of a younger Roman Tyrell buried in the soft cushions of the couch on a cold winter's night. For some reason, it warmed me.

I followed Mercutio's grandmother into the kitchen smelling of warm apples and cinnamon from a pie in the oven. My stomach twinged. My mother would often bake apple pie for my father and me.

She waved at the rustic wooden table just big enough for four people, indicating that I sit. "Did you want some tea or coffee?"

"I'm fine, thanks." I chewed my lip. "I'm actually here to ask about Roman."

Mercutio's grandmother pulled off her faded red apron and hung it on the hook on the back door before she sat down opposite me at the table. "Are you a girlfriend of Roman's?"

I felt my cheeks flush.

Before I could say anything, her eyes lit with understanding. "I see," she said as she nodded at me.

She had the wrong idea. I had to correct her. "Mrs. Brevio—"

She laughed. "So formal. Please, call me Nonna." She smiled at me and her warm brown eyes suddenly appeared younger than her obvious years. I wanted to blurt out my entire confusing predicament. Somehow, I thought that she'd understand. She'd know what to do.

I held my tongue.

"Nonna," I tested the term on my tongue as I debated what I was going to say next. "I'm not his girlfriend," I said truthfully. For some reason, it hurt to say it.

"But you care about him," Nonna stated as if it were fact.

I swallowed. "I'm confused about him."

Nonna nodded and folded her wrinkled hands together on the table in front of her, a dusting of flour on the backs of them. Her fingers were tiny and compact, her nails cut short and clean. "Roman has always been misunderstood. Even by himself. Even from a young age I could see there was a war raging inside that boy." She sighed, then glanced up at me as if expecting me to say something.

"That makes sense, seeing the family he was born into," I blurted out.

She gave me a sad smile. "He was always different from his other brothers. He was born premature, you know."

I blinked at Nonna. "No, I didn't know that."

"Twenty-six weeks. They weren't sure if he was going to make it. But he defied the odds. He was still such a tiny thing when they brought him home from the hospital." She smiled, her eyes going all misty with the memory. "Even as he grew he was always smaller than his brothers. He was his mama's favorite, perhaps because she nearly lost him."

"He was close with her," I guessed.

"Very." A deep sadness closed over her face and the wrinkles around the corners of her mouth deepened. "Maria was a beautiful woman with the largest heart. She just loved the wrong man."

I remembered the news articles about Maria's murder. A knot developed in my throat. I knew what it must have felt like for him to lose his mother at such a young an age.

"I tried to do my best for Roman afterwards, but...he was never the same after that. There was a darkness in him that wasn't there before." Nonna sighed, a low and aching sound. "I just don't know how a young boy recovers from something like that."

The back door swung open, cutting off our conversation. "I'm home, Nonna," a deep voice called. Mercutio strode in, two grocery bags in his hands.

"Mercutio." I stood up from my seat, gazing past his shoulder, my heart half terrified, half wanting to see Roman behind him.

But Mercutio was alone.

Mercutio froze when he caught sight of me, his eyes narrowing to slits. "What's going on?" He glanced over to Nonna sitting beside me, his gaze searching her face. "Nonna? Are you okay?"

Nonna let out a snort. "Mercutio, don't be so paranoid. This is one of Roman's friends. She came here to speak to you."

Mercutio turned his attention to me, his dark eyes now hard. "Perhaps *Ms.* Capulet and I should speak alone," he said.

Nonna stood up, patting my hand. "It was nice to meet you, dear. Go easy on our Roman, will you? He needs someone like you to understand him."

A thread of guilt wound through me. I shouldn't have made it seem like Roman and I were friends. Mercutio placed his bags down and crossed his arms over his chest, glaring at me over Nonna's shoulder. He knew I hadn't been presenting myself truthfully to his grandmother.

"It was nice to meet you, Mrs. Brevio," I said.

"*Nonna*, please." She gave me one last smile before she walked out of the kitchen.

Leaving me alone. With a hostile-looking Mercutio.

"*Detective* Capulet," he said, spitting my title like it was a curse. "Why didn't you show her your badge? Why didn't you tell her you were a detective investigating Roman?"

Because I wasn't here in an official capacity. But I couldn't admit that. He'd kick me out in two seconds flat if he knew I had no real reason to be here. No reason except for my ridiculous unwavering obsession over a certain dark-eyed friend of his.

I stood up so that I was on his level, meeting his stare. I wouldn't be intimidated by him. "I didn't want to scare her. Would you have preferred I bring up the corpse we found—"

"No," Mercutio snapped, his eyes going to kitchen door. "She doesn't need to hear any of that."

I nodded. "Then we agree, let's keep this between us. Please, sit, Mr. Brevio."

"I told you everything at my interview."

"I still have more questions." Just one, actually.

He didn't reply. I decided to take a chance and play hardball with him. I let out a sigh. "If you'd prefer we can go back to the station and do this there?"

Mercutio stared at me for a second, then looked back to the door before taking the farthest seat from me, keeping the table between us. "You have two minutes."

I let out a breath as I sat. He had agreed to give me two minutes. Two minutes wasn't a long time. Better cut straight to the chase. "I think there's something more going on here. I think that Roman might be mixed up in something he doesn't want to be mixed up in."

Mercutio let out a humorless laugh. "Did you figure that one out all by yourself?"

I ignored his comment. I wasn't here to argue with him. "I want to offer him a way out. A way to escape his family. You and I both know that he isn't like them."

Mercutio narrowed his eyes at me. "What game are you playing here, detective?"

"I just want the truth. I want...to help him."

Mercutio stared at me, the anger that had been so apparent faded into a suspicious mask. Whether he believed me, I didn't know. "Let me guess, you went to him first with your generous offer and he shut you down. And now you're coming to me."

"I know you care about him. Don't you want to help him get away from his family?"

"All you're going to do is get him killed," Mercutio said.

"I can protect him."

"Not from this." He stood up, his chair scraping the floor. "Your two minutes are up. Get out of my house."

I had failed. I stood. "Please, just talk to him about it."

Mercutio said nothing as he herded me out and slammed the door behind me. I was beginning to think that coming here had been a mistake.

~

I should have known when I returned home later that night from grocery shopping that I had been followed. But I hadn't been paying attention. My head was a whirr, tumbling over and over what Mercutio had said about Roman.

I juggled my grocery bags and purse, struggling with my keys at the lobby before finally letting myself in, part-tumbling, part-shoving my way into the empty foyer, my footsteps echoing against the marble floor. I heard the door behind me catch rather than click shut. I didn't have time to turn around to see who had come in after me. In an instant, I felt him right behind me.

It all happened so fast I had no time to scream. A gloved hand came over my mouth, a strong arm closed around me like a vice. I dropped my bags and grabbed at the steely arms holding me captive, but it was no use. I might have well have been wrapped in chains.

Just take my purse! I wanted to scream, but I could barely breathe behind his large stifling hand wrapped in leather. My captor kicked open the door to the boiler room next to the stairs and shoved me inside. Dear God, was he planning to rape me in here? Kill me?

I had to calm myself down, figure a way to escape. The door clicked behind us, leaving me alone with him. Inside the old boiler room was hot and suffocating. Something was rattling in one of the ancient machines rusting against the far wall. The walls were thick concrete to muffle the noise from the outside. It would muffle the noise of whatever *he* was going to do to me.

His hand came off my mouth. I sucked in the hot, steamy air of the tiny room and prepared to elbow him. He spun me, slamming me against the concrete wall, winding me. The single lit fluorescent bulb in the middle of the room flickered, casting a sickly glow across the face of my assailant. My eyes widened. I inhaled sharply. Roman Tyrell was glaring at me with murder in his eyes.

"*You.*" He stabbed a finger in my face. "You come into Nonna's house and question her son? You pretend to be my *friend* to try and get information out of her?" He was beautiful, even drowning in fury.

He slammed the wall beside my head with his palm, the fury and aggression of it making me gasp. A tiny shot of actual fear went through my body. My skin felt sensitized a hundred times. When he leaned in close, his minty breath on my cheeks made me shiver.

His eyes bore into mine like burning coals. "You want to come after me, come after me. Just leave Mercutio and Nonna out of it."

I found my voice. "I...I don't want to come after you."

His eyes narrowed into slits. "Then what do you want?"

I swallowed. Should I tell him the truth?

He slammed his hand against the wall again, making me jump. "Answer me. And don't you dare lie. I will know if you lie."

"You confuse me," I confessed with a whisper.

He flinched as if that was the last thing he expected to hear me say.

I continued before I lost my nerve. "Everyone tells me they know who Roman Tyrell is. 'Stay away from him. He's a bad man. Dangerous. Evil. He was born with a gun in his hand and violence in his heart.' But...the man I spent the night with was not a killer. The man I spent the night with was good."

For a mere second, his mask of rage fell, dropping like a curtain. I glimpsed the hopeful, vulnerable man underneath. Then his mask was up again so quickly I almost thought I had imagined it.

"You think I'm *good*?" He began to laugh, a cruel growling sound, his eyes sparkling with amusement.

He was mocking me. My cheeks burned at his reaction. "Mercutio and Nonna wouldn't love you if you weren't," I blurted out.

His laughter cut off. "Nonna and Mercutio don't see everything."

"You wouldn't love *them* if you weren't good."

Suddenly his hand was wrapped around my throat, his movement so quick it was a blur. He held me against the wall like that, his grip firm enough to remind me that he was in complete control and just tight enough that I could barely breathe.

He leaned in close. I thought for a second that he might kiss me. I should have been terrified. Instead my body vibrated with awareness at his nearness. "Don't mistake me for an angel, Jules. I'm the shadow you run screaming from."

"Yes," I whispered. "You're dangerous. But not evil. You're *not* evil, Roman."

His lip curled up in a snarl. "I see. You think you can come in and save me. This isn't some stupid high school fantasy. You can't save me. I'm not your prince. I am the monster in this story."

"What if I don't want the prince…" I dared to say, my voice coming out so soft I could barely hear it.

He flinched as if I'd slapped him. The air between us began to sear. I'd finally admitted that I still wanted him. I lifted a hand to his face. If I could just touch him…

He caught my wrist easily in his free hand and slammed it against the wall, pressing into me further. I could smell his cologne mixed with his male scent and the hint of sweat.

His lips brushed my ear. "Damn you," he hissed. "You have no sense of self-preservation, do you?"

"I'm not in danger from you," I whispered back against his neck. "You'd never hurt me."

He pulled back and glared at me, but the fury seemed forced. "I am Roman Tyrell, son of Giovanni Tyrell. You'd do well to remember that."

"You don't scare me," I lied.

"I should." He ran the tip of his nose along my cheek, slowly, to my ear. That single touch sent a wave of fire across my skin. My nipples pressed painfully against my shirt. Then his lips were brushing over my earlobe and his breath was down my neck.

He spoke softly, deep and low, like he was trying to seduce me. His words betrayed his real intent. "You'll stay away from my family and me, detective. If you know what's good for you."

He pushed himself away from me and strode out of the boiler room, leaving me shaking and breathless against the wall.

Did that just happen? The erratic thudding of my heart seemed the only evidence of his appearance.

"Stay away from my family and me, detective."

Well, Mr. Tyrell, I did not respond to threats. The easiest way to make me chase after something is to tell me I should let it go. "Stubborn" or "bullheaded" my father often called me with an affectionate smile on his face.

Underneath the surface of Vinnie Torrito's gang-related execution was something more complex. Roman Tyrell was the key to unraveling it all.

As I pushed myself off the wall a flash of silver on the floor caught my eye. I bent to pick it up. It was a small card. It appeared to be an invitation.

We cordially invite you to...
The Fated Grand Opening

Midnight, Friday, August 25th
Dress code: Evening Wear & Masks

There was an address on the other side.

It was a party invitation for next Friday. Roman must have dropped it. Did he do it on purpose? Did he want me to find this? Was this his way of inviting me?

I shook myself. He just told me to stay away from him. It must have been an accident. What should I do with it? I certainly wasn't going to return it...

I should just throw it away.

I glanced once at the boiler room door as if I expected Roman to come back for it at any moment. He did not return. I slipped the invitation into my pocket.

The next day another package arrived for me at work. A long white box just as before. No message, no note, no return address.

My stomach fluttered as I opened the lid. As I expected, I found a second perfect blood-red rose.

JULIANNA

I 'd been sitting at the large meeting room table in one of the offices for hours, cheap laminate chipping off the corners. Across the table I had spread out all the files we had on the entire Tyrell family and their associates. Each file was open with photos and papers fanning out across the table and stuck up across the walls, my notes in glaring red marker pen. I'd been combing through each file, memorizing each one, my stomach curdling as I read about the Tyrell family's cold-blooded rise to power. How could Roman Tyrell grow up in such a family and yet turn out so different from them?

"Hey, Jules." Dene, one of the tech guys, stuck his head into the meeting room, making me jump.

His eyes cast across the room and his eyebrow lifted for a second. I know what it looked like. It looked like one of those shrine rooms we always seemed to find when we busted a crazed stalker.

"I'm in the middle of a case," I blurted out. "This is for a case."

He let out a whistle. "Damn. I'd hate to be the one you set your sights on."

I stabbed the lid of my pen closed. "Do you have something for me?"

His gaze snapped towards me. "Er, you'll want to see this."

"This better be good."

I followed him into the tech room, where he had lined up black-and-white security footage on several large monitors. I recognized the hotel. It was the one that Roman and I had spent the night in. Oh, shit. I completely forgot about the hotel security footage. *I* was on that footage. The blood drained from my face. I felt like I might pass out.

"When did we get the footage from the hotel?" I asked, trying not to hyperventilate.

"Earlier today."

"And you didn't tell me?" I asked, my voice going high.

Dene frowned at me. "I'm telling you now."

At that moment, Espinoza walked in and stood next to me, blocking my exit. Even if he hadn't, I still couldn't have run. I was frozen to the floor. I could only watch in horror as Dene rolled the footage from that Saturday night.

On screen, Roman entered the hotel lobby, unmistakable in his stature and the way he walked, commanding the attention of everyone in the space. Slung over his shoulder was me.

"Same kind of hair as Rosaline," said Espinoza. "Pity we can't see her face."

"She's got great legs," said Dene.

I ignored that comment. "Do, er, do we get a shot of her face anywhere?" I asked, trying not to let my voice shake.

"No. Just her sweet ass."

Espo slapped the Dene on the back of his head. "Have some respect, bro." He pointed to me.

"Oh, er, sorry, detective," Dene said, sounding a little embarrassed.

"It's fine," I muttered, hoping he didn't notice that I couldn't look him in the face.

The camera angle flicked to the lift, then to the top floor's suite. I was still hanging upside down, my hair in my face. I had never been so thankful that Roman had been such a caveman that night.

"They go into the Presidential Suite at eleven-oh-three," Dene said. "They don't leave the room, either of them, until seven the next night."

"Do they get any visitors?" Espo asked.

"They order room service on Sunday, twice."

"Just like Rosaline said in her statement. Looks like she's telling the truth. Show us the footage of them leaving."

"Here." Dene pointed to another screen where Roman was walking back out of the room, the duffel over his bag. The time stamp was seven eleven p.m. He disappeared off screen. My gut tightened. I would come out next, maybe five minutes after him.

"Where's the girl?" Espo asked.

"Well, this is the strange bit..." Dene said, his eyes flicking over to look at me.

Oh my God. I was so screwed. In a second they would both watch me walk out of that hotel room.

Hopefully I could argue that it *was* Rosaline and not me. We did look similar. It wasn't like the footage was perfectly clear. Right?

I could barely breathe as Dene sped up the tape and the minutes flew by. Here it was...seven sixteen p.m. I stared at the screen, waiting for the door to the Presidential Suite to open, revealing my face.

But it never did. The video played on and on until the cleaners came the next morning.

"That's it?" Espo asked. "She never comes out?"

Dene shook his head. "It's the strangest thing. I checked the footage for the rest of the day, even the day after just to be sure, but we never see her leave the room."

Somehow I'd dodged a bullet. I slowly let out a breath of

relief. But how did this happen? I had walked out a few minutes after Roman. Why wasn't I on the tape?

"Is there another exit?" Espo asked.

Dene shook his head. "Not unless she climbed off the balcony."

"Has someone messed with the footage?"

"If they did it was a pro job."

Roman. Roman must have done this.

He was protecting me. Protecting my career, my job, my reputation. My heart began to warm. He did care.

I shook myself internally. What was I thinking? Roman didn't do this for me. He did it for himself. If word got out to his family that he'd been intimate with a detective, they'd have reason to mistrust him. They might even kill him.

I couldn't get rid of the nagging thought that he'd done it to protect me. It was stupid. Arrogant, even. Still, I couldn't help but want to thank him. In person. My heart skipped a beat at the thought of seeing him again.

Stupid heart.

Espo let out a growl. "Dammit. His alibi holds. The chief isn't going to like this."

I stared at Espo. He was beginning to sound like my father. Condemning a man before he was proved guilty. "Here's a novel idea," I said, my voice biting at the air. "What if his alibi holds because he *didn't* do it."

Espo stared at me like I'd grown two heads. "If I didn't know any better, I'd say you were on his side."

"No, I'm on the side of 'innocent until proven guilty.'"

"Roman Tyrell *is* guilty."

I threw my hands up in the air before storming out and locking myself in my meeting room again. I shoved the files aside until I found the one on Roman Tyrell.

No arrests except for drunken brawling. No criminal record. He'd not even been associated with the Tyrells until his father basically kidnapped him as he was about to leave the country. Roman wasn't staying in Verona of his own free will. Of that I was sure.

I stared at one of the few photos of Roman Tyrell we had on file, taken from a video camera still in the interrogation room that day I found out who he was. His thick brows shading intense eyes that stared back at me. He was volatile, aggressive, dangerous even. But he was not a cold-blooded killer.

What does your father have over you, Roman?

Why won't you let me help you?

These questions plagued me. They plagued me until Friday, August twenty-fifth arrived. That night I was trying to sleep, but a certain frustrating dark-eyed man was on my mind and a particular invitation was burning a hole in the bottom drawer of my bedside table. I told myself I wouldn't go...

It was a masked ball. I had the perfect outfit. No one would recognize me.

No. I should just leave Roman the hell alone just like he warned me to.

I could just slip in quietly. No one needed to know. I wouldn't even need to approach Roman. It was a just a chance to watch him without him knowing. Perhaps his father would be there. Perhaps I would overhear something, see something...

Screw it. I was as far from sleep as I could possibly be. What could possibly go wrong?

JULIANNA

Fated was a slinky bar taking up the entire top floor of an inner-city heritage building. The outside was all almond-colored stone and high arches. Inside it looked more like an exclusive party thrown in some billionaire's penthouse than a bar; snow-white walls decorated with large gilded mirrors reflecting the beautiful people in classy gowns draped over plush couches and leather chairs, waiters in coattails carrying flutes of bubbling gold liquid and glasses of honeyed amber over ice.

I might not feel like I belonged but I at least looked the part. I wore a long silver dress that clung to my hips and fell to my ankles like a waterfall of cut crystal. An intricate silver mask of lace-like metalwork wrapped around the upper half of my face like a frosted winter branch. My honey hair was combed back into a bun. The dress and the mask had been my mother's. I had never worn them before. I had never had a reason to. Until now.

A small thrill rushed through me as I made my way through the glittering masked crowd. I felt eyes slide across me and yet I felt invisible. Anonymous. Free. I was no longer Detective

Julianna Capulet. I could be anyone in here. My feet felt light as if I was stepping on lily pads.

I slipped from room to room, searching for those familiar dark eyes. Just as I was giving up hope that he was here, I spotted him. He was standing in a small group, looking regal in his dark suit, matching midnight shirt and tie. He was cloaked in a simple midnight mask. I stood watching, mesmerized as he carried himself like a king presiding over his court, his subjects hanging over his every word, hungry for scraps of his attention.

The music changed. He looked up and his eyes found mine.

Oh my God.

I spun, grabbing a flute of champagne off a passing tray. My sudden movement startled a couple beside me. I gave them a forced smile. "Nice bar, huh?"

They turned back to each other, ignoring me completely.

I gulped down some champagne, wincing when the bubbles fizzled up my nose. *It's fine. I'm sure Roman didn't see me. Even if he did, it's not like he would have recognized me. Stupid. Why did I spin around like I had been caught?* That action alone could have caused more suspicion than my masked face. I'd just turn back around slowly, casually and…

He wasn't there. Where did he—?

A strong hand grabbed my arm, wrenching me against a firm chest. Roman glared down at me, his dark eyes flashing like black diamonds from behind his velvet mask, which I could see were now featured like a raven's. "What," he growled low and full of menace, "are you doing here?"

I sucked in a gasp. "You recognize me?"

His eyes rolled over my body. "I'd recognize you anywhere. Your eyes. You can't change them. You can't hide them." He leaned in close. "I can see the *goodness* shining out of them." He said *goodness* like it was an insult.

"I'm not as good as you think I am."

"Oh really?"

"Yeah, really." I leaned in closer, drawn in by his scent and his pure masculine presence; a thrill of fear mixed with lust shot through my body. I finally admitted to myself, I may be turned on by the danger of being here. Any one of his family might recognize me like he had.

It was the same kind of rush that I sought out by joining the police academy. The same kind of rush I felt when engaging with an assailant. The fear didn't make me freeze like it did some people. It made things sharper, clearer. Just like now, even in the low light of the crystal chandeliers, I could see Roman's pupils dilating, his Adam's apple hitching as I slid a hand onto his arm. He was remembering what it was like to be this close to me, just like I was remembering too. *Skin on skin. Wet tongues dancing. Hot flesh colliding.*

Heat flooded my panties and turned my core into an aching ball. My heart began to bang against my ribs. His lips parted, a reaction I mirrored. If I leaned in any closer... If I just tilted up my face...

"Roman, bro!" a male's voice called out. I jumped back. Roman played it much cooler, smoothing out the front of his expensive suit jacket and acknowledging the man beside me with a nod of his chin. They spoke briefly in low tones. I noticed Roman subtly shifting his body between me and his acquaintance. Like he was protecting me.

Don't be stupid, Julianna. He's trying to hide you.

The other man wore a dark gray suit which didn't fit him as well as Roman's did. His cheeks carried the first flush of liquor from behind a simple pirate's mask. I didn't think I recognized him. I kept my eyes averted and gulped the rest of my champagne, setting the empty glass on a tray as it went past.

As soon as the other man strode away, Roman grabbed me and closed the gap between us, causing a shiver to run down my spine. He lowered his mouth to my ear. "Get out. Now."

"I know you did something to the security footage at the hotel," I blurted out.

He glared at me, his eyes darting around us before locking onto mine. "I don't know what you're talking about."

"I watched it," I said in a low voice. "Somehow the footage of me leaving your hotel room is missing. That's evidence tampering."

He leaned in, his eyes glittering, his voice filled with amusement. "Are you going to turn me in, detective?"

"No," I admitted.

"Then we have nothing more to say to each other about it."

"Except...thank you," I whispered.

He looked taken aback for a second. Then he snorted, his top lip pulling up into a sneer. "Don't think I did it for you. I did what I had to do to protect myself. I just happen to be protecting you at the same time."

He was lying. I could see underneath the bravado he was trying so desperately to cling to.

"Roman!" another male voice called out over the music.

Roman cursed under his breath and I swear I heard my name cursed as well. A group of three men swarmed us, taking up space like they owned the bar. They all had dark hair and dark eyes like Roman's, their faces partly obscured by the same raven mask as Roman had on. I froze. Oh, shit. These men were Tyrell men.

Two of them were flashing wild grins as they scanned the crowd, barely noticing me. The third one, however, was staring at me. I suddenly felt naked. I wrapped an arm across my waist, not that it would stop him from seeing me.

I chanced a glance at him again—still staring. My gaze landed on the familiar scar that came out from under his mask. It was Scarface. Abel Montero. The Tyrell butcher. The man who'd been chasing Roman through the graveyard. The same man who had forced Roman into his father's limo at gunpoint. The one who almost caught me at Roman's apartment. My blood froze. I tore my eyes away from his probing ones. I had to stay calm. Don't react. Don't panic.

I tried to look bored. I tried to look for a waiter with more champagne just for something to do with my hands. Or for my nerves. Of course, there were none to be found when I needed them. I found Roman watching me, then glancing at Abel, a furrow between his brows the only thing betraying his anxiety.

One of the other men clasped Roman on the shoulder. "We got some shit to talk about. Some shipments—"

"This is not the time, Benvolio," Roman growled. "Talk to me later." He waved at the group of ladies dressed in slinky minidresses standing to one side who were looking our way. "Go keep them company for me." Right. They'd been the ones he had been standing with before he came over to me. That's why they were batting their eyelashes at him and glaring at me like they wanted to murder me.

Benvolio looked over to them, his chin dipping as he gave them an exaggerated once-over. He whistled. "*Dayum.* If you don't want them, I'll have them."

"Dude," one of his friends said, shoving Benvolio aside. "Plenty to share."

"No way. Dibs on them all."

Roman snorted as the two grinners sauntered across the room. Then he called out after them, "You're just keeping them occupied until I get back."

Roman's words stung, reminding me that I wasn't wanted here. I didn't belong here. I didn't belong with him. I swallowed the hurt down and forced myself not to react.

"You look familiar," Abel said. He hadn't moved. His gaze hadn't left mine.

My skin broke out in a cold rash. I was about to be exposed. And it was all my fault. I didn't dare look at Roman.

Abel took a slow, measured step towards me. I fought the

urge to turn and run. "Who are you?" he asked. His fingers twitched as if he was thinking about snatching my mask off.

If he exposed me I would be in serious trouble. I had no weapon with me. I had no backup. He couldn't harm me here. Not in front of all these witnesses. He had to take me somewhere quieter to do that. I couldn't let him take me.

I already knew where the exits were; I had noted them all when I walked in, a force of habit. I readied myself to run.

Roman stepped between us, his wide back like a shield. "Run along, dog, and stop bothering the pretty lady. You're ruining the mood by showing her your face."

Abel snarled at Roman. I tensed as I watched the two of them glare at each other, aggression rolling off both. This was a pressure cooker and it was about to blow. I had to do something. Anything.

I touched his arm. "Roman," I said in a Russian accent. I almost cringed at how fake it sounded. God knows where *that* came from. "It iz too beautiful a night for fighting. Besidez, blood vill ruin zis dress."

Roman spun slightly to look at me over his shoulder. He raised an eyebrow at me, the hint of amusement on his lips. "You heard Natassia," he said to Abel.

Natassia? Right, the Russian floozy that I was pretending to be.

"Natassia?" Abel peered at me over Roman's shoulder.

"An old *friend* from Europe who's in town to visit. Now scram."

Abel studied me, suspicion clouding his eyes. "Sure. Natassia. Enjoy your stay in Verona."

I sniffed and turned my head away from him, a dismissal. I felt his one last searing look before he disappeared into the crowd.

I let out a long breath of relief. Roman's face twisted into a scowl. "Are you happy? You almost got yourself killed." He grabbed me and began to tug me across the room. I pulled against him. "What are you doing?"

"You're dancing with me."

Bossy arrogant brute. "You know, most men would *ask* a lady if she'd like a dance."

"Last time I checked you *liked* it when I told you what to do." He yanked me flush against his chest, securing me there with a possessive arm around my back. His fingers felt like they were searing through my dress.

The memory of our night together flashed before my eyes, flooding my body with heat. I shivered as he laced the fingers of his other hand through mine. He began to move to the music, a slow house instrumental with a mix of Caribbean drums and brassy saxophones. I resisted for a second before I gave in to it.

Of course the bastard could dance.

Damn, he smelled good, too good, his familiar dark cedar perfume surrounding me. I resisted the urge to lean my head against his chest, to press closer, to melt against him as we swayed to the music.

"You have some nerve coming here," he hissed in my ear.

"I wanted to talk to you." To see you again. To hear your voice. These things I could not voice. Admitting I wanted to talk to him was enough.

"Talk. You have my full attention." He spun us farther away from the crowd and closer to the far edge of the tiny dance floor.

"Let me help you."

He tensed but he didn't miss a beat. "You want to help me? Leave me alone."

"You say that, but I don't think you mean it. If you really did, why do you keep finding reasons to contact me?"

He let out a short laugh. "Why do you women always read too much into everything?"

I flinched at his insinuation.

"I ask you to come to Paris and you think it's a relationship. I hide you from Abel and you think I'm protecting you. I send you a rose and it means I'm in l—" he broke off.

"You trusted me once. Trust me again."

"Why do you care?" he muttered.

"The same reason you do," I whispered, taking a gamble.

He faltered and missed a step. I stumbled into him. Our eyes locked. For a second, I saw the flash of hope underneath. For a second, I thought I'd gotten through to him. Then the emotionless mask slammed down over his features. A second later he caught up to the music and we were moving again like nothing had happened.

"This is a setup," he said, his voice frosty like ice.

"I wouldn't do that to you."

"Wouldn't you?"

"You *know* me, Roman."

He snorted. The music changed, growing faster, more aggressive. His movements followed and my dress whipped out around my ankles. "Yes, I know all about you. Newly assigned detective. First major case. You want to get out of your father's shadow. You need so desperately to prove yourself."

I flinched as his words found their mark, the sore spots deep inside me. "How do you know...?" Someone had been talking about me to him.

He dipped me. I felt weightless for a mere second, complete trust in the strong arms holding me up. I gasped as his other hand rested flat against my stomach then ran up between my breasts. My body broke out in a prickly heat. I fought a groan as his hand brushed the bare sensitive skin above my plunging neckline. My nipples tightened and pushed painfully against the material.

His hand gripped around my neck firmly and pulled me up against him, keeping his grip around my neck. The heat in my body turned liquid and trickled between my legs. His eyes

SIENNA BLAKE

burned into me. My gaze dropped to his mouth. Closer. Closer, and…

He sneered. "I always make sure I know exactly who I'm up against."

His words stabbed me in the heart. I shoved him but he wouldn't let me go. All the while he kept twirling us around the dance floor like nothing was wrong. "Is that what you really think? That we're enemies? That we're against each other?"

His grip on my neck tightened. It didn't hurt but it was starting to restrict my breathing. "Tell me I'm wrong, *detective*. Tell me how it could be any other way."

"Fuck you, Roman." I shoved him again. This time he let my neck go. His other arm stayed around me so I didn't get far enough away from him.

"You did." His eyes glittered with a cruel light. "I heard you liked it."

I inhaled sharply. I only realized my hand had lashed out when the crack of my palm on his skin rang out and his head jerked to one side. He let go of me completely and cold air rushed up between us. The hum of voices dropped over the music that kept playing. Suddenly I could feel the room's eyes on me like hyenas closing in.

Shit. What had I done? I had attacked the Prince of Darkness in his own territory while he was surrounded by his men. I was alone and weaponless. I was an idiot. But he'd made me blind with fury.

"Grab the bitch," someone cried. Roman's men began to push their way through the room toward me from all sides. I was so royally screwed.

"No!" Roman said, his voice cracking out through the room. Everybody stopped in their tracks. He turned his eyes to me. "It barely tickled."

"You can't let her get away with—"

"That was her free pass. A gift from me to her. Her last one.

244

Because," he sneered, "we all know the weaker sex need all the help they can get."

There was sniggering and nods from around the room. My skin burned from outrage. Was that what he thought of me? Of all women? That we were weaker? I fought against this bullshit as a female cop. I couldn't believe I was hearing it from him.

It's an act, Julianna. He's trying to protect you.

Roman grabbed my arm. "Let me escort you out, *Natassia.* Make sure you don't get lost on the way out." I heard the hidden meaning in his words. If he didn't walk me out, chances were that one or more of his men would attack me in an attempt to gain favor with him.

I let him pull me through the crowd, my body gone numb except for the burning around the skin where he touched me. Even though I had slapped him, he still wanted to make sure I got out of here safely. Or maybe he just wanted to protect his dirty little secret. I didn't know anymore.

I thought he would leave me at the door, but he paused by the bouncers and instructed, "Nobody leaves until I get back." They nodded and shielded the doorway with their bodies.

Until he got back? Roman shoved me into the elevator. On the ground floor, he walked me right out of the building. The night air was crisp and clear. Very few people were strolling around the building, but a short line of cabs waited alongside the grand circular lobby that gave this building an appearance of a luxury hotel.

I tried to snatch my arm back from him but he wouldn't let go. It was like a mouse tugging against a tiger. "I don't need to be escorted to a cab."

"Yes, you do." He let out a grunt of exasperation. "Stop struggling or I will put you over my shoulder." *Again.*

I flinched and fought a shiver as yet another memory assaulted my senses. Stupid, stupid body. Why wouldn't you stop reacting to this infuriating man? He was frustrating and dangerous and totally off limits. Not to mention gorgeous and powerful, and underneath that gruff exterior I knew there was a caring soul.

The caring soul shoved me into the back of a cab and slammed the door. He leaned through the front window, startling the driver who looked like he'd been midway through a little nap.

"Carlos Pinto," Roman said, tapping the plastic badge stuck against the dashboard. "I know your name, your taxi number. I could get your home address and the names of your family members just like that." He snapped his thick fingers in the driver's face.

"Stop threatening him," I yelled. Roman needed another slap.

He stabbed a thick finger towards me. "Shut up and let me keep you alive."

I slumped back into the cracked leather seat. The inside of the cab smelled like that fake pine smell.

Roman turned back to the driver, who was leaning away, pressing himself into the far window. If his window had been open, I bet he would have crawled out just to get as far away from Roman as possible. "See that girl in the back there?" Roman said. "I need you to get her home safely. Don't go straight there. Circle the block several times, make sure you aren't being followed. If anything happens to her, I'm coming after you."

The driver said nothing. He looked like he was about to pee himself.

Roman pulled out his wallet and held out a small wad of folded bills to the driver. "That should more than cover it."

I sat up. That was *way* more than the fare would be. There had to be at least four hundred dollars there.

The taxi driver's eyes widened, the promise of money—lots of money—suddenly making him brave. He straightened in his seat and took the bills. He almost looked like he wanted to salute Roman. "Yes, sir."

I wanted to roll my eyes. When did this man ever *not* get what he wanted?

Roman nodded and pulled his body out of the cab. He stood on the curb, his unreadable eyes staring at me through my open window as the cab driver started the engine.

A lump developed in my throat. "Roman...?" What did I want to say? Thank you? I'm sorry?

He shook his head slightly. *Say nothing.*

The cab pulled away from the curb. I twisted in my seat and watched out the rear window as Roman grew smaller. He didn't move, he just watched as we drove away, our gazes locked until he disappeared out of sight.

I slumped back in my seat. What the fuck just happened?

He saved my life. He made sure I wouldn't be followed. He does care, despite his protests.

He let you go, a voice inside me said. He only saved me because he wanted to protect himself. He had all those skimpily dressed ladies to "go back to." *Face it, Jules, he had you. Now you're not interesting anymore. You're just a pain in his backside.*

I couldn't help the sting that this truth caused me.

JULIANNA

I kept anticipating a third rose all week. But as the second rose wilted, so did my hopes.

"Newly assigned detective. First major case. You want to get out of your father's shadow. You need so desperately to prove yourself."

Roman's words kept echoing through me, sending a fresh wave of hurt every time they did.

"I always make sure I know exactly who I'm up against."

I had tried three times now to convince him I was on his side. Each time I had failed. It was clear he didn't want my help. It was clear where he thought he stood.

"That was her free pass. Her last one."

He had drawn the line. It was war between us. Next time he would not take my attempts to help him with so much civility. Why the hell couldn't I give up on him?

I sank most of my time at work into investigating the Tyrells. Someone had to know something. I called all the sources I'd gathered during my days as a beat cop, asking what they knew about Giovanni Tyrell and the new heir to the Tyrell empire. It seemed when it came to the Tyrells, nobody wanted to talk. I knocked on doors in Little Italy where the body was dumped to see if I could get any more information. More often than not, doors were slammed in my face.

I went through old case files in which the Tyrells had been lead suspects. I found thirteen unsolved cases of Veronesi men shot through the head, execution style. Same caliber bullets used as the kill shot. Bodies all dumped in various black spots of the city: Little Italy, the industrial estates, washed up downstream in the marshes of Verona River. I compared the slugs but none of them seemed to match each other. The striations, the groove markings on the bullets were all different.

These were all long shots. And I was running out of long shots.

We were fresh out of leads. Unless a new piece of evidence came up, there was nothing more for me to do. It seemed it would be the last I would see or hear of Roman Tyrell. At least until another body showed up.

I archived Roman's file, along with the Tyrells' and Vinnie's, in the bottom of my drawer at work. If only I could do the same with my thoughts about him.

I had to stop this. It wasn't healthy for me to be pining over him. I had to find myself a real boyfriend, one I could actually go out in public with. One who wasn't the heir to a Mafia kingdom. One whose job it wasn't for me to bring down.

Perhaps that's why I ended up saying yes to dinner with Christian on Saturday night. It was a moment of weakness.

Christian looked nothing like Roman. With golden hair and classic good looks, Christian was the sunshine to Roman's shadows. As the son of a prominent businessman, he was a media darling and Verona golden boy. I tried to imagine myself sitting here at Belmont, the only Michelin star restaurant in Verona, with Roman instead of Christian. I almost laughed at my own pathetic stupidity. I had to stop thinking about Roman. I had to stop comparing every single thing about him and Christian.

I forced a smile and nodded as Christian spoke at length

about his new job in the mayor's office, his political prospects and how he hoped to run for mayor of Verona one day. I stifled a yawn behind my hand that was holding a dessert spoon, but I could see from the furrow in Christian's brows that he had noticed it.

"I'm sorry," I said. "It's not you. It's this case that's been bugging me. I haven't been sleeping well." That wasn't exactly a lie. I had left out that it was my *prime suspect* that was bothering me and causing me to lose sleep. Nothing to do with the case.

Christian reached over the table, past our shared chocolate fondant that I'd barely touched. He grabbed my hand and kissed the back of it. "You work too hard."

My body barely reacted to Christian's touch. No zing. No fireworks. No electricity. I sighed internally. He was a lovely, handsome man who could be good for me. Why couldn't I bring myself to be interested in him?

He's not Roman, a voice inside me said.

I shoved that thought away, pulling my hand away from Christian's on the pretense of wiping my mouth with my cloth napkin. "I hope you don't mind if we cut tonight short, but I'm exhausted," I said with an apologetic look.

His lips pinched for a second before his expression smoothed over. "Of course. Anything for you."

As he settled the bill I leaned back in my chair and stared out the glass window to my right. The waiter had seated us in a small alcove on a slightly raised platform right at the front of the restaurant, glass encasing us. I felt like I was on display, with the people outside able to see me clearly as they walked past.

My gaze fell upon a figure in the shadows across the street. *Roman's watching me*. I shivered, my eyes fluttering shut. When I opened them, the figure was gone.

If it had even been him in the first place.

I was an idiot. I was thinking about Roman when I shouldn't be, seeing him where he wasn't. I needed to get over this obsession with him before I did something stupid. Correction: before I did something stupid *again*.

In the passenger seat of Christian's car, I slumped back and closed my eyes. Christian shut my door behind me and got into the driver's seat, but he didn't start the car.

"Julianna?"

I opened my eyes and turned to look at him. "Yes?"

I could see his face in the dark, shadows filtering across his features. He was handsome, his features classically put together, but for some reason he didn't make my stomach flip when I saw him. Not like it did when I caught sight of a certain dark, dangerous man.

Perhaps I just wanted Roman because I couldn't have him. Because I *shouldn't* want him.

I brushed that theory away. I had been drawn to Roman from the moment I laid eyes on him. Before I knew who he was.

I was so caught up in my own thoughts, I only realized Christian was leaning in for a kiss when his lips touched mine. For a moment I didn't move because I was too shocked. Then I didn't move because I wasn't sure what I should do. I *should* kiss him back. I should *want* to kiss him back. Christian was the sensible choice. He was good for me. Why couldn't I want him like I wanted Roman? Why couldn't my body catch alight at his lips on mine?

Perhaps if I kissed him back, some feelings would arise? I parted my lips for Christian and felt his tongue slip into my mouth. Where was the surge of heat and need? Where was the feeling that I was falling? Flying? That I might stop breathing if he pulled away?

I gently pushed Christian away with my fingers on his chest and the kiss ended.

He gave me a shy smile. "I've been wanting to do that for a while," he admitted before he started the car.

I tried to push away the unease in my stomach. It took several minutes of driving before I could pinpoint what it was that I was feeling. Guilt. I was feeling like I had betrayed Roman by kissing Christian. Well, that was ridiculous. Roman and I were *nothing.* He made that quite clear the last time I saw him. I didn't owe any loyalty to him. Still, the tightness in my belly wouldn't go away.

~

My phone beeped with a message as soon as I shut my apartment door behind me. I didn't check it right away. It was probably Christian telling me again that he had a wonderful time. It was just the sweet kind of thing that Christian would do. He was lovely and sweet. Why didn't that excite me? Excitement wasn't everything, right?

I only picked up my phone again after I'd showered and changed into the shorts and t-shirt I usually slept in. The message wasn't from Christian.

Roman: Are you awake?

I stared at the black text. It had been his first attempt at communication with me in a week. Was I awake? Why, so you could confuse me again with your hot and cold routine? No, thank you. I was done. I should just ignore him. That's what I would do. Ignore him. I threw my phone to the bedside table and tried to settle into a book.

My awareness kept drifting off the page and back towards that damn message on my phone.

Damn him. I typed out a curt text back. I hit send before I could stop myself.

. . .

Me: What do you want?

Stupid. Why was I even replying to him? Communicating with Roman was wrong. If anyone ever found out…

My phone started to ring. Oh shit. It was Roman. *Don't answer it!*

I answered it. "What?" Well, that came out breathier and less intimidating than I intended.

Roman's deep voice eased into my ear, all rumble and bass. "I just wanted to see how you are?"

I frowned. "I'm fine."

"Good."

"Good."

There was an uncomfortable pause. "Well," I said, "if that's all—"

"Have you been thinking about me?"

My mouth dropped open. What kind of game was he playing now? Should I lie and say "no"? That might end this conversation prematurely. Did I want to admit the truth? No, I didn't want to give him the satisfaction of knowing I'd been thinking of him. Damn him for being so presumptuous as to ask a question like that.

He broke the silence first. "I've been thinking about you."

Inside, I screamed. I wished he were here so I could choke him. "You're giving me whiplash."

He chuckled. "Is that some kind of sex thing? I am open to anything."

I shook my head, trying to ignore the sting because *this* Roman on the phone—open and flirty—sounded too much like the Roman I had started falling for. "You kick me out of your apartment, then you send me roses. You tell me you should stay away from me, then you admit you've been thinking about me. I can't keep up."

"I should stay away from you."

"There you go again! Whiplash."

"I said I *should* stay away from you, not that I *wanted* to."

I let out a soft growl. "You are so frustrating."

"You should stay away from me if you know what's good for you."

I could punch him in the face. Seeing as he wasn't actually here for me to do it, I just stuck my tongue out into the dark. It made me feel slightly better.

"Do you like him?" he asked.

"Who?"

"Your date tonight. He looks like a stiff."

What the fuck? I sat up in bed. "You followed me?"

Roman snorted. "I just happened to see you as I was walking by."

I thought back to the feeling of being watched at the restaurant. Roman *had* been outside. It *had* been him there watching me from the shadows, intruding, unwanted, into a private moment I was having with my date. I should be furious. Instead it sent a thrill rushing through my blood. Stupid body.

"Of course I like him," I lied. "What's not to like? He's handsome, sweet and he doesn't give me whiplash like *some* people."

"But he doesn't kiss you like I do."

My mind flooded with the memory of Roman's kisses, all night, all over my naked body. I began to sweat in my sheets. My breasts became too sensitive and uncomfortably full. I felt like I'd suddenly developed a fever. And yet, I shivered.

No, I wouldn't play into this. I couldn't.

"He's a great kisser."

"Liar."

"I'm not lying."

"If he was such a great kisser, why did you leave him standing on the sidewalk at the end of the night?"

My skin prickled. Roman had been watching us outside my

apartment. He lied. He hadn't just been walking past. He was there outside the restaurant watching us kiss in the car, then watching us again outside my apartment at the end of the night as I avoided a second kiss. He *had* been following me.

"If you were mine," he spoke in such a quiet voice I almost didn't hear him, "you'd never leave me on the sidewalk."

If you were mine... If I were his, I'd never leave him on the sidewalk.

I could never be his.

I jumped up from my bed, throwing my sheets off me, and ran to my window. I had left it partly open, my curtains pushed to the side to let in the breeze. I could smell the scent of the city: cigarette smoke, car fumes and the hint of hot frying oil from a fast food café down the road. The street below looked dark. Nothing moved. Was he down there still, watching my window? Could he see me standing here looking for him? I swear I could feel his eyes on me again. Watching me. The place between my legs that was empty of him throbbed.

"Send me a kiss goodnight, Julianna."

He *was* out there in the dark. I stared out, biting my lip, trying to see through into each shadow to the beautiful secret hidden within. "Where are you?" I whispered, my body buzzing.

"In the dark, little rabbit. A place you shouldn't follow me into."

I shouldn't. I really shouldn't. Oh, but I wanted to...

Send me a kiss goodnight, Julianna.

I remembered his lips on mine. My eyelids fluttered shut as I lifted a hand up. I had meant to touch my lips, to blow him a kiss, but on the way up my fingertips brushed across the swell of my breast and I hissed. God, that felt good. I was so sensitive, so ready, my body burning at the knowledge that his eyes were on me.

The darkness behind my eyelids made me bold. I brushed my nipples again. In my ear I heard him moan, the same sweet noise he'd made all that night. He was watching me and he liked what he saw.

Before I knew what I was doing, I slid one hand firmly across my other breast and pinched down on my sensitive nipples the way his teeth had that night. Pleasure and pain rocketed through me. A louder moan slipped out of me.

"What are you doing?" He sounded like he was choking.

What was I doing? I wasn't thinking straight. All the blood had rushed out of my brain. My body rushed with hot desire making me dizzy. "Remembering what you did to me," I admitted.

He let out a low, pained groan into my ear, the vibration of his voice sending tingles through my body, the same way it had when he'd moaned against my wet folds. All sense of decorum fled from my mind as my body trembled with need. I slipped my hand down my body and into my shorts, gasping when I touched that sensitive bud. I gripped on to the phone, my link to Roman, and slid my other fingers along my wet aching slit, the pleasure running down my legs making them shake.

"Jesus fucking Christ." His breath became heavy in my ear. "If I were there…"

If he were here…

If we could just have one more night together, one more night without being Roman and Julianna. One more night being anything but a Tyrell and a Capulet.

"If you were here…?" I shouldn't be asking. I shouldn't be doing this.

It was too late now. He didn't sound like he was going to stop us.

"If I were there," he growled, "you wouldn't need to remember. I'd bury myself so deep inside you, you'd never get me out." *Too late.*

I impaled my hips onto my fingers, pretending it was his cock and a shudder went through me. It wasn't enough. I needed *him.*

I needed him more than I'd ever needed anything in my life. Food. Water. Air. I needed him more than I needed to breathe right now. "Come here, then."

I heard him inhale sharply. There was a long pause.

My hand stilled. My eyes shot open, searching the darkness below for him, heat rising to my cheeks. "Roman?"

"You'll be the death of me," I heard him whisper before the line went dead.

ROMAN

I t had been a mistake to watch her from the dark of the empty apartment across from hers. Lying in my bed, my mind assaulted me with the memory of watching her hand moving between her legs, of her head thrown back, sweet panting in my ear.

If I were there...

Come here, then.

I grabbed my aching cock in my fist and worked myself into a fury, wrecking myself upon her memory, collapsing in a fever after my release, begging for sleep. Sleep didn't come. And she tormented me, still. Perhaps this was the penance for my sins.

It was early. Much too early. The sun was barely peeking up over the horizon, splashing the glass and concrete buildings of Verona with her bloody brush. I threw off the sheets that were sticking to me from my sweat. I showered, dressed and went out walking. I didn't know where I was going. I just knew that one foot in front of the other was the only thing stopping me from going mad.

I found myself sitting in the pews at the back of Waverley Cathedral attached to the graveyard where my mother and brother were buried. Fitting, as it was where I would end up one day. Too soon, I was sure. Everyone attached to me ended up here before their time, torn from this earth in a flurry of bullets and blood.

That's why I needed to stay away from Julianna. I didn't want her to end up here too.

But she was making it so damn difficult. She was just...everywhere. Showing up at my apartment, at Nonna's house, at Fated...asking all the wrong questions, saying all the wrong things, staring at me with hope in her beautiful amber eyes, acting like...acting like she cared about *me*. Telling me that I was *good*. Making out like she couldn't believe that I could have killed a man.

Well, I did, Julianna. I shot him in cold blood and stole his life. I chose my life over his. Would knowing that be enough to drive you away? Would spilling this secret finally make you understand that I am not worth saving?

I stared up at the statues of Jesus on the cross. He sacrificed his life for us. I couldn't even sacrifice my lustful desire for a certain detective to keep her safe.

"Roman! Is that you?" a familiar voice called from behind me.

I stood up, spinning, my hand going automatically for the gun hidden at my back. I froze as I spotted the familiar figure dressed in a black button-up shirt and the telltale white collar. Bad Roman. I was about to draw a weapon at a priest in a church.

"Father Laurence." I dropped my hand and smiled. I didn't have to force it. I was genuinely glad to see him. In the eight years since I left Verona for the anonymous freedom of Europe, his fine hair had gathered more silver strands and his kind chestnut eyes seemed wearier than ever before, but otherwise he looked just the same. "It's good to see you again."

"Likewise, my boy." I clapped the older man on the back as he pulled me in for a hug.

Father Laurence had been close friends with my mother since

childhood. He had been the one to marry her to my father. He had been the one to bury her.

He pulled back and smiled, his kind brown eyes crinkling at the corners. "Let me look at you." He studied me, clucking softly. "You went away a boy and came back a man." Affection filled his voice. "I barely recognized you." We sat down side by side in one of the pews.

"Well, you look exactly the same."

The Father snorted, such an odd sound to hear from a man of the cloth that it almost made me laugh. "You're just lying to be kind. I've aged much too fast since you left." His face fell. "Verona has become a darker and darker place. It's been more of a struggle to keep the people's hopes afloat."

He didn't have to convince me. I could see how far my father's twisted roots had dug into the community.

He placed his hand on my shoulder, his face growing solemn. "I'm sorry about Jacob. It was...a senseless tragedy."

It still felt like someone had closed a fist around my throat when I thought of Jacob. I still held on to the memories of him when we had been kids, when he still acted like my brother. I still loved *that* Jacob. Sometimes I wondered if I could have saved him from himself. Maybe I should have stayed and tried. Would I have made a difference? I doubted it. I couldn't save myself.

I swallowed down the knot in my throat. "Thank you, Father. He will be missed." My voice sounded hollow, even to me.

"I saw you at the back of the service at his funeral, sneaking into the church after everyone was seated," Father Laurence said softly. "You didn't stick around afterwards for the wake."

"I had to run off." That wasn't exactly a lie.

He nodded slowly. "I hear your father has convinced you to stay in Verona."

"That's one way to put it."

Father Laurence frowned. "But you're not happy to be back."

"Would you be happy if you were me?" I asked, my voice a bitter note. "It's only a matter of time before..." I trailed off.

He slipped his hand on my shoulder and squeezed. The single touch gave me more comfort than I'd ever gotten from my father. I wondered what my life would have been like if my mother had chosen someone like Father Laurence as a husband.

After my mother married my father, Father Laurence joined the priesthood. They said he did that because he loved my mother; he would never love anyone else. Despite the rumors, my mother and Father Laurence had remained close. I had always dismissed the stories as just that. But sometimes I wondered how close they had been... Or perhaps it was easier to believe that I might not have Tyrell blood in my veins.

Father Laurence gave me a weighted stare. "Nothing is inevitable. We all have a choice, Roman."

Some people did. Not me.

"I don't know how to say no to him."

Father Laurence sighed. "Giovanni Tyrell is a difficult man. He's gotten worse since your mother, God rest her soul, passed away."

I didn't even have the energy to nod.

He studied me, frowning. It felt like he was looking right into me. He always could. That's why he was the one I turned to for advice. "That's not the only thing on your mind, is it?"

I leaned forward and ran my hands roughly through my hair. "There's a woman."

Father Laurence, unlike most people, knew when to be silent. He was silent for long enough that I began to fill in the noiselessness with the things that were clattering around in my head.

"I can't stop thinking about her. When I'm awake, I crave her. At night, I dream about her. I need her. Want her. How do I make it stop?"

"We all have desires, Roman," he said slowly. "There's nothing wrong with that."

Coming from a man who was strong enough to control his worldly desires. I, on the other hand... "This is different. *She* is different. She's..." I laughed when I realized I could never put her perfection into words. I could try. "She is so good that... No, she *is* goodness. She has so much goodness in her that she sees it in everyone else." She saw it...in me. Of all the tainted, stained, wretched creatures on the planet, she saw something good in *me*.

Realization flooded his eyes. "You love her."

"No!" I swore out loud, my voice echoing around the inside the church, but the Father didn't admonish me. "I just don't want her getting caught up in my shitty life." This was all I would admit to him. To myself. "She is not someone I should want."

The Father frowned. "Why?"

So many reasons. "She's the daughter of my enemy. We are on opposite sides of the law. She hates me. I hate..." I swallowed down the knot in my throat. "I am supposed to hate her."

Father Laurence sucked in a breath, a sudden look of realization crossing his face. "Julianna Cap—"

"Don't. Don't say her name." Hearing her name stabbed like a knife. I rubbed my face with my hands. How the fuck did I get into this mess? How the fuck did I get out?

"You don't think you deserve her." It wasn't a question.

I let out a curt laugh. "I *don't* deserve her. She's doesn't deserve to be poisoned by me or my family. The best thing I could do for her is to leave her alone. But...I don't think I can. I don't think I want to."

"Does she know how you feel?"

I shuddered. The only reason I'd been able to hold on to my own leash is because of the hatred I saw in her eyes when I insulted her or rejected her, even though it tore me to pieces to do it. I only wished I could take all the hurt I caused her for myself. "I can't tell her. She can never know." I snapped my face towards Father Laurence. "You won't tell her either. You won't breathe a word to her."

Father Laurence was unaffected by the look I gave him. He made me feel like a puppy pretending to be a wolf. He was one man who truly wasn't afraid of me. "Of course I won't."

I let myself relax. He was also one man I truly trusted.

"You know," the Father continued, "she could be good for you."

I almost choked on my own tongue. "I'd be the end of her. Don't you remember who my family is? I'm a danger to her just by wanting her, just by thinking about her, by breathing her name out loud."

"She also has a say in this."

I shook my head and made a noise of disgust in my throat. "How selfish am I that I could consider ruining her just so I could have her?" I wanted to possess her. To own her. Even if it meant I would end her life with my darkness. I wanted to soak myself into her soul, so deep she'd never get me out. I was *this close* to letting myself do it. Wasn't this proof enough that I was evil?

Father Laurence placed his hand upon my shoulder. "What if it wasn't you who darkened her life, but she who lightened yours?"

She could. Her light was strong enough to save cities from themselves. The Princess of Light.

I shrugged his hand off me and let out a humorless laugh. "Let's face it, Father. I'm not worth saving."

JULIANNA

I couldn't believe what I'd done. Every time I thought of how I touched myself at that window my body shivered with fever. Not just from the echoes of lust in my body, but of the shame, of the bitter-burnt rejection when I asked—no, begged—for Roman to *come here,* and all he did was to hang up.

Days went by. I didn't hear from Roman. No texts, no calls, no surprise visits. And no roses. No damn roses. I hated that I would have given anything to get the silky folds of another fragrant flower nestled in a white box. I doubted I'd hear from him again. I refused to message him. I had my pride. My cheeks seared as my actions flashed before my eyes again. I cringed. When would I ever get over it?

I kept my windows locked and my curtains closed at night, a sign to him, if he was even still watching, that I simply didn't care. I was determined to just forget about him.

Easier said than done.

I pushed through the building door into my lobby at the end of a long, frustrating day. The sound of the elevator dinging closed caught my attention. I was about to yell out for the occupants to hold the doors when I caught sight of the unmistakable frame of Roman, dark shirt, dark jeans, a grim look on his face. Nora was in there next to him. He looked up and right at me just before the elevator doors closed.

What was he doing here? With Nora?

But I knew. I had broken into his world and rattled his cages when I manipulated my way into his apartment, when I entered Nonna's house, when I had dared to walk masked among his friends at Fated. He was now doing the same to me. This was payback. *No more free passes.*

I sprinted for the open stairwell and leapt up the stairs, taking two at a time. They spat me out onto my floor, my hand going to the gun in my holster. I heard a familiar gruff voice. Nora's door shut behind him, muffling him. She's in there with him, alone. If he hurts her...

I readied my gun as I moved swiftly to her front door. I pressed my ear against the door to listen for a brief second.

"No, don't." I heard Nora's voice through the wood.

I couldn't wait. She was in trouble. I tested the handle. Thank God, it was unlocked. I shoved open the door and leapt into her apartment, gun first. "Freeze!"

Nora jumped, the jam jar in her hand slipping and crashing to the floor. Roman didn't seem so startled. He lifted his hands in the air, one of them holding a cereal box, the other a bunch of bananas. There were grocery bags sitting on the kitchen counter. I pointed the barrel at Roman. "Turn around."

He gave me a smirk before turning. His black t-shirt stretched across his wide back and fitted jeans hugged his firm, round butt. No gun tucked into his belt. Where was his gun?

I caught Roman looking at me over his shoulder. "If you wanted to check out my ass, you could have just said so."

My cheeks burned.

Nora dropped her hands down on her hips and let out a tut. "What in tarnation do you think you're doing? Leaping into my apartment waving a gun like that. You scared the bejesus out of me. You could've given me a heart attack."

I stared between Roman and Nora. Roman, the bastard, was watching me with amusement.

"I thought you were in trouble. I thought he..." My words died in my throat when I realized how ridiculous I sounded. Nora had no idea that the Prince of Darkness himself was standing in her kitchen helping unpack her groceries.

"You thought I was going to harm your neighbor?" Roman asked, his features tightening, his hands still in the air. "Is that truly how little you think of me?"

Now I just felt bad.

"Jesus Christ, Julianna," Nora said. "Stop pointing that thing at him. You've been more jumpy than normal lately." She leaned towards Roman and spoke to him from behind a hand, loud enough for me to hear. "I keep telling her she just needs to get laid."

My cheeks burned. I didn't care how relieved I was that Nora wasn't in any danger, I was going to kill her myself. If I didn't die of embarrassment first.

A grin began to form on Roman's face. "Isn't that funny," he said, his eyes locked on mine, "that's what I keep telling her."

I'd have to kill him too.

I lowered my weapon but I didn't slip it into my holster. I wasn't ready to lower my guard just yet. Roman placed the box of cereal and bananas on the table before stuffing his hands in the front pockets of his dark jeans, a deceptively boyish move. Trust me, there was *nothing* boyish about this man. I hated myself for running my eyes greedily over his wide frame, his firm chest, his tousled hair getting caught in his long, dark lashes. Damn him for looking so good. My heart gave out a little kick of agreement. And damn you, heart. You're supposed to be on *my* side.

I glared at Roman, the anger and shame from the way he'd

rejected me the last time we spoke resurfacing to heat the underside of my skin.

If I were there...

Come here, then.

"What are you doing here?" I demanded, my voice hard. "What do you want?"

You didn't hurt me enough the last time we spoke? Come back to rub it in? You will not find a stupid little girl pining over you, Roman Tyrell.

"Julianna Abigail Capulet," Nora snapped. "I'm embarrassed for you. There's no reason to be so rude to this nice young man."

Roman Tyrell was a nice young man. And the devil was just a guy in a red suit.

If only she knew the truth about Roman. I wasn't about to tell her. Not while the Mafia prince was standing here smirking at me.

"I was struggling with my groceries when dear Roman offered to help. He was waiting for you outside the building."

I stared at Roman. "Why were you waiting for me?"

He shrugged, making his shoulders appear even more rounded, then shot me a roguish grin. I bet that grin got its fair share of use. I bet it worked too. Well, it wouldn't work on me. "I just wanted to see you again."

Liar. He wanted something. I could see it in the way he eyed me, like a cat eyeing a mouse. I wasn't going to like whatever he came here for.

"Now that you're home, Julianna, you two kids can catch up. In your apartment. Alone." Nora gave me a big obvious wink and began to herd us both out of her apartment. "I can handle these groceries myself now, thank you."

"Are you sure I can't help clean up?" asked Roman, indicating the mess of jam and glass on the floor. I almost snorted. Suck up.

Nora, the flirt, just swooned at him and clasped her hands

together. "Such manners! They don't make men like you these days."

"It won't be any trouble, ma'am."

"Oh, go on now. I'll be fine, thank you." She even had the nerve to bat her eyelashes up at him. Roman bowed—bowed? Who did he think he was?—to her before holding an arm out to me. "Ladies first."

I glared at him. "And turn my back on you? Not a chance in hell."

"Julianna!" Nora admonished me again.

Roman dipped his head at Nora, an amused twist to his lips. "It's fine. She just wants to watch the view as I walk away." He winked as he sauntered past me.

The nerve! I was left gaping after him.

Nora shoved me out the door after Roman before I could protest. "You have fun with this handsome young man, Julianna." She sent me a grin, wiggled her eyebrows, and gave me a thumbs up before she slammed the door in my face. Leaving me in the corridor alone. With Roman Tyrell.

JULIANNA

I stood there staring at Nora's closed door, debating over whether banging on it for her to let me in would seem smart or just cowardly. I could feel Roman's stare burning into my back.

"You're going to have to face me at some point, Jules."

I squeezed my eyes shut. *Dear God, if you exist, please let him be gone when I turn around.*

I turned around slowly. And opened my eyes.

Roman was still standing there, a grin on his face, his gaze roaming over me. He winked at me when I caught his eye, immune to the daggers I was throwing at him. How was it fair that a man could be equally gorgeous and infuriating? I wonder if he'd still be smirking if I shot him.

Suddenly I was conscious that I was at the end of a long day. I hadn't showered. I probably looked like shit. I was scared to smell myself.

"What the hell do you think you're doing here?" I hissed in a low voice, because I knew that nosy Nora would have her ear glued to the other side of that door.

Roman cleared his throat and nodded at something to my

left. One of my other neighbors was opening the door to her apartment, her buggy and three-year-old appearing as the door widened. I hid my gun at my side. This was not a conversation that we could have now. Chances were high that a concerned neighbor might call the cops on us. Wouldn't it be a fun thing trying to explain why I was arguing with the heir to the blood empire right outside my apartment?

I growled and shoved past Roman, cursing my own body when tingles radiated from where I touched him. I unlocked my apartment and stomped inside. Maybe if I shut the door on him he'd just go away?

He jammed his boot into the doorway with lightning reflexes when I tried. Goddamn it. I glared at him. He smiled serenely at me.

"Get your foot out."

"Let me come in."

"Not by the hair of my chinny chin chin."

His smile turned wolfish. "Then I'll huff and I'll puff, and I'll blow you until you scream my name."

My cheeks heated as I got a flash of his face between my thighs. "That's not how the rhyme goes," I said through a clenched jaw.

"Let me in, Jules. I promise I won't bite. Not unless you ask nicely."

Curse him. He wasn't about to take his foot from the doorway. I could shoot it. But then I'd have to explain myself. And paperwork. I hated paperwork.

"I just want to talk," he said. "Five minutes, that's all I'm asking for."

Better to get this over with. "You get two."

"Four."

"Two."

"Fine, two." He shook his head, a small smile on his lips. If I didn't know any better, I'd say it was pride on his face. "You drive a hard bargain."

Despite my better judgment, I stepped aside and swung the door open. "Get in before I change my mind."

Roman strode inside my apartment. I locked the door behind him. He stood in my living room as casually as if I'd invited him in for tea. "Your neighbor Nora thinks I'm handsome," he said, flashing me a smirk. "Do you think I'm handsome?"

"Nora is a sixty-something year old senior with bad eyesight."

Roman laughed. "I notice you didn't deny that you thought I was handsome."

Arrogant bastard. "As handsome as you are infuriating."

His grin widened. "And we all know how infuriating you find me."

I rolled my eyes. "One minute and forty-five seconds left. What the hell do you want, Roman?"

"Would you believe me if…" There was suddenly a softness to his voice. It seemed out of place with the rest of him. "If I told you I just wanted to see you again?"

I blinked. "Why would you want that?"

"I…I can't seem to stop thinking about you."

Wait. What now?

He frowned, looking almost confused. "It's very frustrating. Highly inconvenient."

"You poor thing," I breathed. He can't stop thinking about *me*. Just like I can't stop thinking of him.

"Usually I don't have any trouble getting over… But you…" he trailed off.

I let out a laugh. "This is a trick. A trap. A way to get me off your case."

"Why would I do that? I've heard that I've officially been cleared from the Torrito case. My alibi checks out."

"This is some kind of game, then."

"Trust me," he muttered. "If I could have avoided coming here, I would have."

What was that supposed to mean? "You mean to tell me that all your other *lady friends* weren't available at this moment?"

He grimaced. "I don't care about them."

"Good," I blurted out before I could stop myself.

"I don't even want them to touch me." His face twisted into a mask of anger. "What are you doing to me, Julianna? What the fuck are you doing to me?" He blamed me. He hated me for haunting him just as he haunted me. He took a step towards me. Genuine fear gripped my body.

"Stay right there." I lifted my gun out of instinct.

"What is it about you? Why you?" He ignored my gun, stalking even closer. So close that his cedar and musky cologne filled my nose.

I only realized I had been retreating when my back touched the door. I sucked in a breath. "Don't come any closer or I'll shoot."

Of course, he didn't listen. He stepped before me, grabbed my gun barrel and shoved it against his chest, right over his heart.

My finger twitched towards the trigger. He was a known criminal from a known criminal family. He was in my home. I was just defending myself. No judge in the world would ever convict me if I pulled the trigger.

The anger slipped from his face, replaced with a look of resignation. "If you're going to shoot me, Julianna, just do it. It'll save you and the rest of the world a whole lot of hell."

I knew at that moment that there was a part of Roman Tyrell that wanted to die. He wasn't fearless as I suspected; a part of him didn't care whether he lived or not. Or perhaps a part of him didn't think his life was worth it.

My shoulders sank. My hand sagged. I couldn't shoot him. Because fight it as I might, I knew that his was a life worth saving. I pulled my finger away from the trigger and loosened my grip. *You win, Roman. You win.*

He moved the gun out from between us. I let him. He slid it onto the table beside the door, clanking against the bowl where I usually threw my keys. He closed the distance between us, the heat of his warm chest pressing right up against mine. The back of my head knocked up against the door. The breath caught in my throat.

"I can't stop thinking about that night," he said, his eyes drilling into mine. "I wish I had come over when you asked…"

No. Don't do this. I don't know if I have the strength to stop you. "Don't say that."

"I can't get you out of my head. You plague me when I'm awake. You haunt me when I'm asleep. The memory of your beautiful naked body echoes in my brain on repeat until I can't take it anymore and I have to… release the pressure."

Oh my God. Did he just admit…?

He lifted a hand and tucked a lock of my hair behind my ears. That simple touch set off a shower of sparks inside me. "Do you like hearing that I touch myself when I think of you?" His fingers stroked my cheek and heat fissured through me. If he touched me in the right place, I'd break apart. "Do you like knowing that it's your name I hiss upon my release?"

I couldn't speak. I could barely move, a stunned doe in the headlights.

He reached around my neck and gripped my hair, holding my head still. His eyes glittered with pure intent as he went in for the kill. "Ask me to come over again."

I made a mistake. I shouldn't have let him in. His flirtatious teasing earlier was just a cover, a trick to get himself inside. Here was his real intention. His gaze dropped to my lips and he lowered his mouth.

Kiss me.

"Don't," I whispered, a pathetic attempt at stopping him. It was all I had. My body was betraying me, aching for him, wet for him, begging to unfold for him.

His lips missed my mouth and I could have cried. He brushed them against my ear, sending shivers down my spine. "I would *never* take what's not being offered. Ask me to come over."

"No," I said, my mutinous voice coming out like a breathless plea rather than a command.

His hand remained in my hair, holding me to the door with that single touch. I could get away if I wanted to but...I didn't want to.

He nipped down the sensitive pulse in my neck. My mind was screaming *what the fuck are you doing?* but my body refused to budge. My knees began to shake when his tongue joined his lips and his teeth, searing a line across my collarbone, down, down, down the V of my shirt. He licked a line across the inner swell of my left breast. I let out a soft cry.

"Ask me," his voice rumbled against my breastbone, heightening the pressure in my aching wet core.

I was going to lose my mind. I could barely hang on to the only sane part of my brain that knew it would be a long, hard fall I'd never recover from.

"You wanted it before. You still want it. Let's put our lives aside. Let's give in to this attraction," he continued between kisses that ran up my other breast, then towards my chin. He was saying everything I had wanted to hear days ago.

If I were there...

Come here, then.

He was here now. He was here now, offering himself to me. Take it. Take *him*.

Something stopped me. The delicate wound of his previous rejection throbbed in my chest. What if I gave in, exposing my desires to him? What if he changed his mind again? I wasn't sure I could bear it.

"If we gave in..." His tongue flicked my earlobe, causing my eyes to roll back into my head. I gripped on to his shoulders like he was the only thing holding me on this earth. "We could get it out of our system."

My eyes snapped open as the truth hit me like a bolt of lightning. I could fool myself into believing that being with him would get him out of my system. I knew deep down it wouldn't. He was already under my skin, soaking into me like ink. There was no getting him out. Giving in to him now would mean falling further. There'd be no safety net when I landed. Not for me.

While I was just a game he hadn't won yet. If I gave in to him, he'd soon get bored. Like he'd gotten bored with all the other women he'd been with. All it would take for him would be to fuck me out of his system.

"Get out," I hissed, my voice low and deadly.

He pulled back, frowning at me. "You're angry with me."

"You come into my house, proposition me for sex," I said, my voice growing louder. "And you have the nerve to look confused as to why I'm upset? I am not one of your party whores."

He winced. "You make it sound so sordid."

"Really? How would you put it?"

"An agreement between two consenting adults."

"Get out. Get the fuck out."

"You have to understand why I can't offer you anything... more," he said quietly.

"Who said I wanted more?" I snapped, his words already finding their mark in my heart. Of course he would never want anything more from me than just sex. Bastard. I shoved him back with all the strength of my anger.

He let me go. For the first time in the last ten minutes I felt like I could breathe properly. I felt like I could think. I almost did a stupid, *stupid* thing saying "yes" to him. I grabbed my gun and yanked open my door, holding it open for him to let him know this conversation was over.

He raised an eyebrow, a small smirk back on his face. "So that means you'll think about it?"

"How's this for my answer." I pointed my gun at his dick, still hard through his jeans. "If I see you here again, that's where I'll shoot you."

JULIANNA

I slammed the door behind Roman and slumped against it. What the hell had just happened?

Roman Tyrell, mobster prince, possible murderer, definite criminal, propositioned me for sex. That's what happened.

And I said no.

Damn right, I said no. Roman and I could never have *just sex*. We were too intense, too much fire and lightning, too much under each other's skin. He was daring me to come out of the shelter and dance to the beat of our thunder. I wasn't sure I'd live through it.

Even if we did admit that we wanted to be together, our circumstances, our families, this city would never let us. Our attraction was hopeless. Pointless. That's why I said no. To give in was futile. We could never be anything *real*. No matter how much I wanted it.

My heart ached in my chest. Despite the logical arguments against *us*, hope still fluttered in my soul. I wanted to go after him, to tell him I made a mistake in kicking him out. But my feet were concrete, weighed down by the bog of how we could ever conceive to be together.

Yes. No.

Right. Wrong.

God, I was a mess.

A knock on my door jolted me out of my thoughts. Oh God. He was back. The arrogant man.

I swung open the door, gun pointed. "What do you—?"

It wasn't Roman. It was Nora standing there. She looked at me, my gun, then raised an eyebrow. "You going to let me in, honey? Or are we going to talk about that sexy young man who was just in your apartment out here for all the neighbors to listen in on?"

I let her in, locking the door behind us. When I turned around Nora was watching me with those light brown eyes of hers. Age may have wrinkled her face and shrunk her body, but her eyes were still young and full of life. They didn't miss a damn thing.

"You shouldn't have let him into your apartment," I said, my voice a little hard. Nora followed me into the kitchen. I slid the gun onto my counter and started the kettle. It was a well-worn habit with the two of us. She always said she liked her coffee like she liked her men: strong, rich and black.

Nora settled on one of my bar stools on the other side of my kitchen bench. "Roman said he was a friend of yours."

I wasn't about to let Nora know the details of who Roman was. I didn't want to scare her.

Maybe she needed to be scared a little bit. What if it had been someone worse than Roman who she'd let into her apartment? "Just because someone says they're my friend doesn't mean it's true. You know, 'stranger danger' and all that?"

Nora snorted. "I've been around long enough to know who's dangerous and who isn't."

My eyes almost bugged out of my head. Was she for real? She didn't think Roman Tyrell was dangerous?

Nora tilted her head at me. "By the way you were waving that gun around I take it you two didn't kiss and make up."

"No." He was an asshole. There was no apology for that.

"Are you telling me that you and he aren't..." Nora wiggled her perfectly-groomed silver eyebrows.

My mind went back to the few minutes that Roman had me against the door. My cheeks flamed. "No."

The smile widened on her face. Her eyes took on that sparkle of glee whenever she ferreted out a new piece of gossip. "But you want to. You," she wiggled a manicured finger at me, "like him."

"I do not."

"Oh, please. I can see the way you two look at each other. As if you're already tearing each other's clothes off in your heads. It's downright indecent." She fanned herself. "And hot as hell."

"He's dangerous, Nora. Don't ever let him in again."

She grinned. "The hot ones usually are."

I let out a growl of exasperation. There was no convincing her otherwise when she had her head set on something.

Her eyes widened, a look of realization coming over her features. "Smack me down. He was the one who asked you to go to Paris with him!"

Dammit. What should I tell her? I couldn't admit Roman was the Paris guy or she'd never let it go. I couldn't tell her he was a friggin' gangster or she'd be scared out of her mind. Actually, she'd probably be turned on as hell and push me even further towards him. I realized my mouth was flapping open like a fish. I slammed it shut.

Nora nodded. "Hot, charming, dangerous and loaded enough to take you first class to Paris. Why the hell haven't you jumped all over that? I'll take him if you don't want him."

I cursed inwardly as I slammed down two cups and spooned in coffee. "It doesn't matter whether he was or wasn't the Paris guy, nothing can ever happen between us again."

Nora crossed her arms over her chest, a frown beginning to

form on her face. "Are you really that set on keeping yourself unhappy?"

I sighed and poured the hot water into the cups. "It's not that I don't want to. It's that I can't."

"Is he married?"

"No."

"Gay?"

I laughed snorted. "Definitely not."

"Then what's the problem?"

I stirred our coffees as I debated how to answer this question. I settled with, "It's complicated."

"It always is." Nora took the cup I handed her and placed her other hand on my arm. "Take it from a woman who's lived twice as long as you have, 'the course of true love never did run smooth.'"

The next few days dragged. Every time my phone rang I half expected it to be Roman, making some inappropriate flirty comment as if nothing had happened. When I came home at night, I half expected Roman to be waiting for me in my apartment. Each time he wasn't there, my heart sank lower and lower. Until I almost regretted kicking him out of my apartment. *Almost.*

Things at work seemed to have quieted down for now. Quiet enough that I was stuck doing paperwork. Which made me nervous. The ruling families, including the Tyrells, seemed to have been very quiet lately, too quiet. Like the calm before the storm. We had yet to see the full retaliation for Jacob Tyrell's murder. One of the sources on the street claimed a truce between the Tyrells and the Veronesis had been negotiated. I suspected the war was coming. Giovanni Tyrell was not one to back away. And he was not one for truces.

Early one morning, as I walked the short distance from my car to the station, I felt a strange tingling on the back of my neck. *Roman?* I spun, glancing around the street, looking to find the pair of eyes that was trained on me. I startled a passerby, who weaved around me before continuing on his way. I peered into every doorway, every street corner, every shadow. As far as I could see there was no one.

When I left work that evening—the sun had set, the only light drifting down from streetlights, the law-abiding workers retired to their homes, the ones that remained had shifty-eyes, scanning for trouble—I felt that feeling again. The hairs on the back of my neck rose as I walked through the shadows to my car. Even though I couldn't see him, I knew he was watching.

Roman?

He hadn't given up on me. He hadn't let go. A small relief bubbled up inside me. I had the urge to call out to him, to let him know I was watching. I didn't. I licked my lips, which had gone dry at the knowledge of his eyes on me. And sent a hopeful look into the dark. *Please talk to me,* I threw out into the night. *Don't let this be over.*

I walked slowly to my car, willing him to show himself. I kept glancing into my rearview mirror as I drove home, looking for him tailing me. I felt him. But I didn't see him.

After dropping off my work things and showering, I had dinner at my father's place. My father didn't cook. We ate Thai carry-out from white cardboard cartons with cheap wooden chopsticks on his couch because his dining table was covered in work files. I chewed on too-soft pad Thai and listened to him ranting after I told him we still had no evidence linking anyone to Vinnie Torrito's murder.

"Those damn Tyrells. They think they run this town." My father's face reddened as he spoke, his chopsticks holding a piece of pork waving about, scattering rice everywhere. "They're so damn arrogant, flaunting the law thinking they're too smart to

281

get caught. One of these days their arrogance will cause them to make a mistake, then...I'll get them. We just need one to turn and we'll get them all."

I wanted to argue for Roman, that he didn't really want to be involved with his family's business. "Surely not all the Tyrells are like that," I said carefully.

My father gave me an incredulous look. "Are you that naïve, Julu? Of course they all are. They're bred from birth to be monsters. I won't rest until every single one of them is behind bars."

I bit back the urge to argue with him—what happened to innocent until proven guilty? I had an odd feeling like...like I was betraying Roman by staying silent about the accusations against him.

Whose side are you on, Julianna? Your father's or Roman Tyrell's?

My father studied my face. "You think I'm wrong, don't you?"

I said nothing but my lips pinched in answer.

He mopped his forehead with a napkin. "When your mother *died*," his voice choked on the word, "I made a vow that I wouldn't stop until every single piece of scum was locked up. I vowed that no other family would have to go through what we did." His face had turned a shade of red, his breathing gone heavy. "So far I've failed. Now that I'm chief, I have a real chance to make a difference."

I understood now. All his late nights and weekends at work, his obsession with locking up the Tyrell family. He was on a crusade in my mother's honor. He had turned himself into a weapon to fight crime. My thoughts flashed to Roman Tyrell again. What if that weapon aimed at someone innocent?

It was late by the time I returned home. There was only a small parking lot for my apartment building. It was first come, first served—the price you paid for inner city living. Tonight, it was full—not surprising for a Friday night—so I had to park a few blocks away. A single streetlight dribbled a pool of sickly light onto the gritty pavement as I locked my car, tucked my keys and phone into my pocket. I was tired and confused, my insides warring with each other about my father and Roman.

"Spare change, miss?"

A figure hunched over limped towards me, a hood covering his face.

"Sorry," I said and began to turn away.

He let out a small moan and bent over, almost collapsing. Was he sick or just drunk? Either way, I couldn't just leave him.

"Hey, are you okay?" I lunged towards him, my arms out in case he fell.

An arm grabbed me from behind and a hand clamped down on my mouth, hot, stale breath curdling the air over my left shoulder. I reacted without thinking, all my training kicking in. Keeping my elbow close to my body, I jabbed my thumb back over my left shoulder. I felt the soft give of his eye. He let out a scream and leaned back out of instinct. At the same time, I tucked my body around, away from the elbow of the arm that clasped my mouth, causing his hand to slide off me, leaving him wide open. I slammed the heel of my left hand into his balls. He made a wheezing noise, letting go of me as he bent over himself. I slammed my heel down on his instep and snapped an elbow to his bulbous nose, hearing a satisfying crack. He let out a scream. That'll teach him to pick on someone his own size.

The click of a gun being cocked back made the blood freeze in my veins. The "homeless" man straightened, holding a pistol out in front of him. I realized then he had been a ruse. These two had been working together.

"Freeze or I'll shoot." I didn't recognize his voice. Or at least, I didn't think so. I assessed the man standing in front of me—his face hidden in the shadows of his hood—then the barrel of his gun. Even if he wasn't a crack shot I was too close for him to miss. I gritted my teeth and lifted my hands up in surrender. I had to pick my battles. Bide my time.

The countless homicide scenes, lifeless women with their clothes torn and underwear missing flashed through my mind. I shoved those images aside. They probably just wanted my wallet. Losing a few hundred dollars in cash was better than ending up dead. "You want my wallet? Just take it."

The man with the gun laughed. "It's not your wallet we want."

A shiver of fear went through me.

The guy behind me moaned. "Bitch broke my nose." He grabbed me and spun me. His fist clocked me in the chin. Pain burst through my head as I stumbled back. I landed hard on my wrists, my knees bruising. My head spun from the punch. I scrambled away. I didn't get very far. Bloody Nose grabbed me and shoved me onto my back. He slammed his body down on me, pinning me down. His hips digging painfully into my lower belly. Bile rose in my throat from his heavy, unwanted weight on me. I could smell the sourness of his breath.

He grinned, showing off the blood staining his crooked teeth and over his cracked lips. "We should have a bit of fun with her before we take her to the boss."

The boss? This was not a random attack. Someone had sent these two after me, specifically. They had been the ones watching me earlier, not Roman.

His forearm jammed into my throat cutting off my oxygen. He jammed his knee between my legs and his beefy rough hand thrust between my legs, tearing at my skirt. I tried to scream but all I managed to get out was a choked cry. Any trace of humanity had fled from his uneven bug-eyes. I shoved, scratched, beat, yanked at his forearm to no avail. Air. I needed air.

"Hold her down," Bloody Nose said.

The man with a gun slipped it into the back of his pants as he strode towards me. I heard chuckling as he crouched over me. He grabbed my arms and yanked them above my head, stretching me out like I was on a torture rack. I was exposed. Bloody Nose tore at my panties, his dirty fingernails scraping my skin. Panic slammed against my ribcage. I kicked out. I tried to scream. My struggling only seemed to please him, only served to grind more dirt into me from the gritty ground.

My jaw throbbed. My lungs felt raw from clawing for air. Stars sparkled in front of my vision. I was losing consciousness. At least I would not be awake while they took turns violating me.

Suddenly his forearm was gone. I sucked in air into my burning lungs. He was gone. He'd been pulled off me by a third man, his wide frame encased in a black Everclear hoodie, the sleeves pushed up to his elbows, and dark jeans. Everclear smashed his fist in Bloody Nose's face as he roared. "Nobody touches her, you son of a bitch."

The familiar voice sank into my bones and hit me in my gut. *Roman?*

Relief flooded my body. I had never been so damn happy to see anybody before.

I heard the crack of bones and Bloody Nose went limp. He fell to the ground, lifeless.

The man holding my arms down let go of me, fumbling for the gun in the back of his pants as Roman charged towards him, knocking him off his feet. They tumbled to the ground. Roman pinned my attacker down. He smashed his fist into Gun Man's face and ribs, the sound of hard flesh against wet bloody flesh and the crack of bones filled the air. All of Roman's calm, cold facade had gone. The leash he kept on this part of himself had been unchained. Dear God, he wasn't going to stop.

I rolled to my feet, wincing at my bruises, and ran over to him. "Stop it, Roman, you're going to kill him." I grabbed his arm, trying to pull him back. It was like trying to yank back an oak branch.

He whipped around to me and leapt to his feet, leaving the man a bloodied mess on the ground. Roman's hoodie fell around his neck so I could see his face now, thick lips pulled back, teeth bared, eyes wild, flecks of blood splattered across his sharp cheekbones. "They were going to *rape* you."

I swallowed hard. "I'm fine. Just a bruise or two."

His wild aggressiveness should scare me. His ability for violence should have me scurrying back. For some stupid reason I wanted to lean closer, mesmerized by the heaving of his thick chest and the way his clenched fists were making his forearm muscles stand out in brutal definition.

Roman stepped right up to me and cupped my cheek. His touch was gentle yet firm, the warmth sending a shiver up my spine. I could smell his familiar cedar cologne mixed in with masculine sweat. He tilted up my head to inspect the damage to my jaw. "The fucker," he muttered under his breath. "I could kill him."

I bit my lip, hoping he was joking. For Roman to kill a man because he hurt me was *wrong*. Some part of me, some sick deep-down part of me, was giddy at the idea.

"I'm fine, Roman. Really." I reached up to grab his thick damp fingers so I could pull his hand off my chin. To my surprise he didn't let go of my hand. His fingers laced into mine. We stood facing each other, fingers entwined as if we were standing at my doorstep after a date. Holy shit. I was standing in the middle of an alleyway holding Roman Tyrell's *hand*. What alternative universe had I just stepped into?

"They were going to rape you, kidnap you, do God knows what else to you," he said, as if that justified everything.

I squeezed his fingers, so warm and strong. "But they didn't. Because you were here."

Roman's shoulders relaxed and his scowl turned into a smirk. "You can reward me for saving you later." He kneeled beside the bloody, unconscious man on the ground and began to search his pockets.

The adrenaline of earlier began to wear off and the logical side of my brain began returning to me. Something very obvious finally struck me. "Wait a minute." I frowned. "How did you happen to be here?"

He paused, just for a second. "I was just walking past."

"You just happened to be walking past an area two blocks from my apartment?"

He flashed me a grin. There was not a shred of embarrassment on his face. "What can I say, I like the area."

"Bullshit." I folded my arms across my chest. "Were you following me?"

He snorted. "I just saved you from being raped, kidnapped, and probably murdered. A 'thank you' would be nice."

I flinched. He was right. The horrifying possibilities flashed before my eyes. I shuddered. "Thank you."

Roman straightened and stepped right up to me, toe to toe. I could smell his intoxicating cologne again wafting around him like incense. It took all my willpower not to lean in closer. He tapped my nose with his finger. "See? That wasn't so hard, was it?" Before I could answer he waved something in my face. "Found it."

I stared at the battered black wallet in his hand. "A wallet?"

And P.S. how the hell did he manage to change the subject so quickly?

"Not just a wallet." He opened it, pulled out a set of cards, then handed me a driver's license. It had a picture of the man who was currently at our feet. "Eduardo Sanchez," Roman said, tapping a finger at his photograph. "I don't recognize him. Do you?"

My attacker stared out of the photo at me with a scowl on his face. He had thick dark stubble across a beefy chin and a set of dark eyes glaring out from under caterpillar brows. He radiated the kind of bitter anger of a man who'd not been dealt a fair hand by life. I had barely seen his features while he'd been attacking me; it all happened too fast and it was too dark, now his features were covered in blood. If Roman hadn't thought to search for a wallet, I'd have no idea what he looked like. Some witness I would have made.

I wracked my brain for any flickers of recognition; perhaps a perp I'd arrested before or someone I'd seen walking the streets lately? He must have been following me for a while looking for an opportunity to jump me. I came up empty. I shook my head as I handed Roman back the card. "What do we do now?"

Roman shoved the wallet in his back pocket and turned to the unmoving body on the ground. "We go find out who this fucker is working for."

With incredible strength, Roman lifted the deadweight of Eduardo Sanchez and tossed him over his shoulder, his arm muscles flexing with effort. Damn, he was strong. Incredibly strong.

"Come with me," Roman commanded me from over his shoulder, his voice hard, allowing for no argument.

"What about the other guy?" I glanced over to the first attacker. I could see his neck was bent at an unnatural angle, his eyes open and staring at nothing. *He's dead.* I paused, waiting for the shock to hit me.

I felt nothing. I should be feeling upset or something. Roman had murdered him. In front of me.

No, not murdered. Defended you. He defended you from being raped.

Roman sidled up beside me. He was quiet for a second. "You okay?"

Yes. No. I don't know.

"Fine," I said, my voice wooden.

"I'll take care of him later," Roman said.

"But—"

"Jules, we gotta get out of here. There may be more of them."

Right. I didn't think about that. I glanced around, trying to peer into the shadows, the hairs on my arm standing on end.

"Stay close." Roman strode towards the end of the alley, Eduardo slung over his shoulder.

Still half stunned, I kept up wordlessly alongside him, my eyes darting around for any signs that we were going to be attacked again. The alleyway seemed to hiss, growl and leak around us like a creature that was waiting for a chance to devour us.

Roman stopped at the back of a black Mercedes parked on the side of the dark street. One measly streetlight was left working, a sickly light drifting around the lamp like smoke. This was Verona. Certain areas—the *good* areas—wanted for nothing; they had wide sidewalks, manicured parks and maintained streets. But the inner city—the parts filled with everyday people, the ones whose voices couldn't yell loud enough to reach the ears of those in ivory towers, the ones who kept the city running like overworked cogs in an insatiable machine—lay forgotten and crumbling away. I wanted to grind my teeth at the injustice of it. It was one of the reasons I loved being a cop, to give those who "didn't matter" a voice.

"You're going to have to get my keys out of my pocket for me," Roman said.

My gaze dropped to the pockets of his fitted jeans, then back up to his face. I frowned. Was this a trick?

"If you haven't noticed, my hands are full." Roman flashed me a grin.

I sighed. "Which one?"

"Left."

I sidled up beside him and slid my hand into his pocket.

"A little further in. Yeah, deeper. That's it."

My fingers brushed against something firm that was definitely *not* keys. Oh shit! I snatched my hand back. How the hell could he be semi-hard at a time like this?

Roman didn't look embarrassed at all. He merely smirked at me. "Oops. I mean the other left pocket."

SIENNA BLAKE

I scowled at him. "You did that on purpose."

"I won't deny it if you don't deny you enjoyed it."

"I did not," I spluttered, my cheeks flaming.

"Can you get the keys? You're wasting time." He shifted his right hip toward me and wiggled it. Goddamn him. With all the caution of someone feeding a snake down a hole, I slid my hand into his right pocket, my lips pinched as I glared at him. My fingers brushed against keys but I only managed to push them in further. I gritted my teeth and pushed my fingers in deeper, grasping for the keys while trying *not* to touch his obvious arousal again.

Roman let out a small groan. "If you keep that up, I'm going to drop him and grab you instead."

My cheeks colored. I snatched the keys out—finally—and let out a breath.

"Pop the trunk."

I blinked at Roman. "What?"

"The trunk. Pop it."

"Why?"

Roman let out a grunt. "Are you going to argue with me every damn step of the way? Just do it before I drop him. The fucker's getting heavy."

I opened the trunk. Roman dropped the man's unconscious body into the trunk like a bag of potatoes. He slammed the lid down.

"What the hell?" I glanced around on the street to see if anyone had seen him dump the body in the car. No one was around. Or if they were, they wouldn't "remember" anything. I knew from experience that most people preferred not to get involved. Too many witnesses had a history of disappearing. That was probably why nobody came to help when I started yelling.

Roman snatched the keys from me. "I don't want him waking up while I'm driving and causing trouble."

Roman was right. Shoving him in the back seat would cause unnecessary risk to us. I didn't have any cuffs on me. It was the best way to secure him while we took him to the police station to interrogate him.

The car beeped unlocked, making me flinch. I was so jumpy. I steadied my breath and wiped my clammy hands on my skirt. I knew all the physical things that victims went through after an attack: heightened reactions to noises, paranoia, weakened heart rate, cold hands, sweating, rapid breathing. This was the first time I'd ever experienced it myself. I now had a new level of empathy for all the victims I'd ever interviewed.

Roman must have noticed because one of his hands slid onto my arm. "You okay?"

Why did he have to notice everything? I nodded, my throat deciding to knot. "Fine."

He stared at me for a second. "If you're going to freak out, I'd like some advanced warning."

"I said I'm fine," I hissed through clenched teeth.

He stared at me for a beat. Then nodded. "Okay."

He walked around to get into the driver's seat, leaving me rooted where I stood, half confused, half in shock. The car rumbled to life and the window of the passenger seat rolled down. Roman leaned across the seat so I could see his face through the window. "Get in," he commanded.

Me, alone in a car with Roman Tyrell. The last time he and I were alone together... The car looked too small for the two of us.

"I can follow you in my car."

"You're two seconds away from going into shock. I'm not letting you drive anywhere."

"I'm fine."

He stared at me through thick dark lashes. "Are you scared of being alone with me?"

"No," I said, just a little too quickly.

"Then get in." His eyebrow lifted. "Don't make me do this the hard way."

This was a bad idea. I pursed my lips and glanced around again to see if anyone was looking before sliding into the car. As soon as I shut the door, the locks activated and the window rolled up, trapping us in together. Great, locked in a car with a body in the trunk and a possible psychopath in the driver's seat. What could possibly go wrong?

Roman tugged the attacker's gun from the back of his pants and leaned over, practically in my lap, his mouth inches from mine. I pressed back into the seat, trying to get some distance. "What are you doing?"

"Relax, Jules," Roman said, his voice taking on an added caramel texture. If I didn't know any better I'd say he was trying to be seductive. He popped open the glove box and deposited the gun into it. "I took the bullets out already." He gave me a wicked look, his gaze dropping to my mouth before dragging back up to pin me with his dark stare. "Just in case you felt trigger happy."

I rolled my eyes. And tried desperately to remember how to breathe properly.

After what seemed like an eternity, he straightened back up. I relaxed into the passenger seat and shut my eyes, letting my heart return to a normal pace. I felt us pull away from the curb and let the soft turns of the car rock me into a calmer state.

I would never admit it, least of all to him, but I was glad to have Roman here telling me what to do in his infuriatingly overly confident, bossy tone. It's what I needed right now. My mind was too rattled to think properly. With him here I knew I would be taken care of. I was...safe.

Oh my God. I felt safe with Roman. Completely safe. That was ridiculous. He was a violent criminal gangster, for Christ's sake.

Despite all attempts of my mind to convince me otherwise, I just knew Roman wouldn't let anyone hurt me. He saved my life.

Because he was stalking you, Julianna.

Not stalking. Watching. Looking out for me.

Twist it any way you want, it's still *stalking*. This should terrify me. Instead, this thought sent an illicit thrill through my body. Roman Tyrell watched out for me even though he shouldn't. Like my own dark guardian angel. He cared about me even though he shouldn't. Just like I cared for him.

I opened my eyes a crack and looked over at him. My stomach fluttered like a fan every time I caught flashes of his chiseled profile when we passed underneath a streetlight. He really was breathtakingly beautiful. And totally occupied with driving. I took this opportunity to roll my gaze over the rest of him. Rounded shoulders, firm chest, thick torso, hard bulge...*hard* bulge? No, wait. That was the bulge of a gun in his hip holster.

"Like what you see down there?" Roman asked, a hint of amusement in his voice. Dammit. Of course he'd noticed me staring.

I tore my eyes away, my cheeks heating. "I was looking at your gun."

"Sure you were."

"You didn't use it earlier." *Way to state the obvious, Julianna.*

The skin around his mouth tightened. "I only use it when I need to. I didn't need to with them." In other words, he was such a badass he didn't need a gun against two armed attackers.

"Do you have a permit for it?" I blurted out.

Roman let out a long laugh. "Jules, we have a man locked in the back of my trunk. Are you really concerned if I have a permit for my gun?"

Point taken. I sank back into my seat. I frowned as I glanced back to his piece. I couldn't see it well because of the dim light, but I guessed it was a Glock .40 or something similar. Nice choice of weapon. A random question appeared in my mind.

"You look like you want to ask something," he said. Observant bastard.

"Do you Mafia guys name your weapons?"

He glanced at me out of the corner of his eyes, eyebrow raised, a smirk playing at his lips. "Only if the weapon is really, *really* special."

"Did you name this one?"

He looked like he was trying hard not to laugh. "Jules, I only have one weapon that deserves naming. And from what ladies have said when they've seen it, I'd have to call it 'Holy Shit, That's So Big.'"

I rolled my eyes.

"You roll your eyes a lot at me."

"You warrant it every time."

"One day the wind's gonna change mid eye-roll, then what'll you do?"

I rolled my eyes again just to prove a point.

He hummed. "It might be an improvement."

I sent a punch into the side of his arm.

"Ow. You know, you're a very violent person. Are you sure you're not the one with Tyrell blood in their veins?" He asked this lightly but I could tell underneath was a hint of bitterness.

"Very funny. My violent tendencies only seem to come out around you."

"Those aren't the only tendencies I bring out in you." His insinuation wasn't lost on me. The way his eyes flashed dark and hungry wasn't lost on me either.

I turned my head to stare out through the window. Roman turned off into an industrial estate. I pinpointed where we were on the map of Verona I had in my head and frowned. "This isn't the way to the station."

"We're not going to the Police." He said the word Police like it was a bad smell.

I sat up in my seat, a rash of fear prickling my skin. "Stop the car."

"No."

I grabbed at the door handle but it wouldn't open. He must have put the child lock on. Dammit. "Stop the damn car."

Roman cursed under his breath. "Stop trying to get out."

"Where are you're taking me?"

He glared at me out of the corner of his eye. "Do you want to know who's trying to kidnap you? Do you want to know why?"

"Of course I do."

"If you take him in, you have no chance of finding out."

"That's not true."

"Don't bullshit yourself, Jules. You've dealt with cases like this before. When does the bad guy ever talk to the cops?"

Almost never. These guys were trained not to squeal. They were always more afraid of their "boss" than what law enforcers could do to them. Jail time looked like a breeze compared to their fate if they talked.

I swallowed hard, almost afraid to ask. "So where are we going?"

"Somewhere quiet where we can talk to him."

I bit my lip, warring with myself. I *should* take Eduardo in. It was the *right* thing to do. But...

Roman was right. If I wanted answers, I had to talk to him first. No police station, no cops, no law. A strange rush traveled under my skin. Some part of my brain told me this was wrong, but somehow it felt like the right thing to do. I had always hated how the good guys had to stick to the letter of the law while the bad guys got to scribble lines all over it. Tonight I was leveling the playing field a little bit. Tonight it was personal.

"Just talk?" I asked.

"In a matter of speaking." Roman shot me a look. "Don't worry, I won't tell anyone. You get to keep your pristine reputation."

SIENNA BLAKE

What was that supposed to mean?

Roman pulled into an unlit lot and turned off the engine. The sudden silence in the car was so loud it was pressing into my ears. He switched off the headlights. My world went dark for a moment before my eyes began to filter in the pale moonlight. I flinched when I found Roman leaning into me, staring at me in the dimness, his minty breath swirling around my cheeks. "Jules..."

We could have been two love-struck teenagers parked in a secluded spot on their first date. "Yes," I breathed.

"Lock yourself in the car." He climbed out of the driver's seat and walked around the back, disappearing behind the trunk lid when he opened it.

What? I climbed out after him. "Where are you going?" I skidded to a halt beside him. Eduardo was slung over his shoulder again.

"Get back in the car." He slammed the trunk closed with his free hand.

"No. You're not leaving me behind."

His eyes narrowed at me. "You don't want to watch this."

"What are...?" The realization of what he was going to do suddenly became clear through my shock-addled brain. "Oh my God."

"Did you think I was going to bring him to my apartment for a nice little chat? Make him some tea, perhaps?" Roman gave me a hard look before he strode towards the dark warehouse.

I jogged after him. "Are you going to hurt him?"

Roman turned towards me, gravel crunching under his heel, managing even with a limp body over his shoulder to make it look graceful. "Jules, he tried to *take* you." The aggression rolling from him in hot waves made me shiver. "If I have to beat him to within an inch of his miserable life, I will find out who hired him and why. That's why you're staying outside in the car."

"No."

"If you stay outside you can plausibly deny you know anything about it."

"I'm already lying to them about you. What's one more lie?" I blurted out.

What's one more lie? This was a slippery slope. I was already losing my grip.

Roman let out a growl of frustration. "Inside this warehouse...I might have to say some things...do some things... You shouldn't witness it."

I bristled. "I'm not an innocent little girl, you know? I've seen my fair share of—"

"That's not what this is about."

"Then what is it about?"

His features twisted, etched with anguish. Something was tearing him up inside.

"Tell me, Roman." I stepped closer to him, pleading with my eyes for him to trust me.

He opened his mouth. Eduardo let out a soft moan.

"Damn you, he's waking up." Roman strode forward and kicked at the warehouse door. It crashed opened with a bang that made me jump. He disappeared into the darkness of the warehouse with his burden across his shoulder.

I hesitated at the entrance. Maybe I didn't want to see what Roman was about to do. Maybe I didn't want to get involved.

Despite these thoughts, I felt a tug drawing me to follow him. Whatever Roman was about to do, he was doing *for me.*

But why? Why was he doing this? He didn't have to get his hands dirty. Least of all for me.

I glanced around at the darkness that seemed to swallow everything around me and shivered. I couldn't stand being out here alone, I'd rather take my chances inside. I ran in after him.

JULIANNA

The inside of the warehouse was bare, just a few cranes lay dying on the gritty floor, their reaching arms like cancer-eaten bones. Roman must have turned on the lights, sickly pools trickling down from one of the exposed beams, dust motes floating like lost souls in the musty air that smelled sharply of corroding metal. This place hadn't been used in months.

Roman dropped Eduardo on the ground by a thick studded metal pillar flaking with rust. Eduardo twitched and let out another moan.

Roman spotted me, his shoulders tensing. He strode towards me, brows furrowing. "I told you to stay outside."

"And I said no."

He let out an exasperated grunt. "I don't have time to argue with you. At least make yourself useful. Make sure he doesn't go anywhere." He walked into the shadows.

"Where are you going?" I called after him, the sudden loss of his presence making my hair stand on end.

"Back in a sec." His voice echoed through the darkness.

I stared around me, my shock feeling like it was rattling

awake again. The light above me acted like a spotlight. In the edges of the shadows I swear I could see monsters waiting to jump out at me.

Stop it, Julianna. You're being silly. There's no one here except for you and Roman.

Oh, and the bad guy lying on the floor.

Roman reappeared with rope which he thrust into my hands. "I'll hold him against the pole and you tie him up."

"What?" I stared at the rope in my hands, now feeling as icky as a snake.

"Would you prefer to hold up his weight while I tie him up?"

I stared at the 200-odd pound dead weight in the form of an unconscious man on the floor. "I guess not."

Roman grabbed Eduardo under his arms and hoisted him up to sit against the metal pole. "Do it."

I eyed the man and the rope. Where were my damn cuffs when I needed them? Okay, tie the man up with the rope. I'd seen this done countless times in the movies. This should be easy. I began to uncoil the rope around the man, but Roman was in my damn way. I had to tuck my arms around him to get the coil of rope around the man and the pole without tying Roman up too. Being this close to Roman, my arms around the width of his warm muscular torso, his scent in my nose...it was muddling my brain.

Rope. Bad guy. Stay focused, Julianna.

"You're doing it wrong," Roman said sounding amused.

I let out a huff. "Excuse me if I have no experience tying bad guys up."

"You'd make a terrible criminal. Remind me never to hire you."

I gawked at him, almost dropping the rope.

He rolled his eyes. "Kidding. I'm kidding, Jules."

Finally, I managed to tie the rope around Eduardo's torso and arms securely enough to the pole so he couldn't move or get away.

I brushed my hands and stared at the man I had just *tied up.* Jesus Christ. What the hell had I gotten into?

Roman was staring at me, a dark look in his eyes.

"What?" I asked.

He shifted his weight. "What you're about to see...the man I'm about to become...he's not..."

I suddenly understood. Roman hadn't wanted me to follow him inside the warehouse because he was afraid of what I'd think when I saw him do what he had to do. He was afraid that I'd run away screaming, that I might never look at him the same way again. For some reason, Roman Tyrell cared what I thought of him.

"I know, Roman," I said simply.

His eyes widened as if my answer surprised him, as if he couldn't believe what I was telling him. I let him study my face for signs of a lie. When he was satisfied, relief flittered across his features, a warmth glowing that I thought might have been lost to me. "Jules..." he said so softly, it felt like a caress across my heart. There was so much that was unsaid, from both him and me.

"Just do what you need to do," I told him.

Roman nodded, before a hardness closed over his features creating that same cold mask I'd been introduced to in the inter-rogation room. He looked terrifying with the light casting down on him from above, cutting shadows across his features. He looked callous, without remorse, almost...evil. Alarm bells rang out inside my body. *Run!* my instincts screamed.

I forced myself to stand my ground. *This is* not *Roman.*

Roman knelt in front of Eduardo, who was moaning, his head rolling to one side. For a single moment I felt sorry for the man who was about to wake to a nightmare. Just for a moment. Until I remembered what he had tried to do to me.

Roman slapped Eduardo across his face, the crack echoing into empty space.

Eduardo let out a cry, his eyelids flickering. "What the fuck," he mumbled. He began to struggle against his ropes, his face twisting with rising panic as he rose to consciousness. His eyes snapped open. Then grew into two bloodshot moons. "R-Roman Tyrell."

In that moment, I almost felt jealous of Roman. Imagine having that kind of reputation, that kind of power that went with your name or your face. As a woman I had to fight for every ounce of respect from other men, especially with guys that I arrested or interrogated, and unfortunately, with other male police officers that I worked with.

Roman's features were diamond hard, a bitter disgust curling his lips. I realized he hated being seen as a monster, although he played the part so well. He hated his reputation, his last name.

How long does the world keep telling you who you are before you stop fighting it?

"You know who I am," Roman said in an even tone. It wasn't a question. A mere statement of fact.

The man nodded, his head jerking like one of those bobble-heads on a dashboard.

"You've heard what the Tyrells will do to men who displease us?"

The man swallowed hard. Then nodded again.

"Then you know that I can be the devil or I can spare you. That choice is up to you."

"W-What do you want?" he stuttered.

"I just want to talk."

"*Talk?*"

"I will know if you're lying to me. Let's start with your name."

"Toni."

"Lies!" roared Roman. The man flinched as if he'd been struck. Roman fisted his hand into Eduardo's shirt and twisted,

301

choking him with his own collar. "Didn't I tell you I would know if you are lying? Let's try again. What is your name?"

"E-Eddie."

"Good. Very good, Eddie. Eduardo Sanchez, isn't that right?"

Eddie's eyes widened. "How do you—?"

"I know your name, your social security number, your driver's license number, which bank you use, your home address. I know you have a wife, prettier than you deserve, and you have three kids, all girls. I bet they're a handful."

Eddie's eyes became saucers and his lip trembled. My stomach turned to see a grown man reduced to such raw terror.

Roman nodded as if to confirm, yes, he knew all this. Yes, Eddie, you should be very scared. "I know all this and more. But what I really want to know is who sent you to kidnap her?"

"I–I don't know."

Roman's chin dropped an inch. He let out a heavy sigh. "I had hoped, Eddie, you would not disappoint me so soon." Roman pulled a knife from a strap on his side. He held it up between himself and Eddie. Holy shit. It was a thick, glittering, double-edged blade, one side serrated, the other smooth. The kind of blade that hunters used to gut animals.

Roman placed it to Eddie's neck and pressed, a small line of blood appearing. Eddie let out a whimper. I bit down on my lip. *This isn't the* real *Roman.*

"Let's try again," Roman said, his voice growing hard, *"who* sent you to kidnap Julianna?"

"I don't know."

The blade pressed a little deeper, and the line became a trickle. "One more time, who hired you?"

"I swear, I—"

"Open up." Roman pinched Eddie's broken nose, making him yell, and shoved the end of the blade in his open mouth. Eddie choked on the flat of the blade pressing down against his tongue, blood trickling from the corners of his mouth where the blade cut him, tears shining in the corner of his eyes.

"Roman," I cried, my hands flying to my chest. Dear God. Was he going to kill this man in front of me? I'd seen the coldness of death dozens of times but I'd never been present for a live execution. My stomach curdled as the air suddenly filled sharply of urine. Eddie must have pissed himself.

This isn't Roman. He's playing a role.

He's playing it too well.

"See this lovely lady?" Roman growled. "Thank her. Even though you tried to *rape* her, she wants to spare you. She is an angel. I..." he leaned in close, barely inches from Eddie's face. "I'm no angel. I am the devil made flesh. And I would kill for her."

I would kill for her. My body broke out in shivers at his admission.

I stared at Roman, but his focus was on Eddie. The only hint that he realized what he had just admitted was a slight pause before he continued. "You will tell me what I need to know or I will cut you into pieces starting with your useless tongue." Roman grabbed Eddie's wallet with his bladeless hand. He flipped it open and shoved the picture of Eddie's family in his face. I remembered seeing that picture when we had gone through his wallet earlier. It must have been a Christmas photo, the five of them gathered at the foot of a sparsely decorated tree. "After I'm done with you, I will feed you to my dogs. Then I will find your wife and I will fuck every single one of her holes until she's cursing your name. And your beautiful daughters, they will watch. They will watch and they will know that it was your fault. That you could've saved them but didn't."

My blood curdled. Eduardo made a sobbing noise around the blade and it cut into the corners of his mouth even further.

Roman snatched the knife out of his mouth. "What was that?"

"Okay, okay." Eduardo's eyes glistened with wetness. "I'll tell you. Please, leave my family out of it."

SIENNA BLAKE

Roman didn't relent. He jammed the tip of the blade under his chin. "Then. Start. Talking."

"I don't know who hired us..." he coughed and spat out blood. "We went through a handler."

"Who is your handler?"

"Please," he mumbled. "He'll kill me."

Roman paused, a heavy silence where the only sound I could hear was Eddie's wheezing and my own blood pumping in my ears. "Tell me who your handler is and I'll give you and your family safe passage out of Verona. You'll have a chance to live. Refuse to tell me and your chance dies here."

"You're lying."

Roman leaned in. "I swear on my mother's memory. If you know anything about me, you'll know how much my mother meant to me."

"S-Safe passage?"

Roman nodded. "Safe passage. And cash to get you started wherever you end up."

Eddie swallowed hard, his Adam's apple bobbing across the thin wound on his neck. His left eye was now almost swollen shut so it was only his heavily lidded right eye that skittered over Roman, not daring to look at him directly, as he calculated the odds of his choices.

Finally, he nodded. Smart man. I wouldn't take my chances against Roman Tyrell either.

"Your handler's name."

"I don't know his real name. Just that everyone calls him...G-Goldfish."

Roman's eyes fluttered shut. "Fuck," he muttered, under his breath.

Goldfish. It sounded familiar but I couldn't place it. Obviously it meant something to Roman, something bad, but I couldn't ask him about it now.

Roman recovered himself, his face turning hard and cold

again, wiping away any trace of his previous flash of emotion. "Why do they want her?"

"I don't know. Tate and I were just hired to grab her and take her to a drop-off point. I swear to God I don't know anything else."

Roman leaned in close, almost as if he was about to kiss the man. "If you're lying to me..."

"I'm not." Eduardo winced. He must be in a lot of pain. "I swear."

Roman glared at him for one long, hard minute. Then he nodded and pulled the knife away. I let out a sigh of relief. My knees suddenly felt wobbly.

This whole time I'd barely breathed. This whole time it had felt like time had slowed. Like I had been shoved underwater, watching everything as if through a dream. Now the trance smashed to pieces and every sound grated on my nerves; Eddie's wet breathing, the grit underneath my shoes, the echo of Roman's knife as he slid it back into its sheath.

Roman held up the picture of Eddie and his family between their faces, stabbing the photo with a blood-smeared finger. "I'll keep this, just in case." Roman shoved the photo into his back pocket before he dropped Eddie's wallet onto his lap. Eddie slumped against his ropes.

Roman stood and spun. The second his gaze found my face, he winced. I must have looked shaky and pale. I certainly felt it. Like if the wind blew too hard I might have blown away.

Roman tore his gaze away from me and strode out of the warehouse, a dark storm raging in his eyes. I stared out after him.

What should I do? Should I go after him?

"After I'm done with you, I will feed you to my dogs."

I wanted to stay in here, to hide. God, I never wanted to look at him again.

SIENNA BLAKE

"Then I will find your wife and I will fuck every single one of her holes until she's cursing your name."

I wished I had stayed outside. Why hadn't I just stayed outside? I wished I hadn't seen what I had just seen and heard what I'd just heard.

"And your beautiful daughters, they will watch. They will watch and they will know that it was your fault. That you could've saved them but didn't."

I recoiled at the memory. I couldn't. I thought I could deal with it but...

You selfish woman, a harsh voice inside me said. *Do you know what it took for Roman to act like that in front of you? He did that* for *you.* Whatever I was feeling, Roman was feeling worse. Right now he needed me.

I turned and ran out after Roman.

Just outside the warehouse door, I found Roman standing with his hands clenched in fists, forearm muscles straining. He was glaring into the blackness like he wanted to tear the night apart. He didn't move, didn't make a noise except for his loud inhalations of air.

"Roman," I eased to his side. He didn't acknowledge me. Cautiously, I touched my fingertips to his back. "Are you okay?"

His lips pinched into a tight line. That was my answer. We stood there, me barely touching him, him barely moving for what seemed like an eternity. I could feel the heat of his tense muscles in my fingertips. I wanted to touch him further, to place my whole palm on his back, perhaps even run my hand along him, to soothe him. But I didn't dare.

I found Roman studying me out of the corner of his eye. I suddenly felt self-conscious. I dropped my fingers from his back, missing his warmth already.

"Do I scare you?" His throat bobbed as he swallowed. He was trying to hide it, but my answer mattered to him.

"No."

306

"I'm sorry you had to see that."

I shook my head. "I was the one who wanted to stay."

His shoulders sank and his fists loosened as some of the tension left his body. Why was he so relieved? Why did a man who only wanted sex from me care so much about what I thought?

"Who is Goldfish?" I asked.

Roman's mouth twitched.

"You know him, don't you?"

He still didn't reply. He didn't even look at me, but I saw the flash of pain cross his face before it disappeared.

"Is he dangerous?"

Roman let out a low growl. "No more dangerous than most."

"But you know who he is," I pushed.

"It's not important."

"But—"

"I'll take care of it."

His dismissal was as sharp as a razor blade. Roman didn't trust me enough to confide in me.

Roman took out his phone and dialed someone. "Yeah, I know it's late. I need help." There was a pause. Then he rattled off the address of this warehouse before ending the call.

"Who is that?"

"Someone I trust." That seemed to be the end of it. "You should make a report in the morning. Let your father and your partner know that two men attacked you. They'll be able to protect you better than I ever could." I could hear a touch of bitterness in his voice.

"You did a fine job of doing that tonight," I said quietly.

He looked sideways at me. "I can't always be there..."

"Why did you help me?"

"I wasn't going to stand by and let them..." Roman's face twisted as he spoke. "In the warehouse, with my knife in his throat, all I could think was what if he had succeeded in taking you? What

307

if he put his hands on you and I hadn't been there? What if he'd beaten you, raped you? It took everything I had not to kill him."

I swallowed. "But you didn't."

"I wanted to. I wanted to slide the blade back into his brain and twist it."

Roman just admitted he wanted to kill a man. I should be fleeing from him. But underneath my instinctive fear, my body vibrated, my flesh felt raw and sensitive, the blood rushing hot around my veins. I couldn't deny it. I was turned on.

Turned on? What the hell was wrong with me?

"Aren't you going to arrest me, detective?" Roman stared at me with black fire in his eyes, a confrontational edge to his voice. If I didn't know any better, I'd say he was deliberately pushing me.

"No."

"You should. Kidnapping, assault, you could even get me on attempted murder. You could use me to bring down my whole family."

He *was* baiting me. Testing me. Whose side I would choose?

My father flashed into my mind. This was everything that he needed to put Roman Tyrell away. I could see it now, that rare flash of pride on his face, *that's my girl,* when I locked Roman Tyrell in a cell and single-handedly brought down the rest of the Tyrell empire. It would make my career in a heartbeat. I'd be promoted. Gain the respect I had wanted for so long...

None of that seemed to matter. When I thought of doing that to Roman, my heart ached so hard I thought it might break. I couldn't bring him down. Even to put away the Tyrells, I couldn't sacrifice Roman.

Are you listening to yourself, Julianna? Roman almost killed a man.

But he didn't, I argued with myself. Everything he did tonight was for *me*.

"You saved my life," I said to him. "I owe you. I won't turn you in. This can be…our little secret." My list of secrets was growing rapidly. Where would it end…?

Roman leaned into me, his lip curling up into a scowl. Every cell in my body told me to back up. But I forced myself to remain where I stood. "You don't seem to have any instinct to protect yourself around me. It'll get you killed."

I narrowed my eyes at him. Was he disappointed that I wouldn't arrest him? Did he think I was weak? "You seem to want to push me into either running away from you or arresting you."

"It's just easier if we remember which *side* we're on."

I flinched. I knew what he was referencing. I'd pulled a gun on him after he'd broken into my apartment to talk to me. So much had changed since then. "I don't think we're on different sides," I admitted quietly.

I saw a flash of what I took as hope in his eyes. He stepped closer, his body turning towards me. I mirrored him without thinking. He was beautiful, even with flecks of blood across his face. Even in the pale light coming from the open warehouse door, I could feel his dark, hooded stare burning into me. He pushed back a wayward strand of hair behind my ears, his touch searing into my soul. "Jules…"

"You're hurt," I cried, noticing his busted bloody knuckles. I reached for his hand.

The sound of tires crunching on gravel tore us apart. A black Ford Taurus pulled up in front of us. Friend or foe? I glanced over to Roman but he looked as impassive as ever. My heartbeat climbed in my chest as the driver's door opened.

Mercutio stepped out. His eyes widened as he took me in, torn clothes, scrapes, his gaze lingering on my jaw. The pain had faded during Eddie's interrogation, the stress and adrenaline pushing it to the background. Now it returned with an aching throb.

Mercutio narrowed his eyes at Roman. "You didn't tell me the cops were involved."

"They're not," Roman said. "She is here as a victim. Someone tried to kidnap her tonight."

Mercutio opened his mouth, then shut it. He eyed me suspiciously but remained tight-lipped.

"Take her home," Roman said. "Make sure you're not followed. Make sure her apartment is cleared before you leave. I owe you one." Without even a goodbye, he turned to go back inside the warehouse.

"Wait." I grabbed his arm. His thick bicep tensed underneath my hand. "Where are you going?" I could feel Mercutio's eyes on us.

Roman didn't pull his arm away but he didn't move any closer, his face and voice just as impassive as his actions. "To finish what I started."

I didn't want to go without him. I didn't want to leave his side. Somehow in the last few hours he'd become a safe place for me.

Roman lowered his voice. "Don't worry. I trust Mercutio. He'll get you home safely."

It wasn't that... How did I even explain? But I couldn't. Not without sounding like a fool. I forced myself to release my grip from him.

Roman looked back to Mercutio. Something seemed to pass unspoken between them. Then he was gone inside the darkness of the warehouse.

JULIANNA

I could feel Mercutio's disapproving glances at me as we rode in his car towards my apartment. It made my skin feel itchy. That, the adrenaline crash, the stress of almost being kidnapped, my confusion about Roman, the lateness of the hour, all conspired to put me in a foul mood. "If you have something to say, spit it out," I snapped.

Mercutio focused back on the road. "And have you arrest me for speaking my mind? No, thanks."

I'd gotten this kind of animosity from civilians before. "For this car ride, pretend I'm not a cop."

"Yeah, right. I don't trust cops."

I let out a sigh and tucked my head against the glass. "Suit yourself."

Mercutio said nothing. Several minutes went by, the street lights brightening up the skin behind my closed lids in a series of flashes. I felt my body grow heavy, sleep lapping at the edges of my consciousness.

"Why is he helping you?"

I opened my eyes at Mercutio's question. Why indeed? I looked out the window at the familiar city streets flashing past.

We were still several minutes away from my apartment. There was no way to avoid this conversation. "I don't know," I admitted. "I've asked him. He won't tell me."

"You're putting him in danger."

I rubbed my face. The last thing I needed right now was a lecture. I needed sleep. And an aspirin. And for Roman to stop confusing the shit out of me. "He's a danger to himself."

Mercutio gripped the steering wheel so tight his knuckles went pale. "You don't understand what his father would do to him if he found out that he *helped* a cop."

I straightened up in my seat. "Don't you think I know that? I told him he shouldn't be doing all of," I waved my hand around uselessly, "...*this* for me."

"You have something on him. That's why he's helping you."

I wanted to punch something. Nothing I was saying was getting through to Mercutio. But I was quickly losing the strength to argue. I let out a sigh and leaned against the cool glass again, letting it soothe my jaw. "Believe what you want."

Mercifully, Mercutio didn't say another word until we came to my apartment. He parked in the tow away zone in front of my building. I almost said something about illegal parking, then clamped my mouth shut. He wouldn't be staying long. I halted when he followed me out of the car.

"I'm coming in with you," he said, his tone making it clear that it was the last thing he wanted to do.

"I'm fine."

"No," Mercutio said firmly. "Roman asked me to check your apartment before I left. That's what I'm going to do."

I folded my arms across my chest. "You'll have to get through me to get into my apartment."

Mercutio gave me a small smile. "No offense, but I'm more scared of him than you."

I let out a sigh. The quicker I let him in, the faster he'd be gone. "Fine, but wipe your feet on the mat before you come in."

In my apartment, Mercutio checked each room including the closets. His phone rang and he answered. "Yeah, we're here at her apartment."

It was Roman. It had to be. My ears prickled.

"I'm just doing that now but it all looks clear." There was a pause where Mercutio's eyes darted over to me. Did Roman want to speak to me? "Yeah, no worries." Mercutio hung up.

I frowned as a wave of disappointment rolled over me, making me uneasy. I wanted to hear his voice in my ear even just for a few seconds. Why did he call Mercutio and not me?

Because Mercutio's his best friend and you're just a girl who is turning into a problem for him.

"Was that Roman?" I asked, trying for casual and failing. My voice sounded too tight and unnaturally high.

"Yeah."

"Is...is he okay?"

Mercutio froze, then shot me a look before he opened my linen closet; no monsters in there. "He's fine."

Fine? I wanted to know where he was. Was he okay? What was he doing? What happened to Eddie? Fine was not enough. It appeared "fine" was all I was getting. I held my tongue as Mercutio finished checking my apartment.

"See? No boogeymen," I said, holding the door open for him. "You can go now."

Mercutio paused just outside my front door and turned to me. "Do you care what happens to Roman?" Mercutio's eyes, sharp and intelligent, were studying me.

There was no use denying it. "Of course," I said quietly.

"Then stay away from him."

JULIANNA

I jolted awake when a floorboard creaked, grabbing for my gun that I'd slid under my pillow after Mercutio had left.

"It's just me." Roman's voice made my whole body sag with relief.

I spotted his huge frame silhouetted against my open bedroom window. An overwhelming sense of safety fell over me like a blanket.

"What the hell are you doing leaving your bedroom window unlocked?"

"I hoped you'd come…" I trailed off. My sleepiness was making me too honest.

He stiffened. "What if it hadn't been me, huh? What if they sent someone else to finish what they failed earlier tonight?"

I sat up in bed. The sheet dropped off my torso, revealing the red silk nightie I'd slipped on earlier. I thought I heard Roman's breath hitch. I felt his eyes roaming over me and I flushed. The nightie had been an unwanted birthday gift from Nora. I'd never worn it before tonight. I was glad I did. I pulled the weapon I was still clutching into view. "I have a gun."

There was a pause. Roman let out a soft snort as he shook his head. "Unbelievable."

I moved the gun to the bedside table. Suddenly my hands were too empty, so I gripped the edges of my sheet, my fingers playing with the hem. "What are you doing here?"

"Just wanted to make sure you were okay. I wasn't going to come in. Then I found your window unlocked."

There was an awkward pause. There was so much I wanted to say, to ask, but all of it seemed...inappropriate. My unasked questions hung in the air like pale moths.

"I should—"

"I'm sorry," I blurted out at the same time.

"What for?" he asked.

"For ever judging you incorrectly."

He let out a curt laugh. "You didn't get it all wrong. I'm still a bastard."

I gave him a small smile. "Not where it counts."

Roman's stance softened and his chin dropped. At that moment, he seemed almost...shy. "Thanks."

"What for?"

"For looking closer than anyone ever has."

Our eyes met. The air snapped with tension. All at once I felt like I might suddenly take flight, my chest and stomach both fluttering like frantic doves. And yet, I felt like I was drowning, a liquid heat rushing up to swallow me whole.

"Sleep, Julianna," he said, his voice croaking on my name. He turned, his wide frame blocking my view of the open window. My stomach lurched. *No, please, don't go.*

"Wait!"

He paused.

I cleared my throat. My heart was thudding around in my throat, making it hard to find my voice. I wiped my clammy palms on the sheet. What the hell was I doing? What was I asking?

"Will you stay? Here. With me."

He didn't move. I wasn't sure he was breathing. Or was that just me?

"I don't want to be alone tonight," I admitted.

In the dim he nodded, once. He moved quietly, almost hesitantly towards me, every inch he closed between us seemed to pressurize. The bed dipped when he sat beside me. I sucked in a breath as my head spun. *You just let Roman Tyrell into your bed. You practically begged him to stay. Have you lost your damn mind?*

He rolled me so I was lying facing away from him. Then tucked himself around me, the front of his strong thighs pressing against the backs of mine, one arm slung over my waist. Dear God. I've missed him.

Before I knew what I had done, I'd turned around to face him like a sunflower reaching for the sun, half-mad with the need to be closer to him. I could have cried when the front of my body melded against his. He stiffened against me, let out a muttered curse. But he didn't push me away. There we lay, our bodies pressed against each other.

I shouldn't have turned around.

I shouldn't have asked him to stay.

I shouldn't have left my window open for him.

"Roman," I whispered against his shoulder as I drowned in the nearness of him. "What happens next?"

I lifted my head to look up at him. His eyes were furrowed with pain, his beautiful lips pressed thin as he gazed at me. "Sleep," he managed to croak out.

There was nothing left. Only unanswered questions.

What if...

If only...

The answers were ones that we didn't want to face. At least not right now.

I closed my eyes. In the complete darkness behind my eyelids, I gained the courage to press further into him. His body burned hotter than anyone I've ever met. It seared me to my bones and yet the heat was like a balm to my aching soul. I inhaled his scent of cedar and man, letting it fill my lungs.

I was in the arms of a man who basically admitted to stalking me, a man who threatened to cut someone to pieces with a knife, a man whose presence beside me put me in grave danger from his family, and yet I felt safe. Safer than I'd felt in a long time. I couldn't reconcile these conflicting thoughts, so I just let them go. I needed him here with me tonight. Everything else I could deal with tomorrow.

I didn't know how but I soon drifted off to sleep.

ROMAN

T was lying in bed with Julianna Capulet. And we weren't
naked.

Well...this was new.

I could do this. I could just lie here with her and not—

She shifted her leg over mine, her thigh now pressing right
against my dick. I stiffened, the awareness flooding down my
body. Fuck, I missed her honey skin and soft, warm curves. I
reached for her, halting just before I touched her.

*Don't be a dick, Roman. She was attacked tonight. The last thing
she needs is for you to attack her too, you horny bastard.*

But she asked you to stay. That's practically an invitation to—

Keep your damn hands to yourself, you selfish fucker.

I gritted my teeth against the feral desire that gripped me,
threatening to break my control. She wasn't making this easy.
What the hell did you even do with a woman in bed if you
weren't fucking her?

Cuddles. I seem to remember one of the women I dated
complaining that she wanted to cuddle in bed. How was I
supposed to "cuddle" her without crushing her? I carefully placed
my arm around Jules. She tucked herself further into the crook

of my arm, her soft hair nestled against my chest, smelling like some kind of tropical flower. She sighed, a soft, happy sound. For some reason it made my chest cavity puff up. Damn. This was nice. Real nice. I could get used to this.

I woke up with a start.

My eyes took a second to adjust to the dim, the touch of dawn only just lightening the window. The strange window. This wasn't my bedroom.

I became aware of the soft body beside me. Julianna. I was in her bedroom.

Shit. I hadn't meant to fall asleep, but she'd been so warm and perfect. I stared down at the sleeping beauty. Her face was soft and completely relaxed.

I realized with a start, this was the first time I'd ever *slept* beside a woman without fucking her. What the hell did that mean?

Nothing. It means nothing. Now stop thinking and get the hell out of here before she wakes up.

I slid myself slowly out of the tangle that was our bodies. She let out a soft moan as she shifted. I froze. Thankfully, she kept sleeping as I crept out her window.

The city was already awake below me. It was already too light. I was too exposed up here. Anyone could see me looking like a criminal slipping out of her window and onto the fire escape. Anyone. I took a risk going to her apartment last night. I took an even bigger risk in staying.

No more risks, I told myself. *Stop being so fucking weak over her. She's not worth it.*

But even I knew that was a lie.

"What the hell happened last night?" Mercutio's voice rang out.

I stiffened. Mercutio was standing in my living room, a blanket rumpled on the leather couch. He must have come here after he dropped Julianna off. He'd been waiting for me.

I shut my apartment door behind me. "How did you get in here?"

Merc tilted his head. "You gave me your spare key, asshole, and you didn't answer my question."

"Julianna got jumped by two hired guys last night."

"And you just happened to be there?"

Smart fucker. "Yeah."

"Some coincidence, huh?"

I gritted my teeth. "Some coincidence," I repeated.

Mercutio's eyes narrowed. He knew I was full of shit. "Who hired them?"

"I don't know. I just got the handler's name."

Mercutio snorted. "I bet he just gave you that name freely. Who's the handler?"

Goldfish. Your father. I wasn't going to reveal this piece of information to him until I'd verified it. Mercutio thought his father was reformed, just hiding out somewhere. It'd kill him to know his father was back in the game. I repressed the guilt at lying to my best friend and shrugged. "The less you know the better."

"What do you think you're doing with her, Roman?"

"I don't know what you're talking about." I kept my mask on as I walked into my black marble and stainless steel kitchen to mix up a protein shake. I would take out my frustrations on a bag once he left.

"Don't fucking bullshit me. I'm your best friend." Merc followed me into the kitchen and stood with his arms crossed over his chest. "You stayed with *her* last night, didn't you?" He said *her* like she was some kind of virus. I wanted to throw him against a wall for talking about her like that. But showing any reaction would just confirm my guilt.

I didn't answer. Mercutio was someone I promised myself I'd never outright lie to.

Merc let out a string of curses. "Did the pussy in Europe give you shit for brains? She's the police chief's *daughter*, Roman."

I was all too aware of that.

"If your father doesn't find out, hers will."

Yes, I knew that too.

"You and she can *never* be anything. Just the idea of it—"

I slammed my protein shaker down on the countertop, every single one of his words stinging as they found their mark. "Don't you think I know that?" I bellowed. Mercutio was the last person I wanted a lecture from.

"Then why—"

"I don't fucking know. I've tried to get her out of my head. Believe me, I've fucking tried. I've tried to stay away from her since…"

Mercutio stared at me. His mouth dropped as a look of realization crossed his face. "She was the one you left at the hotel the day you were supposed to leave Verona. She's your Perfect Girl, isn't she?"

I nodded, just once.

Mercutio grabbed at his hair as if he were about to tear it out. "Why would you even take her home?"

"I didn't know who she was, okay? She didn't know who I was." As if I would mess around with her on purpose. Did he think I had a death wish?

Mercutio backed up until he hit against the bench top, scurrying away from me as if I were a leper. "Holy fuck, Roman."

Yeah that pretty much summed up my situation.

"Holy fuck," Merc repeated, "you're in love with her."

His words slapped me like a cold palm across my face. My head snapped to face him. "I am not in—"

321

His words sank in. My chest seared and clenched as if someone had put a round of bullets into it. I tried to shake them away. I was not in love with her. I couldn't be. The heir to the Tyrell empire could not be in love with the police chief's daughter.

I grabbed my shake and tilted it back, drinking the entire thing down, then wiping my mouth with the back of my hand. I really needed to hit something.

Merc was still staring at me with a woeful look on his face. "Dude, what the hell are you going to do?"

I know what I should do. I should walk away from Julianna. Leave her the hell alone.

But I couldn't. I'd tried. I just wasn't strong enough. What choices did I have left?

I shook my head. "I don't know, Merc," I admitted. "I don't fucking know."

~

After Mercutio left I changed into a pair of navy sweatpants. Every time I closed my eyes I saw the two men attacking Julianna. I saw the gun pointed at her, the terror on her face when she realized there was no way out. I saw Eddie grabbing her, then hitting her. I could almost *feel* the bruise on her swollen jaw. My blood boiled and the aggression spilled over as I remembered them holding her down. I slammed my fists into the punching bag I kept in my spare-room-turned-gym.

Eddie had gotten off way too easily. For a second it felt like the knife was in my hand again, the tip of it inside his mouth aimed at his brain. If Julianna hadn't been there next to me, I might have killed him right then.

See...violent tendencies. Just like your father.

My father's face flashed through my mind as I laid into the bag, sweat pouring off me. Goldfish had been his employee until he went underground, but I'd heard rumors that his supposed confession was just a ploy orchestrated by my father to get the case thrown out. Could Goldfish still be working for my father? Could he be the one who tried to snatch Jules last night?

He couldn't... He wouldn't...

An unwanted memory flashed in my head.

"She's the daughter of the new chief of police. A very...interesting girl."

"She doesn't seem that interesting," I said as casually as I could.

"Her father is a righteous man. He's stubborn enough to believe that he can clean up this city. Incorruptible, they call him. But I think I just found what he'd be willing to bargain for."

"What are you talking about?"

"No one is incorruptible. Everyone has his price. You just need to find their weak spot and know when to push."

My stomach turned as I imagined Julianna being used as a pawn in my father's hands. "What are you going to do to her?"

"Nothing. Yet."

I staggered as a horrible truth slammed into me. My own father ordered her capture.

ROMAN

I drove like a man possessed to the outskirts of Verona, my head churning the whole way. My father might have had something to do with this. My own goddamn father. How could Julianna ever forgive me if this were true? How could she still care about—?

I slashed that thought in half before I could finish it. Julianna had a moment of weakness last night when she asked me to stay with her. She didn't care about *me*. How could she?

Giovanni Tyrell still lived in the house I had grown up in, a vast, cold fortress of marble and granite. At least when my mother had been alive, she had left warm human touches on the place, vases of sunflowers and wild violets, rich, colorful landscape paintings done by local artists, soft rugs and sunny throws over every sterile piece of furniture. Under my father's sole care, it looked like a soulless luxury hotel.

I stormed down the wide corridor, the stomp of my boots echoing off the marble and stark white walls, ignoring the maid calling after me. "Sir! Mr. Tyrell! Please. He's not to be disturbed."

Abel blocked the doors to my father's study where my father

ate his breakfast while he read the day's papers. He always had. He was, if anything, a creature of habit.

"Get out of my way," I growled.

Abel didn't move. I didn't slow my strides as I shoved past him like a linebacker, breaking through the defense. He made the mistake of grabbing the back of my shirt. I turned and decked him square in the jaw. He let go of me, stumbling back with a grunt. I didn't stop to assess the damage. I burst through the door into my father's study.

Giovanni Tyrell sat behind his expensive mahogany desk dressed in his royal blue bathrobe, our family crest, an eagle with vines, emblazoned on his chest pocket. There was a plate of croissants, tiny pots of butter and jam, and a pot of black coffee at his elbow. Papers spread out in front of him. My father didn't even flinch at the sight of me. In fact, he almost looked bored as he tore off a piece of pastry and stabbed it into his mouth with his thick fingers, chewing slowly and thoughtfully.

I stood before his desk, chest heaving, fists clenched at my sides. "Somebody is trying to snatch the police chief's daughter."

Behind me I heard the maid and Abel both apologizing for letting me in. My father waved them away and they backed out, still mumbling apologies.

The door clicked shut behind me. My father turned his dark glittering eyes on me. Just like when I was a boy, a bolt of fear went through me. "Why does this matter to you?"

Lie, Roman. Because your life and hers depends on it. "Targeting the chief's daughter, a detective in her own right, a detective who just happens to have both of us under suspicion for a recent murder, puts the crosshairs of the police on our back, something which I thought you didn't want to happen. It's bad for business, isn't that what you said?"

"She has a dangerous job. Bad things happen to people in her position."

I gritted my teeth. That wasn't an admission. That wasn't a denial either. "I just want to make sure it wasn't *our* stupid move."

"You've got some balls coming in here and accusing me of being stupid, son."

"Are you admitting you tried to have her kidnapped?"

"No."

"I'm supposed to be your heir. I should have been consulted if this job was ordered. It needs to be called off, now."

My father's eyes narrowed at me. "If I didn't know any better I'd say you were concerned about this detective woman."

I snorted and forced as much derision as I could in my snarl. "I'm concerned about not driving our business into the ground because we've pissed off the chief of police so much that he makes it his mission to bring us down. I'm the one who's supposed to take over after you're gone. I don't plan on taking over a pile of rubble."

For a few terse moments, my father and I just glared at each other.

I suddenly felt very vulnerable standing in my father's office, in his house, surrounded by his men. What if he had ordered Julianna kidnapped? What if he found out I'd been the one to save her?

A smile crawled across my father's face, causing a bolt of fear to go through me. I feared his smile more than his anger. "I knew I was right to bring you back into the fold, Roman. I knew you would step up into the role. I think you might be ready to see more of our operations."

I tried to ignore the chill that ran down my spine. The more of his operation I saw, the harder it was to get out. I felt the darkness reaching for me.

"You still haven't answered my question about the chief's daughter," I said.

My father took a long, almost delicate sip of his coffee. He placed the china cup down before folding his fingers in front of him. "No. I have not authorized the capture of the lovely detective Capulet."

I didn't believe him. "So who would it be if not us? The Veronesis again?"

"She's a detective. She has arrested and pissed off a number of bad people. Maybe one of them did it? Now, get out of my study so I can eat my breakfast in peace. Unless there's something else you'd like to accuse me of?" My father leveled a stare at me.

"No, Father." I almost thanked him but I bit my tongue. My father would slap me if I thanked him, if I thanked anybody for anything. I was a Tyrell. I was entitled to whatever I wanted. Thank no one, apologize to no one. That's what he always taught me.

I turned, eager to see this house in my rearview mirror. It felt like the lion's den.

I was almost to the door of my father's study when his voice made me halt. "How did you know, by the way?"

A knot developed in my throat as I turned back to look at him. "Know what?"

"How did you know that someone ordered her capture?"

Shit. I was so furious at the thought that my father could've been the one behind this, I barely thought twice before coming over here. I just wanted answers. Now I may have betrayed myself.

I shrugged, keeping my face casual. "I have my sources just like you have yours." I walked out of his study before he could ask any more questions.

Abel scowled at me as I strode past him, but I ignored him. As I showed myself out, I felt the eyes of my father's men stationed around the house. My senses tingled with anticipation. None of them pulled a weapon on me. Or tried to stop me.

Did I believe my father? Did I believe that he had nothing to do with this? If he did order her capture, then he just lied to me.

He lied to me, which meant that he didn't trust me. If he didn't trust me, then I was already in trouble.

If he tried to kidnap Julianna, he'd try again. Not so soon after a failed attempt. But he wouldn't wait too long either. Being around her was too risky. I had to stop watching her if I knew what was smart. I couldn't step in to save her again if it meant exposing myself. I had to stay away from her.

But telling myself to stay away was futile. It was clear from the way I had launched at the two attackers last night without concern to myself that I'd do anything to protect her. Even risk my own damn life.

JULIANNA

I rubbed my forehead with my fingers where a headache was building. I knew I shouldn't have reported this. I glanced up from where I sat behind my father's desk, Espinoza sitting on my right. "I said I'm fine."

"You're fine?" my father repeated, his voice hard and rattling with fury. "Julianna, somebody tried to kidnap you."

"But they didn't succeed, did they? I'm sitting right here."

"Sitting right there with a bruise on your jaw the size of Texas." My father exhaled so loudly it reminded me of a bull.

My jaw let out a throb as if to agree with him.

"Do you have any ideas on who would be behind this?" Espo asked. It was the first thing he'd said since I'd revealed last night's drama.

Goldfish. Whoever that was. "I don't know."

"I bet it's the goddamn Tyrells," my father said, emphasizing his words with a fist slamming on the desk.

I stared at him, indignation at his prejudice tightening my grip on my chair arm. The Tyrells couldn't have done this. Roman was the one who saved me.

A worm of doubt threaded through my stomach. What if his

father or someone else in their organization was doing this behind Roman's back? It was possible.

Or Roman's playing you, a small voice said inside me. *He organized his men to try to kidnap you so he could come in like a hero. Do you really believe he just happened to be there?*

I shoved that voice down. I didn't care how stupid it sounded, I knew Roman. He wouldn't harm me.

"Why would the Tyrells do it?" I asked.

"The Tyrells have a vested interest in you because of your investigation into Vinny's murder case."

"Which stalled. They know that. What did they have to gain by kidnapping me? It would be a stupid move on their part."

My father's chair creaked as he sank back into it. "I'll have a plainclothes officer stationed at your apartment building while you're off duty."

I could feel the protective walls clanging up around me, just as they had for the years after my mother died. My father had gotten so strict and paranoid he barely let me out of the house then.

How would you see Roman again if you were being watched?

I shoved that inappropriate thought aside. "I don't need a bodyguard," I said firmly, "I have a gun."

"If somebody's trying to kidnap you—"

"It was probably a random attack," I lied. I hadn't told them about the attempted rape.

"And if it wasn't?"

"I managed to thwart the attempt last night, I will thwart the next one *if* it comes." My voice began to rise. "I will not be made a prisoner." *Again.*

My father looked at Espo, obviously trying to garner some support.

I stared at him with my own unspoken plea. *Please, Espo. Don't let him cage me.*

Espo took his time in speaking. "Obviously when she is at

work, I'm with her," he said. "Julianna's building is secure. As long as I escort her home after work every day and she doesn't go out alone at night, I don't see why she needs a protective guard. There's no evidence that Julianna was even targeted."

I had lied to them. I had told them that I had saved myself. I'd made myself sound like a regular G.I. Jane when in fact it was Roman who had been the hero last night. I wondered for a second what they would say if I told them the truth.

Probably have me committed.

My father sank his face into his hand and rubbed at his forehead.

"I'll be careful, I promise," I said. "Besides, I know you're short-staffed. You don't have a man spare to guard me. How would it look to voters if you took a uniform off his normal duties to play my shadow because of one random attack?"

My father leveled his stare at me. His lips pressed together. He didn't like it but I could see the resignation on his face. "Don't go around alone at night again, okay? I'll come to your place for dinner from now on."

I nodded, relieved that I had managed to escape with my freedom. Espo and I stood to leave.

"Espinoza, can I have a moment alone with my daughter, please?"

Espo nodded and left the room. I lowered myself back into the seat, my nerves jumping with anticipation. What did he want to talk to me about?

Does he not believe my story?

My father sank back in his chair, his amber eyes watching me carefully from under his bushy brows. Suddenly he seemed so much older now than I remembered him ever being. I could see the weariness in the bags under his eyes, in the permanent crease between his brows. This job was a set of thick chains slung across his shoulders, weighing them down.

He finally spoke. "I promised your mother that I would look

after you. That I would raise you right. Protect you when you needed it." He let out a soft laugh devoid of any amusement. "I don't know whether I've done a very good job."

I straightened in my chair. I wanted to launch from my seat, run around the desk and throw my arms around him. That's not how our relationship worked. "You did the best job a father could do. But I'm not a little girl anymore. Some things I need to take care of myself. Some things I need to decide for myself."

For some reason, I thought of last night when I let Roman into my bed.

Some mistakes I needed to make by myself.

~

When I finished work, Espo drove me home. I tried talking to him on the way but he answered in monosyllables. I knew something was up.

He pulled up outside my apartment building.

"You gonna tell me what's up or do I have to beat it out of you?" I said with a light teasing note to my voice.

Espo glanced at me out of the corner of his eye and pursed his lips. "You gonna tell me what really happened last night or do I have to beat it out of you?"

I froze. He knew something. I forced a confused look on my face. "I don't know what you're talking about."

He turned his torso to face me completely. "You're telling me you fought off two grown men with just your fists and your gun. And they both happened to get away before you could cuff them."

I gritted my teeth. "Just because I'm a woman doesn't make me helpless. You of all people know that I can take down a grown man larger than me."

"A grown man, yes. Two? That would've been a miracle."

"Oh ye of little faith."

"Don't give me that. I know when you're lying."

"I'm not lying."

"You know, a dirtbag by the name of Tate Jackson was found with his neck broken a few blocks down from where you said you'd been attacked."

"Oh yeah? What's that got to do with me?"

"You sure you were just off Grosvenor Road when they jumped you?"

"I am."

"It was dark. You could have mistaken the road you took back to your apartment."

"I'm not mistaken," I said through gritted teeth.

He let out a breath. "Okay. Whatever. You don't want to tell me what really happened, that's fine. I'm only your partner."

Way to lay down the guilt, Espo. "I told you everything. There's nothing else to tell."

Espo stared for me for a long moment, a hard pinch to the skin around his mouth. "Fine." The tone of his voice told me it was *not* fine. "See you tomorrow, *partner.*"

I felt like I'd been punched in the chest. I got out of the car, making sure to slam the door hard behind me, and walked into my apartment building without looking back.

Damn you, Roman, for coming into my life and messing it all up. Now I was outright lying to my father, my friends and my partner. My partner now suspected that something was up with me. I didn't know how much longer I could keep hiding secrets from them. I just hoped that when it all came out, when it all blew up in my face, no one I cared about got hurt.

JULIANNA

D ays went by. I didn't see or hear from Roman. The bitter pit grew in the base of my stomach. I thought that it had meant something for him to stay with me on the night I was attacked. I thought that maybe he cared. Only I'd woken up that next morning to find Roman gone, the only evidence that he'd even been there at all was the hint of his cologne on my sheets.

The truth was clear. He had stayed out of pity. I thought I was being open and vulnerable with him, instead I'd come off desperate; I had practically begged him to stay. I felt dirty, used, as if we'd slept together. Perhaps it would have been better if we did. Maybe I would have been able to brush it aside as a one-night stand. *For the second time.* I thought I deserved...something. Not this silence.

One evening, I found myself at Waverley Cathedral. Instead of walking around the back to the cemetery where my mother lay, I went inside the building. I needed to talk to someone living. I made my inquiries with an altar boy who was cleaning up the rows of old candles and was directed towards a room upstairs.

The door was already open. Father Laurence was sitting at his desk, pouring over the text of an ancient-looking open book.

I cleared my throat. "Father Laurence?"

He looked up, pulling his glasses off the end of his nose. "Julianna." His face broke into a smile. "Come in, please." He stood up, his chair making a scraping noise against the stone floor, before he walked around his desk towards me, his church robes swaying around his feet. "What a pleasant surprise."

He held out his hands and I took them. They were warm and slightly rough. He squeezed my fingers and leaned in to place a kiss on my cheek. He smelled of the church incense and of old books.

"I'm sorry to bother you, Father," I said.

"Not at all. Come. Sit." He directed me to an old couch, his visitor's couch. I'd sat on this very couch so many times after my mother had died, just taking comfort in Father Laurence's presence. My father had been so devastated by my mother's death that he had no room for my grief. I couldn't talk to him about her or even say her name. Father Laurence had given me that space I needed to grieve. He had been a confidant ever since. He was the one who gave me the courage to leave home and pursue my dream of joining the police academy.

Father Laurence studied me as he leaned back against the brown leather. "Now, what's on your mind?"

I inhaled and tried to figure out how I was supposed to start. Whether I should even start.

My eyes came to rest upon the bookshelf made of sturdy wood against the opposite wall. This was new. Filling one shelf was books, their spines reading *The Alchemy of Herbs, Herbs for Healing* and *The Power of Plants*. On the other shelves were glass jars filled with dried leaves, roots and flowers. "You've started studying plants?"

"Yes. Plants, herbs and their medicinal uses. But come, Julianna. You didn't come here to talk about my hobbies."

I sighed. "There's this boy. No, not a boy, far from a boy. He's most definitely a man Although, he often acts like a boy." I stopped suddenly, realizing I was rambling.

"You like him."

"Yes. I mean, no." I let out a frustrated noise. "I don't know."

"And he...likes you?"

"Sometimes I think so. Then other times... He's hot, then he's cold. He's the most confusing, frustrating man I've ever met. He's bossy and stubborn and jealous and he has such a temper on him. Sometimes I wish I could just..." I shook my hands as if I were choking his neck.

"I see," Father Laurence said quite simply.

Did he? Because I couldn't.

"Have you told him how you feel?" he asked.

Told Roman how I *feel*? I almost laughed. Then I felt like crying. I squeezed my eyes shut and shook my head.

"Why not?"

"I... I don't think I should. I don't know if it's right... But I don't know how to make this feeling stop."

Father Laurence let out a small hum.

I stayed in the safety of the darkness of my lids until Father Laurence spoke again. "Many years ago, I was in the same position you find yourself in now." He paused.

I opened my eyes. Father Laurence was staring at the floor, his eyes misty as he weighed his next words.

"Did you tell her?" I asked.

The corners of his mouth turned down. "No." That single word seemed to contain all the gravity of the world. "I failed to tell the woman I loved that I loved her. I failed to fight for her. Because at the time, I told myself it wasn't *right*."

"Why not?"

"At first, it was because I didn't want to risk the friendship we had. I was scared. Eventually, it was because she married another man. She died before I could tell her." Father Laurence raised his eyes to mine. I was startled to see they were wet. "It was and still is the single greatest regret of my life."

"Father..."

"Life is over much too soon," he said. "If you love him, Julianna, don't hold it back."

～

Father Laurence's words were banging around in my head as I dug around in my bag for my apartment keys. My phone rang. My heart did its usual skip at the thought that it could be Roman.

It was Christian. He'd already called a few times since our date and I hadn't returned any of his calls. I debated whether to ignore it. *Roman's ignoring you and look how that's making you feel.* I shoved these feelings inward and picked up the call, juggling the phone and my bag. "Hey, Christian."

"I heard about what happened. I can't believe someone tried to kidnap you. Thank God you're okay."

"How did you...? My father," I muttered, answering my own question. "Thanks for your concern, Christian. But I'm fine."

"What are you doing tonight? What if I come over and make you dinner? You shouldn't be alone."

I opened my door and froze. I wasn't alone. Roman was standing in my living room, waiting for me.

JULIANNA

Roman, as usual, looked incredible in dark denim and a fitted black t-shirt that stretched over his muscled arms. His hair was mussed and he had a scowl on his face, his hands jammed into his pockets.

I slammed the door shut behind me before one of my neighbors could see him. What was he doing here? Did he forget something? Did he find out something about my attackers?

"Hello? Julianna?" a distant voice called.

Shit. Christian was still on the phone.

"I-I'm fine. Really. Thanks. I gotta go." I hung up on him. I slid my phone and bag onto the side table. Roman still hadn't said anything. "What are you doing here?" I asked him.

"I shouldn't be here."

My eyes darted to the living room windows. He had drawn all the curtains. No one could see in. It was just him and me. Alone. A shiver fell across me. "No, you shouldn't."

"But I don't care."

"What?"

He just stared at me, hardly blinking. I don't think I'd ever seen him so serious. "It's what you do to me."

338

I blinked as my brain struggled to comprehend what the hell he was saying. "What do I do to you?"

"You make me not care about anyone or anything else. It's just you, you, you. You're all I want. You...You make me fucking crazy."

My stomach tightened, my head spinning at his admission. *You make me crazy too,* I wanted to say. I could barely breathe, let alone speak.

"I've tried to figure out," he began to advance on me, his face beginning to twist, a sharpness to his voice, "what is it about you? Why you? Of all the women to make me..." he trailed off.

I backed up until I hit the door. He was in my face, crowding me. I could scream, but I was pinned frozen by his wild stare.

"Why the hell did it have to be *you?*"

He wanted me. He didn't want to want me. Everything twisted inside me from my throat down to my core.

"I didn't ask for this either," I spat out.

"All the while I thought I was the dangerous one," he said, his eyes never leaving me. "You had me all fooled."

His finger gripped my chin, tilting my face up. His eyes dropped to my lips.

Kiss me.

Don't kiss me. If you kiss me, I'm done for.

"W-What are you doing?" I whispered.

"I can't stay away from you," he said, sounding pained. "I tried but I can't." His gaze rose to pin me with a stare so intense my toes curled. "I'm done trying."

Yes.

No.

My control. I was losing it. I was slipping.

Oh God. I am so screwed. I clung on to his words the last time he propositioned me. *"You have to understand why I can't offer you anything...more..."*

I swallowed and forced myself to look away. "No, Roman. One more night between us would—"

"I don't want *one* more night," he growled, leaning in so that his chest pressed against my swollen breasts. Dear God, he was everywhere. His scent and his heat rolling over me, his breath against my cheeks, his erection pressed against my belly, making my empty core ache. "I want all of them."

He wants…*what*?

"Give me all of your nights, Julianna," he murmured against my cheek. "*Be* with me."

My head spun and my heart slammed against my ribs so hard I thought he must feel it. *Me. Him. Together.* This felt so right. God, but it was *so* wrong…

"We don't make any sense," I whispered.

He pulled back to look at me, his eyes glistening with a tenderness I'd not seen before on him. He was standing here, naked and vulnerable before me. "Why does it have to make sense? This isn't something you plan for. This isn't something you schedule into your life with someone who meets a predetermined set of criteria. It just…happens."

"It just happens," I repeated, feeling the truth echo deep in my heart.

His fingers traced the bruise at my jaw so tenderly I almost wanted to cry. That was when I realized his fingers were shaking. "A couple of times in your life you meet someone and it just…clicks. Everything just clicks."

"Or just once," I said, barely a whisper.

A flash of surprise stole across his face. He nodded, barely a nod. "Or just once."

He moved for me as I moved for him. Our mouths crashed together. We were hungry and desperate, the frustration and longing built up over the last few days, exploding from ourselves, melting our two bodies together. There was no space between us but somehow I could not get close enough.

He slammed me up against the door. He tore his mouth from mine and began to bite down my neck as he pushed my shirt up off my body. "I've been wanting to fuck you against a door since that day you walked into my apartment wearing that silly red dress. So brazen. So arrogant."

"You're the bastard who answered the door in a goddamn towel," I hissed back at him, grabbing at his belt and undoing the zipper of his pants. I found his cock waiting for me, thick and hard as a rock. I wrapped a hand around it and he groaned, a noise that rumbled like thunder.

"You're the one who showed up unannounced." He palmed my swollen aching breasts and sucked at the peaks, making me groan. "I knew you wanted me even then."

"I did not."

"Liar." To punish me, he bit down on my nipple hard. Pleasure mixed with pain ricocheted through me, causing me to cry out. Wetness pooled in my already damp panties.

"You are the most arrogant man I've ever met."

"You are the most frustrating woman I have ever met." His fingers found my underwear under my skirt and in one swift move, he tore them apart.

I gasped as cold air hit my bare pussy. "Fuck you. You owe me a pair of panties." He grabbed my ass and I wrapped my legs around him. I moaned into his mouth and my fingers tangled into his hair, as his erection pressed against my aching core.

"Fuck you for making me wait for you." He thrust into me in one swift movement, pleasure and a hint of pain shuddering through my body. He didn't hesitate. There was no pause for me to get used to his size. He fucked me up against the door, the wood vibrating against the frame with every thrust. I felt every inch of his thick cock inside me, dragging against all my sensitive insides, lighting up my body with heat and pleasure. More, more, more, my body cried.

"Is that all you've got," I said, sneering at him, taunting him, baiting him. My hands dug into his shoulders as I hung on to him.

His eyes sparkled with hunger. "You're going to regret saying that."

"I doubt it."

He gripped my hips and slammed into me, hard and cruel and vicious, his fingers digging into my hips, causing tiny points of pain. I loved every violent stroke. I loved every brutal thrust.

We were soaring together, high and wild among the stars. From way up here, all the arguments against *us* seemed like mere power and dust. Roman and I were gods together. Immortal together. Floating among stardust. Spinning new universes with our bodies.

And when you fall back down to earth, a voice warned, *what a pretty tangle of blood and limbs you will make together.*

No matter the consequences, I told myself, *this is worth it. He is worth it.*

My body shook as my orgasm built. I bit into his shoulder. He cried out as I drew coppery blood. If it were at all possible, he fucked me harder in response. There were no words left. My head rolled back against the door and my vision went white as a red hot sun exploded inside me. I'm sure I screamed. He kept pumping into me over and over again, feeding my orgasm, shooting his own release into me in hot pulses.

We slid down to the floor, a sweaty tangle of limbs and raw lips.

ROMAN

I remember my father once telling me that my mother was the most beautiful creature he'd ever seen. She *was* beautiful. But as far as I was concerned, all women had something beautiful about them. How you could pick out one above all the others, I couldn't understand.

Until now.

There was something about Julianna. She just seemed to glow, as if the light inside of her was so strong, so pure, it lit up her skin. I found myself mesmerized by her dainty fingers, the soft curve of her lower back, the hollow at her neck. If God was an artist then she was his masterpiece. The slightly crooked tooth, that tiny freckle on her chest, it was all perfection.

I loved the teasing, sweet scent of her freshly washed hair, the way her skin gave way under my fingers, the way she threw back her head when she laughed...they were layer upon layer of melodies, all singing to me. She was my siren. My lighthouse.

She cuddled into the crook of my arm as if she accepted my protection. As if she needed it.

Mine to protect. This whisper grew and grew inside me until it rang in my soul like a bell and my chest swelled with purpose.

And yet, a sour knot sat in my gut, a bitter seed taken root. Would she still want my protection if she knew what I'd done? Would she still look at me the same? Could she love a murderer?

I almost laughed at myself. Stupid boy. Of course she wouldn't. I was a monster hiding under a façade of a man misunderstood. She had fallen for it.

I didn't deserve her. But I was a selfish, selfish man. I would keep her. Hold her tight. For as long as I could. Until the day she figured it out and she ended me.

JULIANNA

hen I woke up Roman was gone. As if he was never here. As if last night was just a dream, a glorious, wonderful dream broken by the harsh morning light filtering through the edge of my curtains.

But a dull, empty ache lay between my legs, my nipples tender from his teeth, my ass from his palms. I rolled over to his side and pressed my nose into his pillow. Cedar cologne and man. If I could bottle up that combination, I'd make millions. Memories of last night flashed through my mind, making my body ache all over again.

My stomach gave an uneasy flutter. Why did he disappear this morning without saying goodbye? Did he regret last night? Did he realize it was stupid for us to risk a relationship?

Something crinkled as I moved. It was a small note on white paper crushed under my arm.

Tonight. Make sure no one follows you.

. . .

Underneath was an address. Roman had told me about his mother's secret apartment. This must be it.

Tonight. I'd see him again tonight. Butterflies took off in my stomach. I had to bite my lip to stop from laughing. Roman and I. We were really doing this.

~

Something had been bothering me since my kidnapping attempt two nights ago—had it only been two nights ago? At work, when Espo had gone out for lunch, I opened our arrests database. From Roman's reaction to the name Goldfish, I suspected that it would be someone who had a reputation in the Verona underworld, likely someone who had a record. I typed in "Goldfish" and hit search.

I sat back in my chair as I waited for the results, glancing around me at the few officers who were at their desks, nodding at one of them who caught my eye. All of this, my job, my reputation, my career, I was risking being with Roman Tyrell. If we were ever caught…

I imagined the worst, trying to bathe myself in these stupid risks I was taking, a part of me hoping that these realities would snap me out of the insane decision I had made last night. That I would continue to risk if I went to him tonight.

Somehow, all these consequences just lapped around me like inconsequential waves. My deep longing for Roman, which began at the very sight of him, had in these last few weeks grown into something…greater. Like a mountain risen out of the sea. I was tied to him like he was to me.

And where could this relationship possibly ever go, Julianna? spoke a bitter voice inside me. *Do you think you'll marry Roman and have his children? Will both your families be present at your wedding?*

I shoved these thoughts away as my search results came up. I had no answers. A single entry was headed, Tito "Goldfish" Brevio.

Brevio? I frowned as I clicked it to open the file.

There was an arrest photo of a man in his mid-fifties, softening skin around his mouth, a few dark freckles on his cheeks. He had an almost bored look as he stared at the camera, his head slightly tilted.

My blood drained as I read the details of his file. This is why the name sounded so familiar. Goldfish was Mercutio's father.

Before he went into hiding, he worked for the Tyrells.

JULIANNA

Nobody followed me that night. I made sure of it. I doubled back and went a circuitous way to make sure. I slipped inside a small nondescript building on the edge of downtown Verona.

What am I doing here? My feet padded on the old worn carpet of the lobby. This was a far cry from Roman's real apartment. *The handler working for the man who tried to kidnap me works for the Tyrells.*

Used to. He might not work for the Tyrells anymore. *Think of how surprised Roman was to hear his name. If Giovanni Tyrell was after you, Roman had nothing to do with it.*

Stupid girl. You really are so naïve and foolish.

I rode the elevator and stepped out onto the landing of the fourth floor before making my way to the faded gray door marked 17, the fluorescent light above me flickering ominously. I was here to confront Roman. I had to look him in the eyes when I told him what I knew. I had to watch his reaction. Then I'd know for sure.

I knocked. He answered the door within seconds.

For a moment, he just stared at me from the doorway, relief

clear in his eyes. He pulled me into the apartment, locking the door behind us. He wrapped his arms around me, his face burying into my neck. "Fuck, you smell so damn good. I thought I might go mad today wondering if you'd come. I wanted to stay until you woke this morning but..."

I didn't move to hug him back. He pulled back, one of his hands pushing back the hair from my face. "What's wrong?" He searched my face. His own cracked into an icy mask. "You've come here to tell me that we are a mistake, haven't you?"

"Tito 'Goldfish' Brevio," I said simply.

Roman tensed against me. "I wanted to tell you..."

"But you were afraid at how it'd look?" I finished for him.

He paused. "Yes."

"Did you know?" My voice had turned to ice. "Was this some kind of ruse to gain my trust?"

"No!" he said, his features twisting. "How could you even think...?" His lip curled up. "No, I understand exactly why you would think that. There's no reason why you should trust me."

I let out a small breath of relief. I knew from his reaction, Roman hadn't been in on it. "Is Tito still working for your father? Am I in danger from your family?"

His nostrils flared with rage. Before I could back away he grabbed my face in his hands. His touch was firm, bordering on painful. The power in his grip, raw and coiled, triggered a deer-like reaction in me and I froze with a gasp.

"I will never *ever* let anyone hurt you, least of all my own fucking family. I would kill them all, my cousins, my brother, even my own damn father, before I let them touch a single hair on your head. Do you understand me?"

I. Couldn't. Breathe.

I could barely think. My mind had gone.

Fuck, I think even my heart stopped.

He took a deep, shaky breath. When he spoke again his voice was calmer. "Do you understand me?"

I nodded. Or at least I thought I did.

"Words, Julianna. I need to hear them."

"Yes," I croaked out. I had to clear my throat, it had gotten so dry. "I understand."

"Good." His grip relaxed but he didn't let go of my face. "You don't need to be scared of me. Ever."

"I'm not," I lied. The truth was, I was scared. I was downright terrified. But not because I might lose my life...

I was scared I'd lose my heart.

I was terrified at how hard I seemed to be falling for him, even though it didn't make any rational, logical sense, and that I just didn't seem to care about the consequences.

Most of all, I feared the day that we'd be torn apart.

"Good," he said again. On his face was a shadow of a smile.

His eyes dropped to my mouth. His thumb brushed along my bottom lip. A shiver ran through me, my nipples instantly hardening. How was it possible that one tiny touch from him was enough to fill me with such *want*? He knew too, the bastard. His eyes glistened with smug hunger as they rolled over my body.

I felt myself blushing. "Aren't... Aren't you going to show me your mother's apartment?" I had barely registered anything when I came in.

"Later." Roman picked me up and wrapped my legs around his waist before pressing me up against the door.

"And this?" I picked up a small photo frame made of knobby unbaked clay edged in seashells. It had been broken once into a dozen or so pieces, but it had been glued back together. It framed a photo of a stunning woman and a young boy. I recognized those eyes. This must be Roman when he'd been a boy. And his mother.

Roman laughed as he came up behind me, snatching the

photo frame out of my hands and placing it back on the shelf. He spun me to face him and draped my arms around his neck. "You're a very curious creature."

"Only because you never like to give anything away about yourself. The surest way to stop me from asking questions is to tell me everything."

"Never. If I do, you'll stop being curious about me."

"I'll never stop being curious."

His eyes traced down my body. He let out a low growl. "Have I told you how incredible you look wearing *just* my shirt?"

I laughed. "Only about a thousand times."

"Prepare to hear it a thousand more." He leaned down to kiss me but I dodged his lips.

"You still haven't told me about the seashell frame."

He let out a long sigh and wrapped his arms around me, kissing the top of my head. "I was ten. I made it for my mother using shells that I'd collected from her favorite beach. My brothers teased me for being so sentimental and broke it. I thought she had thrown the pieces away but...she must have hidden it here and glued it back together."

"You loved her so much, didn't you?"

"But it wasn't enough."

I turned to face him. "What does that mean?"

Roman's face cracked, a deep pain flashing in his eyes. "I loved her but I couldn't stop her from dying."

"You couldn't have done anything, Roman."

He shook his head. "You don't understand." It came out a whisper.

"Understand what?"

"The newspapers were right. I killed her."

JULIANNA

My breath turned to stone in my windpipe. "What do you mean, you killed her?"

He rubbed his face and began to turn away.

I grabbed his arms, forcing him to face me. I could not believe that Roman killed his mother. I couldn't. "Roman. Tell me. Please?"

He inhaled sharply and dropped his hand from his face, revealing glassy eyes. "That night she was supposed to sit up on the roof of the house with me. It was our spot. Our thing, to look at stars. She had gotten a call from my father. I knew it was him because she had that look on her face when she got off the phone, tight mouth, unfocused eyes. She told me she had to go somewhere, she wouldn't tell me why. I was upset that she was ditching me. I had yelled at her that she didn't love me and slammed my bedroom door in her face. I heard her apologizing through my door, begging me to unlock it, to hug her before she left. But I didn't and she gave up. I felt like such a shit. So I ran downstairs to catch her before she left."

Roman took in a deep breath and let it out audibly. I realized then that I had been holding mine. He sat on the bed, his shoulders slumping, as if the weight of his story was so heavy he could not hold it any longer.

I sat down next to him, pulled his hand into both of mine and squeezed. *I'm here.*

"I heard her muffled scream," he said, "as I approached the garage. I froze in the doorway. She was in the front seat of her car, struggling with someone in the backseat. He had his hand over her mouth, a knife in his hand."

I sucked in a breath. "Did you see his face?"

He shook his head. "He was wearing a mask. The driver's door was open, an unlit cigarette fallen on the floor."

"Your mother's cigarette?" I asked.

He nodded. "She started smoking a few months before. I hated it. She only ever smoked in the car...or when she was out..." he trailed off.

"Roman, you don't have to tell me any more."

He shook his head. Despite the pain showing through the cracks in his face, I could see that he needed to speak, to finally pull this burden off his shoulders and share it. I waited for him to continue. We sat in silence. We sat so long in silence I thought he would not go on.

"She must have pressed the cigarette lighter on as soon as she got into the car. She plunged it into the back of her assailant's hand, burning him. He screamed and let go of her. I remember seeing a red circular burn on the back of his hand. She scrambled out of the car and tripped to the ground. Her eyes locked on mine. She screamed at me to run! Run! All the while I was screaming at myself to...to *do something.* To *stop him.* But I couldn't move.

"He was too fast. He was suddenly behind her, grabbing her. I still couldn't move. I just *watched* as his knife sliced across her neck."

"Roman, you didn't kill her. *He* did."

"I did nothing to stop it."

"You were *only* twelve."

"I was old enough." The pain reflected in Roman's broken eyes reached into my chest and squeezed at my heart. He looked just like a boy at that moment: lost and scared. I swallowed back my tears. No child should ever, ever have to go through something like that.

"He sliced her throat and then he dropped her. He just stared at me for a few seconds, black beady eyes from two slits in his mask. Then he ran. Only then did I go to her. But it was too late... Her blood was spreading all around her. Afterwards, I didn't say a word to the police. I just remembered what my father always said, 'never to talk to the coppers'. I said nothing. He got away with it."

I wanted to tell him not to give up hope. That one day his mother's murderer would be brought to justice. But it would be a lie. I couldn't even bring my own mother's murderer to justice.

"I loved her so much," he said, "but it didn't matter. I couldn't protect her..."

So he couldn't protect me, I filled in what was left unsaid. A missing piece fell into place. This was why Roman kept pushing me away. He was afraid of loving me. He was afraid that he couldn't protect me. He was afraid that one day he would lose me the same way that he lost his mother.

I turned back to the seashell frame and traced the faint broken cracks that now seemed so obvious. If only hearts were as easy to fix. "I wished I had known her," I said.

He gave me a small smile, the tension slowly lifting as he wrapped his arms around me and pulled me into his lap. "She would have loved you."

I felt a tiny sun glowing in my chest. "You think so?"

"Yeah. You're as stubborn as she was."

I slapped his arm.

He let out a soft chuckle. "I didn't say that was a bad thing. You're alike in a lot of ways, actually."

"Oh?"

"You're both beautiful, radiant, independent, stubborn. And..." he added quietly, "you care too much for all the wrong men."

I began to protest but something in his eyes appeared distant and dulled, his arms suddenly stiff like a wooden puppet. He had shut himself off to me in an instant.

It hit me like a knife in the gut. He truly believed he was the wrong man for me. Nothing I could say or do would ever convince him otherwise.

I realized then, the greatest danger that we faced was not his family, but himself. Our relationship would never survive. Because he would never believe he was worth it.

JULIANNA

My phone screamed in my ear. I groped around, struggling to scramble my way out of the mire of sleep. I caught the source of my unfriendly awakening. As I answered, the clock on my phone read three-oh-seven a.m.

"Sorry to call so early, Capi." It was Espo. Which meant only one thing. Another body.

"It's fine, I..." I sat up, blinking in the dark. I was hit with the realization that the shadows around me were unfamiliar. I was naked, the sheets tangled around my legs, but I was not in my bedroom.

Roman. I had stayed the night at Roman's secret apartment. I hadn't intended to but...the glorious hour I'd spent with him turned to two, three... I must have fallen asleep.

I glanced to my right. Roman's side of the bed was empty, the moonlight filtering across the bare crumpled sheets. Did he leave?

"We got a body on the outskirts of Verona. I'll pick you up in ten."

"No!" Shit. There was no way I could get dressed and rush home in time to pretend that I had been in my apartment all along. "I can meet you there. Text me the address."

"Seriously, Capi. Your apartment is on my way anyway."

I cringed. "I'm, um, not at my apartment."

There was a pause. Then Espo's voice came on with a chuckle. "You sly dog, you. Capi's gettin' laid," he sang.

"Okay. That's enough from you." I slid out of bed, grabbing my clothes flung about the room, my cheeks burning when I remembered how they all got there.

"Tell me where you are and I'll pick you up from there."

"No, it's fine. I'll catch a cab."

"Seriously. It's no big deal."

"I'm not on your way."

Espo sniffed. "You don't want me to meet this mysterious new man of yours."

If only he knew how close to the truth he was. "Don't be silly, Espo," I hissed. "It's faster if I just meet you there. Text me the address." I hung up and threw the phone on the bed. Dammit. I didn't have a change of clothes with me. I'd have to wear the same ones from yesterday. My underwear, where was my underwear?

I didn't have time to search for it. I cringed as I tugged on my pencil skirt sans panties and tucked in my button-up shirt as best as I could in the dark. I'd have to buy a new pair on my break.

"Roman?" I slipped through the apartment, following the muffled rhythmic sound of slapping. I located the source of noise behind a closed door, a thin stream of light showing the underside. I opened the door and poked my head in.

It was a bedroom converted into a small gym. Roman was bouncing around a boxing bag wearing only low-hanging shorts and a pair of black boxing wraps. His glorious chest and arms were on display, pumped up from exertion and glistening with sweat. Desire warmed my lower belly. I found myself licking my lips at I stared.

Roman caught my eye. He stopped punching and clung to the bag to stop it from swaying. "Sorry, did I wake you?"

I shook my head. "What are you doing up?"

He looked away, wiping his forehead with the back of his hand. "I couldn't sleep."

I knew him well enough to know that this wasn't the whole story. Something was bothering him.

"Something on your mind?" I walked into the room towards him, drawn in by his pure masculinity and the intoxicating smell of his sweat mixed with his signature cologne.

He ignored my question, his brows furrowing as he eyed me fully dressed. "Where are you going?" He glanced over to the clock on the wall. "At three in the morning?"

"I got a call from work. They've found a body."

I moved in to kiss him but he avoided my grasp. "I'm sweaty."

I didn't care. He obviously did. I frowned at him, my fingers itching to touch him but feeling like for some reason beyond the excuse he'd given me, he didn't want me to. "Will I see you later?"

He nodded. But he didn't say when. I turned, a knot building in my stomach, and walked through his apartment towards the front door. Something was wrong. Why wouldn't he touch me? I had a sudden flash, a premonition, the feeling that a dark star of fate was descending towards us.

"Jules," I heard as my hand touched the doorknob.

I turned, surprised at how close he was. He'd barely made a sound as he followed me through the apartment. There was something heavy in his eyes. Before I could decipher it, he grabbed my chin with his fingertips and kissed me. His lips were firm, hungry, his kiss swift and heated. If I hadn't been so surprised I would have moved closer to him, grabbed him, taken the closeness he had deprived me of before.

He pulled away, his fingers lingering on my jaw before they dropped away. "Be careful."

I studied his face, his dark hooded eyes, his pinched brows, his clenched jaw, trying to uncover the hidden meaning to his words.

I forced a smile. "Always."

JULIANNA

I slid out of the cab, pulled up along a deserted road on the outskirts of Verona. Response team cars littered the side of the one-lane dirt road, an arthritic fence lining one side, an unkempt field stretching out from the other. The familiar yellow tape fluttered in the early morning breeze.

It was still too dark, sunrise still hours away. Spotlights had been set up, turning pieces of rock into bladed shadows. The forensics team was milling around, their flashlights scanning the ground, taking photos, gathering evidence into bags and plastic containers.

Under a large spotlight, Lacey was crouched over a prone body on the side of the road facing the field. Espo was kneeling by her side, no humor on his face, no flirtation evident. The victim was lying on his stomach, the back of his head a bloody mess of bone and gray matter, the spotlight glistening off the blood like rubies. It was like some twisted gothic stage play. Except this was real, tension strung tight across the dark morning.

Lacey looked up as I approached. The skin around her eyes was stretched and the hollows of her cheekbones seemed more pronounced. She would have been one of the first they called, so she'd have had even less sleep than me. She frowned. "Are you wearing the same clothes from yesterday?"

I flushed. Here we go.

"Oh yeah," said Espo, amusement in his tone, "*someone* didn't go home last night."

Lacey gave me a surprised look, a flash of hurt underneath it. She and I had gotten close since she started work at the precinct. I should have mentioned a new love interest to her. "Who's the lucky guy?"

I shrugged, trying very hard to appear nonchalant. All the while my stomach was doing flips. "Just a guy."

"She won't give out any details," Espo said aside to Lacey.

"Really?" she replied.

"Which makes me think there's something wrong with him."

Lacey let out a gasp. "Like maybe a hump on his back."

"Or a peg leg."

"Or he's bald."

I rolled my eyes. "Guys, I'm standing right here."

"Or," Espo turned his sharp twinkling eyes towards me, "he's someone we know and she's embarrassed."

I felt the blood drain from my face as Espo's eyes bored into me; they seemed to tear away every shroud I'd covered my secrets with. For a moment, I wondered if he *knew*.

I cleared my throat. "I think we should focus on our poor victim rather than my boring love life." My voice came out tight and higher than I intended.

Lacey and Espo gave each other a conspiratorial look before Lacey turned her attention to the body lying on his stomach. "Hispanic male, mid-thirties, no wallet, no ID, no phone. Found here less than an hour ago by a passing car." She pointed up the road where two kids, who appeared to be teenagers, were huddled together wrapped in heavy blankets despite the warm summer breeze, staring at the ground. Poor things. Seeing a dead body was not something normal people got used to.

I got a flash of my attacker with the broken neck. I shook it away and kneeled beside the victim. A sharp smell hit my nose. I noticed then the victim appeared to be damp. "Is that...bleach?"

"Ten points to Capi," Espo said. "Appears our killer tried to *clean up* after himself."

I rolled my eyes. "You're so *punny*."

"Espo," Lacey said, "can you help turn him to his side. I just want to check lividity."

Espo nodded and carefully rolled the victim towards me. My stomach dropped as I stared at his familiar yet bloodied face.

Eddie Sanchez.

One of the men who tried to kidnap me. The one that Roman threatened in that warehouse. The one who gave us the name Goldfish.

"I wanted to kill him." I remembered Roman's face as he spoke these words to me, all twisted features etched in black hate.

I swallowed hard and stared at Eddie's open eyes, the unthinkable rising to the surface of my thoughts no matter how hard I tried to push it away.

Roman Tyrell *did not* kill Eddie Sanchez. He promised on his mother's memory that he'd get Eddie to safety.

"Jesus," Lacey said, "his zipper's undone. His...*thing's* hanging out. Like the poor guy just stopped for a piss."

"Jules, you okay?" Espo was frowning at me.

"Fine." I tried to school my features into one of professional distance. No one could know that the victim was one of the men who tried to rape and kidnap me.

"Do you know this guy?"

I shook my head, a little too hard, a little too quickly.

Lacey continued, "COD is a gunshot wound to the back of the head. Execution style. We'll know more once I get his body back to the morgue. There's a lot of blood here and lividity is fixed so it's safe to say that he was shot here."

"Do you know time of death yet?" I asked. If time of death was last night, then I know Roman couldn't have done it. He was with me.

"I'm estimating some time two nights ago, but I'll know more once I get him back to the lab."

My head spun. That was the night that Roman had supposedly taken Eddie to safety. Roman had come to my apartment after he'd dropped Eddie off. But I had no idea what time that had been.

I shoved those thoughts away. *No*, I told myself firmly. *No more of that.* Roman Tyrell was not a murderer. He did not kill Eddie Sanchez just like he didn't kill Vinnie Torrito.

I rode to the station with Espo as the skyline of Verona began to lighten, a great unease sitting like a jumbled ball of live wires in my belly. I pretended like I was taking a quick nap, slumped in the passenger seat, forehead leaning against the window, eyes shut. I could sense that Espo kept glancing over at me.

"So...new boyfriend, huh?"

I sighed internally and opened my eyes. No point in trying to pretend I was asleep.

What would Roman say if he knew someone had called him my "boyfriend"? Was he my boyfriend? It seemed such a juvenile term for what he was to me. "I wouldn't call him a boyfriend, exactly."

"Good for you. About time you got a little sumthin' sumthin'."

Roman's fingers sinking into my wet folds...his tongue flicking against my sensitive bud...his thick cock rubbing against the deepest parts of me... I turned my face to look out the window in case Espo could see me flushing.

"Same guy who sent you those roses?"

My flush turned into an ache in my chest. "Yeah."

"Well, I hope it works out."

No, you don't. Not if you knew who it was.

At the station, I excused myself to go to the bathroom. In the privacy of a stall, I dialed Roman's burner cell he'd kept just for me. With every ring of the dial tone, my unease grew. *Come on, pick up.*

It rang out.

Dammit, Roman, where are you?

I tried again but there was still no answer.

JULIANNA

Me: Roman, call me when you get this. It's important.

JULIANNA

Me: Why aren't you answering my calls? Call me back. It's urgent.

JULIANNA

Me: Please, Roman. Where are you? Just tell me you're okay.

JULIANNA

Two days.

It was now two damn days since I'd left Roman that early morning at his secret apartment. I'd had no messages. No missed calls. Not a word from him.

I couldn't sleep the last two nights. I kept tossing and turning, staring past my open curtains, willing that his familiar figure would darken my window.

He never came.

My stomach was so twisted in knots I couldn't eat. I just kept thinking that something...something terrible had happened. I could feel it in my twisted gut.

Why wasn't he answering his phone? Was he hurt? Was he... dead? Wouldn't I feel it if he'd been ripped away from this earth?

"What's up, girl?"

I shook myself out of my thoughts. "Huh?"

Lacey stared at me, her thick eyelashes blinking, the fluorescent lights of the morgue causing shadows in the creases of her frown. "Have you even heard a word I said?"

I gave her a sheepish look. "Sorry. Just things on my mind."

"You don't say." She gave me a once-over. "Care to share?"

I shook my head. "It's nothing. Just tell me what you've found out about Eddie."

Lacey stared at me for a moment longer, lips pressed together. She seemed to be debating whether to push me.

"It's just personal stuff. Family stuff," I said quietly.

Lacey nodded, then turned to the body lying on the slab, a large Y-incision stitched up with thick thread making him look like Frankenstein's monster. I could have hugged her for letting it go so easily.

"See all this bruising?" She pointed to his ribs and cheek. I could almost see Roman's fists as he made those bruises. "Somebody worked him over pretty good. But the bruising was done hours before death."

"So it's possible that whoever beat him up, didn't kill him," I said, my heart skipping a little.

Lacey lifted a perfectly arched eyebrow. "Sure. It's possible."

My head was already whirring. I bolted out of the morgue calling thanks over my shoulder.

I glanced around me as I sat at my desk. Espo had up and ran off somewhere a few minutes ago after he'd gotten a phone call. No one was paying any attention to me. I opened the phone number tracing software on my computer. It was a risk I was taking. Every search created a history log. But I was desperate.

I typed in Roman's burner phone number and hit search, my eyes glancing around me as the results triangulated.

The software made a small noise indicating it was done. My eyes slid to the screen. Nothing. The satellite couldn't locate the phone number. His burner phone was either off or there was no reception wherever he was. *Dammit, Roman, where are you?* I made a vow to head to his secret apartment tonight after work if I still hadn't heard from him. If he wasn't there, I'd go to the Tyrell apartment.

"Capi!" Espo yelled from behind me.

I jolted, closed the trace down on my computer and spun in my seat.

Espo jogged up to me, waving a piece of paper, his face flushed, his eyes bright. He didn't seem to notice my nervousness nor did he stare at me with suspicion. That was a relief. I pushed away my thoughts over Roman and forced a smile. "You look like you just won the lottery."

"You know that witness at the gas station?"

I frowned. We'd canvassed the gas stations and convenience stores around the area where Eddie's body was found. One of the gas stations had turned up a witness who'd claimed he'd seen a car and two men stopping there just before time of death. The security cameras at this gas station were fakes, so no tape. "Yeah?"

"Just got his artist's sketch." Espo slammed the paper down on my desk and stabbed at it with a thick finger. "Who does this look like to you?"

My stomach turned over itself, the pencil lines on the artist's sketch blurring before me. This could not be happening. "Who?" I asked, even though I *knew*.

Espo leaned in, his eyes glittering with excitement. "Roman Tyrell."

ROMAN

Two days earlier...

I made the mistake of checking my phone after Julianna had fallen asleep in my bed. I found a message waiting for me.

Giovanni: Tomorrow we have something important to do. Be ready at 6am. Abel will fetch you.

Fetch me. Like I was a stick he liked to throw around. I imagined smashing my phone. I imagined burrowing myself into Julianna so deep that he'd never find me. I imagined disappearing into the far corners of the earth; all I'd need was Julianna by my side.

Only she'd *never* run with me, she'd made that much clear. Verona was her home. Who the hell was I to her?

Tomorrow we have something important to do.

These words filled me with a cold dread. Whatever it was that my father had planned, it would not be good. Our father-son outings ended in guns drawn or someone dead. Each time a little bit more of me blackened. Each time a little more of me became accustomed to his brand of "justice". I could sense Darkness lay waiting for me, softly laughing, fingernails clicking.

I couldn't sleep after that. My mind folded over and over, arguing for me, against me. The cold truth frosted over my heart as the cold dawn crept ever closer. I couldn't escape who I was.

"Something on your mind?"

I turned away from my boxing bag to find Julianna standing at the door to my gym. Shit. I hadn't meant to wake her. Then I noticed she was dressed. "Where are you going? At three in the morning?" I couldn't help the accusation in my voice.

"I got a call from work. They've found a body."

Today she would be solving a crime. Today I would be committing one. The reminder of how different we were slid into my gut, injecting me with self-loathing. She tried to hold me but I pushed her hands away. She didn't deserve my filth on her clean skin. "I'm sweaty," I grunted, like the creature I was.

A small crease appeared between her brows. "Will I see you later?"

I remembered my hands, the blood under my fingernails after the night I shot Vinnie Torrito. I remember the foul, wretched creature I had morphed into afterwards. Whatever my father was going to have me do today would be worse; I could feel it. I could not let her see me afterwards. Not until I had pulled myself together. Not until I had scraped the remaining gentle, warm pieces of me back into place, patting them down like pieces of clay to cover back up the rotten black core. I said nothing, promised her nothing.

I watched her face fall, her pain evident from my cold dismissal. Didn't she realize how bound I was to her? She had me. She ruled me. Couldn't she see that it was all for her? It was so painfully obvious to me.

I couldn't let her walk away with doubt in her heart.

I went after her. "Jules."

She turned, her hand on the doorknob. I grabbed her chin, tilting her face up to meet my crushing lips. The growing sense of doom sizzled like a poison in my blood. I kissed her as if her lips held the antidote to death. I kissed her as if it was the last time. I had only borrowed her. One day soon I would lose her.

Julianna froze, perhaps shocked at the desperate turnabout of my attention. I wanted to roar and beat my chest, lock her away here with me and never let her out of my sight. That would be the only way I could protect her.

You can't protect her. Just like you couldn't protect Mama.

I let go of her before I scared her any further. Before I scared myself with the violence of my desperation. "Be careful," I said, trying not to let fear creep into my voice.

The smile she gave me back was forced.

Abel was waiting for me on my couch, robed in black like a Master of Death, when I returned to the Tyrell apartment at about ten past six that morning. "Where've you been?" His face was twisted into a snarl, probably from having to wait for me.

"For me to know and for you to find out." I walked past him into my bedroom, barely glancing at him, an obvious dismissal.

He followed me. I could practically smell his acrid breath over my shoulder. "You're late. Your father's waiting."

"Calm down, dog. Let me drop my gym bag and we can be off."

As I dropped my bag on my still-made bed, I felt my burner phone buzzing in the bottom of the bag. Julianna. She was the only one who had that number. Why was she ringing me at six in the morning A strange feeling echoed in the pit of my stomach. Whatever it was, I couldn't take her call now. I'd have to wait until I got back from...whatever my father had planned. I grabbed the gun from my bedside table and strapped it to my hip.

"Where are we going?" I asked when the driver of the limo that drove Abel to fetch me missed the turnoff towards my father's mansion, continuing down the highway out of Verona. Seeds of apprehension sprouted weeds in my gut.

Abel smirked at me from the opposite seat, a slimy thin-lipped smile that made his scar whiten. "For me to know and for you to find out."

Bastard. I strained not to fidget in the leather seat, watching the city hurtling past.

My stomach had become a knot of thorns as the limo pulled up into a small airfield. My father and a small entourage of black-suited men were waiting, a private jet waiting behind them, our family crest emblazoned in gold on the tail and wings.

"I said seven o'clock takeoff," snapped my father to Abel as we got out of the limo.

"Apologies, sir. We were delayed." Abel shot me a murderous stare.

My father grunted and turned towards the plane. I repeated my question to him as I strode beside him, watching our long morning shadows like ominous twins before us on the tarmac.

My father clasped me on the shoulder, pushing me forward to take the short flight of steps up to the jet. "It's time you learn about the true heart of our business, son."

"The true heart?" I sank into a plush cream leather seat inside the luxurious cabin.

My father nodded. "We're going to Colombia."

ROMAN

Six hours later, we landed on a private airstrip, a leveled field in the middle of a dense jungle. Our entourage piled into three camo-painted four-wheel drives and took off down a dirt track through the forest. My stomach was rumbling as I was thrown around in the back seat, the air humid and stifling so that with every breath it felt like I was taking in less and less oxygen. My father sat to my left, Abel in the front seat.

We broke through the jungle and passed through a heavily guarded gate. Up a long gravel driveway surrounded by trees was a monstrous house on a hill, all glass and whitewashed walls making it look like a ripe, unnatural pimple upon the earth. We could have been on the gaudy side of Hollywood hills, except for the wild monkeys that scattered through the trees as we approached. We pulled up in front of the circular driveway. A thickset figure stepped from the door wearing a pressed white shirt unbuttoned at the collar, matching white pants and blue snakeskin shoes. He had an unlit cigar in his mouth.

"Well, well, well," he said in greeting. "Baby brother has finally come to visit me."

Marco, my other brother. I hadn't seen him in eight years. I didn't come back from Europe when the news broke that he had been charged for knifing a man in the back during a bar and had fled the country. That had been six years ago.

"Marco. It's been a while." He seemed smaller than I remembered. Then again, I'd grown a lot in eight years. He looked less like the fearsome and unyielding brother that I remembered, and more like a man who was trying too hard to be a king. His swagger looked borrowed and his ego seemed much too big for him.

Marco shot me a smirk. "It's such a coincidence that Jacob was murdered, leaving you to snatch the Tyrell throne. Have you come to steal the rest of *my* inheritance, too?" he asked, the bitterness clear in his tone.

He should have been the one by my father's side today, not the one exiled to a savage jungle country. He should be the next in line to the throne, the king of Verona and all that surrounded it. He still hadn't accepted the fact that *he* had been the hot-headed idiot who thought that being a Tyrell meant that you were invincible in the eyes of the law; we were, but only if you were smart about it. He was still looking for someone to blame for his demotion, his misfortune. I was the clear target, the usurper to his rightful throne. He couldn't see that the "prize" was really a chain around my neck. He didn't realize that the "heaven" he desired with a sickness was actually hell. My hell.

The air filled with hot tension. I could feel all the men's eyes on me, waiting to see what I would do. I would be judged by my actions. My weakness studied. My faults assessed. I could not look weak or I would be killed in my sleep here by an ambitious soldier. Or by my brother himself.

I leapt out of the jeep and landed toe to toe with Marco, gravel flicking out from my heels. Marco flinched. First point to me.

I lifted my lip in a sneer. "And if I did want to take it, who has the power to stop me? You, *brother?*" I spat out. I rolled my eyes over his body. I towered over him by two inches now. He'd let himself grow soft, his belly tumbling out of the top of his suit pants. "Too bad you let yourself go. I'd gut you before you could touch me."

Marco let out a forced laugh and looked around at our audience. A red flush had crept up his neck. "I was just joking, Roman. Lighten up."

I gave him a tight smile. "I'm not," I said in a voice low enough so only he could hear. "Watch your step, Marco."

"Where's your wife? Where's little Azucena?" my father asked, breaking the tension. Marco cleared his throat, shot me a weary look, and moved past me to walk my father through the open French doors. After he'd fled here, Marco had married a local Colombian girl. Azucena was the daughter that they'd adopted because his wife couldn't have children naturally. She'd be eleven now if I remembered correctly. I'd never met her.

"Sofia's in Bogota with Azucena," I heard Marco say, a note of contempt in his voice. "Spending my money on shoes and dolls and God knows what else. It's just us men."

I followed them through the climate controlled house. It was an attempt to replicate my father's mansion back in Verona; all glaring white and too much cold marble. Abel and the other suited monkeys cleared the rooms before they stationed themselves around the house like a well-oiled circus.

Marco took us out to the back balcony that stretched almost the length of the living area inside, coca plantations like a patchwork quilt across the jungle beyond. My family owned all the land as far as the eye could see, bursting with the flat leaves of the coca plant as green as money.

"We can produce cocaine here at about $1,500 per kilo in our labs," my father said to me as we stood along the balustrade. He cut off the end of a Camacho cigar and lit it, the ruby end sparking as he puffed away. "It sells for up to $50,000 per kilo in

America. A return of over 3,000 percent," he announced in a puff of smoke like some kind of magic trick.

Three thousand percent return. It only cost you your soul.

"Marco oversees the operations from this side," my father said. I glanced at Marco and found him already glaring at me. "If you're to run the American side, you need to know how it works. We'll take you for a tour through the plantation in a little while. But first, we eat."

After lunch, an over-catered affair of imported meats, cheeses, breads, pasta and Dom Perignon, we took the same four wheel drives through the plantations. We passed gaunt sun-leathered workers being carefully guarded by well-fed men with rifles.

"We provide work for the local communities," my father said as we drove past field after lush field. "We've installed street-lights, provided clean running water, built a local school. We've done much to support them. They are much better off."

I could only stare at him as the jeep rattled my bones. He truly thought he was doing good. The drug dealer with a heart of gold. I wanted to puke.

We passed through the workers' camp, a jumble of huts ramshackled together from plastic tarp and plywood. Among the matchbox homes, I spotted a few females in short skirts and tight tops leaning against a wall. Their faces followed us as we passed. Other than that, they didn't move. I caught the gaze of one, long dark hair in a ratty mess, thick, swollen mouth. Something seemed dead in her eyes. My gut twisted.

"Who are they?" I asked.

It was Marco who flashed me a grin from the front seat of the jeep. "Got to provide the workers some form of entertainment."

I tasted bile at the back of my throat. These ladies were hook-ers. Used for sex. "Are they paid for what they do or *forced*?"

"They're fed and clothed," Marco said. "Isn't that enough?"

The horror must have shown on my face because my father

laughed. "Honestly, Roman. Anyone would think you were a bleeding-heart pussy."

"If you like," Marco said with a wicked grin, "we can organize one or two of them to entertain you tonight after dinner."

A realization hit me like a sucker punch to the liver. This plantation had been funding my extravagant lifestyle in Europe the past eight years. I didn't know. Truthfully, I didn't want to know. It was easier for me to focus on my singular problems, to stick my head in the sand. To remain in my comfortable, luxurious ignorance.

I was no longer ignorant. This time I was not running away. I had a new plan.

I would bide my time. Wait until my father had passed, inherit his dirty empire, then dismantle it from the inside. I could do that. I could claw my way into being the kind of man who deserved to walk down the busiest street of Verona, chin held high and holding Julianna Capulet's hand. Maybe even her father could learn to like me. Perhaps, eventually, see me as a son.

I was jolted out of my daydream by a series of yells. The jeep skidded to a halt in front of a large cluster of buildings, the labs where the coca leaves were dried.

"What's going on?" demanded my father.

Marco jumped out of the front seat and snapped orders to a few of his men. Beyond them the yelling continued, the air ripe with tension. Now the Tyrell heritage was clear; with his back straight and a determined furrow to his brows, he seemed even taller. He could have been my father at a younger age.

I slid out of the jeep, my gun in my hands, as Abel helped my father out, his men scrambling from the other vehicles to form a protective circle around us.

Movement alerted my attention. A group of soldiers were dragging a bruised and bleeding man towards us. I almost recoiled as my mind threw me a picture of Vinnie Torrito, swollen with blood under his thin skin, face screwed up in pain. Inside I yearned to tear the unknown man from the rough hands clamping him in place, I wanted to pick him up from his knees. Outside, I numbed my features and stood my ground like a coward.

The man was shaking, begging in Spanish. I caught the words "yo no fui" and "ayúdame, Jesus".

I didn't.

Help me, Jesus.

We were a long, long way from help here. And Jesus never tread upon this land.

Marco strode up alongside the victim and pointed a gun at his head. "This sonofabitch was trying to steal from us," he yelled, his voice like the crack of a gunshot, his face overripe, veins straining at the neck.

Around us, brightly colored parrots fled in terror. The sun hid her face behind a cloud. The faces of workers pressed against all the panes of glass of the buildings.

My father turned to me. "Roman, here is an opportunity for you to show us just what kind of leader you are."

His dark eyes pinned me down. *Don't disappoint me*, they seemed to threaten.

Around me I saw the sneers of my brother's soldiers, heard the unspoken doubt that I had the balls to command as my father and brother did. Quieter, underneath the hostility, I sensed the collective held breath of the powerless workers. Would I be a tyrant just like my father, or would I show mercy?

"What has he stolen?" I asked.

Abel sneered. "Money. Drugs. What does it matter?"

Marco and Abel shared a uniting look, two men who have recognized that each other share a common enemy.

I shifted slightly. "How do we know he stole—"

"*I* am telling you he stole from our family. From us. From

you," Marco said, his voice booming like a megaphone. "Are you calling me a liar?"

I swear I heard Abel chuckle.

My eyes found the man still on his knees in front of me. He was begging now, his soft chanting now broken by hiccups and repressed sobs. His hands were clasped in front of him as best as he could with his elbows being held back. His fingers, despite being dirty, were elegant, long and distinctly feminine. If he had been born in another situation, perhaps he would have been a musician.

My windpipe felt crushed. This man would have no trial. He would get no fairness bestowed upon him. An unlucky birth had given him a cruel past but his future I would single-handedly tear from him. I could show him no mercy. No matter how much my soul screamed for it.

I could feel all their eyes on me. Waiting for my verdict, my judgment, my punishment. If I wasn't harsh enough, I'd be laughed at. Accused of being weak, of having too much of a heart. I'd never make it out of here alive. I'd never live to dismantle this poisonous inheritance of mine.

If I wanted to survive, I had to be ruthless.

If I wanted to bring down the Tyrell empire from within, I had to first become like my father.

I had to walk like him, talk like him, *punish* like him.

I tore my eyes away from the accused and shut off his prayers from my ears.

No mercy.

A greater good. My chest swelled with purpose.

"Bring all the other workers outside and tell them what he's done," I said. "String him up, shoot him in front of them. Leave his body for the vultures and jaguars." A bullet to the head would be the kindest thing for him now. It would be a quick death, a painless one. I would make sure that his family received an anonymous windfall. Measly restitution for the death of a loved one, but it was the best that I could do.

"Excellent plan," my father said. "That'll teach the rest of them never to steal from a Tyrell." He turned to me. Like a father bestowing a toy at Christmas, he said, "You can be the one to punish him."

I was too numb at this point to flinch. This "kindness" from my father, I had been expecting.

"Perhaps," Marco said, his tone deceptively helpful, "shooting him would be too kind." He uncoiled a rough python of a whip from his belt and held it out. "This would make a more painful and effective punishment." His eyes glittered at me, mocking me, daring me to take it.

Don't flinch. Don't you dare flinch, Roman.

I took the whip, weighing the rough handle in my hands. The knotted tail had been stained with something dark brown. Blood.

Marco sneered at me, a hatred etched into his features. He was jealous. His baby brother being raised up higher than him in front of all his men. I needed to be careful tonight that I didn't have my throat slit in my sleep. "Careful you don't whip yourself, *brother.*"

They tied the man up with his back to me. The coward in me was thankful I couldn't see his face.

His crying sounded muffled in my ears as if I were drowning underwater. My vision had taken on a blurry quality. And when I lifted my arm to make the first strike, it didn't feel like *my* arm. I was merely an observer, watching through another's eyes.

The whip came down across his back, opening it to the sky. Violent red blood appeared like a warning. *Stop. Stop!* His screams took on an anguish that fisted into my heart.

To my horror, a rush of power surged through my veins. Power. I held this man's life in my hands. I was a god.

I hated myself for feeling it.

Don't lie, Roman. You love the power. You are a Tyrell. Give in to it. Take it.

I was becoming everything I feared. Everything I had fought so long not to become.

A fury rose out of me. It had nowhere to go except towards the man before me. *You fool. Why did you have to steal from my family? Why did you have to make me do this?* The anguish released from me in the frenzied furious slashing of my whip.

Crack. Crack. Crack.

He screamed louder, his voice echoing across the wide sky like the pained cries of the jungle birds, cries that would later rouse me from my bed. Between screams I could hear the muffled sobs and whispers of the workers behind me. *Monster. Monster. Monster.* They would chase me from wake to sleep like my shadow.

Then it stopped. All the noise ended in a collective hushed gasp. Even my brother, who had been laughing, had fallen into silent horror.

All the noise except for the bark of my whip. Crack. Crack.

Someone grabbed my forearm poised above me and the whip coiled at my feet like an obedient snake.

My father stared at me with gravity. "That's enough, son." *That's enough.*

I turned around slowly. I caught the look on my brother's face: fear. Then Abel's: respect.

My eyes came to rest upon what was left of the man who was screaming no more. I had torn him to ribbons. A mess of flesh stripped off bloody bones remained wrapped around the tree.

Later that night in my brother's den, as we all sat our well-fed selves in armchairs so soft it was like sitting in the lap of angels, I heard the whispers of the devil. *Yo no fui,* he taunted. *Ayúdame.*

Through the nameless ghost of the man I had whipped to death, my father raised his glass to me. "I'm proud of you, son."

I had never felt so lost than in that moment.

JULIANNA

The present...

My heart was beating like an executioner's drum as Espo and I strode down the hallway towards Roman's apartment door, his official one, not his secret one.

"I still think we should wait until there's more evidence," I hissed at Espinoza.

"Capi, we have a witness that puts Roman in a car heading out from Verona on the same road that the body was found on."

I rolled my eyes. "He was a druggie and it was dark. Some witness."

"You know," Espo glared at me, "it's almost as if you *don't* want it to be Roman Tyrell regardless of the evidence."

"You know," I snapped back, "it's almost as if you *want* it to be Roman regardless of the lack of evidence."

Espo lifted a finger to signal to be quiet as we approached

Roman's door. Espo insisted that he and I personally go to his apartment to escort him to the station.

There was nothing I could do. No excuse I could give to avoid it.

I lifted my trembling fist and rapped my knuckles on Roman's door. *Dear God, please don't be home.*

"He won't hear you if you knock like a mouse." Espo slammed his fist against the door making it reverberate, the sound rattling around in my body like a pile of old bones.

The lock clicked like the cock of a gun. The door opened.

Roman stood in the doorway, wide and imposing as always, fitted black shirt over denim jeans. His eyes found mine, boring into me. For a second my heart squeezed in my chest so hard it hurt to breathe. *Thank God, you're alive.*

Now that he was alive, I was free to kill him. *Why haven't you returned my calls in two damn days? Not even a quick text, you bastard.*

There was nothing I could do except keep a calm professional face on.

His unflinching eyes slid across to Espinoza at my side. "Detective Capulet, Detective Espinoza. What brings you to my humble abode?"

"We would like you to come with us down to the station and answer some questions," Espinoza said.

Roman's gaze returned to me. As usual I could decipher nothing in his stoic features. "Care to tell me what this is about, Detective Capulet?" Roman asked, his voice as sharp as a blade.

He thought I was betraying him. If only he had called me back I could have warned him we were coming. I opened my mouth to speak but—

"Roman?" a female voice called from within the apartment. "Who is it?"

A female's voice?

Roman's face betrayed nothing—no guilt, no apology,

nothing—as a honey-haired woman wearing a silky wrap-around minidress appeared beside him.

Rosaline.

When she spotted me, she shot me a smirk and pawed possessively at Roman's side. He put his arm around her.

He put his fucking arm around her.

Inside I raged, a tempest, a storm smashing our ship to pieces. Outside I was too shocked to move or say anything. Bastard! How could he betray me?

Roman wouldn't do that to you, a voice inside me urged. *There must be an explanation.*

Are you stupid, Julianna? He doesn't contact you for two damn days and you find him with her *in his apartment?*

"These fine detectives just want to talk to me for a while," Roman said to Rosaline. "Another misunderstanding, I'm sure." Roman turned back to me, a smirk on his face. "Tell me, detectives, do you actually have any evidence this time of whatever it is I've supposedly done? Or is this just another fishing expedition because of *who my family is?*"

I cringed at his words.

"Oh, don't worry," Espo said, his words cordial yet barbed. "We have evidence."

Roman didn't flinch. His eyes bored into mine, a thousand unsaid things hanging between us. "Let's get this over with."

Roman Tyrell sat in the back of our patrol wagon, a set of thin bars like a wire cage separating us from him. It hurt my heart to see him sitting there, in the seat reserved for criminals and lowlifes. He had his arm slung casually over the back of the seat as if he was being chauffeured in the back of a limo, but I could see the tightness in his jaw, his inner state beginning to leak out.

Sitting in the passenger seat I could feel his eyes boring right into the back of my head. The tension in the vehicle was so thick you could cut it with a hatchet.

"Look at that," Espo said, just a little too casually as he glanced up in his rearview mirror. "Roman Tyrell sitting where he belongs."

Roman said nothing.

"Tell me, Roman, with your brother Jacob gone you're next in line to rule the Tyrell empire, isn't that right?"

"Believe me," Roman said in an even tone. In the rearview mirror his eyes flashed with anger. "I would rather he had lived."

Espinoza let out a short, sharp laugh, devoid of humor. "But now you don't have to share once your old man dies. Total power for you."

"Espo," I hissed at him out of the corner of my mouth, trying not to let my cheeks flare with embarrassment. I couldn't believe what he was saying to Roman. Each word like a stab in my own gut. "Leave him alone."

Espinoza shot me a look. "Excuse me?"

"You're being unnecessarily rude to a suspect."

"Roman is tough. Aren't you, Roman? You can handle it. I imagine your father has had harsher things to say to you, judging by his reputation."

"You're quite right, Detective Espinoza," Roman said. "My father is an unforgiving and unrelenting teacher. I've developed a skin thicker than steel. Nothing you say to me could possibly have any effect other than to stroke your own prejudices."

I began to protest. "I don't think—"

"I don't need *you*, of all people, to fight my battles for me, Detective Capulet."

I was stunned into silence. What the hell was that supposed to mean?

At the station we put Roman in an interrogation room. We placed a very snotty Rosaline, who had followed us in her car, in a spare office to "wait for my Romy away from all the riff-raff".

Usually we made the suspect sweat it out in the interrogation room for some time before we began our questions. Espo and I watched Roman through the live feed of the camera from the tech room. He sat casually in the chair, one ankle crossed over the other. He looked like he hadn't a care in the world, while inside I was in turmoil. I alternated between glaring at Roman on the screen and at Espo beside me. "What the hell was that about in the car?" I blurted out.

Espo narrowed his eyes at me. "I could ask you the same question."

"Excuse me?"

"If I didn't know any better, I'd say you were picking sides and the side you were picking was *his.*"

I let out an exasperated sound. "I'm not picking sides. I just think we have to keep an open mind about our suspects and let the evidence speak for itself."

"Capi, the evidence has spoken. We found a witness who saw Roman that night. You and I both know what kind of man Roman Tyrell is."

I pinched my lips together. There was so much I wanted to say to Espo. About Roman, about the night he saved my life, about how I knew he didn't kill Eddie Sanchez. But I couldn't. So I said nothing. Like a damn coward.

JULIANNA

Espo and I sat opposite Roman in the interrogation room, the cold metal chair biting at my legs through my skirt. Espo glared at Roman. I stared at the table. Roman watched me. He seemed so calm, so collected. Meanwhile I was a fucking mess inside, trying not to let it all leak out all over my face.

Espo pressed the start button on the recording device, spoke our names, the time and date.

He pulled a blown-up copy of Eddie's driver's license photo out of his file. "Do you know this man?" he asked Roman, as he pushed the photo across the table.

Roman leaned over the table and gave the picture a cursory glance. "No." He sank back against his chair, which gave out a low creak under his bulk.

"Of course, he didn't exactly look like that when you last saw him, right? Perhaps this image will jog your memory." Espo slid out a second picture, this time of Eddie's pale, dead face taken from the crime scene, the bullet wound leaking blood, his eyes frosted over and his mouth open as if mid-begging for his life.

Roman glanced down to the second picture.

Nothing. There wasn't even a flash of surprise on his face. Did he know already? Did he have something to do with it?

Roman lifted his eyes up to meet mine. For a second there was an accusation in them. An accusation? At me?

"Hey," Espinoza snapped as he bristled beside me. "I asked you a question."

Roman slid his gaze back to Espinoza, coldness wafting off him like he was made of ice. I shivered inside.

This is just the mask he wears for the world, I reminded myself. *You know the real man. The good man inside. The man who is worth fighting for.*

"Like I said," Roman said, his voice sharp and deadly like the edge of a blade. "I don't recognize this man."

"Lay your hands out."

"Why?"

"Are you refusing?"

For a few terse moments, Roman and Espo glared at each other, an unspoken battle of wills raging between them. At any moment either of them, or both, might lunge over the table and punch the other.

Roman gave Espo a smile that bordered on a smirk before spreading his hands on the table, palms up.

"Palms down," Espo said, his eyes still fixed on Roman.

Roman hesitated for just a second, then turned his hands over.

My heart sank. His knuckles were scabbed over, bruised up as if he'd hit someone. He had. He'd hit Eddie several times the night he saved me.

Espo glanced up to the camera above his head, the red light still on, as if to make a point that we now had Roman's injuries on record.

"How did you get those cuts on your knuckles?" Espo nodded to Roman's hands.

Roman didn't flinch. He didn't even take his hands off the

desk, he just stared at his knuckles as if he were admiring them. "I got into an altercation with a man who was assaulting my girl."

"When was this?"

"Two nights ago, three… I don't keep track of these things."

"And you sure it wasn't *this* guy you hit?" Espo tapped the picture of a very dead Eddie.

Roman let out a long sigh. He picked up the picture, making a show of studying it. I could almost see his mind working. What did we know? What evidence did we have?

If he'd only called me back, I could have warned him. Instead, we had him in a corner.

Roman dropped the picture on the desk. "I'm sure, detective."

"Really? 'Cause I think you beat the shit out of this guy." Espo stabbed the picture with his finger. "Eddie Sanchez. Look again."

Roman leaned back in his chair, cool as anything. "Do you have any evidence linking my wounds to this man's wounds?"

Espinoza shuffled in his seat. "No."

"I see."

Espo leaned in, his chair scraping against the ground. "Someone had the foresight to pour bleach over his wounds, destroying whatever DNA evidence there might have been."

Roman gave Espinoza a smug look. "Really? How clever."

Espo glared back. The tension in the room was strung as tight as a tennis racket. "What was the name of the man you assaulted?"

"I didn't assault anyone. I was protecting my girlfriend."

"Fine, what was the name of the man you were protecting your girlfriend from?"

"I didn't get it."

"You didn't get it?"

"I didn't exactly stop to chat. I was too busy teaching him some manners."

"Bruising on your knuckles shows you must have hit this man several times."

"He was a poor learner. I had to *teach* him several times."

"What a coincidence, a body turns up that had been hit several times before he was killed."

"There seem to be a lot of people around the place who deserve that kind of thing."

"You think Eduardo Sanchez deserved what he got?"

"I already told you, detective, I don't know this Eduardo character."

Espinoza paused. "Where were you two nights ago?"

"With a girl."

"This girl have a name?"

He looked over to me, his eyes piercing into my soul. I stopped breathing. I was fucked if he opened his mouth. He was fucked if he didn't.

I would lose my badge. My father would kill me. But Roman had no choice. He would be alibi-less if he didn't.

I braced myself.

"Julianna," he said deliberately. I could feel Espo bristling beside me at his informality. "You know my girl, don't you? Gorgeous face, long honey-brown hair, a body to kill for."

I gritted my teeth. What was he playing at? Just say my name already. "I'm sure I don't."

Roman leaned across "Don't play coy. She's sitting in this very station now."

My heart stopped beating.

"Rosaline?" Espo said.

Roman smiled. My heart stuttered back to life. Of course, Rosaline. I had totally forgotten about her. He was talking about *his girl*, Rosaline. The image of their arms around each other at his apartment door flashed through my mind.

"You're telling me," said Espinoza, "that your alibi for *this* murder just happens to be the same alibi as the last one we pulled you in here for?"

He shrugged. "Coincidence."

"That's one hell of a coincidence."

"What can I say," Roman looked squarely at me as he spoke, "I really like this girl. Want to spend all my time with her."

I flushed.

"We have a witness that puts you at a gas station on the road leading out of Verona at around midnight. The same road where we happened to find poor Eddie. What do you say to that?"

Roman smiled like he didn't have a care in the world. "My girlfriend, who happens to be the daughter of a prominent Verona businessman, says otherwise. Are you calling her a liar?"

With the interview and audio recording suspended, Espo and I conferred in whispers on our side of the table. Roman watched us carefully.

"I'll go talk to Rosaline right now," Espo said. "Get her side of the story. You stay here and keep an eye on him."

And be left alone with Roman? "I, er, I should go with you."

Espo pursed his lips. "No offense, but you and Rosaline don't really have a rapport. I think she'll open up to me more if I speak to her alone."

That wasn't something I could argue with. I nodded, resigned to my fate.

Espo shot Roman one last glare before he left the room. The door clicked behind them. I was left in the dim interrogation room alone with Roman Tyrell. Had it only been less than forty-eight hours since we had kissed goodbye? How much things could change in so little time.

Roman's face twisted with the first sign of any emotion from him. "Here we are again, *detective*."

"Roman, you don't have to call me that. There are no recording devices on."

"You sitting on that side," he continued, "me right back here on the side I belong. You, the cop. Me, the guilty party."

I lunged forward in my chair, ready to start yelling at him.

"Careful, detective. No one might be able to hear you but they may be watching." His eyes darted up to the camera, the light like a glaring red eye.

I sank back in my chair and crossed my arms over my chest. "You're not guilty," I hissed. "Don't you dare think I believe that. Don't you dare think I wanted to put you in that chair."

The only sign that my words had gotten through to him was a slight twitch to his jaw. "You mean to tell me," he said slowly, "that you *don't* think I killed Mr. Sanchez."

"Not for a second. You were with *me* that night."

"Not the whole night. I had plenty of time to kill him before I came back to you..." he trailed off.

"I don't believe it. You wouldn't kill him."

"I wanted to."

"You gave him your word. You promised him safety on your mother's memory. Someone else killed him after you dropped him off wherever it was that you dropped him off."

Roman studied me for a long moment. Finally, something in his face softened.

"I tried to warn you," I said quietly, my voice low and hard. "I called, left messages. *You* never replied. Then I find you in your apartment...with *her.*"

His lip curled up into a sneer. "Jules, I'm disappointed. What did I tell you about how I feel about other women?"

"You mean to tell me that all your other lady friends weren't enough for you?"

"I don't care about them."

"Good," I blurted out before I could stop myself.

"I didn't even want them to touch me." His face twisted into a mask of anger. "What are you doing to me, Julianna? What the fuck are you doing to me?"

My gaze locked on his. More memories piled in on me. My body heated, my nipples pressing painfully against the fabric of my shirt.

"It's what you do to me."

"What do I do to you?"

"You make me not care about anyone or anything else. It's just you, you, you. You're all I want."

I was jolted out of my memories when Roman's knee brushed mine under the table, sending a crack of electricity up my leg and hitting that space between my thighs.

"You seem...uncomfortable, Detective Capulet." His deep voice caressed my warming skin.

I swallowed hard. "I'm fine."

"I'm not." Roman leaned his chest over the table like he was about to tell me a secret. "I missed you these last two days," he whispered, his fingers trailing across my knee under the table.

I froze, torn between the rush of lust thundering through my brain, short-circuiting it, or the voice in my head screaming that he couldn't be touching me in a fucking interrogation room.

"What are you doing?" I hissed at him.

"This is your reward."

"What?"

"For trusting me. Now...hold still."

Hold still. His hand shifted up my thigh, pushing my skirt further up. His fingertips burning along my inner thigh like they were made of hot irons.

I squeezed my legs shut, trapping his hand so he could touch no further. "Don't."

"Don't make a scene, detective."

Me making the scene? I wasn't the one with his damn hand up my skirt.

"Open your legs."

"No."

He narrowed his eyes at me. "That camera up there can't see my hand under the table, but it can see your face. If you don't want to draw attention," he pinched my inner thigh with his fingers and I whimpered, "you'll be a good girl and open your legs."

Fuck him. But I knew he'd won. I relaxed my thigh muscles slowly, knowing that this was such a bad fucking idea. Somehow not caring enough to protest too hard.

"Wider."

He nudged my thighs with his hand. I let them fall apart.

"Good girl." His fingers brushed against the front of my panties. I gasped as stardust and rockets burst across my body.

"Detective Capulet." Roman's deep voice cut through into my brain fog even as his fingers kept rubbing my clit in circles. "I need you to keep asking me questions."

"What?"

His fingers paused. I almost let out a whimper. His eyes flicked up and back over my head. Right. The video camera. Someone could be watching us from above. They couldn't hear us or see his hand under the table but they could see our lips. I had to keep asking him questions so that everything appeared normal.

Roman stared at me from across the table, hunger in his eyes. "You ask a question," his finger pushed aside my panties, "and I'll give you an *answer*." He thrust a finger inside my wet entrance, sending a hot wave of pleasure through me. God, I'd missed his touch. It had only been two days but it had felt like a lifetime apart.

He stilled. I almost cried out with frustration.

"Question. Answer. Do you understand, detective?"

His words clicked in. If I kept asking him questions, he'd keep touching me. If I stopped so would he.

"What's your full name?" I blurted out, a stupid question to ask seeing as we already had his name recorded, but I was barely thinking straight. His finger began its languid tantalizing thrusting. I sucked in a breath.

"Roman Giovanni Tyrell."

"And your girlfriend's name is?" I said, breathlessly. In and out went his finger.

"You already know that, detective."

"And you...you like chocolate, right?" I was mumbling, saying anything, asking anything that came to mind. Anything to make sure he didn't stop.

He chuckled. "I do like chocolate. Especially when it's melted all over the divine body of my very sexy woman. In fact, when I see her next I might just have to eat her pussy with chocolate." He added a second finger, widening my aching, needy core further.

"Oh dear God," I hissed.

Roman lifted an eyebrow at me, his two fingers paused at the hilt inside me. "Was that a question, Detective Capulet?"

"I...um, how long have you known her?"

His fingers began to draw in and out of me again. I almost cried with happiness. "It feels like forever."

"And how would you...how would you describe her?" I muttered, lost in the waves that were running up and down my body.

"She dims even the stars," he began, his words catching my attention.

His eyes caught mine as I snapped them open.

He raised an eyebrow. "Shall I continue, Detective Capulet?"

God, yes. "That would be good," I stuttered.

The smile on Roman's face widened. He curled his two fingers in, stroking at that glorious spot on the front wall of my pussy while he drew small circles on my clit with his thumb. Fuck, that was so good, the waves of pleasure growing deep and thick. My toes curled up in my shoes. I shut my eyes. Thank God the camera couldn't see my face.

I barely listened as he spoke, describing *her*, me. It was all just a deep, soothing rumble outside of the pleasure cave I was lost in. The pressure built and built until I was trembling in my seat.

"Detective Capulet," he said breaking into my thoughts, "you look like you are so *close* to your last question."

SIENNA BLAKE

"Yes," I breathed out, my body already pulsating around his fingers, sweat breaking out across my forehead. I was going to go over the edge. Right here in the interrogation room with Roman Tyrell's fingers deep inside my greedy, wet pussy.

"Do you...care about her?" I spluttered. I couldn't bring myself to say the word *love*.

His fingers slid out of me, pausing for a mere second. "I'd kill for her." He slammed his fingers deep inside, hard against my g-spot, his thumb vibrating against my clit. His words. His touch. The complete reckless taboo of it. It was all too much.

I came hard, biting down on my bottom lip so I wouldn't scream, so hard that I tasted blood. My vision went white. My pussy clamped around his fingers, my fists scrunching my notepad in front of me as pleasure rolled through me wave after wave.

He pulled his fingers from me as my orgasm faded. I slumped back in my chair and blinked at him. Did that really happen?

Across the table, Roman's eyes seared into mine, a hungry yet satisfied grin on his face. He pulled his right hand up and brushed his two fingers across his mouth, smearing it with my juices. He lowered his hand before he licked the taste of me off his lips.

JULIANNA

Rosaline corroborated Roman's story. Her lies perfectly matched his. Too perfect. He must have known that Eddie's body had been found. He must have known that he'd be interrogated.

Roman disappeared behind a wall of expensive lawyers. We couldn't hold him. Not unless we could find more evidence.

"Don't leave town," Espo said with a scowl as he held the station door open for Roman.

"I wouldn't dream of it," Roman said, his eyes on me. "Not while I'm having so much fun here."

I flushed under his stare and hoped to hell that Espo didn't notice. My mind flashed to what he had done to me in the interrogation room. I shivered at the memory of his fingers inside me. *Damn you, Roman Tyrell. Damn you in the best way.*

Roman was standing in my living room when I returned home that evening. I quickly locked my front door behind me and deposited my bag on the side table. He still hadn't moved or said

399

a word. I frowned as I studied him. His features, which earlier had seemed lightened by my admission that I knew he was innocent, were now grim. An uneasy feeling coiled in my belly. Something had changed since he walked out of the police station earlier today.

"Where have you been these last two days?" I asked, something I'd not been able to ask before now. "I was so worried when I didn't hear from you. No response. Nothing. Then Eddie…"

His features twitched at that name, but he didn't speak. Something was wrong.

"Roman, talk to me." I moved towards him.

He avoided my grasp and we found ourselves circling each other. A flash of pain cut across his face. "I can't do this anymore."

"Do what?"

"I can't pretend to be someone I'm not."

"I don't understand. Why won't you let me touch you?" I reached for him again but he grabbed my wrists.

The cold, cruel mask he wore with such a practiced ease, the one I hated so much, slammed down over his face. "I am a Tyrell." Even his voice calloused over. "It doesn't matter how hard I try to fight it, it's in my blood. I can never get away from it. It's part of me. The only thing you can do is to be smart. Walk away."

I shook my head and yanked against his grasp. "I won't—"

"You have a choice. Be smart. Walk away from me."

"You have a choice, too."

"I have *no* choice." His voice boomed out like a gunshot. He let go of me as if I'd burned him, one of his hands coming up to run through his hair.

I refused to flinch. I refused to be swayed, to give up like he obviously already had. I would fight for both of us. "You always have a choice."

His gaze snapped to mine. His eyes were now the only thing that was alive in him; they burned like they were on fire. "You don't understand."

"No, *you* don't understand. I love you." These words spilled out of me. The words were like a stopper. As soon as they were released out came a pouring bubbling mess of every feeling I had tried to deny to myself. I loved him. I loved Roman Tyrell. I let out a strange, curt giggle as my chest tickled full of fireflies.

His eyes widened for a single moment. For a single moment I thought I had reached him. His tenderness turned to bitter ash. "You can't possibly love me."

"I do." I grabbed his tense shoulders and matched his stare, begging him to believe me. "You're a good man who—"

"A good man." His face twisted, darkness leaking into every crease. He pushed my hands off him. I burned and crumpled with rejection. "Let me tell you what this *good man* did."

"There's nothing you can say that would—"

"I killed Eduardo Sanchez."

The blood drained from my face. My fingers grew cold as they hung from numb arms. "You're lying."

"I am not. I pointed the gun at his head and I pulled the trigger." There was no remorse on his face. No sign of guilt. Just pure, dark hatred. Hatred for me? Or...himself?

I shook my head like I was batting away the words coming out of his mouth. This was a mistake. A dream. A nightmare. This wasn't the real Roman standing here talking to me.

I could not believe it. There must be some reason... "Why? Were you forced into it? Did your father—"

"He could not be trusted to keep what I did for you a secret. You were in danger if he lived."

"I would kill for her." Roman admitted it in the interrogation room. I just hadn't been listening.

"Why are you telling me this?"

Roman said nothing. He just stood there while my world was

401

shaking under my feet. Why would he do this? Why would he admit such a thing, if it were even true?

Realization struck me. "You want to push me away."

"You should be *running,* not walking away from me, Jules."

I shook my head. "You...you were just protecting me."

"I am a Tyrell," he repeated. "I'm nothing but a bloodthirsty monster."

"No," I said. "You are not a monster. You're a good man who did a bad thing. You were just protecting me."

"I am *not* a good man."

"You are. You saved me from being raped. From being kidnapped."

"I killed both those men."

"To protect me. Only to protect *me.*"

He shook his head violently. "Stop turning everything into something *good.*"

"You are good. Deep down, you are."

"I tried to be good for you, but I can't fake it anymore. I am a Tyrell down to the core."

Something had happened; I could see it clearly. Something had happened in the last two days to make him think there was no hope for him. The last flame was extinguished after he left the police station.

I still burned with hope. I had to hope it was enough.

"What happened while you were away? What happened this afternoon?"

His eyes glittered with hatred. "I woke up."

I grabbed his neck, sliding my other palm on his cheek. "Roman," I pleaded, "you are *not* your father."

Believe me, you have to believe me.

I saw the flash of surprise in the lift of his brows. For a second I thought I'd finally gotten through to him...

His eyes turned to stone, dead and lifeless. "Jules, don't embarrass yourself any further," he said slowly like I was a child being lectured. "Just accept it. You and me." He pushed my hands off him. "It's over."

It's over. Two words like twin swords, piercing me through the heart. "You... You don't mean that."

"This was fun. But I'm bored now. I...I want someone else."

"I don't believe you. You're just saying that to make me give up on you. I won't give up on you."

"I'm not yours to fight for anymore." He swallowed hard, as if his words were only half chewed. "I'm going to marry Rosaline."

Rosaline. An image of his arm around her flashed through my mind. Bitter hot jealousy tore ragged edges along my veins. This could not be happening. This could not be his decision. "Your father," I blurted out as realization struck me. "Is your father making you marry her?"

"I'm marrying her because I *want* to."

"You can't... You... You don't love her." Was I trying to convince him? Or me?

His lip curled up in a scowl. "Why? You thought that I loved *you*?" His cruel words were knives, each one aiming to be my death blow.

I inhaled sharply, my eyes filling with tears, my heart fluttering like a dying butterfly, hanging on to the thinnest silk thread of hope. "Please. Don't do this, Roman."

"It's already been done. The date is set. Six weeks from now. Don't expect an invitation."

My heart crumpled in on itself. Shock gave way to raw, agonizing pain. I felt my body trembling, shattering apart. He had given up. My prediction, our fate, my worst nightmare had come to life.

Fuck him for giving up. I would not give him the satisfaction of watching me fall to pieces. I would not let him see me cry. "Get out."

His mask crumpled. He didn't really want this, I could see it underneath his peeled back edges. He had already decided that he would never be good enough to be loved. I'd lost him the moment I'd met him.

"Jules..." his voice, suddenly soft, was little comfort. He reached out for me. How dare he try and soothe the wounds he made?

If he touched me I'd fall apart. I'd give in. I'd beg him to stay. I could not bear to beg him.

"Get out and don't ever come back," I screamed, my voice breaking as anguish tightened its clawed fist around my neck, letting just enough air in to keep me mercilessly alive.

He drew back his hand. I got to keep what little pride I had left. He looked like he had many more things to say. He didn't give voice to them. He walked quietly to my door and I turned my back on him; I couldn't bear to watch him leave.

Then he was gone.

JULIANNA

Roman Tyrell may have ended things with me, but I felt as if he'd died. Or perhaps it was easier for me to think of him that way. If he was dead, there was no hope left for us. Hope kept me hanging on to a sunken ship even as it pulled me under.

I still dreamed that he would slip into my open bedroom window.

I still felt his eyes on me when I was awake.

Sometimes I thought I caught his scent on the breeze.

Despite my grief, the cruel world just kept turning. The sun kept rising and falling. The waxing and waning of the moon marked the passing of weeks. Other people found love, got married, had babies. Other people hugged their families: mothers, fathers, husbands at the end of their work day. My pain remained motionless, a crystalized ball in my chest while I stayed numb around it.

I shouldn't mourn a man who admitted he'd killed another. Even if it was to protect me. I shouldn't *want* a man who broke another man's neck in front of me. Even if it was to stop me from being raped.

I shouldn't.

But I did.

Roman had only done what I'd secretly wished to do. To wield a sword of justice. To play judge and executioner to the scumbags who escaped punishment. No one was any worse off with them gone. They had deserved it. Nobody could ever convince me otherwise. I had held the hand of too many victims, heard the broken sobs of too many of the victims' families, watched too many shattered souls trying to rebuild their lives again after being destroyed.

So, no. I didn't mourn the scumbags that he'd killed. Knowing about Roman's involvement didn't make me want him any less. The truth was, I had fallen in love with Roman Tyrell and I didn't know how to crawl out of love. Every time it felt like I had made progress, I would be reminded of him and I'd slide right back down. It was an irreversible love. An unbreakable love. Completely unconditional. Beautiful and terrible all at once.

The leaves began to turn. The nights became colder, cold enough to need blankets on my bed. I kept a brave face on. Lacey occupied my lunchtimes at the station. Espo kept driving me to and from work. My father took to eating dinner at my apartment several times a week. On weekends, Nora sat on my couch and tried to coax me to come out to the markets and the movies. Sometimes I went, just to keep up the front that I was okay. Mostly, I didn't and we just stayed in nursing cups of tea while she chatted animatedly, being content to let me stay silent. I was surrounded by people who cared about me. Still, I managed to feel like a ghost. I walked through my days chasing distractions, yet I couldn't shake the feeling that I'd misplaced something important.

It was only at night, in the silence, that I was unable to hold back the tide and thoughts of Roman rushed back in. The night breeze blew in the smells of the city through my open window, but they didn't bring him.

I missed him with an ache that burrowed down to my soul. I missed his touch. The way he smelled. The way my world shrank down to just us when we kissed. Every day that went past was one day closer to the time when another woman would make him her husband.

~

Rosa Sanchez looked smaller than she was. Her head hung, staring at the floor as she walked, her shoulders rounded as if she were trying to hug herself, her thin, oversized gray sweater swimming on her slim body. She sat in front of me on the old worn couch in the witness interview room, knees pressed together under her long skirt, a cup of plain black tea untouched before her.

"Thank you for coming in, Mrs. Sanchez. I know it must be hard."

She didn't answer. She kept glancing past me, out of the glass window facing the interior of the station, where her three girls were being kept entertained by Espinoza. They were six, eight and twelve. The two youngest were laughing shyly into their collars at the faces that Espo was making and the way he clambered over the chairs. The oldest just stood there, mouth pinched, watching him with wary cynicism.

Espo would make a great father one day, if he ever settled down. What kind of father would Roman make?

I shook that question off, turning back to Rosa. Back to my job. "Your girls are fine," I said in a soft voice. "See?"

Rosa looked over at me, meeting my stare for the first time since she arrived. I could still see the mistrust in her black eyes, her arms crossed over her body. That was understandable. I was a cop. Her husband had been...a questionable man.

I pressed on. "We just need to ask a few questions about Eduardo."

"Eddie," she corrected in a timid voice. "He used to hate it when anyone called him Eduardo. Only his mother called him—" She stopped speaking suddenly, flinching, her eyes going to the door as if she expected he would burst through at any minute.

She tugged at her sleeve, covering up the purple and yellow mottled bruise around her arm. Understanding knotted around my stomach. She had all the signs. The bastard. My insides simmered. If Eddie wasn't dead already, I'd kill him myself.

I slapped myself internally. *You'd* kill him, *Jules?* This was not what good people thought. This was not how good cops reacted.

"When did you last see Eddie?"

Rosa chewed her lip. She didn't answer.

I leaned in. "You can talk to me," I said softly. "He can't hurt you anymore."

A laugh burst out of Rosa's mouth, which she tried to stifle with her fingers. She dropped her hand into her lap. "I know he can't," she said, her eyes suddenly shining. "The bastard's dead."

I was missing something. "Of course."

"He was home earlier that night. He got a call during dinner. He left without finishing. Around seven thirty, I think. He didn't tell me where he was going."

"What did you do?"

She frowned. "We ate dinner, me and the girls. Washed up. Put the girls to bed. Fell asleep around eleven."

"You didn't go anywhere?"

Her frown deepened. "No. Where would I go?"

"So you were...at home, asleep, between midnight and two a.m.? Is that what you're saying?"

Her eyes widened with shock. "Y-You think I shot him? I didn't do it. I didn't do nothing."

I studied her reaction carefully. Most innocent people asked for their lawyers. There was fear in her reaction. Maybe...guilt.

She was hiding something.

Maybe Roman was lying. Maybe he hadn't pulled the trigger.

Maybe she was the classic battered wife. She had put up with his abuse until she couldn't take it anymore and *bang!* she snapped.

I didn't want her to be guilty. What would happen to her kids? Her girls?

I had to follow every lead, that was my job, even if I didn't like where they led.

"Can anyone corroborate your story? Neighbors? Friends?" I offered. *Give me something so I can rule you out.* "Did anyone call you at home? Did anyone stop by?"

"No." Her fingers fidgeted at her hem. "It was just me and the girls at home. I was asleep," she repeated. "I didn't kill him. I didn't do it. I didn't even know about the money."

Money?

I straightened. "What money?"

Rosa made a small choking sound. She'd said something she shouldn't have.

I leaned in. "What money?"

Her lip trembled even as she pressed them shut.

"Rosa, I want to help you. I want to help you *keep* your kids. I can't do that if you don't tell me what's going on. If you're not honest with me, then that's what I have to tell social services."

Her eyes widened. "You can't take them. You can't." She began to rise out of the chair, her eyes flying to the window again. I placed a hand on her knee, forcing her to remain seated.

I hated using her kids against her, twisting the truth to get answers out of her. But it was for the greater good. "If you tell me the truth, Rosa, nobody will take your kids."

Her wet eyes snapped towards me. She wanted to believe me. "Just tell me about the money."

She sniffed and nodded.

I leaned forward.

"After Eddie died, I got a call from an insurance company. Turns out that Eddie had taken out an insurance policy on his life two years ago. Now that he's dead, it all came to me."

"How much?"

"A million dollars," she whispered.

I nodded. "Okay. There's nothing wrong with that, Rosa."

"You don't understand."

"Understand what?"

"The insurance man came to my house. I needed to sign some papers so I could get the money. I saw the insurance policy, the one that Eddie took out."

"Yes?"

Her lashes lifted, her eyes locked on mine, confusion swirling around in them. "It wasn't his signature."

ROMAN

I pulled over into the gas station, the single sign of life along this lonely stretch of road leading out of Verona. I snatched the cap off Eddie's head, ignoring his cry of annoyance.

Trust the fucker not to have the gas tank of his getaway car full. Idiot.

"Wait here," I commanded.

Eddie Sanchez, sitting in the passenger seat of his own car, nodded. His nose was already swelling. His left eye was bulging like the end of a rotten eggplant.

After I untied him at the warehouse, we took my car to his car, still sitting several blocks from where he had attacked Julianna. We swapped cars under the cover of night.

It was a risky move on my part, pulling over for gas, but I couldn't risk getting stuck out here.

It was past one a.m. We were the only customers at the station. I filled the black late model Ford with gas, keeping my head low. I could see one of the tires was softer than it should have been. I tsked my tongue against my teeth. Eddie didn't treat anything with respect, this much was clear.

I was in and out in less than five minutes, picking up something I

411

needed from the shelves before I paid cash, pulling the cap on my head down so that the rim covered most of my face from the camera positioned high over the cashier. It must have been my lucky night that the young pimple-faced cashier paid more attention to his tiny TV, blaring some cop show on his counter, than to me.

I got back in the car and pulled back onto the road. The farther we got from Verona, the more Eddie seemed to relax. It didn't take long for him to start talking like we were buddies.

"Are you banging her? The hot cop, I mean?"

It took all my willpower not to shove my fist in his mouth. "I'm not banging her, as you so eloquently put it," I said through gritted teeth.

"She's so fucking hot. Shit. I can see why you helped her. Like, maybe she'll suck your dick to say thanks."

How much longer did I have to listen to this fucking degenerate? I said nothing, hoping he'd get the hint and shut the fuck up.

But Eddie, the dickwad, was obviously not the sharpest tool in the shed. He was just a tool. He kept talking, kept making it easier for me to do what I needed to do.

"The ones who start out saying no, like they're pretending to be good girls or some shit, they're the ones who usually want it the most."

Just keep talking, fuck stain. Keep making it easier for me.

I eyed the passing landscape, dark and soulless. We hadn't passed another car for miles. The road looming long and straight ahead showed no oncoming traffic. There were no street lights to light up the bleak darkness, no houses around, just a long stretch of farmland on a single lane road. Good enough.

I slammed on the brakes. Eddie went flying forward, smashing himself against the dashboard. Fucker should have listened when I told him to put on his seatbelt.

"Jesus fuck man," he moaned around a flood of blood coursing out of his already broken nose, "why the hell did you do—"

I held the gun to the side of his head, shutting him up with a gasp. I cocked the gun. It made a lovely cracking sound. "Get out," I said, my voice a hard, mean growl.

"Aw shit, man. I didn't mean any of that shit I just said. I just talk—"

"Get. Out. Now."

"Okay. Okay." Eddie tumbled out of the car, his hands up in the air. I slid out of my car door, my gun still pointed at him in case he tried to run. Go on, run. Just try, I taunted silently.

The idiot was still rambling as he stood on the side of the gravel road when I strode up to him. "Turn around."

I saw, in the glow of the internal car light, the second that Eddie realized that I wasn't just kicking him out of the car.

"Fuck, man. Don't do it. I won't say shit, man. I swear."

"Turn. The fuck. Around."

Eddie kept whimpering, blubbering as he shuffled around as if his shoelaces were tied together. He was trying to tug on my heartstrings— as if there was something for him to pull on—moaning about being the only support for his wife, for his daughters.

After Merc left the warehouse with Julianna, I'd pulled a favor and got a background check on good ol' Eddie Sanchez before I'd untied him. There had been several complaints from neighbors about late night rows from their house. His kids and wife all had files at the local ER from their various "accidents".

Wife beater.

Child abuser.

Even if he hadn't tried to rape Julianna tonight, the fucker deserved to die.

I'd pulled another favor—I hated to admit it but sometimes having the surname Tyrell helped. I had a million dollar life insurance policy taken out on Eddie Sanchez, backdated to two years ago so it didn't look fishy. Guess who the sole beneficiary was on the policy? His wife.

So yes, Eddie, you will be a real fucking support to your wife and kids. When you're good and dead.

"Pull your zipper down," I said, the barrel of my gun pressed to the back of his skull.

Eddie froze, his shoulders hunched up around his ears. "W-What?"

"You heard me."

"M-Man, I ain't gay. I ain't—"

"Do it before I give you a second asshole."

His zipper cut over the low hum of the car engine, still on.

"Now pull your dick out."

He let out a pained whimper over the rustle of his jeans.

I shifted my fingers on the grip and tried to block out his sobbing. I wondered if his daughters would mourn him. Or would they sag with relief when they heard he'd died, knowing that their beatings would stop. Knowing what I did, they would probably do both and it would tear their tiny insides apart. Bastard as Eddie was, he was still their father. I was about to take him away from them.

I forced my finger onto the trigger. To my surprise, a trickle of sweat beaded on my forehead.

Come on, Roman. It's not like this is your first kill.

But Vinnie had been forced on me, my father's gun at my back. The second attacker, Tate Jackson, whose neck I'd broken earlier, had been an accident. I hadn't meant to kill him. I was just so fucking furious when I saw his hands on Julianna, when I heard the tearing of her clothes, when I knew, knew, what he wanted to do to her.

"You promised me you'd get me to safety," Eddie garbled. "You promised."

Do it, Roman. Do it to make sure this scumbag never reveals what he saw tonight—the heir of the Tyrell Mafia empire saving the life of a cop.

Do it to protect her.

"I lied." I pulled the trigger.

The bullet rang out like a bang, echoing out into the night. Eddie dropped forward like a sack, his dick hanging out of his pants like the poor unlucky fucker just stopped for a piss.

For a second I just stood there, my gun still pointed at where Eddie's head once was, whips of smoke reaching for the heavens from the end of my barrel.

No weapon, no evidence, no witnesses, *a voice echoed in my head, spurring me to action.*

There were no witnesses to worry about.

I would take the gun with me, throw it into the river on my way as I drove back to Verona.

As for any evidence I might leave behind... I strode to the seat behind the driver's side where I had stashed the two cans I'd bought in the gas station earlier. Eddie hadn't even noticed I'd returned with them, to his detriment. I grabbed the one marked "bleach". Good old household cleaner. Will remove all scum, stains and DNA evidence.

I washed Eddie down before I climbed back into Eddie's car and gunned it back onto the road.

The other can was marked gasoline. This car was going to make a pretty bonfire.

Sometimes, when I wasn't thinking of Julianna, I replayed that night over in my head as I lay in bed staring at my ceiling.

I wasn't going to lie to myself. I was glad Eddie was dead. One less rapist scumbag for the world. Did that make what I did justifiable? Did that make me a hand of justice in a way?

He was still someone's son. Someone was going to miss him. Someone was going to mourn him.

"You are a good man, Roman."

Julianna's words taunted me. Haunted me. How could a bright angel see any light in me?

"Let me tell you what this good man *did. I killed Eduardo Sanchez. I pointed the gun at his head and I pulled the trigger."*

Every day since I confessed to her I half-expected, half-hoped I'd be arrested. The knock on my door never came. Even with the way I left things, even after I deliberately caused her pain, she would not turn on me. I didn't fucking deserve her. She was better off without me. Soon she would see that.

415

JULIANNA

I didn't tell anyone that the signature on Eddie Sanchez's insurance policy was forged, not even Espo. I promised Rosa that I wouldn't. That woman had been through enough. She had three young girls to look after and that insurance money would go a long way. I didn't give a shit that it was the *wrong* thing for me to do, I would not tell. I would not take that money away from those girls.

A forged insurance policy. A million dollars. A dead husband. Was it possible that Eddie's death had nothing to do with Roman?

Or did Roman have something to do with this mysterious policy?

My father had just left. I sat in an armchair by my living room window, staring out into the night. A fist rammed against the door.

Roman.

My heart rocketed into my throat. I smoothed down my hair as I hurried to the door and flung it open.

It wasn't Roman. Everything alive in me sagged.

Nora didn't wait for me to speak before she pushed past me into my apartment.

"Why don't you come in then?" I muttered under my breath before shutting the door.

When I turned to face her, she had her arms crossed over her chest. "You've been walking around with that mopey look on your face for the last four weeks."

After Roman left my apartment the night he broke my heart, Nora, like a bloodhound, had come over demanding to know details. I had made up some vague excuse, "our careers don't match" as to why Roman and I ended our relationship.

She grabbed my cordless house phone and waved it at me. "Call him. Tell him you miss him."

I wasn't going to get her off my back unless I told her the truth. Or at least, some sort of semblance of truth. "Nora," I said slowly, choosing my words carefully. If I revealed too much, the poor thing might have a heart attack. "Roman isn't who you think he is."

"I know *exactly* who Roman Tyrell is."

I stared at her as my brain skipped like a scratch in a record. Nora couldn't *know* know. If she *knew* she'd be yelling at me for putting myself in danger by associating with such a criminal.

She let out an exasperated sigh. "Roman Tyrell, youngest son of Giovanni Tyrell. Public enemy number one according to your father. Did I miss anything?"

"But…" I shook my head, trying to knock this new piece of information into place. "I don't understand. You knew who he was all along? Aren't you mad at me?"

Nora tilted her head. "Did I ever tell you about Pappy?" Pappy had been her husband of almost thirty years. He'd passed away the year before I had moved into this building. Nora and I had connected over our shared experience of deep loss. In the years I'd known her, she rarely spoke about him.

I shook my head.

417

"My parents hated Pappy when they met him. He was dirt poor. He was a welfare kid with an absentee father who grew up on the wrong side of Verona." Nora's eyes turned misty and unfocused as if she were remembering. "But I loved that son of a bitch. He loved me. I didn't care what anyone said about him; I knew he was a good man. He loved me, supported me, protected me until the day he died. I still love him."

"I never knew."

Nora narrowed her eyes at me. "I know you, girlie. You ain't stupid. If you see something in Roman, that means that he's fit to spend time with. He's a good man too. No matter what anybody says."

I let out a bitter laugh. Would she still say the same thing if she knew he had killed to protect me? "What I think of him doesn't matter. It will never work between us."

"If the love is strong enough, it will survive anything."

"Except that he doesn't love me."

"Bullshit."

"He ended it, Nora," I cried with a frustrated smack of my palm against my thigh. The physical pain helped to distract me from the one in my heart. "*He* ended it. Why would he do that if he loved me?"

"Because he's scared."

"I'm not that scary," I muttered.

"He's not scared *of* you." Nora let out a sigh. "The most terrifying thing any of us can do is to fall in love. Why do you think they call it 'falling' in love? The greater the love, the harder we will fight against it."

Roman and I had been pushing and pulling against our feelings, against each other this whole time. Had he been falling in love too? Was this why it was all so...terrifying?

That was ridiculous. We'd been fighting against each other because we weren't meant to be together. This thought was a knife that sliced the raw wound open again.

"It doesn't matter," I said, tasting bitterness on my tongue. I wiped under my eyes, angry at my tears. "He's gone."

"He'll be back."

I shook my head, my heart weighed down with the knowledge that even though I would never give up on him, he had given up on us. "No, he won't."

ROMAN

A soft, warm hand slipped across my stomach as I slept.
Julianna.
My heart let out a thud. My bright angel had come back to me.

I let out a small groan as the hand slipped lower. A weight shifted over me, soft thighs slid on either side of my thighs. My cock stirred. *Jules...don't stop.*

Something nagged at the back of my mind. She...felt wrong. There were too many angles. She wasn't soft enough. She smelled *wrong*; the sharpness of too much spicy perfume hit my nose.

I sat up, instantly becoming alert. I grabbed her wrists, pulling her hands off me. She let out a soft, excited cry. The familiar voice sent a coil of annoyance through me. I collected both wrists into one hand and reached out to turn on the designer bedside lamp of my Tyrell-owned apartment. Apparently, a free-for-all apartment. The golden glow fell across a face I'd be happy never to see again.

Fucking Rosaline.

I knew I should have stayed at my mother's place instead of

coming back here. She was straddling my lap wearing a black leather teddy that barely covered her fake breasts in a series of straps that strung up onto a studded choker. Her hair was pulled into two pigtails and her heavily made-up face was pulled into a look of triumph.

My loving *fiancée*, I thought with a sneer. "What the fuck are you doing here?"

Rosaline gave me a look of fake innocence, batting her false eyelashes at me. "Can't a wife surprise her husband in bed?"

"You're not my wife," I growled.

"Yet." A lascivious look flashed in her dark, sinful eyes. She ground herself onto me, trying to get a rise out of me. Literally. That was never going to happen.

I pushed her aside, causing her to yelp, and damn near leapt out of the king-sized bed. I grabbed my steel-colored bathrobe, wrapping it around my half-naked frame. "How the fuck did you get in?"

She shrugged. "I had a copy of your key made since you were so rude as to not provide me one."

How the hell did she get a hold of a key to copy? Mine hadn't been out of my presence. "Whose key did you copy?"

She pouted her sticky pink lips.

"Rosaline?" I warned.

She crossed her arms. "Benvolio let me borrow his key."

For fuck sake. I made a mental note to slap Benvolio upside the head the next time I saw him. Also, to get my locks changed. Abel had a key. Benvolio had a key. Now Rosaline. Apparently, my keys were candy that was handed out like it was Halloween.

I pointed at the door. "Get out."

She crawled on all fours on my mattress, wiggling her ass. "Aww, baby, are you still mad at me?"

I snorted. "Mad is a temporary situation. Hatred is a better word for what I feel for you. Even that is being generous."

She crawled towards me, giving me a shot right down her cleavage. "There's a fine line between love and hate, baby."

Jesus fucking Christ. "Rosaline, get the fuck out of my apartment."

"Or what? You'll call the *cops*?" she sneered.

I flinched at the thought of Jules breaking down my door to find Rosaline in my bed dressed like that.

She continued, "Besides, you can't kick me out of *my* apartment."

"It's. Not. Yours." I ground out. If only she was a guy so I could break her nose and throw her out the window.

"What's yours is mine, remember?"

"Not yet."

"But soon, baby. Soon." She tweaked one of her nipples and let out a small moan.

I crossed my arms over my chest. "Yeah, well, until then, leave me the hell alone."

"Are you sure about that?" She reclined on the bed, dropping her knees out so I got a shot of her black panties. Crotchless.

Dear God. It was past one a.m. I wasn't getting back to sleep anytime soon. It looked like I wasn't going to be getting my bed back soon either. I grabbed jeans, a dark t-shirt and my jacket. I would change in the damn elevator rather than stay here another second.

"Where are you going?"

"Out," I called over my shoulder. "You better not be here when I get back."

"I don't like this place, Roman," Mercutio said.

"Why?" I slammed down another shot of whiskey and indicated to the lanky, bearded bartender to keep them coming. These days it seemed that I had to drink down a stomach-pumping level of alcohol just to get a buzz. Even then I never got numb enough. My head was slightly fuzzy from the booze, my body buzzing with hot, pressurized aggression. Aggression I hadn't been able to release despite the daily pounding of my boxing bag until I dropped to the ground covered in sweat.

We were in a flashy club downtown called Covert or Espionage or something like that, a place with a dance floor that lit up from underneath. The clientele was mostly gyrating Barbies in crop tops and tight jeans, wearing lip liner the thickness of crayons, and overly tanned guidos with tight white pants and too many top buttons undone.

It was a place I *never* went to. Partly because I hated the kind of Eurotrash pop anthems they played at an ear-splitting volume. But mostly, I never came here because I wasn't exactly wanted in here. It was a slip in management that I'd been let past the front door. A slip in management that I was sure they were about to regret.

Mercutio frowned at me. "What are you staring at?"

He turned his head towards the group of men in black jackets in the roped-off VIP area that I'd been eyeing since we arrived. Merc snapped his face towards me, his eyes wide with realization. "This is one of the Veronesis' clubs."

Indeed. We were deep in enemy territory. I'd told Mercutio not to come out with me tonight, but lately he seemed to have become like my second shadow. Anyone would think that he was...worried I'd do something stupid.

"It's a free country." I slammed down another shot, wiping my mouth with the back of my hand. There was only one Veronesi brother in here tonight, surrounded by his wanna-be goons, all dressed like him in black leather jackets and jeans, all with slicked-back hair. Just one would work.

Mercutio elbowed me to get my attention. "You don't think I see what you're trying to do," he hissed.

I knocked his arm away. "What am I trying to do, Einstein?"

"You've been a suicidal prick since you broke things off with her."

"Jules, don't embarrass yourself any further. It's over."

"I'm going to marry Rosaline."

"You thought that I loved you?"

I hissed under my breath as the heartless things I said to her echoed back in my head. Every cruel word was a knife I would have gladly taken myself. But they were doubled-ended blades, making twin wounds in both of us. The way her face had crumpled, the tears threatening to spill over, the way she had trembled; these memories were a whip that I punished myself with over and over again. I was an asshole and I hated myself for it. I deserved every foul, wretched thing coming to me.

"This is not about *her*," I said through gritted teeth.

"Oh, really?"

After I'd left Jules, I found myself at Mercutio's place, punching the gym bag he kept in his garage. It took only seconds for him to come out and casually ask me what was up. I had spilled my pathetic guts to him, a moment of pure weakness. Something I was regretting now.

Her, her, her. Why did everything have to come back to *her*? Why couldn't she leave me the hell alone for one goddamn minute. The only peace I seemed to get was when I was throwing punches. I did not want to be throwing punches at my best friend. The Veronesis, on the other hand...

"I just wanted to try out a new place," I lied. "I guess it was just fate that we ended up here."

"Fate?" Merc gave me an incredulous look. "You're kicking fate in its teeth."

"So what if I am? It's my life."

"It's *your* life?" Mercutio grabbed the front of my jacket. "You selfish prick—"

"Well, well, well." A cold, gruff voice cut through us like butter. "What do we have here?"

Mercutio let go of me and spun. Standing before us was Dante Veronesi, built like an Italian soccer player with lean, muscular limbs, the peek of a tattoo showing on his forearm from his jacket pushed up to his elbows, green eyes under heavy dark brows, a permanent scowl on his face. Of all the Veronesi sons, Dante was the dangerous one, the ruthless one, the reckless one, the one you'd never turn your back on. He was the one I had hoped to run into tonight.

He had a man flanked on either side of him, both shorter and stockier, but less scary-looking than Dante, the bulges under their jackets a sign that they were both armed to the teeth. Merc and I were outnumbered. Instead of being scared, a shot of adrenaline rushed through my veins like I'd taken a hit of cocaine.

Merc, the idiot, stepped in between us. "We don't want any trouble. We were just leaving. We didn't realize this was your club. No disrespect intended."

"I don't know, Merc," I said, pushing him aside and glaring defiantly at Dante. "I knew this shithole was Veronesi territory as soon as I smelled the inside of it."

"Jesus Christ," Mercutio muttered.

Dante's lips curled, his entire face contorting with anger. "You have some nerve coming in here and running your mouth. I think someone needs to teach you some manners."

I plucked a pink umbrella from a cocktail that a passing woman was carrying. "Who?" I waved the umbrella at Dante. "You and your entire boy band?" I flicked the cocktail adornment at him. It bounced right off his nose.

"You son of a bitch." Dante lunged at me.

Before I could get off a punch, several strong arms grabbed me from behind. More of Dante's men must have come up behind us. If I hadn't been so stupid, so blinded by my self-destructive urges, I'd have realized he might have arranged that.

I readied myself for Dante's hit, but it never came. For some strange reason, Dante's men were holding him back too. "Dante," one of his men hissed with a warning. "Not now."

My eyes followed their line of sight. There was a slightly older man, dressed too formally for a club, walking around slowly, his eyes sharp and peeled, looking at everything except the girls gyrating on the dance floor. An undercover cop.

Dante leaned in and stabbed a golden-ringed finger into my face. "You are one lucky motherfucker. Any other night and your head would be hanging from that chandelier."

"You'd try. That's as far as you'd get."

He snorted, dismissing me with a hand. "Get him out of my sight."

This was not ending here. I elbowed one of the men who was trying to shove me towards the exit and lunged towards Dante. Unfortunately, the other guy was still hanging on to me. "I challenge you, Dante Veronesi!" I yelled as loudly as I could. Everything seemed to freeze. I swear I heard gasps all around me. "You. Me. Outside. Right now."

Dante glanced around, his gaze finding the undercover, then leaned in. "You want to duel outside my club. Right when there's an undercover cop in here? Do you think I'm stupid?"

"You could have fooled me."

Dante nodded his head. "I see. This is a trick. We duel and the pigs swarm this place. They'll have grounds to investigate further until my family is brought down."

"No. No cops. You and me, outside."

Dante laughed. "You want a duel, so be it. But not here. Midnight tomorrow in Little Italy. Dead Man's Alley."

Mercutio inhaled sharply. "Roman, you can't—"

"Done," I said.

Dante grinned. "See you then. Unless you chicken out beforehand." He waved his hand in dismissal. I let myself get dragged away.

Mercutio and I were thrown out of the club into the back

alleyway. It stank of piss and the sole streetlight had long since been broken.

"This is real leather, assholes," I yelled at the retreating bouncers as I brushed down my jacket. They didn't bite. Looked like I wasn't getting my fight tonight. I was resigned to taking it out on my boxing bag later. Again.

The door to the club shut, cutting the music down to a dull thumping. "Do you believe those guys, Merc?"

Mercutio stood there staring at me, a stunned look on his face.

I let out a sigh. Time for the lecture. "What?"

But he didn't yell or rage or rant at me as I expected. It would have been so much easier if he had just yelled. Instead his face crumpled into one of disappointment, lancing me right in the gut. Why was it so easy for everyone to be disappointed in me?

"Roman," he said. "What have you done?"

JULIANNA

Espinoza and I hadn't been making any headway on the Eddie Sanchez case. We had a body but there was no workable evidence. There were no witnesses to the actual shooting and no weapon.

We got our hands on security footage from a pawn shop across the street from the Sanchez apartment. We saw Eddie take off in his car at around seven thirty, just like Rosa said. Rosa never followed him out. She was scratched off the list of suspects.

That left only Roman Tyrell and the unreliable witness who saw somebody *like* Roman at a gas station several miles away from his actual murder site. It was thin evidence, at best.

My cop instinct kept wanting to blurt out Roman's confession. It kept bubbling up onto my tongue at the most inappropriate moments. I *knew* Roman had killed Eddie. I knew it had been him at that gas station. I knew he somehow manufactured that insurance policy so that Eddie's family would be taken care of after he died.

It didn't stop me from missing him. It didn't stop me from loving him.

It was past ten thirty. We'd both just clocked off work. Espo was driving me home. For the first time in a few weeks, we didn't just drive in silence.

"I'm telling you, it's a tragedy," Espo said from the driver's seat.

I leaned back in the passenger seat as Verona's downtown flashed by, flexing my toes in my black leather work boots. "Why can't Lacey and Jasmine from toxicology be lunch buddies?"

"Jasmine will put Lacey off me forever. You know how girls like to talk."

"Oh, right. Didn't you date Jasmine for like, three minutes, a few months ago?"

Espo let out a low hum. "Best three minutes ever."

I made a face. "Ew. I don't need to know."

Espo rounded the street onto my block. "Dammit, I knew it would come back to bite me on the ass."

"You don't get any sympathy from me, man whore."

"But you can do damage control. She'll listen to you. I know Lacey will say yes to a date with me if you put in a good word."

"Which I won't do because I actually like her."

"Oh, ha ha, wise guy."

I let out an easy laugh. Espo and my relationship had been strained when Roman was in my life; Espo knew I was hiding something. Partners had to trust each other with their lives. Hiding things eroded that trust, putting our lives at risk.

Bantering like this almost had me convinced that we were back to normal. Almost.

He pulled up near my building. There was an awkward pause.

"So, er," I asked as casually as I could, "you want to come up for dinner?" Truth was, I missed Espo. I missed our easy friendship. Everything was so confusing, so conflicting, so damn hard in my life. I was tired of hard. I missed easy. "Chinese food courtesy of my personal chef, Ming's?" I may or may not have deliberately mentioned the name of Espo's favorite Chinese takeout.

Espo pressed his hands to his heart. "Ah, Ming. The one girl who never lets me down."

I ignored his hidden jab, even as it snapped against me like a rubber band. "So, Ming's, then?"

"Sure, that sounds great." Espo's phone began to beep. He let out a groan. "If this is a dead body, I will kill someone."

"If that's a dead body, I'm pretty sure someone beat you to it."

He pulled out his phone and stared at it, chewing his lip. "Damn, I..."

I rolled my eyes. "Let me guess, it's a woman and she wants you to come over. Is it Lacey?"

A guilty look crept over his face. Not Lacey.

I waved at him. "Go, Espo. I can eat Ming's all by myself. At least one of us should be getting laid."

Espo gave me a sad look. "Sorry it didn't work out with the rose guy."

I shrugged, even though it hurt. "It happens. Plenty of fish in the sea and all that, right?" I lied.

It took twenty-five years for me to find someone like Roman. It might take another twenty-five to forget him.

No, that was a lie. I'd never forget him.

At least I was comforted by the fact that she might make him happy.

ROMAN

From the corner of the alley across her street, I watched as Julianna and her partner pulled up in his unmarked dark police sedan. My chest tightened at the sight of her lovely profile, honey hair tied back at the nape of her neck. She laughed at something Espinoza said. My stomach twisted. *See, she's happy.* It'd only been a month and she'd moved on. *You were easy to forget.*

She was not. She was branded onto my heart, stained into my soul.

If I was going to die tonight at Dante's hand, then at least I could say that my life had been worth it because she had been mine. At least for a time.

Espinoza placed a hand behind her seat and leaned in. Close. Too close. What was he doing? My stomach clenched when I remembered what Benvolio had said about them. *"They're fucking, dude. That's the word on the street. And you know what they say, where there's smoke, there's fire."*

Was it true? Was he fucking her? Was he the reason I'd been so easy to forget? How dare he. She was mine. For a second, rage

SIENNA BLAKE

blinded me. I strode out of my hiding spot, determined to rip them apart.

Julianna opened the passenger door and stepped out of the car.

He didn't follow.

I stopped right there at the edge of the sidewalk. He wasn't going in with her. If Julianna looked over right now, she'd see me.

But she didn't. She walked into her building, giving Espinoza a tiny wave once she was inside. I backed into my hiding spot again just before Espinoza could spot me. When we both lost sight of her, he pulled away from the building.

She'd be walking into her apartment right now.

My gaze found the skeleton fire escape, a rickety ladder of rust and spider webs scaling up the side of her building, parts missing. Perhaps I could climb up her building one last time...

I could feel the heaviness of death around me. If I could just... touch her one more time. If I could talk to her...

Don't be stupid, Roman. You came here to make sure she was okay, and she is. The best thing I could do was to leave her alone. She probably wouldn't even spare a thought for me when she read in the papers tomorrow that Roman Tyrell's body was found washed up downriver.

I didn't follow her into her apartment. I slid back into the shadows, walked back to my bike, and prepared myself to meet my fate.

ROMAN

L ittle Italy had once been a bustling trading spot for the immigrant population of Verona. After my father rose to power, it crumbled into a quivering mess of seedy bars, strip clubs, and illegal gambling dens. Mostly it was abandoned, the forgotten homeless squatting in derelict buildings. The few reputable restaurants still open shut their doors well before nine p.m. With alleyways like twisted warrens and the kind of dark that sucked up the pathetic glow of streetlights, Little Italy was nearly deserted after midnight. It was a notorious spot for things that went on that the gentile population of fair Verona didn't want to know about. Dead Man's Alley was right in its rotting center.

A distant clock sounded three times, signaling midnight.

"Where's your dueling partner?" Dante's voice rang out, distorted by the hungry wind. His silhouette extended from the shadows from the other side of the alleyway. Two others followed. Shit. Dante had come with two of his men. If he was as ruthless as they say he was, he probably had more backup somewhere else.

Where was Mercutio? He was supposed to meet me here ten

minutes ago. I pulled out my phone. I'd missed a call from him. I would have been on my bike, riding across Verona when he called, the ringing lost under the roar of the bike's motor and the wind in my ears. He was probably calling to tell me he wasn't going to show up. Too late for me to call him back now.

He let me down. He never let me down.

You've let him down plenty. It's no wonder that he decided not to stand by you for this.

As much as I wanted to, I could not hate Mercutio for not showing up. He was right not to come. He was right not to attach himself to a sinking ship. He deserved better than to die along with me. *Live, Mercutio. Live a better life as a better man than I ever could.*

I gave Dante a casual shrug. "I didn't think I needed to hide behind my men. Unlike *some* of us."

Dante bristled.

Jesus, Roman. Do you ever just keep your mouth shut? Not that it would have mattered. Dante wasn't the kind of man to let me go if I asked. He'd make me beg, then he'd laugh as he killed me anyway.

He stopped about five meters from me, his men standing by his side like a pair of bodyguards. "Are you ready to join your dead mummy, Tyrell?"

I gritted my teeth and pushed aside my jacket to reveal the gun holstered to my hip. "Let's get this over with."

Dante nodded, a sneer lifting his mouth. He opened his arms out to the sides, revealing a single gun holstered to his side. His men helped him shrug off his long trench coat, one of them taking it from him.

We stared at each other across the dim moonlit night, the moon reflecting off the water. I saw my death in his eyes, two deep holes dug into cold dirt. My mind turned back to Julianna's face. *"Don't do this, Roman,"* her image begged me.

Too late. Too late to start again. Too late to say goodbye. Too late to change.

"On the count of three," one of Dante's men called, "shoot."

I shifted my weight, testing my balance. I was a good shot, a good aim. But I had heard things about Dante Veronesi. His father had built his sons their own shooting range when they had been mere children. I had heard that Dante Veronesi could shoot the center out of the king of diamonds from a hundred yards.

"One..."

Everything seemed to slow around me, my heartbeat in my ears became long and overwhelming. Was it too much to hope that there was a heaven and that my mother would be waiting for me?

"Two..."

Who was I kidding? If there was a heaven, then I wasn't being let anywhere near it. My fingers twitched by my gun. My vision sharpened down to two hateful eyes.

A gunshot fired, pain tearing across my left arm. I sprinted for cover behind a pile of crates as more shots whizzed past my head. The shots had not come from Dante but rather from somewhere else in the dark. My arm throbbed but I ignored it, drawing my own gun.

"You cheater," I yelled. I cursed as a shot hit somewhere near my right, causing splinters to spit at me. "Where's your honor?"

I heard Dante laughing. "You idiot. Your precious *honor* is just going to get you killed. Did you really think I was going to pass up the chance to end the Tyrell line?"

I shot out wildly from the corner of my hiding place. A barrage of bullets was their deadly answer. I was forced to crouch low as chips of wood exploded around me.

"Surrender," he called. "I'll make your death quick and painless. This is just business, after all."

I wiped the sweat off my forehead with the back of my hand. They had me surrounded. This was not a duel, but an execution. I wasn't getting out alive.

JULIANNA

One hour earlier...

The second I stepped out of Espinoza's car, the smile slid off my face. Lately it hurt to smile, like I was somehow out of practice. As I made my way into my building, my thoughts turned to Roman. I wondered what he was doing tonight. He probably wasn't alone like I was. He had Rosaline to keep him company. His *fiancée*, I thought bitterly.

I had barely gotten my key into my door when a deep male voice called my name. I'd been so lost in my thoughts that I hadn't heard him come up behind me.

Startled, I spun, drawing my gun at the same time. I didn't expect to see him. Mercutio Brevio was standing behind me, a serious look on his face.

"Whoa," he said as I pointed my weapon at him. He raised his hands, showing me his palms in an act of placation. "Don't shoot."

"Mercutio?" I frowned. He didn't like me. The last time we

saw each other he told me in no uncertain terms to leave his best friend the hell alone. The reminder of Roman throbbed like a wound across my heart. "What are you doing here?"

Mercutio's dark eyebrows drew together. He looked away. Whatever he was here for, he was struggling with telling me. Whatever it was, it took a lot for him to come here. I lowered my weapon but I didn't put it away, my eyes darting over his shoulder to make sure we were alone. "What is it?"

He shuffled his weight, his eyes darting around the hall. "Can we talk?"

"Talk."

"Inside your apartment?"

I flinched. Was this a trick?

Mercutio must have sensed my hesitancy because he opened his jacket, then patted his body. "Look, I don't have any weapons on me." He eyed my gun, now pointed at the floor. "I hate the damn things. Besides, I'm positive you'd kick my ass if I tried anything."

I didn't move. Mercutio might not have a record, but that could just mean that he'd never been caught.

Now who's being prejudiced, Jules?

"Please. It's about Roman."

Fuck. My heart felt scraped raw, my nerves fraying over just hearing his name. God, when would I be able to place him in the past? When would the wound stop feeling so fresh?

I tried to remain as calm as possible. I was sure that I failed. I nodded, my throat in a knot. I unlocked the door and let us in, holstering my gun.

"What about him?" I asked as soon as we were inside, my voice steadier than I expected it to be.

"Roman's in trouble."

"Trouble?" My stomach felt like someone was wringing it out.

"In less than an hour he's going to be facing off against Dante Veronesi. A duel to the death." My heart skipped a beat at the word *death*. "Dante is a ruthless cheater. Killing the only living heir to the Tyrell empire will cement his place as favorite with his father. He's never going to let Roman walk away."

"But the truce—"

"The truce means jack shit. They both blew that sky high. I can't go to his family. They'd turn the duel into a bloodbath and use it as an excuse to incite a war."

I cursed. *Damn you, Roman.* I swallowed hard, as bloody images ripped from crime scene photos flashed before my eyes. What the hell was he thinking by challenging Dante to a duel? They were illegal, first of all; a modern-day flashback to when men used to duel with pistols that the local Mafia had copied to sorting out their feuds. Second of all, what a stupid thing to walk into without backup. "Why are you coming to me?"

"I have no one else to turn to. No one else to help. I know...I know you care about him." *Even though you shouldn't,* was the accusation. "He'll listen to you."

"I don't know if he told you but he..." I hesitated. How much of our relationship did Mercutio know about? I chose to play it safe. "Roman and I don't exactly talk anymore."

"Just call him. Talk to him."

"He won't listen to me." I said, my voice coming out flustered. I wanted to help, but Mercutio was kidding himself if he thought that a call from me was going to convince Roman not to do such a stupid thing. He always did what he damn well wanted. "We didn't exactly leave things on good terms."

"He still...still cares about you."

That was a lie. Why would he break up with me? Why would he say those horrible things to me?

"Please," Mercutio said, "he is the only brother I've ever known. I know he can be an asshole at times..."

I snorted.

Mercutio gave me a wry half-smile. "Ok, he can be an asshole *most* of the time, but he doesn't deserve to die alone at the hand of the Veronesis. And he *will* die if you don't do something."

I squeezed my eyes shut. Could I put my pride aside?

My mind sent me an image of Roman on the ground, bleeding out, reaching for me. *"Jules..."* his voice croaking before his eyes went dead. My heart seized. Mercutio was right. I couldn't just sit here and do nothing. I had to try. Even if I was the last person he'd ever want to hear from. I couldn't live with myself if I did nothing.

I grabbed my bag, rummaging through it for my phone. My phone, where was it?

Dammit. My phone. I must have left it at work.

Shit shit shit.

"Where's your phone," I demanded of Mercutio. I grabbed it from him and called Roman. I'd say anything. I'd beg, if that's what he needed to hear.

Come on, Roman. Pick up.

It went to voice mail. My heart clenched when I heard Roman's voice asking me to leave a message.

Shit.

I hung up and turned to Mercutio. His face was drawn, tension pulling his jaw tight. "He won't pick up." I handed his phone back to him. "We have to go stop them."

Mercutio winced as he glanced at the clock on my wall. "We won't get there in time."

"Where is this duel taking place?"

"Dead Man's Alley, Little Italy."

Dead Man's Alley. Shit. That place was dark, the buildings around it abandoned with plenty of places to hide. Dante could have snipers hidden anywhere. Walking into that with just Mercutio and me would be suicide. We needed help. We needed backup. I gritted my teeth. It meant doing something that Roman would hate me for later. Better that he hates me than him being dead.

"We can stop this duel in time if we call for backup." I lunged for my cordless phone sitting on my counter.

"No," cried Mercutio. He grabbed my hand, stopping me from dialing. "No cops."

"*I* am a cop."

"No *other* cops."

"Merc," I called him by the nickname I'd heard Roman call him, "if you want to save Roman, we need help. It's too dangerous to do it alone."

Mercutio shook his head and swore. "I knew I shouldn't have come to you."

"Merc, we are running out of time. Do you want Roman to live or not?"

He let out a curse. "He's going to kill me…"

Us. He's going to kill us for getting the cops involved. Better angry than dead. "At least he'll be alive *to* kill us."

He let go of my hand so I could dial. "You do what you need to do."

I chewed my lip as the number rang, hoping to hell I was making the right decision.

My father picked up on the second ring.

I didn't stop to chat. "There's going to be a duel between the Tyrells and the Veronesis in Little Italy in less than an hour."

"Where did you hear this from?"

"A source. We need to send a team there now to stop it from becoming a bloodbath."

"A source?"

I withheld an exasperated noise. "A reliable source. Dad, we need to move on this now. I need a minimum of four units."

There was a pause on the other end of the phone. "I thought there was a truce going on between them."

"Obviously it didn't hold." Why was he taking so long to agree to send backup?

"Dead Man's Alley in Little Italy, you said?"

"Yes." Finally.

"It's abandoned there. Just a bunch of empty buildings over-looking the alley. No restaurants or commercial spots around the place."

"Yeah?" Mercutio was frowning at me with a look on his face like, *what's taking so long*. I turned my back on him. "So?"

"No innocents will be injured in the crossfire."

"The Tyrells and the Veronesis will kill each other if we don't stop them."

"Perhaps that's for the best."

"*What*? What the hell are you talking about, Dad?"

There was a pause. A long, heavy pause where I held my breath, the hairs on my arm raising as the anticipation built. He sighed as if I was being slow. "Sometimes," he said laboring over each word, "you have to know when to hold back, Julu. Some-times you have to let nature take its course."

Blood drained from my face. What the actual fuck? "Dad, you're just going to sit back and send who knows how many men to their deaths?"

"They are criminals, not men. And I am not sitting back. I am allocating resources."

"You have to send backup now."

"I do not have the luxury of reallocating uniforms to stop a bloodbath between criminals when I have innocent people who need their attention more."

Tears stung my eyes. My father— my *own* father—was going to let Roman die, a man I knew was good, because of all the bad ones. "One unit. Give me one."

"I'll send a unit there later to pick up the pieces of whoever is left."

My stomach coiled into a tight spring of resolve. Screw him. He might not send anyone to help. But I wasn't going to stand by and let this injustice happen. "Fine. Then I'm going in there by myself."

"Julianna, don't you—"

I slammed down the phone, a prickly heat underneath my skin like a rash. I couldn't believe it. My own father.

I turned to Mercutio, who was staring at me in despair. He wouldn't have been able to hear what my father said, but he would have gotten the gist of it based on my reaction. "We're fucked, aren't we?"

It wasn't over until it was over. "I have an idea, but it might get bloody."

Something passed between us. I saw the deep love he had for Roman mirrored on his face. And I knew that we were both prepared to die for him.

Mercutio nodded.

I grabbed my car keys. "Let's go."

ESPINOZA

Something rang out in Espinoza's car, a soft musical tone. He frowned as he accelerated through a green light. That was not his ringtone. It wasn't his phone ringing.

It sounded like it was coming from his passenger seat. Espo wondered for the moment whether he should stop the car and find it.

He could do it when he got to Desiree's apartment. He didn't want to keep *her* waiting. She'd sent a rather racy detailed message of what she wanted to do to him. The ringing had stopped anyway, silence filling up the car.

Too silent.

For a second the dull hollowness in his chest had a chance to step out into the fore. Desiree was beautiful, but she wasn't really someone he could talk to. Not like Lacey. Smart, funny Lacey, who was so easy to make blush. Smart, funny Lacey, who would run if she knew the past he kept buried.

The phone started ringing again, cutting through his thoughts. He frowned. Whoever dropped their phone in his car must be desperate to get it back. Espo sighed and pulled over to the side of the road. What was the bet this was some girl's phone she'd deliberately "dropped" in his car to make sure he called her again? It wasn't the first time one of them had done something like that.

You're such a cynic, Espo.

He got out of his car and walked around to the passenger's side. It had begun to ring again when he grasped the slim phone that had fallen down the side of the seat.

It was Julianna's phone. There was the small chip along the back where she dropped it that time at a crime scene, almost hitting the corpse on the head. She must have dropped it again tonight when he was taking her home.

He turned the screen over and was surprised to see the caller was "Dad".

The chief.

Espinoza hit answer.

"Don't you dare go after them yourself," the familiar voice roared from the speaker.

"Chief?" Espo asked.

There was a pause. "Espinoza?"

"Julianna dropped her phone in my car."

The chief swore. "Espinoza, you've got to stop her. I called her back on her home phone, but she didn't answer." The desperation in his voice tugged at Espo. He'd never heard the chief sound like this.

Espinoza's blood turned to ice as he listened to what Julianna was about to do. Throwing herself in between the Tyrells and the Veronesis! He knew something had been off with her for the last few months. He should have listened to his gut. He should have gone with her to her apartment for dinner from Ming's. Now she was acting crazy. Practically suicidal.

He had promised to look out for Capi when they had first been partnered, but he didn't count on how much he'd grow to like her. She'd practically become like a little sister to him. It wasn't about his duty anymore. If anything happened to her…

"I'm on my way." Espo sprinted to the driver's seat and slammed his foot on the accelerator before his door was even closed. "I won't let anything happen to her, I swear."

ROMAN

The present...

They say your life flashes before your eyes during those cold, stark moments just before death. Instead of my life, I saw the faces of those who had been cursed to love me. Proof that the money you wasted or hoarded, the women you fucked, the parties that had you drinking and dancing until dawn meant nothing, reduced to ghosts and ashes before life's ultimate humbler. I had convinced myself I needed no one. How funny that at the end of it, the ones you have are *all* that matters.

Bullets chiseled the flimsy crates that I hid behind into splinters. The faces of those who had imprinted onto my soul haunted me like the ghost I would soon become. How clear things were now. I saw every lost chance for me to tell them what they meant to me, shining like fallen gems. I saw how I had pushed them away instead of pulling them closer. *Stupid, Roman. If only you hadn't wasted your time on Earth.*

446

I shot out wildly over the side of the crates. A barrage of bullets was immediately returned. With my back against the crate, my hope running out, I sent out the last messages I wished I'd been able to deliver in person, hoping that somehow my silent thoughts reached them.

My mother. *I'm sorry I wasn't a braver son.*

Nonna and Mercutio. *I'm sorry I wasn't there for you these last eight years.*

And...Julianna. My perfect Julianna, her honey-hair and angel's soul shining brightly in my mind. My heart twisted with regret most for her.

I'm sorry I hurt you.

I'm sorry I lied.

I'm sorry I couldn't deserve you.

I'd spent my entire lifetime running away from the people that mattered because I had been afraid to lose them. I would lose them anyway. I almost laughed out loud. Hindsight can be cruel in her clarity.

But no matter. I wouldn't feel a thing soon. Even my regret would soon be dust and ash.

I fired another shot and crouched back behind the crates. Shit. I was running out of bullets. Only half a dozen left in my last clip. I wasn't going to hold them off for much longer.

"Police," a loud female voice commanded from behind me. "Nobody move."

Bullets start shooting towards this newcomer. I heard a curse from behind me. Then a return fire. For a few terse seconds the lady cop and I fired together at the Veronesis. I almost felt like we were on the same side.

Now that I had backup, I could get off a few more accurate shots. I heard a cry and knew I had managed to hit one of them.

Someone must have called the cops. Or more likely, an unlucky beat cop was patrolling the area and heard the gunfire. *You should have called for backup, sweetheart. We're both dead now.*

Headlights suddenly flooded the alleyway from behind Dante. I squinted as my eyes adjusted to the ghostly light. A police siren began to wail, the flicker of red and blue lights reflecting off the glass windows. Someone *had* called the cops. The police car accelerated straight through the alleyway with a squeal of tires.

Dante and his men scattered, running like rats from the sudden attack, just a blur of silhouettes to my eyes. They darted into dark hidden doorways in the abandoned buildings around us.

The car kept gunning forward towards me. Shit! I sprinted aside to the closest doorway in the wall of the alley. The damn thing was locked. Even as I kicked the metal enclosure, it would not yield. I was going to be hit. There wasn't enough room.

An awful skidding noise tore through my ears as the car braked to a halt, meters from me. The mist swirled up around the headlights. The sirens cut off, the red and blue lights still flickering. The silence was deafening. The driver did not move to get out.

"Hands up where I can see them, Roman," the lady cop yelled from behind me.

My heart gave out a kick. That voice. The way she spoke my name.

I turned slowly, my breath held in anticipation, my hands in the air. It couldn't be Julianna. It was just my mind thinking she sounded like Jules, a byproduct of my desire to see her. *You'll see, idiot. You'll have been busted by a beat cop who looks nothing like Jules.*

I squinted through the dark at the lithe figure pointing a gun at me. Julianna Capulet. My stomach turned to lead.

She strode towards me. Despite the figures I knew must be hiding in the darkness, watching from their safe hiding places, I felt like she and I were alone.

"Jules?"

"Shut up," she hissed. She grabbed my arm and spun me,

digging her gun into my back. She pulled my gun from my hand and I let her. But she didn't cuff me. "Move."

She steered me towards the car. I squinted as we got closer to the harsh glare of the headlights. That must be Espinoza in the driver's seat. Why wasn't he getting out to help her? Where were the other police?

Julianna nudged me with her gun. "Get in the back."

I stared around us. No other cops. No other cars. "Where are the other police?"

She cursed under her breath.

"Jesus Christ, Roman," I heard a male voice mutter from the darkness, "do you ever just do what you're told?" That voice, I knew that voice.

The figure stepped out of the driver's seat. That wasn't Espinoza. I squinted harder.

I blinked hard at him. "Merc? What are you doing here?"

"Saving your ungrateful ass." Merc glanced around us nervously. "Now hurry up and get in the damn car."

When had he started working for the police? Was he...under-cover? Had he been hiding this from me all this time? But where are the other cops?

"What are you—?" I broke off when the realization slammed into me. Merc wasn't working for the cops. This hadn't been a police raid. Mercutio must have gone to Julianna, told her about the duel I had stupidly instigated and somehow convinced her to help him. They had concocted a plan to save me. She had stood in the line of fire for me. He had driven a car straight through the middle of the Veronesis for me.

My head spun. What if she had been hurt? Shot? Or *killed* because of me? What if the Veronesis had shot at Mercutio driving the car instead of fleeing? I would have never forgiven myself. I'd rather I'd died at Dante's hand than have them risk their lives in such a reckless way.

I spun around towards Julianna, causing her to let go of my

SIENNA BLAKE

arm behind my back. I was so angry I wanted to smash my fist into a wall. She had risked *her life* saving mine. Why? Why would she come here?

"I never asked for your help," I growled.

Her face fell but any guilt I might have felt was crushed under the tempest of my rage. They shot at her. Dante and his men fucking shot. At. Her.

They weren't here for me to vent my murderous rage.

Mercutio. Mercutio had forced her to come. How? He must have blackmailed her. The idiot would do anything for me. Even taint his precious morals to save my unworthy ass.

"You," I spun towards Mercutio, fists curled tightly, ready to take out my anger on him. "You brought her here."

"Get in the car," Julianna grabbed my arm, forcing my attention back to her. Her touch burned me right to my blackened soul. She slid her gun into her holster. "We can argue about this later."

Later. Later would be the smart thing to do. But my anger was raging now. It needed a target. Like fast-flowing lava will cut a path down the side of the mountain, my rage would not be denied its path to hell.

I grabbed her shoulders, shaking her. *She could have died. She could have been hurt,* drummed through me like a war chant. "Why did you come?"

Her face cracked. She didn't think I wanted her here. She didn't think I was happy to see her. She didn't know that it had been her face I wanted to see more than anything when I thought I was going to die.

She recklessly put herself into danger for *me*. She wasn't supposed to risk her life for me. I was supposed to do that for her. What use was I otherwise?

She pushed at my arms, trying to unlock my grasp, but my hands just tightened on her. I was vaguely aware that I was

450

holding on to her just a little too tightly. "Why the fuck did you come here?" I repeated.

"What the fuck do you think *you* were doing challenging Dante Veronesi to a duel?" Something between a sob and a cry tore out of her. "You could have been killed. What would that do to Nonna, to Mercutio, to me?"

"You?"

"Yes, asshole." Her voice broke as she beat my chest with her fists. "To *me*."

To her.

She cared. Despite the hell I had put her through.

This was my second chance at life. My second chance to grab on to the things that mattered. I had run away from her just like I'd run from everyone else I'd ever loved. I would not make that same mistake again.

"Damn you." I yanked her towards me, a little too hard. She stumbled and fell against my chest. Everywhere she touched me felt like it was on fire. "You were supposed to stay away from me."

"I couldn't just let you die." Her fists still beat against me, although this time there was no real intent behind her attack except the hunger flaring in her eyes. She still wanted me, even after all I had done...

I dropped my face towards her mouth.

"Stop," a voice boomed out, cutting through us. "Or I'll shoot."

JULIANNA

*S*top. *Or I'll shoot.*

I would recognize that voice in my sleep. It washed over me like boiling water on icy glass, sending cracks right through me.

Espinoza.

He was standing at the far end of the alleyway where I had come from, legs in a wide stance, gun pointed.

I knew how we looked; Roman gripping me too tightly, leaning in too closely, me beating at his chest. It looked like Roman was hurting me. It looked like I was trying to make him let go of me. Espo didn't know the truth that lay beneath us. He only saw what was on the surface. He only saw what his prejudice would allow him to see.

Everything slowed down to a sticky crawl, like the world was suddenly drowning underwater. My heartbeat thudded, low and muffled in my ears.

Several things happened at once. Espinoza cocked his gun, the black evil eye of it focused on Roman.

"No, wait!" I screamed as Roman shoved me behind him,

trying to shield me with his body. His movements were too fast. You don't make fast movements in front of a cop with a gun.

Don't shoot! But before I could get these words out, the boom of Espo's gun was reverberating through the air in sticky waves, drowning out my scream.

Something collided with Roman's body from the side. Mercutio. Mercutio had thrown himself at Roman. They were both going down. Down towards the dirty black earth.

ROMAN

Espinoza pointed his gun at me. I could see hate contorting his face, his prejudice twisting my actions into something nefarious. He would never believe that I wasn't standing here assaulting Julianna. I imagined him pulling the trigger only a split second before he did.

Bang!

I braced myself for pain. I was hit from the side as Mercutio slammed into me. I had almost forgotten he was there. We hit the ground like a fallen tree. For a split second I remained still, my body frozen with shock, waiting for a starburst of pain and the inevitable burning ache.

When I was sixteen, my father had bought me a Glock 19. He made me practice loading a full magazine over and over again until I could do it in under ten seconds without a speed loader. When I succeeded, my father took the Glock from me, a slight smile of pride on his face, and turned it over in his hands. Then he pointed it at me and shot me. The bullet had lodged in my shoulder.

It had been one of his lessons. He had wanted me to feel what it was like to be shot. He wanted me to learn to handle the burning pain, like someone had shoved a red-hot poker through my arm. He made me tie off a tourniquet myself, torn from my own bloody shirt. He glared at me every time water dared to leak from my eye. I'd passed out well before his off-the-books doctor approached me with a scalpel and a pair of tweezers.

In Dead Man's Alley, I lay on the gritty ground, Mercutio's weight on me. I felt none of this pain. My relief was shattered by a wet, sticky sensation on my chest and the tang of metal in the air. Blood. Not *my* blood.

No no no, my mind begged uselessly. I rolled my best friend off me and onto his back, everything else forgotten.

"Merc." I hovered over him, ignoring the grit cutting into my knees. A sticky mess spread from his chest. This could not be happening. Mercutio refused to even *hold* a gun. What kind of God would let this happen?

"I think I got shot." Merc coughed and redness spluttered from his lips. Shit. His lung had been punctured.

"No shit, Sherlock." I pressed my hands over his chest. If I pressed hard enough, if I spread both my hands, if I fucking *willed it* hard enough, he would stop bleeding. He had to stop bleeding.

He looked down at his chest, at his lifeblood pouring out of him. "Man, it looks bad."

"It's not that bad."

"Don't lie to me, it's bad." He coughed again, more blood bubbling up, and winced.

"Why did you come here, you son of a bitch?"

"Someone had to save..." he coughed again. More blood. He ignored my attempts to keep him quiet, to conserve his strength. "...save your ungrateful..." His eyes matted over as swift as a plague. There was no warning. One second he was here and the next...

"Merc?"

Another set of eyes flashed in my head, the rich, earthy irises

SIENNA BLAKE

now dead and black as burned grass. *Mama?* A strange cold numbness fell over me as I slapped Mercutio's cheek, trying to wake him, my bloody hand leaving a smudged print just like a young boy's finger painting. *Wake up. Call me an ass. Yell at me. Tell me off, for fuck's sake!*

"Espo, stop!" Julianna screamed. She had launched herself between me and her partner, standing by me like a guard.

It hit me that the polished steel of Julianna's gun was the same color as the matching sweaters that Nonna had once knitted for Mercutio and me. It had been the first Christmas I'd spent with them since my mother had died. He always got a new sweater. This was my first. Merc had scowled when Nonna had pushed it down over his head. I had pretended to make a fuss too, but I had worn that sweater every day until it smelled. Mercutio would never know that I still kept that stupid sweater, packed in a box in my mother's apartment, now too small for me.

Nonna. My stomach twisted. How was I supposed to tell Nonna? How would I ever explain how I got him killed? How could she ever forgive me? All it took was a twitch of one finger. One careless, single movement. The entire futures of three people—Mercutio's, Nonna's and mine—were torn out of the pages of time.

My eyes focused past Julianna's legs to Espinoza, towering like an executioner. "Stand aside, Capi," he demanded. There was no remorse in his cold, hard voice. None. There was no paling of his skin, no slight quiver in his voice, like there had been in mine. He had been trained to kill. And he did his job. Who was the monster now?

"I won't," Jules said, widening her stance.

His face twisted in confusion, his eyes darting between Merc and me on the ground, and Julianna. He couldn't understand why she was protecting *us*.

Mercutio was dead by his hand and he was *confused*.

This was his fault. His. Not mine.

456

A fury unlike any I'd ever felt before rose through me like a demon taking possession. I was no longer Roman but a demented succubus demanding what was right. Retribution. Justice. An eye for an eye. Mercutio's soul was still hovering above us, torn from this Earth much too soon. It was only fair that Espinoza would be the one to escort him up to heaven.

Julianna's gun glinted in her holster like the wink of an eye. Mercutio would never wink at me again. He'd never roll his eyes at me when I was being an ass. I snatched the gun from Julianna's hip. It weighed nothing in my palm.

I saw Espinoza trying to aim for me, but Julianna was in his way. She would not move no matter how he screamed at her. He did not fire. He would not risk hurting Jules. For that I had to thank him. It was not enough to redeem him.

I had a clear shot of him under Julianna's arm. I meant to aim for his heart. I meant to tear from him the thing he had torn from me. But my hands were wet with Mercutio's blood and the nose of the barrel dipped. I pulled the righteous trigger. The second death crack sounded into the black, sticky night.

The hole appeared in Espinoza's stomach and blood flooded his shirt. An eye for a bloody red eye. Julianna screamed, but it sounded so far away. She screamed as her partner began to fall, like a tree felled, heavy and straight.

The instant he hit the ground, all my brittle fury smashed apart like a vase, scattering into splinters, leaving me in consequences' cold spotlight, tangled in the web of the blackened fate I'd spun myself.

Julianna let out a broken sob as she dove to Espinoza's side. She placed her hands over his wound like I had done for Mercutio mere seconds ago. The pain of Mercutio's death tore through me again, this time joined by the pain I saw on Julianna's face.

I had shot Julianna's partner. Her close friend. Her Mercutio. The gun dropped from my hands.

I am a Tyrell.

As if in answer, the night sky broke open with the scream of police sirens. I pushed myself up to my feet. I felt woozy, drunk from how the last minutes had scattered our four connecting lives in different directions.

The sirens were fast approaching. They'd be on us in minutes. Seconds. I stumbled towards Julianna, my empty hands reaching for her. Grasping for her. My life buoy, like a flash of honey hair over an angry black sea. If I could just grab hold of her.

Before I could reach her, Julianna grabbed another gun from her side, my gun that she'd taken off me. She pointed the single black eye towards me. An eye for an eye, until the world is drowning in blood.

Julianna had finally turned on me. We were finally on the two sides we were meant to be on. *I* had pushed her there. I wanted to fight it, to fight her.

I could not conjure any justification. I was a criminal and deserved to be treated like one. I lifted my bloody palms and tried to convey with just my eyes—my voice had been crushed in the sorrow clogging my throat—that I wasn't angry. I understood.

"Jules…" *I'm sorry.*

"Leave." Her top lip pulled up into a snarl even as her bottom lip wobbled and her hand holding the gun trembled. "Before I change my mind."

She was letting me go. She wasn't arresting me.

Even as relief broke over me, it couldn't wash away the stains of my unworthiness. I didn't deserve her mercy. Angel as she was, she bestowed it upon me anyway. Perhaps she could forgive me. I couldn't leave without knowing she could one day forgive me. Perhaps love me again. "Just tell me—"

"Leave now," she hissed, even as her voice broke. "Leave Verona. Go where you'll never be found. Because the next time I see you, I *will* bring you in."

Her answer was clear. She could never forgive me. Nor did I have any right to expect forgiveness. When I shot Espinoza, I severed the bond between us too.

Useless apologies gathered on my tongue. The fierce wailing of the police sirens blaring down on me silenced me and had me stumbling backwards. I shot one last look at Mercutio and Julianna, sending silent goodbyes to them both, before I slunk deep into the blackened bitter shadows where I belonged.

JULIANNA

Roman slid into the shadows. The instant he disappeared, my anger was jerked out of me as if it were tied to him with a piece of string.

I dropped the gun and turned back to Espo on the ground. Shit. He was losing so much blood. Too much blood.

I pressed my hands to the mess on his stomach. "It's going to be okay, Espo. Just hang in there."

"Why didn't you step aside?" Espo asked, his face screwed up. I was the reason he hadn't been able to defend himself.

"I just...couldn't."

"But..." he winced, "why did you let him go? You had him, Capi."

"I... He..." How could I explain to Espo? How could I excuse the man who had him lying there on the verge of death?

I shook my head.

"It looked like... You *know* him." The accusation was clear in his broken voice.

How could I deny it? How could I keep lying to him when the truth was so clear? I couldn't.

I nodded. "He's not who you think he is," I said, trying to justify myself. My voice sounded weak and limp.

The sirens screamed and tires screeched as help arrived. Relief flooded me. Help was here.

Espo blinked at me, becoming still. "He's the rose guy...isn't he?"

I nodded my head. "I'm so sorry," I whispered.

Betrayal clouded his eyes. My stomach stabbed with a thousand swords of guilt. I couldn't explain any further. Strong arms pulled me back from him as Espo was swarmed with paramedics.

ROMAN

I destroyed my phone and tossed the pieces away so I couldn't be tracked. I drove half out of my mind, somehow finding myself at my mother's secret apartment. I ricocheted through the rooms with all the lights still off and stumbled into the shower with all my clothes on. I leaned my forehead against the cold tiles, watching Mercutio's blood swirling down the drain.

It was only then I realized I'd broken all my father's rules about leaving a crime scene.

No evidence, no weapon, no witnesses.

He'd be so disappointed in me.

It was on the radio when I stepped out of the shower.

"...a gang-related shootout in Little Italy between officers and what was believed to be members of the alleged Tyrell crime family. Mercutio Brevio, son of the infamous Tyrell accountant, Tito Brevio, was shot and killed. Detective Luiz Espinoza was shot at the scene and is in critical condition. No other perpetrators were apprehended at the scene.

Police are combing through the evidence but have no suspects as of this moment..."

I grabbed the closest thing to me, a vase, and threw it. It

smashed across the wall in a shower of cream and red. Mercutio was *not* part of the Tyrell crime family. He was *not* a criminal. He was the best man I'd ever known. A good man. A nonviolent man who didn't deserve Tito Brevio as his father and me, the monstrous Roman Tyrell, as his best friend. How easy it was to assume that he was just like the two of us. He wasn't.

But he'd go down in the eyes of the public as just another criminal.

Nonna.

The blood drained from my limbs, pain ripping through me. Nonna would know by now. Dear God, I hope they were gentle when they told her. I hope they were kind.

I had to go to her, screw hiding. I had to comfort her, to fall apart alongside her, the only other person in this world who felt like I did right now.

Don't be stupid, Roman. She wouldn't want to see you again. She'd curse your name. Hate you. It was your fault he's dead.

It was my fault.

Mercutio died for me.

I began to pace, pace, pace in this cramped apartment. Replaying every second of those fated moments in my head. Trying to bend the bullet's trajectory. Each time failing. I watched Mercutio die over and over.

Every time it ripped me apart.

JULIANNA

I sat with my elbows on my knees, staring at the orderly squares of linoleum across the hospital floor. The plastic seat creaked underneath me every time I shifted even slightly. I didn't know how long I'd been sitting there. Minutes. Hours. Outside, the dawn had come and gone, but inside this hospital, time didn't seem to move.

"I'm sorry. He lost too much blood..."

God, the lights here were too harsh. They burned my eyes. I squeezed them shut, red staining the backs of my lids.

Damn you, Espo. Why did you have to show up when you did? Why did you have to shoot? You fired at an innocent man. You *killed* an innocent man. It was your own fault. Your prejudice killed you. *You deserved your bullet.* Even as that thought rose to the surface, guilt spread across me like spilled oil. How could I think that? How could I blame Espo? He'd only been protecting *me.*

I should have told him about Roman. I should have made Roman's true character known. I'd stayed shrouded in my cowardly silence while a good man like Roman Tyrell was crucified by the world. This was my fault.

My eyes drew to the dark red half-crescents stained under my nails. I had washed Espinoza's blood off my hands, but the evidence of my guilt was still there. I had stood in his way. I had stopped him from defending himself.

How could I have moved if it meant that it would have been Roman lying in the morgue instead?

In that cursed alleyway, clutching at Espo's life as it bled away, I had blamed Roman for all of it. I had sent him away with callous words and the accusatory point of my gun. The broken look on his face haunted me. His best friend had just been killed and in that moment, all I could think of was my own wretched grief, blinded to my own part to play in this black tragedy. At the time when he needed me most, I let him down.

My shoulders slumped around my heart, crumpling in on itself from sorrow's weight. So many pointed fingers. So many moments when it all could have been prevented. Now we had two deaths on our hands. The blame was a heavy chain that fell across all our shoulders. Nobody was innocent.

"Julu!"

My head snapped up. My father, his tie askew, his hair disheveled, strode down the hallway towards me.

"Dad," slipped out from my lips like a prayer. I launched into his arms and clung to his neck like a nine-year-old who had just woken up from a nightmare. Any minute now I would wake up. Any second now...

He shushed at me, a sound like soft waves. "I'm sorry, Julu. So sorry. Espinoza was a good man."

I nodded into his neck, letting his soft sweater soak up my tears. "I don't know what to do, Dad," I whispered.

"His mother's been notified," my father said, his thumb rubbing against my back. That was my father. Strong and calm even when things were falling apart around him. "She's coming in with her brother."

I nodded. I didn't even think about who might need to be notified. I was so lost right now.

"Don't worry," my father said, his voice vibrating with its first timbre of anger. "We'll get the bastard who did this."

I froze.

"There are no usable fingerprints on the gun," my father continued. "But you saw who did it, didn't you?"

Roman. Roman did this. But it wasn't his fault. It wasn't his fault.

I tugged away from my father, my thoughts jumbling around in my brain. I was a witness. I could not keep this quiet. I had to tell the truth. Right? It was my duty to say what I saw.

Could I turn on Roman? Could I speak up against him knowing it'd be my words that would slam the bars closed on him for life? He shot a police officer. No judge in the world would be lenient. Even if it wasn't all his fault. He was just reacting against Espo killing Mercutio.

How could I justify what Roman did? He killed out of anger, out of revenge, out of a sense of justice. How could I let Espinoza's death go unpunished? How could I ever face his mother again knowing that I had the power to send her son's murderer away and chose not to? How could I remain a cop?

My father gripped my shoulders. "It was Roman Tyrell, wasn't it? Wasn't it?"

I had to turn him in. This was my job. My duty. I opened my mouth to speak the words. The memory of Roman's broken face as I sent him away flashed in my mind. Somehow, I knew he wouldn't be angry with me if I turned him in. He would understand. Because that's who he was. He would be expecting it. The part of him that didn't see his own worth, embracing it.

It's okay, Jules, I could almost hear him whisper. *You do what you have to.*

This wasn't his fault. It wasn't. We were all to blame for creating a perfect storm resulting in two deaths. Even me.

They would never see it this way if I told them the truth. That's not how the law worked. The law pinned the blame on the man who pulled the trigger, not on the unseen forces compelling him to do it.

"Julu?" My father frowned deeply at me.

I couldn't do it. I couldn't send Roman away for life. The thought of it made my heart twist in agony. It was wrong, even though it was the "right" thing to do.

"It was dark." My tongue grew thick with my lies. "I didn't see..."

My father let go of me like my skin had become poisonous. His face twisted from disbelief to incredulity to anger. "What are you talking about?"

"I don't know who shot Espinoza." My voice came out strained and weak. I hated lying to him. But it was the lesser of two evils.

"The bullet pulled from Mercutio's body was fired from Espinoza's gun. Espinoza's death was a retaliation killing by Roman Tyrell. Admit it." Disapproval radiated off my loving father, stabbing me across my torso.

But I wouldn't break. I couldn't. "I don't know. I didn't see."

"You're lying."

"I'm not."

"Are you *protecting* him?"

"He isn't what you think."

"He is a *Tyrell*. They are monsters."

If he just *knew* Roman like I did, maybe he would give Roman a chance. "He's not like the rest of them. Father, if you only—"

"He killed your partner," my father roared.

"Espo's not innocent. He shot Mercutio, who didn't even have a weapon on him."

My father bristled. "So it was okay for Roman to kill him?"

"No, I just mean..." What did I mean? This gray brand of justice was never going to rest easy with my father, with the law.

467

Espo had killed Mercutio, an innocent. In turn he was killed. An eye for an eye. It was a clean brand of justice. "Roman doesn't deserve to go to jail."

"He killed your goddamn partner, so why are you protecting him?"

My shoulders sagged as tears sprang to my eyes. I was never going to get through to him.

My father grabbed my shoulders and shook me. "Tell me the truth or I swear to God I will have your badge." His voice boomed out through the hospital corridor. Several nurses and orderlies gasped. I felt all eyes focused on our public display. My face flamed with heat. So much for keeping up appearances. "I'll arrest you myself for obstruction of justice."

My stomach twisted. "You wouldn't."

"I would."

I pushed his hands off me. My father hated the Tyrells so much it made him demented. It was like my father pinned all the world's faults at the feet of the Tyrells. He gave evil a name, a pulse, so it'd be easier to pull down. He couldn't see, blinded by his prejudice, that the world was more shaded than pure black and white.

He shook his head as he paced in front of me. "My own fucking daughter. What does he have on you, huh? What does Roman Tyrell have on you?"

"Nothing."

"Then why won't you speak up against him? Are you afraid of him?"

"No."

"I can protect you. The system will protect you."

"You don't understand."

"Then make me understand."

"He saved me from those attackers. He stopped them from raping me."

"He what?"

"You see, he's good. He's a good man. He's caring and..."

My father stared at me like he didn't even know me. "I can't believe it."

"I love him." It came tumbling out.

There, I said it. I spoke the words. Now I couldn't take them back. I chose where I stood. I would not falter.

"You...*what?*"

I gripped on to the sides of my pants for strength. "I'm in love with Roman."

"N-No." My father staggered back from me.

I stepped towards him, reaching for him, pleading with him. "I love him because I know the *real* him. If you just took the time to get to know him, you'd see what I see."

My father's wide eyes locked on mine. For a second I thought I had gotten through to him. For a single sweet second my two worlds met and coexisted.

His lips curled into a snarl. And my fantasy was shattered. "You don't love him, you only think you do. And he doesn't love you, he's playing you, you stupid little girl."

"That's not true."

"How do you know he didn't hire those men himself to attack you so that he could swoop in and play the hero?"

His words slapped me hard across my face.

"What did he get you to do for him in return, huh? Did he ask you to throw the case on Vinnie?"

"No," I said in horror.

"Did you tamper with evidence?"

"How could you even ask me that?" My gut curled with indignation.

"I don't know. Maybe because my own fucking daughter just told me she was in love with a fucking criminal."

My hands, reaching so hard for that dream where my two worlds coexisted, faltered then dropped uselessly by my sides, drained of hope. My father would never accept Roman Tyrell, not in a million years. There could never be a world where the two men I loved most walked on either side of me. In turning to one, I rejected the other. In loving one, I hurt the other. I could not have them both; they would not let me.

My father leaned in, thrusting his finger in my face. "You tell me right now, who shot Espinoza?"

I stared over his weighted brows, his lips pressed thin, the glare in his eyes daring me not to answer.

It came out barely a whisper. "I didn't see."

His finger dropped. Disappointment rolled off him, weighing down the corners of his mouth. "Hand over your badge."

"Dad—"

"Badge. And your gun."

I unclipped the shield and holster from their positions on my belt. I had worked so hard to get them. I had fought sexism and accusations of nepotism. Now I was throwing it all away.

My father snatched them from me. "Now, get out of my sight."

Somehow, it still felt like the right thing to do.

I shouldn't be here. Even as I tried to walk as silently as possible, my heels still made soft clacking noises against the sterile laminate floor. I kept my head down, avoiding eye contact, walking assuredly as if I was supposed to be here.

I entered the morgue, silent and empty of living beings. Espinoza was lying partly under a white sheet on one of the tables. My step faltered when I spotted him. The only way I was able to keep walking was to focus on my shaky breath.

In.

Out.

In.

I clutched at the metal table as I stood near his head. His

usually tanned skin was so pale. So damn pale that I could see the veins on his eyelids. Even his smart-ass mouth was starkly white against the stubble on his strong jaw.

"Oh, Espo," I whispered. "I'm so sorry." Wetness rolled down my cheek.

"What are you doing here?" A voice came from behind me.

I spun, wiping my face. Lacey was standing at the doorway to the morgue, dressed in scrubs. She looked tired, her eyes red-rimmed from crying. Like mine were.

"I just wanted to see him. To see... To say goodbye."

After a pause, Lacey nodded and walked up to my side. We stood there, two people mourning over a friend, over a good man, who we both cared about.

I'd been hoping that coming here would give me some kind of closure. I was hoping to ask for forgiveness, strange as it was. I knew Espo couldn't hear me anymore. I knew he was gone. I had to find some kind of way to make peace with what I'd decided to do.

"Did you do the autopsy?" I asked quietly. I hoped not. I hoped they didn't make her do it.

She shook her head. "Dr. Carmichael."

I nodded. Dr. Carmichael was a medical examiner who worked the night shift. He and Espo had little contact. Performing Espo's autopsy would have been easier for him. "Did he find anything?"

"I don't think that's something I can discuss with you," she said, her voice turning frosty. She glared at me out of the corner of her eye.

My blood chilled. A single flare of anger attempted to take off —I thought friends were supposed to take friends' sides—but it fell to earth like a kite that wouldn't catch the wind. I couldn't blame her for acting this way towards me. She and Espo had been close too. I knew she'd even had a small crush on Espo, despite her hesitance at his playboyish ways.

SIENNA BLAKE

"I should go." I turned towards the exit.

Lacey grabbed my arm and spun me to face her. Her face was creased with blame, her eyes shiny with anger, her lip trembling. "Why won't you tell them who did it?"

More apologies jammed up into a knot at my throat. Soon I would choke on them.

"Without your testimony, we have nothing," she went on, her voice becoming more harried, more agitated. "Espo's murderer gets away with it."

"I'm sorry," I finally managed to say.

Lacey's face hardened and her gaze went to something over my shoulder. "I'm sorry too."

A firm hand rested on my shoulder and I turned. Two officers in their shiny blue uniforms had been sent to escort me out. I recognized the officer with his hand on me as Detective Pierce. There was an almost sorry look in his cornflower blue eyes. He was just doing his job, even if he didn't like it. Beside him was a new male officer whose name I couldn't remember.

"Ms. Capulet," Pierce addressed me. His formal tone struck me. He usually called me Capi just like Espo did. *Had.* Just like Espo had done. He'd never call me Capi again.

I realized Pierce was still talking to me. "You are not allowed to be here under your current suspension. I'm sorry, but we're going to have to escort you out."

Oh.

Right.

I didn't fight them as they led me out, up past the ground floor desks and the reception area. As I passed, the voices hushed around me. Heads turned. I felt the weight of every pair of eyes staring at me. Passing judgment on me, even without knowing the full story. Some of them were openly scowling at me, soft four-letter words uttered deliberately just within earshot. As if I had been the one to pull the trigger.

Now I truly understood how Roman felt.

JULIANNA

"What do I do, Nora?" I begged her. I was lying on my side, curled up on the covers of my bed.

Tell me. What do I do?

Nora sat by my side, brushing my hair from my forehead as if I were a sick child. I had told her everything. Confessed everything. The things I knew were too big, too swollen to keep inside me. I'd burst if I did.

I was so twisted up in my thoughts, like rope around my body, that I could not see a way to untangle myself. I could not cut my way out.

Should I hate Roman for killing my friend? My friend that would have killed him, the man I love. Or should I vilify my partner, who killed Roman's friend? If I wished that Espinoza were still alive, it would be wishing Roman dead. Roman's death would mean a death of me, too. How could I give thanks that Roman lived if Espinoza was dead?

Nora took my hand and patted it. "The only question you need to ask yourself is…how much do you love him?"

"What does love have to do with anything?"

"Love has everything to do with everything."

I pushed myself up to sitting and sniffed. "I don't understand."

Nora smiled. "My girl." She wiped my cheeks. "Love forgives. Love accepts. If you love Roman, truly love him...go to him."

"But he's gone." *I sent him away.* Why did I send the keeper of my heart away? Why did I banish my only joy?

Nora gripped me with a strength that I didn't know she had. "Then don't stop looking until you find him."

ROMAN

I t was late, very late. The cathedral was locked when I arrived. But locked doors had never deterred me.

I had received a lock-picking kit from my father when I had turned fifteen. He told me I had one week to learn how to open any door or I'd be sorry. Exactly one week later my father locked me in the basement without food, water or light and told me the only way I was getting out was by my own skill. Turns out that fear was a very useful learning incentive.

I was here because I had nowhere else to go. I wouldn't seek refuge with my father. No doubt he had heard what I'd done and was scouring the city looking for me. Perhaps part of me was waiting to get caught.

I sat in one of the pews. The large wooden Jesus stared down at me from his eternal place of suffering. Perhaps it was just my imagination, but he gazed at me with such pity, or perhaps the few candles I had lit about the empty church caused the deep shadows around his eyes. Fuck your pity.

I turned my head and found a pillar closest to me carved with an image of Satan, his face monstrous and warping as if it were melting wax. Here was a figure I could relate to.

"Roman? Is that you?"

I didn't have to turn to know that Father Laurence had entered the main section of the cathedral. I must have woken him.

I said nothing. I didn't have the strength even to hold my own head up under all this crushing guilt. Under all the tormented chants of *if only...*

Father Laurence slipped into the pew beside me, dressed in striped pajamas and slippers. He placed a warm hand on my shoulder. "Talk to me, my son."

I confessed everything. I had no strength to hold it all in. My guards were down, my will wrecked upon the rocks of fate. I told him about Julianna, about the duel, then about what had happened to bring me here. Even as I spoke, some of the heaviness lifted, but still the guilt remained.

I'd shot a man out of fury. I'd killed him out of pure revenge. This was worse than any death I'd dealt before, because no one had forced me to pull the trigger that severed a man's connection to this Earth. Not just any man. Julianna's *friend*.

And Mercutio... My heart twisted in agony every time I thought of him. He had been innocent in all of this. He died to save my wretched life. Why couldn't he have just let me take that stupid bullet? Of the two of us, I deserved it a thousand times more than he did. If he'd just let me take that bullet as punishment, I wouldn't have had to kill a man to avenge him.

"Oh, Roman," Father Laurence breathed. "I am so sorry."

"Pity Mercutio. Pity Espinoza. But do not pity me. I don't deserve it." I stared at the sculpted pillar of the ultimate sinner. "I am no better than Satan himself," I said, quietly.

The Father was silent for a long time. Then he hummed to himself and leaned back in the pew, folding his hands over in his lap. "Do you know what Satan's only mistake was?" he said.

"Going against God, being an evil bastard, that about sum it up?"

"It was not his rebellion or his wickedness that was his mistake."

"Really? They seem like pretty big mistakes."

If my sarcasm affected the Father he didn't show it. His demeanor remained calm and steady. "His only mistake was to believe that God would not forgive him."

Father's words settled on my skin like a fresh layer of snow. It began to melt and seep in slowly, like the end of winter.

I shook my head, not ready to hope that *I* could be forgiven. "By now I should be a wanted man. I'll leave before I force you into an uncomfortable situation." It was the Father's moral duty to call the police, even if the law protected my confession to him. I couldn't hate him for turning me in. Just like I couldn't hate Julianna for eventually speaking the truth about what I did.

Father Laurence patted my hand resting on the back of the pew in front of me. "You will always have a safe place here, Roman. Come, you must be tired."

I stared at Father Laurence as he stood and slipped out of the pew. He couldn't possibly mean to help me. He looked back at me and motioned for me to follow him.

"You'd be harboring a criminal," I said, still stunned at his benevolent intentions.

"Roman Tyrell, all men are sinners. All men are thus equal in the eyes of the Lord."

I still couldn't stand.

He walked back to me. "Come," he repeated softly as he pulled me to my feet. "Things have a habit of looking more hopeful after a good night's sleep."

Father Laurence set me up in a spare room up in the tower of the church. It was simply furnished with a small bed and rug, a tiny toilet in an adjacent room. I lay upon this bed with a thin pillow

477

under my head. The pre-dawn light was still minutes away from lighting up the stained glass windows, so all was dark except for a single candle I'd kept lit by my side. I was already drowning in darkness; I could not stand to be consumed by the night. I was very much alone except for the ghosts of all the men I'd sent to their deaths. I was not a superstitious man, but something about the vaulted ceiling that rose above me—or perhaps it was the ghost of tears and cold finality that clung to the gray stone walls —made me feel as if I were lying at the base of my own tomb.

A knock sounded on the door.

I sat up, thankful for the reprise from my sour self-pity. "Come in, Father."

The door creaked open. A figure, much too short to be Father Laurence, stepped into the small room and closed the door.

"Jules..." I stood, my heart jamming against the back of my throat and wrapping around my spine. If I weren't already standing with the backs of my calves against the bed, I would have stumbled back farther, knocked off my feet at the sight of her.

She was an angel in a dark hooded sweater and jeans, the lit candle she was holding brushing a warm radiance about her face, making her whiskey eyes glow like amber. "I came to speak to Father Laurence. He told me you were here."

The good Father did give me up after all. "Have you come to arrest me? I'll go peacefully."

Her mouth sprang open. "I didn't tell them it was you."

What? "Why? I am guilty."

She lifted her chin, her honey hair falling over her shoulders to frame her face. "If you are guilty, then so am I."

"*You? Guilty?*" I couldn't believe her words. Her only guilt was caring too much for me.

"If I'd only told Espinoza about you, about us, he wouldn't have fired."

"It's not your fault."

"I am as much to blame as you."

I shook my head, disbelief making me lightheaded. "If you're not here to arrest me, then...why are you here?" She was risking her reputation by being here.

"Could you...?" She stepped farther into the room, then hesitated.

"Could I what?"

"Could you find it in your heart to forgive me?"

Forgive *her*? My head spun so hard I was nearly forced to my knees. "Forgive you..." I could barely get the words out, they were so absurd, "for what?"

"The way I sent you away... What I said to you..." She chewed on her beautiful bottom lip, sending a curl of warmth through me.

"Leave now," she hissed. "Leave Verona. Go where you'll never be found. Because the next time I see you, I will bring you in."

She was here asking for...of all things...*my* forgiveness, when I should be begging for hers.

"I'd just shot your partner, your friend." I took a step towards her, partly testing her reaction to my proximity, partly because it physically *hurt* to be in a room with her and not get closer. "Your reaction was angelic considering the circumstances."

"He'd just killed your best friend." She matched my step. "Your reaction was...understandable considering the circumstances."

She didn't hate me. Through my darkness, a ray of light appeared. I could scarcely dare to hope. "Do you think..." Dare I ask? "Do you think...you could ever forgive me?" I kept closing the space between us, desperate to hear the answer and yet terrified of it too.

"That is what love does. Forgives the unforgivable."

My head spun at her words. Could she still love me? After all I had done? "You still l..." I trailed off. I felt so undeserving even to speak the word.

"Still love you? Yes." She lifted her chin, her features stained with sorrow. And yet there, on her face, was everything I'd ever wanted but never deserved. Forgiveness, openness, love. I took it because I could not believe my luck. I took it because I could not do anything else.

I claimed her mouth. I stole her breath into my lungs and let it bring me back to life. I crushed her against me like I could drag her into my body. Her tiny fingers curled into my shirt and she pressed up against the heart that only beat for her. This was my saving grace; that I was good enough to love *her*.

I promised to God, from that moment on, I would do everything in my power to be the man she deserved. To be the man she *saw* in me. To be the man who deserved her love. Even if it took a whole lifetime.

JULIANNA

We lay under a blanket, naked, squashed together on the bed that barely fit the two of us. I was sated and warm and happier in this tomb-like room with Roman by my side than anywhere else without him. The dawn began to spill into the room. We would have to face the world soon. But not yet.

"Why did you break up with me?" I traced his hard, muscled chest with my finger.

He stiffened. "Does it matter?"

"It does to me. You're still engaged to her."

"Rosaline," he growled under his breath.

I gave him silence, the space to speak. He inhaled long and loud before he spoke. "Rosaline knew about you. She said she saw me leaving my apartment late one night and followed me. *I* led her straight to you," he said through gritted teeth.

I traced his jaw and it softened.

Roman turned his dark eyes towards me with a look so intense that my breath caught in my throat. "First, she threatened to come clean about her lies as my alibi. When that didn't work, she threatened to expose *you* if I didn't marry her. I couldn't let her ruin *you*."

I knew there was a reason. I just thought it had been his father who had forced him into a sham of a marriage. I made a face. "So you broke up with me instead of talking to me about it."

He grimaced. "When you put it that way, it doesn't sound very smart."

I rolled my eyes. "Understatement of the century."

"Okay, I was an idiot."

"About so many things."

He tugged me closer so I was sprawled over his body, his warm, hard body under the length of mine causing the lick of desire to rush through me. I could feel him stirring against my hip. "It probably won't be the last time I act like a fool."

"Are you telling me that I better get used to it?"

"How long are you planning to stick around?"

I shrugged. "Just for always or so."

His fingers tightened around me. "Always?"

"Always." I brushed my nose against his as we made a cave with our breaths and sighed happily as the world was shut out for just a little longer. "I don't want to live without you. I tried but I can't. I'm done trying," I said, repeating words he once said to me.

He let out a low growl and kissed me with an intensity that told me he wanted "always" too. Before I could deepen the kiss, he pulled back and gave me a sad smile. "It's a beautiful dream. But it's just a dream, Jules. You're still a detective. I'm still a Tyrell."

"What if it didn't have to be?"

He flinched. "What do you mean?"

"Remember when you asked me if I wanted to run away to Paris with you?"

He licked his lips. And nodded.

"Does that offer still stand?"

His eyes widened. He opened his mouth, then closed it. For once, Roman Tyrell was speechless.

Was he trying to figure out a way to let me down gently? I sniffed. "It's not that hard a question, Roman."

He shook his head, still looking dazed. "That offer was never retracted. But Jules, your career, your father..." All the reasons why I told him I couldn't leave Verona.

"My career is over. I just lied to the chief of police about witnessing a shooting. And," I tried not to let the bitterness show in my voice, but I failed, "it turns out that my father is not the man I thought he was."

Roman tucked me against his chest, his hand stroking my hair. I found myself softening against his solid, hard warmth. "I'm sorry. It's hard when fathers fail us."

He hadn't answered my question. I pulled back to look at him. "So...?"

"It would mean a life on the run. It would mean leaving everything behind."

"It would mean being with *you*. Really being with you. Walking down the street together, holding hands, kissing in public."

"You'd never be able to come back, to see your father or Nora again."

I paused. My heart squeezed. "Nora will understand."

"And your father?"

I gritted my teeth. "He won't. But that's not my problem."

Roman shifted under me, his features pensive. "I just want to make sure you know what you're getting yourself into."

"I know what I'm getting myself into," I said firmly. I had never been so sure of anything in my life. Paris, with Roman. Hell, I'd go anywhere as long as he was with me.

A small, slow smile crawled across his face. "Okay."

Our mouths crashed together. In my heart, there was this warm feeling of certainty that I had come home.

SIENNA BLAKE

"Wait." He pulled back as my greedy hands wandered down his body. "We have a lot to plan."

"Later," I said, pushing him onto his back and sliding down on his length.

～

I could have stayed with Roman all day. Father Laurence had told us we wouldn't be disturbed there. Later, once we were long gone, we would have more than enough time for lazy days in bed.

We agreed to leave Verona together after Mercutio's funeral that afternoon at another church. We'd take out all the cash we had access to, then leave in my car, ditching it for another once we were out of town. Then we'd hole up in a motel in a nearby town while Roman's contact worked on getting us fake passports so we could leave the country without being detected. The rest we'd figure out as we went.

I watched Roman slipping on his dark t-shirt, apprehension coiling in my belly. Now that we'd decided to do this, I didn't want him to leave my sight. What if his father found him? What if *my* father caught him? "Do you want me to come with you?"

"No. It's too dangerous for us to risk being seen together."

I chewed my lip, my stomach doing flips despite his reassurances. "I'll go crazy just sitting here waiting for you. I'll go home, get clothes, say goodbye to Nora."

He caught sight of my face as he slipped on his shoes. He grabbed the back of my head and pulled me against him. "Don't worry," he mumbled against my hair, "I won't let anyone see me." He kissed me long and deep.

I gripped his shirt, not ready to let him out of my sight. "Promise me you'll come back?"

"I promise."

ROMAN

I watched Mercutio's funeral from afar, cowering behind an old oak tree. It was held at the small Catholic church that Nonna went to every Sunday, the Church of St. Michael. She used to make Mercutio and me go with her when we were boys. As we got older it became harder for us to sit still long enough for her to wrangle us into our Sunday best.

The small chapel on the grounds was unassuming, a simple rectangular design with a copper bell hanging from the bell tower. The tombstones here were like small, simple, mismatched teeth across a threadbare lawn, Mercutio's grave sitting open and fresh like a cavity.

I should be the one in the ground. What kind of person did it make me to take happiness from being alive when he was dead? What kind of person did it make me to take shelter in the arms of the woman I loved when the ones he loved paled with his loss? I would return to Julianna and Nonna would return to an empty house.

There was a cluster of mourners around his gravesite. Nonna was among them, her soft, trembling body shaking with grief.

She cried as the priest spoke. She wailed as the coffin was lowered into the cold ground.

I wanted to go to her. To wrap my arms around her shaking shoulders. I wanted to howl alongside her and beat my fists at the ground. I wanted to throw my wretched self at her feet and beg for her forgiveness, forgiveness I didn't deserve.

But I couldn't. I didn't want to cause her any more pain than I already had. I stayed where I was, letting this hurricane wreck the insides of me.

If only I could turn back time, Nonna. I'd have gladly taken that bullet meant for me. He shouldn't have tried to save me, damn him, but he was just too good a man to let me die. He was too good for this world so the angels took him. He belonged with them now.

When it was all over Nonna collapsed in her exhausted state, moaning, held up by her friends and neighbors that I'd met over the years. The crowd dispersed, one by one, like black chess pieces off a board. Then there was no one left except Mercutio, lying alone in the cold, cold dirt.

I remained frozen in my hiding spot.

Out of the corner of my eye I spotted a figure walking towards the grave from between the headstones. A man in a gray suit with a cane in one hand. I squinted through the light, misty rain that had begun to fall. I knew that walk, that swagger.

That was Mercutio's father. Tito Brevio.

Goldfish.

I was told once by my father that the Chinese have the same character for crisis and opportunity. I don't think I'd truly understood why until now. My grief fell below the surface as this opportunity rose like an oil slick. I would find out who Goldfish was working for. I was no longer helpless and aimless. I grabbed this reprieve from sorrow and ran with it.

I snuck up behind him, ducking from gravestone to gravestone as silently as I could, as Goldfish came to stand at the base of Mercutio's grave.

"Ah, son," I heard Goldfish say, his deep voice weighed down by what sounded like pity. "You were such a good boy. Such a good boy. You still ended up here."

I grabbed Tito's shoulder and swung the man around. His cane came for me. I ducked aside, grabbed his wrist and spun him around with his arm twisted around his back. He let out a small wail and dropped his cane into the damp grass.

"Mr. Brevio," I said in a low voice. "It's been a long time."

Goldfish flinched. He looked over his shoulder at me, his graying eyebrows drawing together when he recognized me. "Roman Tyrell," he spat out my name like it was bitter. "What do you want?"

"I just want to talk."

"Yeah? Well I don't talk well when I'm being held against my will."

I leaned in to Tito's ear. "Try to run and I'll blow your kneecaps off."

"I don't doubt it, son."

I let go of him and he scrambled to get some distance from me. He cleared his throat, composing himself as he brushed down his suit and straightened his silver tie. "I heard you were back."

I picked up his fallen cane. He held out his hand for it.

I flicked the head of the cane. A blade came out of the end. I raised an eyebrow at him. "I think I'll hang on to this until you've answered my question." I flicked his weapon closed and gripped it in my left hand.

Goldfish gave the cane one more yearnful glance before focusing on me. "What question would that be?"

"Who hired you to kidnap Julianna Capulet?"

"That lovely young detective?" He raised an eyebrow. "Someone tried to kidnap her, did they?"

"Don't play dumb with me."

"Even if I did know, why do *you* care what happens to Detective Capulet?" There was a glint in his eye as he spoke. He knew something.

"That's none of your business. Now answer the question." I pulled the pistol from inside my jacket and pointed it at him. "Or they'll be digging a second grave next to Mercutio's."

He eyed me over, his eyes stopping briefly at the gun. "You're asking a dangerous thing, boy."

"I'm not a boy anymore."

Goldfish let out a puff of air. "No, you are not. You grew up into a man. Just like your father," he added with a cruel twist to his lips.

"I'm nothing like him."

Goldfish's lip twitched. His gaze felt as heavy as a fallen pillar. "Of course not." He glanced down at the freshly covered grave, a mound of dirt and a new headstone marking the final resting place of his son and my best friend. He let out a sigh. "He grew up too. He grew up into a good man."

"The best," I agreed, swallowing around an acorn in my throat.

"And yet...here he lies. Gone too soon."

I studied Goldfish's face, an older version of Mercutio's, and felt a stab of sadness. Merc would never grow old enough to look like his father did now.

"I was never a good father to him," Goldfish said, so quietly I barely heard it.

"No, you weren't."

His eyes snapped up to meet mine, a tension to his jaw. "I did the best I could for him, which was to stay away. It was more than you did." His words were barbed, but the wounds I had already inflicted on myself were so raw that nothing more could be said to hurt me. "You want to know who ordered the capture of your little girlfriend?"

"Yes."

"Consider this a funeral gift. Because Mercutio would have wanted it."

"Who?"

"Ask your father."

My father. The shock snapped at me and yet it didn't. It already echoed something I knew deep down but was too afraid to admit. "You're lying."

"Why would I lie?"

"Because you've never liked me. Because you're covering for the person you're really working for."

"You want proof?"

Did I? I nodded, slowly.

"$7,275, Nemo's Furniture Removals, the thirtieth of August."

"What's that supposed to be?"

"It's how much the contract was, who it was paid to and the date it was paid. Find the corresponding payment on your father's bank statement, you have your proof. Now," he held out a hand, "may I have my cane back?" I threw the cane to him and he caught it. "I'll tell you one more thing before I go, shall I?"

I nodded.

"The contract is still open." He saluted me with his cane, then turned to walk away. "Happy fishing."

The contract is still open.

My blood turned to ice. They were still after Julianna.

We had to get out of here, tonight.

JULIANNA

I slipped out of my apartment building as dusk was approaching. I'd spent longer there than I had planned. Nora wouldn't let me go, squeezing my neck like she was a child, sniffling into my collar. I pushed away a pang of sadness for the life I would be leaving behind.

The thought of Roman soothed the ache. He was my life now. He was more than I ever expected for myself. I could always sneak back to visit her.

A few leaves flew past me, whipping my hair up. Now to just find a cab. It was peak hour and an available cab would be hard to find. Perhaps if I walked it would be quicker.

A taxi turned the corner towards me. That was lucky. I hailed it and jumped inside the warm interior. It seemed fresh out of the box, unmarked leather seats and the plastic divider behind the driver had hardly a scratch on it. From the back seat, I only had a view of the cabbie's dark hair, a dark blue cap pulled low.

"Waverley Cathedral, please."

The cab driver nodded and pulled away from the curb. I watched the city that I grew up in slide past my window, recognizing the familiar streets and shops with a nostalgic pang. Soon, everything would be new: new city, new streets, new life. I found myself missing my mother. She would have understood. She knew what it was to love deeply. She would have urged me to go, she would have accepted Roman. I know she would have. Not like my father. A seed of bitterness rooted in my stomach. He would never understand. He would never accept Roman and me.

The taxi took a wrong turn into a deserted alleyway. I frowned. Where was he going? I knocked on the plastic divider. "Excuse me? This isn't the way to Waverley Cathedral."

The mechanical locks on the doors clicked like a gunshot. A voice crackled through the small speakers on the side of the cab. "Afraid we're not going there, Miss Capulet."

My blood froze in my veins.

A low hiss grew into a loud one as a white smoke filled the back of the cab, stinging my eyes. I held my breath and struggled with the door. This wasn't working. I spun to my side and kicked at the glass. Break, damn you, break. I could hear the cab driver laughing through the crackle. I couldn't hold my breath any longer. I gulped in sweet medicinal-smelling air. My head spun. Black spots flickered in front of my eyes. I couldn't pass out. I wouldn't. I just had to break this window…

My legs grew weak. The edges of my vision closed in.

I just had to—

Everything went black.

ROMAN

J ulianna still wasn't here. I paced the small room at Waverley Cathedral, grabbing my hair. It was almost nine p.m. She still hadn't arrived back. She was supposed to be here hours ago. I tried calling her several times, my fingers stabbing the keys on my new burner phone, but her cell phone had been turned off. I was about to go insane. My heart tore itself to pieces with helpless worry. Something had gone wrong. Terribly wrong. What was the bet my father had something to do with this.

I couldn't wait here any longer.

Outside Julianna's apartment, I sat in the black sedan I'd stolen. It was supposed to have been our getaway car, the back packed with a few clothes, enough food and bottled water for our drive out of here.

Her apartment was dark. Too dark. Not a soul stirred inside. Still, I had to be sure. I slipped out of the car and locked it behind me. In the side alley, I took a run up and leapt for the bottom rung of the fire escape. I caught it, pulling myself up, before making my way up the rickety ladders to her apartment. I peered through her bedroom window into the gloom – she wasn't home. No one was.

I slid around the building, jumping from ledge to ledge until I got to the single window at the end of the corridor on Julianna's floor. I found the window unlocked, thank God. I pushed it open and slid inside. It was getting late but I didn't care. I knocked on Nora's door, my fist reverberating through the wood. My anxiousness caused me to hammer on it too hard.

I heard a call from inside, "Hang on a damn second."

Hurry up, Nora. There were no seconds to lose.

Nora opened her door, her robe tied around her waist. Her features went from surprise into a frown. "Roman, what are you doing here?"

"Did you see Julianna?"

"Yes, but she left a few hours ago. To meet you."

Shit. The blood drained from my limbs. Cold fear took root in my gut. "She never made it."

Shit shit shit.

Somewhere between here and Waverley Cathedral, Julianna had disappeared.

ROMAN

In the silence of my car, I pulled out my phone and rang a number that I had memorized. A contact I only called in emergencies. A number that I always deleted from the phone memory after I used it.

"I thought I told you never to call me again," a female's voice said through the phone, no humor to her tone.

"It's an emergency," I said through gritted teeth.

"It always is with you."

"Goddammit, D, I don't have time to chit-chat."

She tsked. "Alright already. Calm your farm."

I shoved down the frustrated curt response about to lash off the tip of my tongue. *Control yourself, Roman.* Yelling at D was not going to get Jules back. "I need you to check something in the Tyrell accounts."

"The Tyrells have a number of accounts."

"Check all of them."

"*All* of them?"

"I have an amount and a date. Check all of them."

There was a soft sigh at the end. "I don't know why I keep doing shit for you."

"'Cause you secretly love me." I couldn't help but joke despite the situation.

She snorted.

I recited the information Goldfish had given to me. There was a pause and tapping.

Finally, her voice came back online. "Yup, there it is coming out of one of the Tyrell subsidiaries…$7,275, Nemo's Furniture Removals, thirtieth of August."

My blood turned cold.

Goldfish was telling the truth. My father lied to me. He paid to have Julianna kidnapped.

The contract's still open.

JULIANNA

I rose to awareness like a drowning woman reaching from under the surface of an icy lake. For what seemed like ages, awakeness seemed removed from me by a thin sheet of ice. I fought against it, kicking and screaming for life. Finally I broke through.

My eyes opened. I inhaled sharply, drawing sharp, frigid air into my lungs, and sat up. My head spun. I reached down to steady myself, finding a cold, smooth surface.

Where was I?

My mind scrambled to piece together the last few minutes of consciousness. I had been in a cab before the doors had been locked. I had been knocked out by some kind of gas. I had been taken. By whom?

I squinted through the dim, trying to figure out where I was. It was a room perhaps the size of a small bedroom, empty shelves about the place. A single fluorescent light bulb flickered over me, the only one working, casting a greenish sickly spotlight over me. There was a distinct smell of something rotting. The air felt wet. I frowned. The walls and floor were white and shiny, like marker board. So was the ceiling. High along one wall there were three air conditioning units on shelves. There were no windows that I could see. A large door like a barn door took up part of one wall, sheets of plastic draped before it.

I knew what this was. I was in an old cold storage room.

"I did warn you to be careful, didn't I, Detective Capulet?"

My blood froze.

Protruding from the shadows on one side stood a man whose features looked so similar to those that I treasured.

Roman's father.

He stepped forward so I could see him properly. With a wide frame dressed in a midnight-black suit, leather shoes so polished they shined, Giovanni Tyrell was just as intimidating and imposing as I remembered him to be. His dark hair was slicked back off his stern features, and his sharp dark eyes studied me from under thick brows. It unnerved me that I could see fragments of Roman's face in his.

Several rifles cocked, their barrels pointing out of the shadows, letting me know that he and I were not alone. I slid back, keeping my distance, keeping my features schooled, even though inside I was lashing out like an animal cornered. It would do me no good. I had to bide my time. Gather as much information as I could, then figure how to get the hell out of here.

When I spoke, my voice came out steadier than I felt, thank God. "What do you want with me?"

"Don't take it so personally," he said, his voice rough like the rumble of an engine.

"It's a little difficult not to take it personally when I'm the one being held here against my will."

"You're just a means to an end, my dear. With you I get to kill two birds with one stone, excuse the pun." He grinned, a horrible smile of teeth and stretched lips.

I tensed. "I don't understand. I'm just a lowly detective."

He let out a curt laugh. "Don't play coy with me, girl."

"I'm not."

He pursed his mouth. "You know, you remind me of Maria, my deceased wife, God rest her soul. You both have spunk. A spark. That certain bewitching quality." His features hardened. "And that annoying habit of sticking your nose where it doesn't belong."

The hair on my arms stood on end. Look where Maria Tyrell ended up.

"No matter," Giovanni continued. "In the end, I can turn anything to my advantage."

"What does that mean?" I demanded. "What plans do you have for me?"

"You'll just have to wait and see, won't you?" He turned and exited my cell. I could do nothing but stand there as the nameless guards retreated after him, their guns trained on me until the door was slammed shut and locked.

I had no idea what Giovanni meant. I only knew that his plans could not be good. I had to warn Roman but I had no idea where I was or how the hell I was going to get out.

ROMAN

My father. My own damn father had Julianna.

I pushed through the doors to my father's library, where I had been told he was. The library was a medium-sized room, the walls lined with tall bookcases almost to the ceiling. It was carpeted in a warm green, the color of moss. Around a fireplace were several high-backed armchairs.

My father reclined in his large crimson leather armchair, his slippered feet resting on a matching leather pouf, a round crystal-cut glass filled with amber liquid. He was staring off into space. It was past midnight, but he was still awake as I knew he would be. He'd been an insomniac for as long as I could remember.

Even when I was a child, he often sat in here alone except for his volumes and volumes of books—mostly business and politics. He would often make me read them as a teenager. My father might be an immoral man but he wasn't stupid. He was never violent for the sake of being violent. Every one of his decisions was strategic, calculated and had a purpose. Even the bloody ones. He clawed his way to the top of the underground world using his brain and his penchant for getting his hands dirty. A deadly combination.

For a split second, before he noticed me, when he still thought he was alone, he looked...open and vulnerable, lost in his thoughts. How could someone so evil, so ruthless, so monstrous, look so fragile? So human. So lonely.

I imagined that he was replaying the faces of all the men he'd sent to their deaths. Did they whisper to him as they whispered to me when I was alone? Did he regret the things he did? Did he hate who he'd become? He wasn't always this man. My mother wouldn't have loved him if he was. I wondered if he ever thought back to the first decision he made that turned him down this dark road. Whether, knowing what he did now, he would have made the same decision. I noticed the wrinkles around his eyes, the downward pull of the corner of his lips and the great weight that curved his shoulders. I almost felt sorry for him.

Almost. The sight of him sitting comfortably while he kept Julianna somewhere against her will made my blood boil. If he let his men hurt her, if they so much as touched her, I would slaughter every last one of them myself, damn the consequences.

For now, I had to keep pretending I was on his side. I had to keep playing the dutiful son. The deserving heir. At least until I got her back. When I got her back, God help me...I would burn his fucking empire to the ground with him in it.

I tucked away the river of fire in my veins. I promised the monster inside of me that he would get his revenge, and I composed my features. I was a Tyrell. I knew how to keep my emotions in check. I cleared my throat. "Father."

He looked over, his humanness melting into the stern mask that I knew so well. His lip curled up into a snarl, my standard greeting. "So good of you to return, son," he said, his voice thick with sarcasm. "But then again, I knew you would eventually."

He thought I could never survive without him. He was

wrong. So wrong. Today would not be the day I proved that to him.

I brushed off his jab. I strode over to the liquor cabinet on one wall, opened the stopper of the crystal bottle that he had left out and took a sniff. Cognac. No doubt the finest that money could buy. "Family first," I said. "Isn't what you always say?"

He let out a scoff behind me. "Since when do you actually listen to me?"

If I didn't know any better, I'd say he sounded bitter.

I poured myself a stiff drink and turned to face him. He eyed my freshly pressed black pants and black button-up shirt. I'd showered and changed out of my wrinkled clothes before coming to him. My wardrobe of Giovanni-approved suits and smart-casual clothes hung in the bedroom that had been kept here for me. My attire, at least, he couldn't disapprove of.

"Where have you been?" he demanded. "I had men looking for you."

I snorted. "They didn't do a very good job of finding me."

"Or you did a very deliberate job of hiding from them."

I shrugged. "I was upset over what happened to…Mercutio." I tripped over his name. But quickly composed myself. "I took a few days out on my own."

My father let out a sneer. "Whoring and drinking, I suppose. You look like shit."

So, he'd noticed the bags under my eyes and where they were red from being rubbed. He always found something to criticize. Somehow this time, it stung less. Maybe because I had finally let go of caring what he thought of me. More likely, the underlying fear over Julianna's safety overruled anything else.

I raised my glass in a mock salute. "You just know me so well, Father."

I walked to the chair beside his on the bearskin rug and sat, crossing my ankle over my leg, taking a large sip of the liquor, letting the burn ease down my throat, soothing me.

When I looked over to my father, he was watching me closely. "I hear we have a…guest," I said as casually as I could. I wanted nothing more than to knock him to the floor and slam my fist into his face until he told me where she was. My father would never give her up if he knew that was the thing I wanted most.

My father tilted his head at me. "And how do you know this?"

I shrugged. "I hear things. I have my own sources, you know?"

"What does *that* mean?"

I leveled a stare at him, some of my antagonism leaking out. "It means that some of the men in our business understand the way things are going. They wish to future-proof their standing in my empire."

"*My* empire," he growled.

"For now. I am the heir you are grooming to fill your shoes. After all, nobody lives forever," I said with a lightness that hid the threat underneath.

For a second my father's nostrils flared, a touch of color rising to his cheeks. Then he let out a small laugh. "Spoken like a true Tyrell," he said, his words bitter jabs.

I took a large gulp of my drink so that I didn't lash back out at him, letting the fire going down my throat burn my anger away. At least for now.

"What's the plan for our guest? I'm a little disappointed that I haven't been made privy to them."

"I'm disappointed I haven't been made privy to your whereabouts," my father snapped.

"You're already privy to that, Father. Drinking and whoring. Do you really want the details?"

My father snorted and swallowed the last of his drink in one large gulp.

"So…" I said, steering the conversation back to the burning question. "The girl?"

"She's a negotiation tool."

"With whom?"

"Her father will be missing her in a day or two. I'll have a set of demands for him soon."

"What demands?"

My father tilted his head. "All in good time, son. For now, you are not to leave this compound."

I could push. But I didn't want to make myself seem so desperate to hear the answers. My father wasn't a stupid man. At least I knew that Julianna was alive.

For the moment.

No weapon, no evidence, no witnesses.

Julianna was a witness. My stomach twisted. Whatever he had planned would not end without her dead and taking his secrets with her.

It took everything to stand up and walk away without demanding any more information or that he take me to her, my glass left on the table by the chair.

I had to get her out alive before my father had a chance to execute his plan. I couldn't take any chances. Not with her life.

An idea stirred in my head...

Could I turn against my own father? Leaving him was one thing, but could I betray him? Could I turn my back on my family? Could I destroy my father's legacy, as dark as it was?

I paused at the door to his library, my hand on the cold knob. I turned to face my father again.

"What?" he growled.

"Do you miss Mama?" I asked.

He stiffened. "Why are you asking me such questions?"

"Do you?" I pushed. "Miss her?"

Even from here, I saw the flash of pain in his eyes. He slumped back into his chair, his gaze becoming unfocused. I knew he was thinking of her. "There's not a day goes by that I don't think about your mother."

My gut knotted. In some deep, hidden part of him, my father still loved her. His love for her was like a single pure seed

503

covered by layers of dirt, twisted roots and the thick matted branches of an overgrown forest. "If you could have her back, but you had to give up this..." I waved my arm. "Everything. Your empire. Would you do it?"

Please, Dad, just one small sign of goodness. Show me one. Just one.

He could barely meet my gaze. For the first time in my life, my father dropped his God-like guard and looked like any one of us mere mortals. For a second he looked like a lost boy, grabbing at ghosts.

His face froze over like the fast approach of a winter's frost. "I built this empire with my bare hands. Twenty years it took me to amass this kind of power. This is my legacy. Your mother was determined to ruin that before..." he trailed off. He straightened in his chair, his eyes blazing. "I would not give up our legacy for anything."

That single seed died. Choked to death under that black, hateful forest. There were no more chances left for redemption.

It turned out there was part of my father in me, because when his heart froze over, so did mine. I knew what I had to do. And I would carry no guilt over doing it. I would betray my father, turn my back on my family and burn his cursed legacy to the ground.

I slipped past my father's guards and defied his order not to leave the compound. I stood in front of the white painted house in a leafy suburb of Verona. The windows were trimmed in a deep red, matching the door, a weather vane straddling the terracotta-tiled roof. The dawn was just brushing the edges of the horizon, painting the quaint street in a pastel light. The whole scene was so...quaint. So wholesome.

I felt a flicker of envy inside me at the sight of Julianna's childhood. She told me about falling out of the tree on her lawn, a large towering oak, when she was eight, breaking her arm. Here on this footpath was where she used to draw hopscotch boxes with chalk. I imagined her taking her first ride down this driveway without training wheels on her bike. I smiled despite my situation.

I hadn't been followed here. I made sure of that. Still, I glanced around me again before I walked up the driveway. Standing on the porch, I stared for a moment at the door. I knew the chief was up because I could hear footsteps inside and the slight rabble of the early morning news on a radio.

I had to make him listen to me. Surely he would put his prejudice aside if it meant he could save his daughter. Right? My stomach churned. This would either go right or it would go horribly wrong.

I forced down my apprehension and knocked on the door.

I heard footsteps then the door opened. Chief Montgomery Capulet appeared in the doorway. He frowned at me. "Yes?"

I pushed back my hood. The chief's eyes, so much like Julianna's, flared with recognition. He snatched his gun from his hip and pointed it in my face.

I lifted my palms but I stood my ground. "You could shoot me right now, but then you'll never get Julianna back."

"You son of a bitch—"

"I don't have her. But I know who does. And I know how to get her back."

The chief cursed. "I knew something was wrong when she stopped answering my calls."

"Please, let me in. I'll tell you everything I know."

The chief shuffled his feet, suspicion rolling off him in waves. Still, I could sense his desperation. He wanted to believe me. His eyes narrowed. "Why would you help me?"

"Because…I care about her as much as you do."

"Liar." He stepped forward so the barrel of his gun was inches from my face.

I didn't flinch. I just held his gaze. "Jules told me about how the two of you used to make pancakes for your late wife on her birthday. Blueberry pancakes. She said that you used to take her and her mom camping out on the lake in the Virgin Forest every July. She told me that you and your wife used to put old Louie Armstrong records on low and dance in the living room on Sundays after you thought she'd gone to sleep. She used to watch you both through the stair railings without you knowing and dream of one day finding a love like that." As I spoke, the chief's face softened, his mouth parting wider at each intimate detail I revealed. "Do you want me to go on?"

"She...She told you those things?"

I nodded.

There was a long, terse pause. He lowered the gun but kept it close to his side. He glanced around the street to see if anyone was watching. No one was. I had made sure I wasn't followed. He turned his hard amber eyes, so much like *hers*, upon me before stepping back to let me in.

Once inside, he patted me down before he directed me into the living room of his family home, his gun still in his hand. I could see touches of a woman here—the faded pastel yellow of the walls trimmed with cream, soft gray and yellow curtains in a large floral pattern, fringed cushions on the couches. But I could see the years of being a single man layered on top of it: old yellowing newspapers in piles on the chairs and carpet, dirty coffee cups left on each flat surface, water stains in rings from glasses without coasters.

The chief walked over to the curtains and snatched them closed, surrounding us in darkness. He switched on a side lamp, the light throwing shadows across his face. "Now," he turned to me, "talk."

I told him what I knew about her attempted abduction, the contract that had fallen to Goldfish, the proof that Goldfish had given me of my father's involvement.

The whole time the chief paced back and forth across the carpet, tugging at his hair as he became more and more agitated.

"Where is she being held?" he demanded when I finished talking.

I knew. I had paid dearly for that information.

I grabbed Benvolio's shirt in my fists as he struggled against the rope around his wrists. It had been so easy to incapacitate him. He'd been so damn trusting. He just let me into his apartment and turned his back to me. "You'll fucking tell me where my father is keeping her."

"What makes you think he told me?" Benvolio's voice was shaking even as he tried to keep it steady.

I lifted my lip in a snarl. "The money for her contract was wired from a subsidiary in your *name. Don't even try to deny that you aren't balls-deep in this shit."*

"Alright. Alright."

I let go of him and painfully uncurled my knuckles, stiff from the fists I had made in his shirt and his face.

"She's being held on a farm, southwest of Verona. It used to be a slaughterhouse. There's a cold storage room there that's decent for holding..." he stiffened, "people who we need to hold."

"Address. Now."

He rambled it off. I pulled out my phone and looked it up. Sure enough, it used to be an old abattoir. "Thanks, cuz." I slid the phone back into my jacket and curled my fingers around another piece of metal.

"You'll let me go now?"

Over Benvolio's shoulder, I spotted the photo frame he kept with a picture of the two of us. We had been sixteen then, lanky arms slung around each other's necks. "Of course." I smiled. "We're cousins. Family."

Benvolio let out a sigh of relief. "Get this fucking rope off me, man."

My father's voice echoed inside me. No weapon, no evidence, no witnesses.

The smile faded from my face. I slid out my gun, a silencer on the end, aimed and pulled the trigger.

Back in the chief's house, I cracked my neck, shaking off this recent memory. "I know where they're holding her."

The chief stopped pacing. "Where?"

I shook my head and crossed my arms over my chest. "I want to make a deal. I want it in writing."

He stiffened. "What kind of deal?"

I outlined my proposition.

The chief spluttered, his cheeks turning red. "As if I'm going to make deals with a filthy scumbag criminal like—"

"Careful, chief," I said, "this *criminal* is your only hope for getting your daughter back.

We glared at each other. A battle of wills. Who would give in first? I could see the chief working through his hatred for me and weighing it up against his daughter's life.

His shoulders slumped first, then his breath came rushing out of his mouth in an audible swoosh. "Fine, I'll make it happen."

Relief filled me. The truth was, I would have given up Julianna's location without cutting a deal for myself if it came down to it. Thankfully, it didn't come down to it. Julianna's father really did love her.

I nodded. "Make it happen. You have until dusk tonight."

I turned to leave but Chief Capulet grabbed my upper arm in a vice, shoving the barrel of the gun in my cheek. "Make no mistake, Tyrell, even if I can get sign-off on this deal, I don't trust you. You breathe wrong and I'll take you down. You fuck me over and I'll make you wish you were never born." He leaned in close. "And if anything happens to her, I'll kill you myself."

JULIANNA

I lay in wait in my silent cell, dinner tray in my hands. It was made of a thin metal. The flat of the tray was flimsy but it curled around the edges to make a firm, thicker lip. If I swung it at just the right angle, at just the right spot, it might work.

At least, I hoped it would. It was the only weapon I had. The remnants of my dinner, a plastic bowl crusty with canned tomato soup and bread crumbs and an empty plastic bottle of water, sat in one corner.

My "toilet" was a wooden bucket with a lid that sat in the farthest corner. At first I was embarrassed at relieving myself in such an undignified way. It didn't take long for my bladder to feel like it was bursting and for me to stop caring.

I'd been standing at the edge of the door, waiting, for ages. Hours, it felt like. Although I knew it was more like minutes. They always came back within the hour to pick up my meal things.

Finally I heard the footsteps of someone approaching. I heard the jingle of keys. I readied myself, lifting the tray above my head.

The door to the cold room slid open and a guard stepped in. I swung with everything I had. I smacked the base of his head with the edge of the tray. It made a dull clunk. His eyes rolled into the back of his head and he collapsed to the ground.

I stared down at the guard. He was no more than a boy, really. Maybe eighteen. Nineteen at most. What the hell happened to him that he would choose a life working for the Tyrells?

I had no time to lose, no time to stand around feeling sorry for my captors.

I slid around the corner of the doorway. Right into the barrel of a gun. The second guard lifted his lip in a sneer. Past him was a thin corridor between palettes. I could see parts of a wooden building. I could smell hay and the earthy hint of livestock. I was in a barn. Likely on rural property. I probably wasn't even in Verona anymore. My stomach dropped. How was anyone going to find me out here? The only one who would have known that I was missing was Roman.

"Back in your cage, girlie," the guard said, "or you and me will have problems."

I lifted my hands up. Dammit. I should have known it wouldn't be that easy.

ROMAN

"You're late."

I froze at the doorway to the dining room of my father's large mansion, where my father was seated with Abel to his right. Abel sneered at me from his seat, the one that should have been mine. A few of my father's men stood around at various points of the room, guarding him.

"Sorry, Father." I strode to the empty seat on my father's left, ignoring the look he and Abel were trading. The table was laid with various plates of pasta, steamed greens glossy with melted butter, and a leg of lamb in a baking tray sitting in a thick, rich tomato and olive sauce.

"Where have you been?" my father asked.

For a second I wondered if he knew.

I shrugged as I began to fill my plate, even though I was anything but hungry. "Out."

"Out where?"

I tried not to flinch. My father never questioned where I was. Why now?

"Just...out. Riding around. Clearing my head."

"I did not give you permission to leave the mansion."

I speared an olive on my fork. "I didn't think I needed it." My father had forbidden me to leave earlier. I had to dodge the security cameras, then climb over the wall to get out.

Bang!

My father's fist slammed down on the table, making everything vibrate. "You will look at me when I'm talking to you."

I put down my fork deliberately, swallowed my olive and lifted my eyes. His black eyes glittered with fury. Was he angry because I disobeyed his orders? Or did he know I had sought out his enemy? Did he know I was plotting the downfall of his empire?

If he knew, he'd kill me. No, he would torture me, make me hurt for days before he got bored and finally killed me.

Don't flinch, Roman. Act like you've done nothing wrong.

My father leaned in towards me. "You dare disobey me again and I won't think twice but to punish you."

Let it go, Roman. Just nod like a good boy and keep your mouth shut.

I couldn't let it go. "I'm a Tyrell," I said. "I do what I want. Isn't that what you're always telling me?"

I could feel more than hear the collective holding of breath of the men around the room. Abel hissed under his breath at my insolence. My father glared back at me. The tension twisted between us. Father. Son. The student now becoming the master. The power struggle clear. This had been the first time I'd ever talked back to him and he knew it. I wondered if anyone had ever spoken back to him and lived. I was no longer a boy. I was no longer listening to his word as gospel and "yes, Father," "no, Father" was no longer part of my vocabulary. His usual methods of demand and obey were no longer going to work on me. I could see the slight flash of fear in his eyes. I was no longer his son, a man beneath him, but a man reaching for his own power. An equal. Someone who could easily take his place. Someone to be feared.

I could see the flash of indignation in being spoken back to in front of his men. He wanted to punish me. But I was his only heir and he needed me.

The tension in the room was thick, suffocating. I matched his stare, daring him to do his worst. *Go on, Father,* I egged him on with my smirk, *do your worst. Challenge me. I'm ready. I'm not afraid of you anymore. We'll see who comes out on top.*

My father's lip twitched. He broke out into laughter, breaking the tension. He leaned back into his chair and clasped my shoulder. "Finally, you're getting it through your thick skull. Yes, you *are* a Tyrell. You do what you want, when you want to do it. Let any man here dare to get in your way." He wiped the small beads of sweat off his brow. Across his forehead I could see the fingers of his right hand shaking.

After dinner, I waved off the glasses of cognac that were being passed around and made my excuses. I left the dining room and headed down the corridor to my room, my leather shoes sinking into the plush carpet, my head spinning. A hand grabbed me roughly on my shoulder.

I spun, my body tensing. Abel was glaring at me, the dining room door shut behind him, leaving the two of us alone. Had my father sent him?

I shoved his hand off my jacket. "Touch me again, dog, and I'll make sure you never use that hand."

Abel sneered at me. "You talk a good game. But I think you're full of shit."

"You want to test me on that?" I stepped closer to him, glaring down at him, using my extra two inches to my advantage. He didn't even flinch.

"I think," he said slowly, an excitement glittering in his eyes, "that you're getting too close to people that you shouldn't."

I stiffened, trying not to reveal the flash of panic that went through me. If Abel had any inkling of where I'd been... If he knew I'd been about to run away with Julianna...

If he had proof, then I'd be dead. I shrugged and turned to leave, dismissing him with a scoff. "I don't answer to you."

"Your father's getting suspicious too."

I snorted. "If my father had suspicions, then he'd be the one up in my face." I turned to face him again, my arms crossed over my chest. "You just hate that I'm his son and that I'll be *your* boss one day."

"You don't deserve it," Abel said with a snarl.

"Careful," I said, "your bitterness is showing."

"Maybe. But you'll fuck up soon enough. Just remember," he smiled, "I'm watching."

ROMAN

T he next morning, Abel, my father and I rode in a limo together in silence. The city flashed by as we traveled out of Verona, the roads becoming uncovered and gritty. The apartment blocks turned to houses, then to farmhouses, then to stretches of open land.

Nerves jumbled through my veins. I refused to let myself fidget. There were so many unknowns. So many things that could go wrong. The front of my shirt itched but I dared not scratch it.

The chief pulled out a small black device the size of a pea. "This is a recording device."

"You want me to wear a wire?"

"We need Giovanni to confess to something, anything illegal. To smuggling drugs, to ordering a murder. Just get me something."

I hesitated. Walking into the lion's den wearing the wire was a stupid idea. Too risky. What if they searched me?

But the chief was right. They needed something other than my testimony. My father's lawyers would argue that I fabricated it to cut a deal.

It wasn't his ass on the line, though.

I stared at the tiny black device. I didn't have a good feeling about this.

We pulled up to a deserted farmhouse outside of the Verona outskirts. I stepped out of the limo and slid on my sunglasses as the early morning light shot over the thick trees. In a field, now overgrown with weeds and stalks as high as a grown man, a huge wooden barn rose, paint peeling, thick dust on the windows.

"Where are we?" I asked, pretending I hadn't known about this place. That I wasn't here just last night.

"A property we hold in a hidden subsidiary company," my father said. He directed us towards the large barn door, partly opened in anticipation of our arrival. Several men stood holding rifles in their hands.

"What's this?" I asked as a suited man standing by the door began to wave a metal wand over Abel's body. It ticked as it went over him.

Abel turned and smirked at me as the metal wand was waved over his back. "A bug detector. Sensitive stuff going on inside. We want to make sure that no one's *stupid* enough to wear a wire."

Don't fucking flinch. I stood like a lump of metal as the bug detector went over my father. A bead of sweat rolled down the small of my back. "Is this really necessary?"

My father glared at me. "Yes. For me. And you."

The metal wand waved over him. The man holding it nodded. "You're clear."

All eyes fell on me. I could refuse to be tested. Then I'd probably be strip-searched.

Just get this over with, Roman.

I stepped up to the man and held my arms out, looking bored. "Well, go on then."

He waved the wand over me. Tension coiled in the air as the thing clicked. I felt Abel staring. I knew he was waiting for the wand to start shrieking.

"Just remember," he smiled, *"I'm watching."*

This scan was probably his idea. He'd be the first to put a bullet in me if it went off.

"Turn around, please."

I spun slowly. My vulnerable back was to Abel and my father. All those eyes. All those guns. I felt naked, under a spotlight. I refused to flinch as the wand made another pass over me.

"That's all, sir. You're clear."

I let myself release a tiny breath of relief before I turned to face Abel, his eyes wide with disbelief. He thought he had me.

I smirked. "What? Did you think I'd not pass your stupid test?"

Abel snarled. I strode past him into the farmhouse as if he didn't exist.

Inside I glanced around, pretending to take it all in. It was an old barn with a high roof and open rafters, the hay bales still standing about the place. It had been an old abattoir. The air still stank of soured blood and old death, sending a ripple of anxiety through me.

Abel and my father followed me. The barn doors were shut behind us. I turned to my father. "What are we doing here, then? Playing with hay?"

A small smile played on his lips. "We're going to send a message to Chief Montgomery with proof that we have his daughter."

"Proof?"

"Yes." My father smiled at me, the cruel, gleaming smile of a snake. "You're going to cut off her pretty little finger."

JULIANNA

I don't know how many days I was left in that storage room. Two. Three. The light never changed. I had no watch or clock to help me keep time.

My thoughts flashed to Roman. Did he know his father had me? What would he do? Would he try to rescue me? God, how could he even do that without revealing himself to his father as a betrayer? If his father knew he was planning on leaving, he'd kill Roman. *Stay safe, Roman. Please, stay safe.*

My father must be worried sick about me now. Was he looking for me? Did he have men on the case?

I thought about the bodies found dumped in Little Italy. I imagined my own pale lifeless body, devoid of color and hope, lying in the bottom of a coffin. The bile rose up the back of my throat.

I shook my head. I would not turn out that way. It would all be fine. We'd get out somehow…

It must have been early morning when the door to the storage room slid open, waking me up. I sat up and wiped my face, squinting against the fluorescent light that was never switched off. I had set up a few blankets on the floor in the darkest corner of the room as my bed. That's where I had slept for the last few nights.

The door to my prison gaped like an open mouth.

I expected Giovanni Tyrell. When a wiry figure stepped from the shadows into my cell, I sank back.

Abel Montero, Giovanni's right hand man, the man they called "The Butcher."

His scar flashed white as he smiled at me. "We need an audience with you."

"What if I don't want to come with you?"

"I'm afraid you don't have a choice." A gun appeared in one of his gloved hands. "Would you like to do this the hard way or the easy way? Please say the hard way." He grinned. "I like it when they choose the hard way." His voice slithered down my spine like a snake.

I wouldn't give him the satisfaction. I lifted my hands and shuffled forward. "I'll come willingly."

That just made Abel grin wider.

He led me through a short corridor to where the main barn area opened up. My eyes squinted as they tried to adjust to the increased light. Half a dozen men stood around, some holding guns, all in suits.

All men.

My blood turned cold. My mind flashed back to the night that Eddie and Tate tried to rape me. There was nothing to stop these men from doing whatever they wanted with me. A shiver went down my back.

My gaze fell on the one face I dreamed of and yet, feared to see.

Roman Tyrell.

"Roman," his name tore from my lips in a desperate pained whisper. Every cell of my being yearned for him. I dared not move.

He looked stunning as always, a king of darkness in a

tailored dark gray suit, a black shirt underneath. Coldness wafted off him as he glanced over me. As if he barely knew me. As if he hadn't been embedded in my heart. As if I had no place in his.

This is just a mask. Roman Tyrell loves you. He will get you out of here.

What are you doing here? Did you know I was here? Please tell me you have a plan. All these things I desperately wanted to ask but couldn't. We weren't supposed to love each other. I shoved all my feelings, all my love and desire, back down inside me.

I forced myself to glare at him, at all of them. My heart thumped against my windpipe.

"Welcome, Detective Capulet," Giovanni Tyrell called out.

I said nothing. I could barely breathe. It took all of my energy to keep my heart rate steady. What did they want with me?

Abel reached around me to grip my throat and I let out a strangled cry. He pulled me right up against him. I could feel every inch of his slimy body. Oh my God. He was hard against my ass. I cringed. He was enjoying my fear. Getting off on it.

"When Mr. Tyrell speaks to you, you speak back, you disrespectful girl," he hissed into my ear.

Roman didn't move. He didn't flinch. Although I could see by the tension on his jaw that he was two seconds away from launching himself at Abel and ripping his face off. If he did, he'd give himself away.

I had to act as unaffected by Abel as possible, for Roman. I couldn't let Roman see how disgusted I was, how much this evil man touching me was like having bugs crawling around under my skin.

"Speak, girl. And be respectful," Abel hissed over my shoulder, his nose running down my neck, his disgusting worm of an erection twitching against me. I struggled not to squirm. I would not let him see how much I was screaming inside.

"What's going on?" I found myself asking, my voice quivering much more than I wanted it to. "Why am I here?"

"You're going to help us send a message to your father," Giovanni said.

"Whatever it is," I said as defiantly as I could, "he won't agree to it." Abel tightened his hand on my throat. "Sir," I added, my voice straining. Abel loosened his grip, but only just.

I could see Roman's jaw twitch.

Don't do it, Roman. Don't give yourself away. We just have to get through this, then figure out a way to escape together.

Giovanni smiled at me. "Oh yes, I think your father will agree. Because it'll be a small thing, some money, to get you back. And he'll pay. He'll pay because it'll be small enough that he can pay. It won't be worth involving the police. And he, of all people, knows how badly the police can fuck up hostage situations."

I frowned, glancing between him and Roman. "You kidnapped me for a small amount of money?" I didn't know whether to be insulted or terrified that there was something bigger that I wasn't seeing.

It was Roman who began to laugh. "Stupid girl," he said, his voice hard and cruel. "You don't see it, do you?"

"See...what?"

"The money is a decoy. What we *will* have when we make the exchange are photos, hard evidence, that your father is corrupt."

I gasped. "But he's not. He'd never..."

"Never make a cash trade with a Tyrell?" Roman said, his lips lifting in a sneer. "He will for you, his precious only daughter. His weakness. Love makes us weak, doesn't it? We'd do stupid things for love, wouldn't we?"

He doesn't mean that. He doesn't. He's just playing the game. He loves me. Love makes us stronger. It gives us a reason to keep fighting.

"But I'll know the truth," I said. "I'll tell—"

"The public doesn't care about the truth," Giovanni said. "They just love to lap up the latest scandal. Your father, the 'incorruptible', proven to be corrupt? They will eat that up. Photos don't lie."

They couldn't. My father would be ruined. Everything he'd built would be destroyed. All the criminals he'd ever put away would use his "corruption" as an excuse to get their sentences overturned. All the good he'd done under his command would be turned into a pile of rubble all because of me.

I sank back against Abel in horror.

"Shall we begin?" Giovanni said.

"Begin what?"

"The message to your father." Abel's voice slid into my ear. "Roman has agreed to cut off your finger."

My...*what?*

Giovanni pulled a long butcher's knife from the sheath being held by one of his men. It glinted in the light as he handed it to Roman. Roman took it and turned towards me, his face remaining cold.

My blood froze. Oh my God. He was going to do it. Had he turned on me?

No, Roman would never. He would figure out a way to get us out of this. When? How? If he refused to cut my finger off, he'd be punished.

Abel rubbed his erection into my back. "Go on, girlie," he whispered in my ear so only I could hear him. He let go of my throat to caress my cheek with his gloved hand. "Scream a little. Bleed for me. You're in good hands when you pass out. I bet your blood tastes like your pussy will."

No. No fucking way. I turned my head and sank my teeth into his hand. Soft leather, warm flesh and wetness spilled into my mouth.

He let out a scream and shoved me away. I heard tearing. His glove and part of his palm came away in my teeth. I spat it onto the ground, a mess of black leather and blood.

"You fucking bitch," Abel said. He backhanded me with his

uninjured hand so hard that my head rang. I fell to the cold floor at Roman's feet.

"Back off, dog." Roman stepped in front of me, the knife meant for me aimed at Abel.

Don't defend me, I wanted to scream. *You've given yourself away.*

"I knew it," Abel yelled. "I fucking knew it. You've got a thing for her. You're the one who had Tate and Eddie killed."

Tate and Eddie. The two men who had been hired to kidnap me. Giovanni Tyrell had been behind it after all.

"We need her alive, you fucking idiot," Roman scowled. "We can't return her to her father all broken."

"You're cutting off her finger. What's another bruise or two? Or are you too soft to do it?"

"Enough, Abel," Giovanni called out, his voice calm and steady. "Roman is right. We need her alive. And relatively unharmed. I know that you can often...get carried away."

Only then did Abel back down. "Yes, sir," he said as he clutched his shirt with his right hand, now gloveless and bleeding down his inner wrist in rivulets.

I let out the breath I hadn't realized I'd been holding.

"You..." Roman's voice shook. I snapped my face towards him. He looked like he'd seen a ghost.

I looked towards where he was staring, where the knife was now pointed. To the back of Abel's hand.

There in the center was a raised pink circular scar.

A circular burn.

Like a cigarette lighter.

Roman spun towards his father, his face a crumpled mask. "Why did you do it? Why?"

Giovanni straightened up, his chin thrust abnormally high. I swear I saw a flash of fear in his eyes. "What are you talking about?"

"My mother, my fucking mother," Roman yelled. "Why did you have her killed?"

"I didn't—"

"The night she was murdered, the night I watched her die, she attacked her murderer with a cigarette lighter, leaving a circular scar on the back of his hand. Like the one that Abel has." He pointed at Abel with the knife that was meant for me. "That's why you wear the gloves."

"Fucking bitch," Abel hissed, glaring at me, his other hand covering up the scar as if it were a mark of shame.

"Your *dog* doesn't do anything without your instruction," Roman said, his dark eyes fixed on his father.

Oh, Roman. My heart twisted. His own father had his mother killed. He sat back and watched as the media crucified Roman, as rumors spread around of a little boy so monstrous that he killed his mother at the age of twelve. How could he do that? How could his father do that to his son? The throbbing in my cheek faded as I became overwhelmed with rage for Roman. I burned for Roman. I shook where I sat.

Giovanni's face curled like the withered leaves of a poisonous tree. "She was going to leave me, leave us. She was going to run off with that bitch prosecutor and leave us all behind. But I fixed it."

Bitch prosecutor.

I choked back a gasp. A final piece of the puzzle clicked into place.

Joan. Joan from the taped conversation in my mother's case file. The one I couldn't find a file on. My mother had been talking with Maria Tyrell. Maria wanted to testify against Giovanni in exchange for a new life for her three children.

My mother showed up dead in an alleyway a few hours after Maria Tyrell was killed. This was not a coincidence.

Nobody connected the two deaths at the time because they were two very different women, so far apart in their social circles, both killed in two different parts of the city, each with a different MO. A break and enter gone wrong. A random mugging in an alleyway. A knife. And a gun. Even I hadn't connected these two deaths for this very reason.

I leapt to my feet. "You son of a bitch." I only saw Giovanni Tyrell, the edges of my vision fuzzy and black around him. "You had my mother killed."

"What?" I heard Roman cry, his voice sounding so far away.

"Your mother," Giovanni snarled at me, "shouldn't have tried to take my wife away from me and her boys. She filled Maria's head with such nonsense. She turned Maria against me. She deserved her bullet."

"You know, you look just like her," Abel said to me with a cruel smile. "Such a strong woman until she was begging for her life."

Abel had shot my mother. He had staged the fake robbery in the alleyway where she was found.

"She was a good woman, a loved woman." I began to blubber as my heart tore into pieces. "You had no right. No fucking right." My gaze narrowed to the gun on Roman's hip. I didn't care that I was surrounded by men with guns who would fire back. Rage flared around my body, gripping me tightly in her burning hands. I was reborn out of the flames like a phoenix, a creature of justice. I would avenge my mother.

I lunged for Roman's gun, snatching it from his hip. I swung it towards Giovanni. The warehouse filled with the sound of weapons being drawn and hammers being cocked. There were at least five guns, now pointing their cruel black eyes at me.

"No!" Roman lunged in front of me, shielding me with his body.

I screamed at Roman just as Giovanni yelled, "Don't shoot!" His face turned red as he spat, "Don't you dare shoot my son!"

A violent crash sounded in stereo. The windows burst in as if a bomb had gone off on all sides. Guns appeared at the openings. Shots rang out and wood splintered as bullets ricocheted around the room like ping pong balls.

SIENNA BLAKE

"Jules, get down!" Roman yelled at me, shielding me with his body as I dropped to the gritty ground. The smell of hay and dirt hit my nose.

Giovanni's men ran for cover, yelling, returning fire. It was an ambush. The Veronesis? Or...the police?

How did they know we were here?

In the chaos, Roman and I had been forgotten. We could try to make a run for it.

Something glinted to the right of me. My vision zeroed in on the barrel of the rifle pointed at Roman from one of the broken windows. From the outside, the police wouldn't know the difference between Roman and all the other Tyrell men.

"Roman!" I screamed.

He turned. The rifle fired, the barrel kicking back. Everything seemed to slow.

I saw the bullet hit before it did. I saw the nightmare before it began. In that split second, the life I thought I might have was torn from me. Our future, the one with Roman and me in it, happy, together, disintegrated. I could do nothing, helpless, as it unfolded.

The bullet hit Roman. It hit *him*, but I could feel it ripping through *me*.

He fell to his back on the ground, grabbing at his stomach, looking down as if he couldn't believe what he was seeing, a rush of blood soaking his clothes. He lifted his head, his eyes caught mine. A cold rush flooded over me like I'd just crashed through the ice into a watery grave.

"My son!" Giovanni Tyrell rose from behind a crate, screaming in a battle cry. "You shot my boy, you bastards." He turned to fire, getting off a couple of shots before the first bullet hit him. Three stains appeared on his chest as he toppled to the ground.

The firing seemed to fade around me as I kneeled beside Roman. His stomach was a bloody mess. "Oh God, Roman."

His eyes caught mine. I saw resignation in them. "It's bad."

"It's not so bad," I lied.

"Jules, listen…"

"No." I pressed my mouth to his to shut him up. My hands clutched at his stomach, trying to stop the bleeding. "Help is on its way. Just hang on."

"All those years I thought I was living," his voice rumbled against my lips. "I was merely waiting for my life to begin."

"Stop talking like that, you're going to be fine." This could not be goodbye. I wouldn't let it be. The blood just kept pumping out of his stomach, squeezing between my fingers like grains of sand even as I tried to stop it. What are two hands against a tide?

He grabbed my hands and pulled them off his stomach, his grip surprisingly strong. He brushed my fingers with his mouth, smearing it with liquid the color of roses. "My life began with you. It will end with you."

"Roman." A rising panic choked me. Tears blurred my vision. He was saying goodbye. Fuck him for saying goodbye. This could not be goodbye. "Please hang on."

"I love you," he said. The three words I'd longed to hear. My heart swelled to bursting. Then shattered. "I'm sorry it took me so long to tell you."

"Please," I begged. I begged with every aching piece of my soul. "Don't leave me."

"Be brave for me, Julianna," his voice grew hoarse. "Be happy…" His eyes fluttered shut. He stilled, his fingers unraveling from mine, slipping from all the blood, and fell out to his side.

He let go.

He let go of *me*.

He wasn't supposed to let go.

I heard someone screaming, a long, pained scream of anguish. As if the very core of the universe were ripping apart. I realized it was coming from me.

Someone grabbed me, cruel, strong arms ripped me back from Roman's body. "Miss, you have to let go of him." I would not. I sent out a desperate plea to God, to Allah, to the devil if he were listening, don't let him die. All their lives for Roman's. I would trade all their lives for his.

They dragged me back. I felt my bond with Roman pulling, coming undone like a rope about to snap.

"Let me go," I screamed. "He needs me. He needs me." If Roman could just feel me near him. If my soul could just reach out and catch the tail end of his and pull it back into his body. If our love could do that. It was strong enough to do that, wasn't it?

They wouldn't let me go. The sight of Roman was lost to me as he was surrounded by the dark blue uniforms I used to love so much.

JULIANNA

I sat in the back of a police van, numb, wrapped in a blanket. My father, still wrapped up in his tactical gear, was standing in front of me, explaining...trying to explain.

"Roman came to me. He said he would do anything to save you. Even turn on his family."

My stomach clenched. *Oh, Roman. Why did you have to try to save me?*

"He made a deal with us," my father continued. "He gave us this location where they were keeping you. He was supposed to wear the wire so we could get something incriminating on tape. So we could end the Tyrell empire. He installed the recording device inside the barn last night."

"Looks like you got what you wanted," I spat out. Bitterness coating my tongue.

"He knew the risks." My father sighed. "You were right. Roman Tyrell...was a good man, in his own way. He died a hero."

Finally, my father believed me. But it was too late now.

"But no one will know that, will they?"

My father gave me a guilty look. "It's better if we don't reveal publicly how we were able to get the recording or to find the location of the barn."

Angry tears fell on my gray fluffy blanket. This was so unfair. I could scream, but my throat was choked up. "So he dies a criminal."

"I'm sorry. If it means anything, I think he really did care about you." My father looked at me with such sorrow I almost softened.

I remembered the barrel of that rifle pointed at Roman. I looked up, glaring at my father. "Your man shot him. Whoever shot him did it on purpose. I saw—"

"It was crazy in there, Jules. You don't know what you saw." My father's jaw twitched. Was he lying? Did he know something he wasn't saying? If his team knew that Roman was on their side, then someone had shot Roman on purpose. My father was covering for them.

I pulled the blanket tighter around me. "I'd like to be alone now."

"Julu…" My father slipped a hand on my shoulder.

I flinched from his touch. "Don't call me that."

He sighed, dropping his arm to his side. "You'll get over him, love. You will." He walked back among the officers who were processing the scene.

My heart curled up into a withered pile of ash. I'd never get over Roman. Never.

I had just finished giving my statement inside the station. They'd sent me some jerk-off kid who still had his training wheels on to question me. I had seen a *cop* shoot Roman. No one would listen to me. I needed proof. I needed to know who shot him. Then I could get a confession.

"Pierce," I called to the young officer standing out back of the police station sneaking a quick cigarette.

He flinched, coughing out a cloud of smoke. "Hey, Capulet." He waved the smoke aside as I strode up to him.

"I know you were at the Tyrell takedown earlier today."

He blinked slowly at me. "Right. Yeah, a few of us were there."

"Were you stationed on the north or the south of the barn?"

I saw him pause. "Aren't you off duty at the moment?"

"Were you on the north or south?" I repeated.

"Why does it matter?" He stubbed out his half-smoked cigarette and turned to go back inside.

I grabbed his arm. "Just answer the question, Pierce. Please."

He glanced over my shoulder to the doorway leading into the station. "I was...on the south."

He would have been standing on the same side as the shooter. "Who was stationed on the western-most window on that side?"

He shuffled his feet, his eyes darting about him. "Why are you asking all these questions?"

"Who stood at that window? Tell me now or I'll go to my father."

Pierce scoffed. "He'd be the last person to tell you who stood there."

I froze, my blood turning to sharp icicles in my veins. I grabbed Pierce's shirtfront, not caring that I was assaulting a police officer right outside the police station. "Was it you? Was it you who stood at the that window?"

"No."

"Then who, dammit?" I leaned in. *Who?* If you've ever thought of me as a friend..."

He shushed me. "Jules, keep it down."

"Tell me, Pierce, tell—"

"Okay," he relented, "but this never came from me."

Triumph flooded through my veins. "I promise."

Pierce glanced around before locking eyes with me. "Your father took that position."

My fingers sprang open. I stumbled back. Dread rattled down my bones. Betrayal shot like a bitter poison through my veins, withering my insides.

"Jules...are you okay?" Pierce's voice sounded so far away.

No. I was not okay. I wasn't sure I'd ever be okay again.

My father had shot Roman. He killed him on purpose.

ROMAN

"You can stop pretending to be dead now," a familiar voice said.

Light hit the backs of my lids. A wave of fresh air rolled over me and I sucked it in greedily.

I remembered Julianna's face just before I "died", her eyes glassy with tears, pain ripping across her beautiful features. The image was burned into my retinas. It would haunt me forever. A rush of anger flooded through me as I sat up, blinking as I tried to adjust to the light.

"Easy, tiger," Chief Capulet said. "You'll get fake blood everywhere. Let them take the bag out." He stood by the metal table that I was sitting on, watching as an older man in a white coat unzipped the rest of the body bag I'd been transported here in. Wherever here was.

I sat still as the man in a white coat cut away at my suit and removed the blood bag that had been strapped to my stomach. The plan had been executed to perfection. Almost. Julianna's screaming echoed in my head. She was the one flaw.

I was in what looked like a curtained-off section of a morgue, heavy metal tabletops and square metal drawers along one wall.

The air smelled sharply of antiseptic, but underneath it was the thick odor of stale decay. I guessed the man in the white coat must be a medical examiner—the one who had been roped into faking my death certificate.

They hadn't closed the curtain enough, because just past it, on the tabletop next to me, I spotted a familiar figure. My father, his eyes still open, a look of shock on his face. As if the great Giovanni Tyrell himself couldn't believe he was actually dead.

Turns out you aren't immortal.

Under the numbness that coated my body, a rumbling of something dark and painful rippled. I tore my eyes away from my father's face. I was not ready to deal with this now. Not right now.

The examiner finished wiping my torso of the sticky fake blood. Julianna had almost touched the bag under my suit. I remembered grabbing her hands, gripping them, brushing them across my lips. If only I could touch her hands once more.

You did what you had to. You made the deal for her.

The important thing was she was safe and alive.

The chief's voice broke through my thoughts. "Your immunity comes into full effect as of now. The paperwork is almost done for your transfer into our witness protection program. We'll have a car take you to the airport for a flight tomorrow morning."

Tomorrow? Please, not yet. I wasn't done here. I needed some reason, some excuse, to stay in Verona. Near her. Just for a few more days...

"I want to attend my father's funeral," I said as my eyes came to rest upon his body. "It'll be in a few days, I'm sure. You wouldn't deny me that, would you?"

Chief Capulet gave me a suspicious look as he considered my request, his stare edged in hatred. Even with how he felt about me, he wouldn't deny a son his right to attend his father's funeral, would he?

"Fine," he said finally. "But you'll stay hidden. I'll escort you myself to make sure there is no...funny business."

"Of course."

Julianna's stricken face came to mind. Her screams echoed in my brain. I had promised I wouldn't see her or speak to her again —conditions of the deal to get her back—but I couldn't leave without seeing her one more time.

~

Two days later, my funeral was scheduled right after my father's in Waverley Cathedral. I was escorted from the safe house I'd been hidden away in by two armed guards and the chief himself. I was allowed to remain only on the mezzanine that ran above the church's main floor, the shadows hiding my face as I watched the funeral below. The chief and his men stood a few meters back from me at a respectful distance while I leaned against a pillar, the scent of incense and lilies clogging my nose.

They kept the top half of the coffin open. From up here I could see my father lying in his coffin as if he were sleeping. He looked so mortal from up here. So much at peace. No trace of his monstrous nature left.

The first wave crashed through me, causing me to grip at the balustrade, feeling unexpectedly like a release. It took me a second to realize that I was feeling...relief. I'd spent so long fearing him, cowering from him, hiding from his disapproval. Terrified of what his next "lesson" might be. Despite all these things, I'd also been driven by a need to please him, a task I could never win. Even when I won, I failed.

It was all over now.

It was all over.

My father was dead.

The last moments of his life thundered through my mind.

"My son!" My father screamed, rising like an avenging demon from behind a crate. "You shot my boy, you fucking bastards."

He had died avenging me. Despite his brutal lessons, despite his hard, cruel ways, my father loved me.

He loved me.

Twenty-six years of searching for a sign of his love. He handed it to me, right before he was taken from me. His actions, his behaviors, however harsh, were suddenly colored with another light. The light of a father who loved his sons enough to want to make them kings. Who revered them enough to want to build an empire for them, however bloody. He forced men to their knees around him so that his sons would never have to bow down. He inspired a fear that reached out like Zeus's hands so his sons could be gods on earth.

Something inside me dissolved and blew away. Grief swirled into my body, hitting me like a tsunami. My father was not a monster. He was just a man. Mortal. As breakable and fragile as all of us. Perhaps even more so.

I never understood his ways. I never would. But he was my father and I loved him.

"I forgive you," I whispered.

Family is most important, he'd always told me. I never really appreciated that until now. He had been the last link to family that I had left here. Now he was gone.

I was alone.

I sucked in a shaky breath as Father Laurence finished up the ceremony below. There were only a few scattered heads in the pews. Hardly anybody had shown up. All of my father's family were either dead or exiled. His colleagues either in jail awaiting trial or refusing to show any connection with him. All my father's wealth, his power, his empire...it all came down to nothing, reduced to rubble upon his death. *Oh, Father. If you were alive to see this now, it'd break your heart.*

Alberto Veronesi, his enemy and one-time friend, made his

536

way down the aisle, dressed in a long black overcoat, a single white rose on his lapel.

He placed a heavy gloved hand on the coffin. "Goodbye, old friend, dear enemy. You'll be with Maria now."

My mother.

My father's admission crashed into me, knocking into me from the other side.

He'd had my mother killed. He loved her and he still killed her.

"She was going to leave me, leave us. She was going to run off with that bitch prosecutor and leave us all behind. But I fixed it."

My mother had been about to leave us. Leave *me*.

Everything I thought about her was wrong. She didn't love me. She didn't care. What mother leaves her children behind in the hands of a cruel father? She was selfish and...and...I *hated* her. Bitterness spread throughout my body, gripping me in its clutches like a poison.

Below, my father's coffin was carried out towards the burial site. I stood frozen, white knuckles gripping the balcony, as a silent storm tore me apart from the inside.

When the door closed, leaving the church empty, I slumped over myself. I was tired. So damn tired. I felt like I could sleep for an eternity.

The side door of the church opened. It wasn't so much the sound of the door or the soft foot treads that had me lifting my head, but the *sense* of who had entered.

"Jules..." I whispered.

She was so beautiful. Even with her face pale, wisps of hair escaping from her ponytail, whiskey eyes rimmed with red. Even with her feminine body cloaked in light-swallowing and shapeless black.

I spotted the stairs leading down and started forward. Everything faded except for her. My promises, my deal, my immunity, all forgotten.

Two firm hands wrapped around my upper arms yanked me back. "Don't you dare," the chief hissed in my ear.

"If I could just say goodbye...?" If I could just touch her face one more time. Smell her hair. Feel her heart beating against mine.

"She thinks you're dead. You need to stay that way. If you don't, the deal's off. It's life in prison and I swear to God I will make it a living hell."

How do you say goodbye when you are forced into silence?

When I had made the deal with Chief Capulet, I had been desperate and half mad with the knowledge that my father had Jules. I would have said yes to anything to save her. Even if it meant I had to give her up. As long as she was safe. Alive. That's all that mattered to me.

I gave up my life for hers. I'd do it a hundred times if I had to. It was my sacrifice. It was all I had to give her. Perhaps now I could be...good. Perhaps now I had redeemed myself. I had proven myself worthy of her... I only had to give her up.

They tried to drag me back away from the balcony, away from the edge, away from Julianna.

"Please," I begged. "Please, just one more minute."

By the grace of God, they loosened their grip. My heart squeezed tighter and tighter as I watched Julianna walk down the length of the cathedral, her steps hesitant, until she passed into the section in the back where my locked coffin, weighed down with sandbags, sat waiting for my funeral.

You will learn to forget me, I told her silently. *But every day of my life I will think of you.*

I would die a thousand times if it meant your life was saved.

Goodbye, my precious Jules.

Be brave.

Be...happy.

JULIANNA

I sat in the one of the pews and stared up at the man on the cross. He died for me. Just like Roman had died to save me. The ultimate act of love.

Inside me was just...nothing. Empty space between the nothing.

I closed my eyes and pressed my fingers into my face. This is where I stayed. Long after Roman's funeral ended. Long after everyone had left and the church had grown silent again.

I didn't move even as I heard the patter of soft footsteps coming up the aisle. He or she stopped beside me.

"Miss?"

A boy. Young. I didn't lift my head.

"This is for you, miss."

I said nothing. I didn't care enough to open my eyes.

"I'll just leave it here."

There was a rustle as something was placed beside me. The soft patter of his shoes, slower now, as he left.

I rubbed my eyes, blinking into the dim church. The sun had long since gone down. The candles had dwindled to their last inch. I should...go home.

What is home without Roman?

I glanced down. Beside me was a single red rose.

I started, spun around. But the boy who left this for me was long gone.

A single red rose.

Was this someone's idea of a sick joke?

Roman was *dead*.

Anger swelled up, burning away the numbness that had wrapped around me until now. I grabbed the rose by the stem in my fist, ignoring the thorns that cut me open. "Fuck you!" I screamed and flung it. It smacked against the altar, petals flying off in a shower of red.

I was a cliff whose roots had been ripped away. It would not hold. I would not hold.

The earth opened up under my feet and I fell into the abyss, a bottomless pit I could not escape from.

Fuck you, God. Fuck you, heaven. You don't deserve him. He was supposed to stay with me.

We were supposed to run away to Paris. To live out a long life of love and laughter and glorious heart-stopping sex and... babies. Oh God, our babies. My heart cried for the future we would never have, the home we would never get to make, the children we would never get to know.

I cried because he was stolen from me. He was stolen from this city that would never know him. They deserved to know him like I did. Roman turned on his family, singlehandedly ending the Tyrells' reign of terror in this city.

My father repaid him by taking his life. My father was a murderer, no better than Giovanni Tyrell. Worse, because he hid behind a badge and a good name. My father—*my father*—had selfishly stolen Roman away from his world, this city, from me. My own father. The man who gave me life thought he had the right to take it away.

In my darkness, the storm raged around me. I shivered,

naked, in the center of it. Anger and grief choked me, crushing my lungs. My insides ripped apart, as if my very soul was trying to tear itself from my body, to follow Roman into the afterlife. It hurt so much I doubled over, heaving in breath.

I can't breathe.

I can't breathe.

I can't breathe.

"Julianna, my child." A soft hand slid on my shoulder. Through my universe of pain, I heard Father Laurence's voice. I reached for it like he was my lifeline. Father Laurence would help me.

I inhaled, loud and hoarse like a drowning woman. I had managed to find a sliver of air. A sliver of hope. I exposed my face to the Father, in all its broken rawness. "Please," I begged.

He had to help me. He had to.

He gazed at me with such worry. "Please, what?"

"A gun."

"*What?*" He drew back, a look of horror replacing his pity.

"They took mine from me."

"Julianna—"

"Or a knife. I'm not fussy. A knife would hurt more and it would take longer to die than a bullet but..."

The Father made a wheezing sound and grasped at the pew in front of us. "You can't be serious..."

I trained my eyes on him, my grief solidifying with purpose. "As serious as death."

"Don't be too hasty. You are young—"

"I am young," I spat out, my words bitter. "Which means I have to spend every minute of every hour of every day for the next sixty or seventy years waiting. *Waiting* until I can join him."

"You... You will get over him."

That was what my father said. He lied. He'd had never gotten over the death of my mother, his love, his soulmate. Look at him now, an old lonely, hateful, bitter shell of the man he used to be.

I would not become him.

I could not live with what *he'd* become.

I'd rather die.

"You do not know true love if you think I can go on without Roman. I won't live as a ghost. Let me die like I should. Let me join him."

Father Laurence shook his head. "I can't. I w—"

I grabbed the front of his shirt, my fingers twisting into his robes. "If you do not help me," my voice was as hard as bullets, "I will find someone who will."

He stared at me as I held his gaze, willing him to comprehend how determined I was.

Slowly, his shaking hands slid over mine, his eyes growing resigned. "Okay, Julianna. Okay."

Late that night, I held the tiny vial in my hand. The thick dark liquid inside looked black, but held up to the light, the edges revealed its true nature. Blood red, like wine.

The Father's words came back to me as if he were standing right next to me.

"Drink the whole bottle on an empty stomach. All of it, don't miss one drop. You'll begin to get sleepy in a few minutes. You'll sink into what feels like a sleep, then you should feel...nothing."

I had prepared for my death in a steady, logical motion. I'd cancelled my electricity, my home phone and internet account. I donated the groceries left in my pantry and fridge to the local soup kitchen down the street. I wrote out a will, a suicide note, signed them both and left them on my dining room table.

I went over to Nora's place and gave her one last hug. I threatened to give myself away when I squeezed her for too long. She just thought I was still upset about Roman. She didn't realize my veiled attempt at goodbye.

Just one last goodbye to make. My stomach tumbled around as the phone rang. It didn't matter how much I blamed him, he was still my father. He would hurt enough as punishment when he realized I was dead.

My heart fluttered with relief when my father's phone went to voice mail. His gruff voice came on over the speaker, telling me to leave a message. The same voice that rumbled "I love you" against my forehead when I was a child and he thought I was asleep. It would be the last time I would hear it. He might have killed Roman, but he was still my father and he would mourn me. I knew he would mourn me.

Beep.

"Dad? It's me... I just wanted to tell you that I know what you did to Roman. I know you shot him. I wish..." my voice cracked, "I just wish you'd gotten to know him, the real Roman. He is...*was*...my air. Just like Mom was yours. I can't live without him. I hope you understand. Goodbye, Dad." I hung up before I broke down.

I lay myself in bed, dressed in a long nightgown. The vial watched me from the bedside table as I played the audio recording of my mother's voice one last time, letting her voice infuse me with strength. When the recording ended, the silence was swollen.

It was time.

I picked up the vial. My future felt weightless and so delicate in my hands. A river of fear ran up my arms. What if Father Laurence had been lying? What if it was painful? Or worse, what if it didn't work?

I pushed down these thoughts. If I wanted to see Roman again, I would have the courage to drink every last drop. I focused on his face, clear in my mind. My chest filled with resolve. I unscrewed the top and dropped the tiny cork stopper. It bounced off my bed cover and rolled around on the floor somewhere.

SIENNA BLAKE

I remembered Roman's last words to me. *"My life began with you. It will end with you."*

I lifted the vial up in a toast. "To endings, that are really just beginnings."

I knocked back the vial and the cool liquid hit the back of my throat. It tasted like bitter almonds and grass. I forced myself to swallow it all down.

I dropped the empty vial. I lay back on the covers, staring at my ceiling, waiting.

First, my toes and my fingers began to tingle. Then a tightness, like a frost, closed around on me. My heart thudded as a shot of fear went through me. What had I done? It wasn't too late. I could run to the bathroom and make myself throw it all up.

"Be brave," I heard Roman whisper.

The frost swept over my vision, making all my edges blurry. I embraced it. I began to float. It wasn't long before the blackness took me.

ROMAN

I got into my small pickup truck and wiped the back of my hand against the sweat beading across my forehead. It was only nine a.m. but the sun was as raw and exposed as the land here around this desert town. As empty and vacant as my heartscape. The steering wheel of the truck was almost too hot to handle. I ignored the burn and accelerated down the dusty road away from my one-bedroom shack, windows open to try to cool the inside of the cab.

My name was Remy Montague now. I hated the name. I hadn't shaved since I left Verona, my three-day stubble already transforming my features, making them darker. The sun was already turning my olive skin a deeper shade. The desert dust was in the weave of all my clothes, in the creases of my elbows and stuck in the eyelets of my boots. No amount of cleaning would ever get them out. The desert was already consuming me. Soon I would be nothing but a part of it. This relocation wasn't a new life, it was an exile. This desert town was only a two-and-a-half-hour flight and four-hour drive south of Verona, but it may as well have been another planet.

Even as part of me raged against my purgatory here, another

part of me knew I deserved it. I may not have gotten life in prison for my crimes, but this was another type of prison. The wide-open spaces, the sky touching the edge of the dry, dusty landscape, rocky crops where only the most daring and brave of the desert flowers could grow. They were my bars. This scorching, glaring sky became the walls of my prison. The rattlesnakes, my wardens.

There was not a second since I'd left Verona that I didn't think of Julianna. I prayed that she would not hurt for too long. Maybe it was better that she thought I was dead. It was a cleaner break. It gave her some closure. She could move on. Closure that I would never get.

I drove into town every day to get internet reception so I could check my phone for news on Verona. I couldn't help it. I sat in the same seat on the porch of the only café in town and ordered a coffee, black. Some things didn't change.

I connected to their Wi-Fi, which was spotty at best, and waited. My coffee had cooled to the point where I could sip it by the time the browser loaded. It pained me every time to read about a city I was no longer a part of. But I greedily drank up every headline—a new development proposed, the local elections coming up, a local school attempting the world record for most consecutive turns of a skipping rope—because these things were happening around the woman I loved.

Today was different.

Today's headline was blackened, poisoned words shaped like knives that cut me so that all heat drained from my limbs in a rush.

Chief's Daughter Commits Suicide.

. . .

There was some mistake. There had to be some mistake. Some other chief. Some other daughter.

I clicked through to the article, my finger shaking as it tapped the screen. I glared at the white screen as the Wi-Fi struggled to keep up.

Come on, load, damn you. I only realized I had slammed my fist on the table when it rattled my coffee cup. A few patrons turned their heads to stare at me. I was the grouchy stranger among them who refused to make any friends, and they already didn't like me for that reason.

I didn't give a shit what they thought. Just that this goddamn page would load and the mistake would be cleared up...

The page presented me with cold, ordered font in neat lines.

Detective Julianna Capulet, the daughter of Chief of Police Montgomery Capulet, was found dead in her apartment yesterday by her father. It appeared that she had ingested poison and her heart had stopped. There were no signs of forced entry and she left a note in her handwriting. The police have ruled it a suicide. A memorial will be held for her tomorrow at Waverley Cathedral.

Julianna.

Dead.

Suicide.

Everything in my body seized.

My blood turned to swollen hot lava in my veins. This was Chief Capulet's fault. He should have told her I was still alive. I let out a roar that echoed across the desert plains.

I was alive, Jules.

I was alive.

The unfairness, the sweet life she just threw away, burned in my body. For what? A lie that her father perpetuated.

I was half-blind with rage as I stood, knocking my chair back. I threw money down—too much money—for my half-drunk coffee. I tumbled into my truck and turned it immediately towards the nearest city with an airport, letting my blood roar along with the engine.

I didn't care that I would be imprisoned for life if I were caught. Tonight, I would return to Verona.

I wore a cap pulled down low over my eyes as I pulled up in a cab to the back entrance of the Waverley Cathedral grounds, the morning dusk creeping across the slated roofs of Verona. I caught a glimpse of myself in the side mirror as I got out. My four-day beard darkened my face. Sorrow made my eyes weary. I doubted even Nonna would recognize me now.

The cab crawled away across the crackly gravel. I slipped into the rusted gate that led to the graveyard. I trudged past the rows of bone-like headstones as I made my way to the back of the cathedral building. It wasn't long until I found myself standing at the very place that I first saw her standing by her mother's grave. The plot beside it had been dug up, a fresh headstone stood beside her mother's.

Rest in Peace
Beloved daughter and friend.
She left us much too soon.
Julianna Abigail Capulet

My vision blurred, her name disappearing behind my grief.

I could not believe she was dead. I would have known. I would have felt it, her soul ripping from where it joined with mine when she flew away from this Earth. Was it a trick to weasel me out? To get me back to Verona by the Veronesis who wanted to finish off the last of the Tyrell line?

I knew deep down, these were just the desperate thoughts of a man close to madness. I was balanced on a knife's edge.

Her memorial was not scheduled until later this afternoon. Just as my empty coffin had been, only a few days ago, her coffin would now be in the room at the back of the cathedral.

The cathedral appeared empty as I slipped into the back door, keeping an eye out for anyone who might be around. I walked the same path that Julianna had walked towards the back room. My steps slowed as I neared the door, everything in my body screaming at me to turn back.

I had to keep going. I needed to see her body with my own eyes, even as my heart banged against my ribs. Until I saw her, she was alive somewhere in my mind.

I placed my hand on the smooth wooden door, *be brave*, and pushed my way in.

The coffin sat where mine had, upon a stone table. Unlike mine had been, the lid was open. My vision narrowed so that it was all I saw. They had sent my mother away dressed in mahogany too.

Oh, God, I can't do this.

Yes, you can, Roman. You have to make sure it's her.

I forced myself to step closer, my throat closing up as I neared and the inside came into view. Nestled like a gift in wrapping paper was my Julianna.

She was still so beautiful. At least death hadn't stolen that away. Not yet. Her eyes were closed. She looked just like she was sleeping, except her lips were pale and the veins showed through her thin eyelids. She wore a soft white sundress printed with sunflowers, the same dress I had first seen her in, her hands clasped across her stomach.

It was true.

She was dead.

Because of me.

"How dare you," I slammed my fist down on the stone platform, reveling in the pain that flared up my arm, "your life was not yours to take. It was mine. It belonged to me." I clutched at the edges of her coffin, my fingernails scratching against the wood. I wanted to crawl in there with her and never wake up. "You belonged to me."

I couldn't protect my mother.

I couldn't protect Jules.

I had failed.

Everyone I loved was now gone. There was nothing for me left on this Earth.

Nothing.

My gut twisted with resolve and relief as I made up my mind. I would not go back to my purgatory. "I'll be with you soon, my love," I whispered.

One last touch. Just one. I reached out for her cheek.

"Roman?" a male voice spoke from behind me.

I spun. Father Laurence was standing at the door to the room, dressed in his white priestly robes, a purple sash falling on either side of his neck. I'd been so focused on Julianna I hadn't heard him come in.

His face broke out into one of relief. "Thank God. I knew you'd come back. I tried to get a message to you, but no one at witness protection would talk to me."

"I read about it in the news," I said, my voice wooden.

Father Laurence's face dropped. "I'm so sorry, Roman. You shouldn't have had to hear about it that way."

"I'm sorry about a lot of things." I pulled the gun out of the back of my belt, a gun I had bought off a street thug on my way

here. There were only three bullets in the chamber. That was
fine. I only needed one.

"What are you doing?" the Father asked, his palms coming up,
his face turning pale.

"You need to leave this room. Right now."

Realization sparked in his eyes. "Roman, I can't let you do
this."

"You can't stop me." I raised the gun to my temple, the cold
eye of the barrel biting my skin.

"No, wait," he said. "I beg of you, just one more minute. It's
not what you think."

"What will change from this minute to the next?" I cried,
letting out an angry growl. "Julianna is gone and—"

"Roman?" a soft girlish voice called, heavy with sleep.

I turned my face towards the voice, my breath a solid ball in
my throat. Julianna was lying in the coffin, in the same position
as before. But her eyes were fluttering.

I couldn't speak. I tried.

I felt Father Laurence pulling the gun from my hand. I
let him.

Those perfect whiskey irises looked right at me, right into
me. I wanted her to be alive so much I was hallucinating.

"Roman?" she said, her voice cracking as if her throat was too
thick. It was the most beautiful thing I'd ever heard.

Speak again, bright angel.

My heart began to rattle in my chest like a cage. My body
coursed with fire. But my feet had turned to sand, my body to
wood. I just stared at her. Looking at her. Trying to understand.
What was happening. To fit these missing pieces together. Two
seconds ago, she was dead. My life was over. Now...she was
blinking. Speaking.

Could it be that there was a God? Could it be that there were
such things as second chances? Had He decided I was to deserve
one?

Julianna tried to sit up, her movements weak. She fell back down on her pillow.

"Help me get her out," Father Laurence said.

On autopilot, I stepped up to the side of the coffin and reached in for her. My arms went around her tiny waist. Her arms flung around my neck.

She felt so real.

"Father," I said, "it's the strangest thing. She feels alive to me."

"I'm alive, Roman," the ghost of Julianna said into my ear.

"I'm dreaming, then." I inhaled deeply, taking in her smell of clean skin and the hint of her sweet perfume. I pulled her out of her death-box and placed her on her feet. I didn't let go. I couldn't. She'd disappear if I let her go.

I was losing my mind. Or maybe I was actually dead. I had pulled the trigger and shot myself and this was heaven. Julianna's arms were heaven. So in heaven I must be.

"I'll just leave you two," the Father said quietly. The door clicked shut behind him.

"You're not dreaming," she whispered. "I'm here."

My head spun with all of my wildest hopes and dreams. The relief was so palpable it hurt. Like boiling water over icy glass, cracking my grief to pieces. I just kept whispering her name and rocking her in my arms, holding her so tight I was sure I was hurting her. She didn't complain. She clung to me with her own delicate fierceness.

I pulled back and touched her face. I brushed her hair. I ran my fingertips across her cheekbones and jaw. My eyes sought every freckle, ran over every crease in her bottom lip. Everything was in place.

This was real. She was alive.

I shook my head. "How?" I asked. She began to speak. I shushed her. "I don't care how. Just that you're here and alive. Jules, I couldn't live without you."

"You don't have to."

Our mouths closed against each other's, my tongue swiping across her lips before she let me in. My arms wrapped so tightly around her, pulling her soft, warm body flush against mine. She moaned into my mouth and fisted her hands into my hair, telling me she wanted more.

It was a kiss made of stars and light. Of gunpowder and sparks. A kiss that stirred up a lost hope as fragile as snowflakes. We kissed for what had ended and for what was only just beginning.

JULIANNA

My head spun with lightheadedness. From the toxin's effects. From his kiss.

His lips moved over mine with desperate tenderness, with pained hunger, with crazed relief. Our hearts collided against each other, drumming the same beat, as they had always done. If there was a way to draw him all into me—his scent, his taste, everything—I would.

I couldn't believe it had worked. The Father's plan had worked. The drug had worked, thank you, God. The Father warned me that the toxin was dangerous. He warned me that it could actually kill me. Or that I might never wake up.

I hadn't cared. I was dead anyway if I couldn't find a way to be with Roman.

Now that I was "dead", I was released from the shackles of my previous life. I could go with him, anywhere, be anyone…

"Julu?"

I jolted away from Roman, lips swollen, breath caught in my windpipe. I spun towards the familiar voice. My father, the chief, stood at the doorway in a black suit, tie askew, purple shadows under his red-rimmed eyes. "You're…alive?"

Oh my God. We'd been caught. So close to freedom and stopped just before the line. We were so screwed. Roman broke his immunity deal by coming back to Verona. I knew what this meant. He was going away for life.

Screw this. Screw the system. I did not come this far, risk this much, to back down.

I stepped forward, shielding Roman from my father. "Don't you dare blame him. Don't you dare make this his fault. We wouldn't have had to lie if it weren't for you."

My father just stared at me, an incredulous look on his face. "You... You were going to let me think you were dead."

"It's nothing you didn't do to me," I said coldly.

My father gave me a pained look, a look that squeezed in through the gaps of my shield. "I guess I deserve that."

I glanced past my father. The only way out of this room was through him. How far was I willing to go for Roman?

All the way. I was prepared to die for him. If I had to shoot my own father to get us out of here, I would. We'd have to go on the run. But at least we'd be together.

I turned my eyes back to my father, trying to calculate my next move. He started forward and I flinched, making him pause.

"I won't let you take him," I cried. "If you try to arrest him, I'll—"

"I won't."

"You...won't?"

My father's gaze settled on Roman standing at my side. "You look at her the way..." he cleared his voice, "the way that I used to look at my wife. You really love her, don't you?"

Roman's hand slid around my waist and he pulled me close. "With everything that I am."

My father turned his gaze to me. "You really love him too, don't you?"

I nodded, my throat too closed with emotion to speak.

My father deflated, his shoulders falling. "I have been...an old fool. A short-sighted old fool." He looked at me. "Can you ever forgive me?"

I flung myself into his arms and he hugged me back. "I already have," I said to him. "I love you."

"Oh, Julu," he muttered into my hair, "you're alive."

"I'm alive," I repeated as I laughed, my body filling with warmth.

My father pulled back and faced Roman. "I'm... I'm sorry for forcing you to lie to her. I'm sorry for trying to keep you two apart."

Roman nodded. "You were just trying to protect her." He shot me a look. "I understand the impulse."

"But how did this happen?" my father asked, staring at me. "How are you not...?"

"Dead?"

"I'm afraid I am responsible," Father Laurence stepped in from the doorway, joining us.

"The Father knew Roman was really alive," I said quickly, in case my father turned on Father Laurence with anger.

Roman nodded. "He had to help fake my funeral."

"So, when I begged him for something to end my life..."

"You what?" Both Roman and my father snapped their heads towards me, a mirrored image of shock and horror on their faces.

"I gave her Atropa Belladonna instead," injected Father Laurence, "otherwise known as Sleeping Nightshade, an herb when prepared properly, mimics death."

Roman grabbed my shoulders. "You were going to die for me?"

"You came here to die with me," I reminded him.

His grip loosened. He lowered his forehead to touch mine. "Don't ever die for me again," he whispered.

I broke into a smile. "We will live for each other instead. I'll

come with you, we'll leave Verona and go back to where you
were sent under witness protection."

"Julu," my father exclaimed, "you don't have to go with him."

"Where he goes, I go," I said firmly.

"But your job—"

"You've suspended me," I said. "Besides, I quit."

"You can't just throw away everything."

"I'm not throwing away everything." I turned to look at
Roman. Once again, he left me breathless with his dark, intense
stare and the midnight hair that curled over his collar. "I'm grabbing on to what's important with both hands."

My father sighed. "I've never been any good at telling you
what to do, have I?" My father shot Roman a stern look. "You
better take care of her."

Roman straightened up. "I will, sir."

"It is best that you stay 'dead', at least until the trials. The
extradition request for your brother from Colombia is under-
way. The Tyrell empire will soon be dismantled piece by piece. I
will try to expedite the court process, see if we can't get you both
back here any quicker, but it'll take time.

"How much time?" I asked.

"A year. Maybe more."

"A year?" We'd have to stay hidden for an entire year. We
couldn't come back to Verona for a *whole* year.

"A year is fine," Roman said.

I snapped my head toward him. *Was he crazy?*

Roman smiled at me, a glint in his eyes. "I know just where
we can go…"

ROMAN

J ulianna and I sat in the car parked on the side of the road in a leafy part of Verona, a familiar cottage with a faded blue door to my right.

We'd just stopped at Nora's apartment and surprised the hell out of her. She screamed so loud that I was sure the entire population of Verona knew we were still alive. Hell, my ears were still ringing from her ruckus.

Jules and I agreed we would let Nonna know as well. It wasn't fair to her if we didn't. I could see the soft, cuddly frame of the woman who'd stepped in as a mother figure to me. The same woman whose grandson I'd sent to his grave. I couldn't make myself get out of that car.

"We should go," I said. "It's getting late." I reached to turn the car key but Julianna's hand slid over mine.

"Roman," she said. "It would only be 'too late' if you drove away without telling her you're alive. Don't leave her in pain because she thinks you are dead."

I know. I was being a coward. I was more nervous now facing up to Nonna after what happened to Mercutio than facing my father. *Be brave.* I forced myself out of the car. Jules followed me.

Every trudge up her front path felt like I was sinking in concrete, my feet getting heavier and heavier as I approached the blue door.

"Don't you usually go in the back way?" Jules asked.

The back door was for family. I had destroyed hers. "Usually," I mumbled. I lifted my hand and knocked.

"It's open," I heard Nonna calling through the door. Trust Nonna to still keep her doors unlocked, no matter how much I told her to lock them. She was too trusting.

I opened the front door and stepped into her living room. The smell of cinnamon and vanilla warmed the place, making my stomach twinge. Nonna baked when she was happy. She baked when she was sad. Jules stood close to my side, her presence giving me strength.

"I'll be there in just a—" Nonna cut off as soon as she stepped from the kitchen, her eyes locked on me. She froze, her cheeks paling.

"Surprise, Nonna," I said. "I'm—"

"You're alive," she said, her voice warbling as if she was unsure of whether to be shocked, angry, sad, or to shriek with excitement. She stared at me as if I were a stranger. Perhaps to her, I was.

I gave her an uneasy smile to test the waters. "I'm alive."

She slowly wiped her hands, dusty with flour, on her apron. "Well," she said, a slightly defensive tone to her voice, "I've already packed up all your things that you left here and given them away. Clothes and shoes and video games. Although I suppose you don't fit into those clothes anymore." She placed her hands on her hips.

She'd kept my things for eight years? I didn't go into Mercutio's old room the last time I was here. I bet it was still the same, twin beds covered in comforters decorated with Marvel comic superheroes, large boxes in the corner stuffed with our toys and games.

Jules slipped her hand into mine and squeezed. *Go on.*

"I'm sorry," I said.

"You should be. You should have told me." She glared at me. "I don't have any dinner ready for you."

"I know. I'm sorry."

Tears filled her eyes. She ran over to grab me, pulling me into her fleshy warm arms. Jules stepped back so Nonna and I could have a moment. She broke into an undignified sob on my shoulder. "Oh, Roman. I'm so happy you're alive."

I leaned a chin on her graying hair that always smelled like her lavender shampoo, feeling like I was finally home again. "I'm so sorry I let you think I was dead," I whispered. "I'm sorry for...everything."

Nonna pulled back, wiping her eyes with the edge of her apron, and composed herself with dignified sniffle. "Why didn't you come to me earlier?"

"I thought you might not want to speak to me after...Mercutio." My voice broke on his name.

Nonna's eyes teared up at his name. "My poor Mercutio. Why are you blaming yourself for him?"

"He died saving my life."

Nonna sniffed. She shook her head, but there was an edge of wistfulness on her lips. "That boy would have followed you to the edges of the Earth. He was loyal to a fault. That's not your doing, Roman."

"It was my fault," I squeezed out. "I'm so sorry."

"Did you pull the trigger?" she asked, her voice eerily calm.

"Well, no, but—"

"Then you didn't kill him. You hear me?" she asked, her tone firm and commanding. She grabbed my arm and repeated, "You. Didn't. Kill him."

I stared into Nonna's face, stern and yet warm. I saw sorrow still fresh in the creases of her face. But not a thread of blame. I pulled her into another hug, taking in her comforting "Nonna smell" of baked goods and the hint of lemon cleaner, and let her begin to mend another broken piece of my soul.

JULIANNA

Three months later...

Paris was everything I dreamed it would be.

We were free here. Just two strangers holding hands among the lively fashionable rush, strolling down the cobbled streets lined with chic boutiques and cute cafes, green shutters flung open to the sun or walls draped with ivy. All my senses were pulled left and right; the earthy smell of coffee and sweet, warm pastries, the sharp music of market sellers calling out their wares, flowerboxes spilling with pink and purple geraniums.

I sat close to Roman on the sidewalk of a café in Montmartre, a tree-lined part of the city built on a hill with winding cobble-stone streets. Our cozy rented apartment was above the cafe, in the attic. We came down here every morning for a cafe au lait and a croissant and watched the people stroll by or glide past on bicycles.

Roman held a small tablet out in front of him.

"How the hell does this thing work?" Nonna said with a growl from the depths of a black screen.

I giggled behind my hand. Nonna still hadn't gotten used to internet video calls.

"It's on, Nonna," Nora's voice came through. "See? You just have to turn the video on." Both their faces came on the laptop screen. The four of us let out a cheer.

The last day that Roman and I spent in Verona, my father, Nora and Nonna came to our hotel room to say goodbye. They met each other properly for the first time then. Since then, Nora and Nonna had been inseparable. They often ambushed my father at his place to make sure he was eating properly and that the house hadn't turned to mold around him. It made me happy that they were looking after him and each other.

Nonna's face broke out into a huge smile. "How is Paris?"

My eyes met Roman's. It was a dream. Waking up every day next to him, getting to walk without fear or shame down the streets, holding his hand, and kissing him, oh, the public kisses. I think we've even made a sport of public kissing.

We filled Nonna and Nora in on Paris and the apartment we'd rented here.

"We miss you," Nonna said. "Our lives are so dull without you two."

"Speak for yourself," said Nora.

Nonna snorted. "Did you hear that this floozy here has a new boyfriend?"

"When does she ever *not* have a new boyfriend," I said.

"I'm not dead, so I don't have to act like it," Nora said in a haughty tone.

Sounded like everything back home was as we left it. Roman squeezed my hand under the table.

We spoke for another few minutes before we signed off with promises to call again next month.

I leaned back in my chair, sipping the remainder of my coffee. "I love that Nonna and Nora are friends."

"I love you." Roman stared at me, a small smile on his face.

"I love that we're here in Paris."

"I love you."

"You know, you're getting very good at saying that." I remembered when he couldn't bring himself to say those words to me.

"I'm not afraid to say it. Anymore."

"Well, I love..." I said slowly, tapping my lip with my finger, "...the Eiffel Tower."

"You love that I'm as big as the Eiffel Tower."

I snorted.

Roman grinned. "You want to *climb* the Eiffel tower?"

We stumbled up the skinny staircase and poured into our apartment, a tangle of limbs and ragged breaths. He barely got the door shut behind us before I was slammed up against it. Fuck, I loved doors. Doors were amazing. It was my favorite thing to be crushed between them and him. I had only to look at a door now to get wet.

He kissed me like he was drinking me in. He peeled off my clothes, taking a moment as each article was thrown aside to brush his gaze across my skin and made a small, pained growl of approval. He made me feel so beautiful with the way his eyes devoured me.

Then we were naked, skin on skin, our limbs twisted around each other, the air sweet with our heavy breaths. When he slid inside me, we lost ourselves in each other, then we found ourselves. Right where we were meant to be.

ROMAN

Three months later...

I shifted myself into a more comfortable position on the pillow and tucked Julianna into the crook of my neck, sweaty and deliciously tired. She had that exhausted, satisfied smile on her face, one I loved putting there.

She was so beautiful. And she was mine. How did I get so damn lucky?

Julianna's burner phone rang, vibrating on the white painted wooden bedside table. She went to roll over but I crushed her to me, keeping her there.

"It's probably my father," she said. "I have to take it."

"Let it go to voicemail," I whispered in her ear as I rubbed my hips against her.

She pushed at my chest, laughing. "You're so greedy. Afterwards."

I let out an annoyed sigh but I let her go.

She rolled to sitting, showing off her smooth violin-shaped

back, and answered the phone. "Hi, Dad." There was a pause. She twisted to look at me, a frown on her face.

"*What?*" I mouthed to her.

"It's...it's for you." She held out her phone.

Me? Her father wanted to speak to me? He was cordial enough to me at our small farewell in Verona. He often asked Jules to pass on his hellos. But he'd never asked to speak to *me*.

I took the phone from her and held it to my ear, my stomach doing a flip. "Sir?"

"Roman," the chief's gruff voice sounded so strained. "I have some bad news for you."

Bad news. My skin prickled.

"Your brother's extradition request was denied by the Colombian government. I think he has bought himself his freedom. Unfortunately, that means we can't allow you to take back your old life as we planned. If he found out you were still alive, that you took a deal with us, there's no doubt in my mind he'd take revenge."

The blood drained from my fingers as my life, my and Julianna's life, dissolved in front of me. My happiness, it seemed, was just a castle made of sand. I should have known it was too good to be true. "I see."

"I'm sorry, son."

"Me too."

He hung up. My heart was heavy with the weight of the world on it. Jules was staring at me with wide eyes. She knew something was wrong. I was going to break her heart when I explained. This made me more sad than anything.

I told her, my heart cracking as tears welled in her eyes. "I used to hate being Roman Tyrell," I said. "Now I can't wait to *be* him again."

Julianna curled into my side, her hair falling over my chest.

"There's nothing stopping you from returning to Verona, Jules," I said. "You must miss—"

"No." Her head snapped up.

"You don't—"

"I miss Verona. I'm saying 'no' to going back without you."

"There's no point in us both being exiled."

"I'm staying with you."

"But—"

"End of discussion. What we need to be figuring out is what do we do next." Her voice was firm. She was so full of strength. It was one of the reasons I loved her. She glanced up at me with a hopeful look in her eyes. "Any ideas?"

I shook my head. I had no answers.

The next morning I sat at our small dining table, scanning the Colombian news on the tablet for any word on my brother's activity. Jules was curled on the couch reading a book. We were both quiet today after yesterday's revelation.

My phone rang at my elbow. I frowned. It was a private number. Maybe Nonna was phoning using Skype?

It was too early back in Verona, they were six hours behind us and it was only eleven a.m. here.

I hesitated before I answered.

The voice that spoke was one I'd never heard before, deep yet smooth, a mild accent I couldn't place and slightly formal. "Do not act like anything is wrong, Mr. Montague." He used the name of my new identity. "We wouldn't want to scare the lovely Julianna, would we now?"

Julianna? She was going by the name of Juliet Caraway.

My skin prickled. My fingers went a deadly cold. I glanced over to Jules, her hair falling over her eyes as she curled around her book. "No, we wouldn't."

"Very good, Mr. Montague...or should I call you Mr. Roman Tyrell."

I stood and walked into the bathroom, ignoring Julianna's questioning glance. I locked the door and leaned against it.

"Who is this?" I hissed. "How did you get my number?"

"Do not fear, Roman. I am not here to hurt you. I am here to help."

"Help me with what?"

"I hear you have a problem regarding your older brother...Marco."

"How do you...?" I trailed off. That was a wasted question. If this man, whoever he was, was able to find out my real name and my phone number, it wasn't a stretch that he'd found out about Marco's extradition denial. I moved on to the next best question. "What do you want?"

"I told you, Roman. I want to help."

"Help me how?"

"I work for an organization that specializes in ridding the world of...problems. Such as the one you have with your brother." That was an answer in riddles if there ever was one.

"Oh yeah? How do you propose to solve my problem?"

The man let out a small chuckle. That sound alone managed to raise the hairs on my arms. "Let me put it this way, the organization I work for is called The Church."

My blood turned to shards of ice in my veins. *The Church.* A group of gentlemen assassins. They were deadly ghosts.

"Why... Why would you help me?"

"It's quite simple. Your brother in exchange for a favor."

My throat tightened. "What favor?"

"One yet to be called upon."

"That's not—"

"This is not a negotiation. You have twelve hours to think it over. You'll give me your answer face to face. Tonight. I'm afraid Julianna can't come. You'll have to give her the slip. Can you do that?"

"Roman?" Julianna called through the bathroom door. "Is everything okay?"

I flinched away from the door. "Fine, honey."

He was asking me to lie to Jules, not just about meeting him, but about my brother. I promised I wouldn't lie to her ever again. I promised her.

But this was for our future. I'd be doing her a favor by keeping this horrible solution from her, by sparing her from the dark truth.

"Answer yes or no, Roman," his voice sounded in my ear.

"Yes."

"I'll text you where to meet."

"Give me a name?" I said before he could hang up. "What do I call you?"

"You can call me...Sevastian."

The line went dead.

I pressed my forehead on the smooth surface of the bathroom door. What would I do?

Should I take his offer? Should I accept this bloody solution to my problem? The world was better off without Marco Tyrell in it.

Jules...she'd never agree to it. If I wanted an end to my problem, I had to keep this from her. I didn't want to keep anything from her.

But we couldn't remain in exile forever. *She* couldn't live in exile forever. I could already see the homesickness that Julianna tried to hide. It leaked out from her without her knowing. In the smile that didn't reach her eyes every time she spoke to her father. In the tears she brushed aside when she thought I wasn't looking. She was here for me. I had to do this for her. I had to take this deal. I had to end our exile so Julianna could go home. I had to lie to her. *For* her. I had no choice.

I opened the bathroom door. Jules was standing there, innocent curiosity in her eyes. "Who was that?"

I couldn't do it. I couldn't lie. *I'm sorry, Jules.*

"I have something to tell you," I said. "And you're not going to like it."

We sat on the couch and I began to speak. I watched her face contort as I outlined who The Church was and the details of Sevastian's offer.

She shivered and I pulled her closer so she was seated across my lap. "You know what you have to do," she said quietly.

I nodded. I had to refuse him.

Julianna turned her amber eyes to me. "You have to accept it."

"What?" If I had been standing, I would have fallen over. "But, it means…"

"I know what it means. I know you shouldn't have told me. I'm glad you did. Because now, we can carry the weight of this decision together."

I couldn't speak. I didn't know what to say.

She leaned her forehead against mine. "Let's end this," she whispered. "Together."

JULIANNA

At eleven p.m. that night Roman and I walked hand in hand to Chopin's grave at Pere Lachaise. There were so many colorful flowers covering his resting place, lit softly by the cemetery lights, you could barely see it. A man in a dark suit stood at the foot of the grave, his black hair trimmed into a stylish sweep across his forehead. I could only see his profile: a strong jaw, cheekbones of a Renaissance sculpture and a pair of impossibly defined lips. Could *this* be Sevastian? As I got closer I realized he was humming something familiar. Was that...*Rock-a-bye Baby?*

The humming cut off. Roman and I both halted.

"Do you know that Chopin does not rest entirely here?" the man asked, his voice crisp and deep with a hint of an Eastern European accent. He was staring at the marble statue of the kneeling woman in robes on the headstone. "Chopin's grave contains everything...but his heart. According to his dying wish, his heart was sent back to Warsaw, Poland." He turned to face us, revealing a set of intense cerulean eyes framed with thick dark lashes. I thought I could see a flicker of annoyance in them, but it was gone before I could be sure. "I told you not to bring her."

Roman tensed beside me. "Where I go, she goes. What I know, she knows. Any decisions, we make together."

"Your affection for each other would be heartwarming. If I had a heart. Have you made a decision on my offer?"

Roman and I glanced over at each other, our eyes locking. He squeezed my hand and I squeezed back.

He looked over to Sevastian and nodded.

"Very good." Sevastian turned to leave.

"Why are you helping us?" I asked, stopping him.

Sevastian raised a dark eyebrow. "Would you believe me if I said I was doing it out of the goodness of my heart?"

I almost laughed. "No."

He smiled. "Smart one, she is," he said to Roman. "Keep her."

"And this favor," I said, suspicion coating my voice. "Why a favor? Why not money?"

Sevastian chuckled and shook his head. "So sweet, so lovely."

I felt Roman bristling beside me. I squeezed his hand. *Stay calm, Roman.*

He remained at my side, relaxing slightly, but remaining on alert. He squeezed back. *Just say the word, I'll choke the life out of him.*

"I have money," Sevastian said. "Lots of money. If I ever need more I can get more. Money is worthless to me. Now, a favor bestowed from powerful people, people with...connections or access to information, that is worth something."

As Sevastian spoke, I felt as if a cold draft had been let in through my body. I fought a shiver. Sevastian was not someone I ever wanted to cross.

"You'll get a message from me when it's done," he said. "One more if I am ever in need of your help. Otherwise, you'll never hear from me again."

That, at least, was a blessing.

ROMAN

Twenty-four hours later...

Unknown: It is done.

JULIANNA

Three months later...

We returned from Paris under the cloak of night. I spotted my father standing at the airport arrivals gate, a few plainclothes policemen at his side.

I threw myself into his arms. "Missed you, Julu," he said, his voice tight with emotion.

"Me too."

We pulled back. Roman stood beside me, our few bags at his feet. He cleared his voice. "Sir." He nodded respectfully to my father and stuck out his hand.

I held my breath. For a few moments it looked like my father was going to reject Roman's handshake.

My father grabbed Roman and pulled him in for a hug, slapping his back. Roman stared at me over my father's shoulder, the surprise in his eyes reflecting mine.

"Welcome home...son," I heard my father say.

"T-Thank you, sir."

My father pulled back and gave Roman a solemn nod. "I'm sorry to hear about your brother, Marco."

"Thank you. Colombia is a dangerous place. He had some very dangerous enemies." Roman didn't glance at me but I saw the dark flash in his eyes, sending a thrill up my spine. I knew who this *dangerous enemy* was.

My father and his armed guard escorted us to a hotel, where we were checked in under false names for the duration of the trials. After the tape in the barn was revealed, all of the Tyrell associates were scrambling over each other to make deals and turn each other in. There was very little left of the Tyrell empire.

Roman was on standby. He wouldn't be called up to testify unless the prosecutor felt they needed his testimony in order to secure a win. Thankfully, the evidence spoke for itself.

Until Abel's murder trial for the death of Roman's mother.

Giovanni had admitted on tape to ordering the murder of his wife. But the prosecutor needed Roman's testimony of what had happened on the night of his mother's murder, specifically, his testimony that his mother managed to injure her assailant with a cigarette lighter, leaving a scar exactly like the one that Abel had on the back of his right hand.

"You're going to be fine," I said to Roman, my hands picking invisible pieces of lint off his shoulders.

We stood in a witness waiting room down the corridor from the courtroom where Abel was being tried. I could feel the hardness of the bulletproof vest he wore under his suit. I hated that it was so dangerous that he had to wear one. I was glad that he didn't argue when my father entered the room earlier with a police-issued vest in his hand and demanded he wear it. Just in case.

"Mr. Tyrell?" the bailiff said from the doorway. "They're almost ready for you."

"Be brave," I said, echoing what he once told me.

"I am because you'll be there." Roman leaned in for a soft kiss, then left with the bailiff.

I slipped into one of the public benches in the courtroom. Abel sat at the defense table, a cruel smile on his face. His defense attorney, a weasely looking man in a navy pinstriped suit, sat beside him.

Mr. Snow, the state prosecutor, stood up. He was an older man with a face like Father Christmas but a reputation as a bull-dog. He had worked alongside my mother when she had been alive, so he had a personal stake in this trial. He wasn't allowed to try the case against Abel for my mother's murder because he had been friends with her, but he was allowed to try Abel for Maria Tyrell's. "The prosecution would like to call one last witness to the stand."

"Objection," the defense attorney called as he rose to his feet. "There are no more witnesses on the witness list."

"It's a last-minute inclusion to the witness list. I'm sure once you hear who it is, you'll understand why we couldn't advise the court any earlier."

"That's hardly fair," the defense attorney argued. "I haven't had the time to prepare my cross-examination."

The judge eyed the two attorneys. "I'll allow it, Mr. Snow, but we will break for the day once you've finished your initial questioning. The defense can commence his cross-examination first thing tomorrow morning. I'm sure that's enough time to prepare, Mr. Frisk?"

My stomach churned as the defense attorney nodded and took his seat. *Here it goes.*

Mr. Snow cleared his throat. "The prosecution calls to the stand...Roman Giovanni Tyrell."

The courtroom erupted as everyone began talking at once. It was big news in Verona when Roman Tyrell "died" in the barn shootout. His being alive would no longer be a secret now.

"What the fuck?" Abel burst from his seat as Roman walked calmly into the courtroom following the bailiff. "You fucking rat. I'll fucking get you." Abel scrambled over the table at Roman. I leapt to my feet, preparing to shove my way through the crowd. To Roman's credit, he didn't flinch. The court security guards were on Abel in seconds, holding him back.

"Order!" The judge smacked his gavel. "Order in the court. Bailiff, make sure that Mr. Montero is cuffed to his seat for the rest of the trial."

With the court settled and Abel restrained, Roman took the stand. "I swear to tell the truth, the whole truth, nothing but the truth, so help me God..."

Roman's eyes found mine. I smiled and he straightened, lifting his chin.

I clutched at my skirt as Roman began to tell his story, publicly for the first time, of how he watched his mother die. I was crying quietly into a handkerchief by the end of it. There was not a dry eye on the jury either. I could see something loosen from inside Roman now that he had told the truth he'd kept inside for so long. Hopefully, it would be enough.

At the end of the trial, I stood with Roman at the back of the courtroom, our hands twisted together, as the judge brought the jury back in. The foreman stood, a piece of paper in his shaking hands, ready to read out their verdict.

"Whatever happens..." I said. I wasn't sure how to finish that sentence.

"Whatever happens," Roman said, his voice low and menacing, "my mother *will* get justice."

Our eyes met. I nodded.

"We the jury find the defendant, Abel Montero..."

I squeezed his hand. He squeezed mine in return.

"...guilty of murder in the first degree."

The courtroom erupted. I let out a cry, tears forming as a

palpable wave of relief crashed over me. Roman slid down onto the bench, his eyes unfocused, his Adam's apple working.

It was over. It was finally over.

JULIANNA

L ater that night, we were back in our hotel room. Roman had been quiet all evening. I knew he was thinking of his mother and what his father said in his confession about her leaving their family.

Nora had just been to visit earlier. She brought with her a small box which I asked her to find among my things stored in her spare room.

Roman sat in a chair by the window, staring out over the city lights. The sky was an inky black. Not even the moon was out tonight. I slid my hand on Roman's shoulder, getting his attention. He lifted his face up to me; his eyes were darkened underneath and weary.

"I need you to listen to something." I slid the USB into the tablet, found the file I wanted and pressed play.

A crackling came over the speakers before the voice of my mother came on.

Abigail: "You don't have to tell me your name. Let's call you...Joan. After Joan of Arc. She was a strong woman, just like you."

. . .

Maria: "I'm scared."

Roman sat up, his lips parting as he sucked in a breath. His eyes found mine, wide with question, raw with emotion. *Is this her? Is this my mother speaking?*

I nodded, because I feared that nothing would come out if I tried to speak.

Abigail: "I know. I'd be scared too. Just take a deep breath. Remember why you want to do this."

Maria: "Are you a mother?"

Abigail: "I am. I have a beautiful little girl. She's eight. I would do anything for her. Anything. Be strong for your children, Joan. Be strong for them."

Maria: "Okay..."

We listened to the whole recording. I stood at Roman's side, a hand on his shoulder, ready to be there if he needed me.

Maria: "My husband...he didn't always used to be a bad man. He didn't used to... My boys...my poor boys. He's going to turn them into monsters."

. . .

Maria began to cry. Roman flinched as her pain crackled through the air.

Abigail: "I promise you, I will get you out of there. I will."

Maria: "I won't leave them behind. I won't."

Abigail: "We'll get them out. We'll ensure their safety."

Maria: "If anything happens to me, you'll look after them. You'll make sure they're happy. That they're loved. That they grow up to be good men."

Abigail: "Nothing will happen to you."

Maria: "Promise me!"

Abigail: "Joan, I promise."

When the audio recording stopped, I felt Roman trembling under my palm, the silence growing thick and heavy.

"Your father was lying," I said, emotion coating my throat so my voice came out strained. "Your mother wasn't going to leave you. She was going to take you with her. She turned against your father because she could see what he was becoming. She didn't want that for you boys. She loved you so much she was willing to risk her life to get you away from him."

Roman said nothing. I slid my hand off him and turned away to give him some space. He grabbed me before I could walk a single step. He pulled me into his lap so I straddled him. He buried his face in my neck and wrapped his thick, strong arms around me like a vice. I just held him, while inside, pieces of him stitched together. We sat like that until he stopped shaking. Until his breathing returned to a steady pace.

"Thank you," he whispered.

EPILOGUE

One year later...

S ixteen years. Sixteen years and I'd finally gotten justice
for my mother.
 She could finally rest in peace. Giovanni was dead.
Abel had been sentenced to life in prison for her murder. The
Tyrell empire was no more.

I stood at the foot of my mother's grave, a bunch of fresh
peonies in my hands. I couldn't believe it had been two years
since I stood here on her birthday. I'd met Roman that day and it
changed everything. It had been gray, if I recalled correctly.
Today the sun was out.

"Do you remember I told you about The Innocence Project?"
I said. The Innocence Project had been a scheme that Roman and
I had dreamed up during our yearlong exile in France. It would
be a cause that reviewed and investigated old criminal cases to
find the *real* truth. It would give hope to sons and daughters,

mothers and fathers, husbands and wives of victims of unsolved cases.

"Well," I told my mother, pride growing in my chest, "we did it. The Innocence Project has officially started. We got ourselves a brand new office, hired our first staff member and we got our first client. Roman was just with him."

I let out a long breath when I thought over the last few years. I couldn't believe we were here. "Can you imagine...a man everyone assumed was a criminal is now the one putting them away? I'm so proud of him. He *is* the man I always knew he was. And we finally found a way to turn that blood money into something good."

After Roman announced he was alive, it came out that Giovanni had left a considerable amount of money for him. When I say "considerable", I really mean he could have bought a small damn country with the money his father left him. While he'd been alive, Giovanni had managed to separate this sum of money away from the Tyrell empire just in case his empire ever fell. For months Roman refused to touch it. It sat in an account in his name until I had the brainwave to use it to fund The Innocence Project. The money allowed us to charge only what our clients could afford.

Roman would work the legal side. I would work the investigative side. Together we were a team. I had quit the police department and needed a job. I couldn't work for the police force anymore. I needed to get out from my father's footsteps and make my own path. The Innocence Project was perfect.

Anyway...happy birthday, Mom." I stepped forward and placed her favorite flowers on her resting place.

Roman stepped out from between two gravestones like he had over two years ago, causing me to suck in a breath. He still knocked the wind out of me. He looked just like he did that first time, suave and powerful in his Armani suit, his dark hair swept back off his chiseled features. Perfect lips pulled in a smile just for me.

He didn't hesitate this time. He strode up to me and wrapped his arms around me, kissing me, his tongue finding mine, holding me like I was the most precious jewel in the world. My body rushed with heat like it did every time he touched me, and I curled my fingers into his shirt.

He pulled away, rubbing his nose against mine. He whispered in that gravel and caramel voice of his, "Hello, Mrs. Tyrell."

A thrill went through me. *Mrs. Tyrell.* I loved hearing him say those words. And I was proud to call myself that. I chuckled, wondering how long it would take for me to get used to that name.

We had walked into Waverley Cathedral together hand in hand a few months ago and were married by Father Laurence in front of my father, Nora and Nonna. All the people who mattered.

"Am I late?" he asked.

I grinned. "No, you're just in time." Like he always was.

He slid his hand onto my round belly and bent down so he could mumble against my bulge. When the doctor told us that I must have gotten pregnant on our honeymoon, in Paris of course, just after I stopped taking the pill, Roman practically beat his chest like a caveman. "And hello to you too, little Mercutio Espinoza Tyrell. I missed you and your beautiful mommy today."

I rolled my eyes. "What if she's a girl?"

"My beautiful Abigail Maria Tyrell, I hope you have Mommy's looks." He winked at me.

My grin widened.

"Have you been talking to your mother about me?" He straightened and pulled me back into his arms.

I rolled my eyes. "Not everything I say is *about* you."

"Of course not. Sometimes it's about what you think of me."

I poked his firm chest. He pretended to bite my finger.

"Sorry I'm late, Julu," a voice called out. My father appeared on one of the paths through the gravestones. "I had to stop for some pesky freeloaders." He rolled his eyes but he was grinning.

"Really, Monty." Nora appeared behind him, arm in arm with Nonna. Nora had taken to calling my father Monty. Only *she* could get away with that. "Anyone would think you don't *like* us. When it was *you* who insisted on coming to pick *us* both up."

Lately, I suspected that Nora and my father were getting *really* close. I caught their stolen looks when they thought I wasn't looking. I think they hadn't told me because they were afraid of my disapproval, but I was thrilled for them. I was going to let them sweat it out a little longer before I put them out of their misery and told them that I *knew* and that it made me happier than anything.

I grinned as my family, *our* family, walked toward us to celebrate my mother's birthday with my husband, our growing baby and me.

My father gave me a hug, shook Roman's hand and placed a small white cake box next to my peonies on Mama's grave. "Pancakes," he said as he winked at me.

I smiled even through a pang of sadness. Mama got her birthday pancakes after all.

"I hope you two weren't making out in a *cemetery*," Nora said, giving me a wicked look.

"No!" Roman said in horror. He flushed. I laughed.

I gave her a quick kiss on the cheek. My mother would have loved Nora if they had ever met.

Nora wiggled her finger at Roman and whispered, "Freaky deaky," before giving us both a wink.

"Good Lord, girl, you're about to pop!" Nonna said as she enveloped me in a warm hug that smelled like apple pie. We were all going to Nonna's place after this for dinner. I bet I knew what was for dessert. Roman's favorite. "Roman, you're not making this poor girl work all day, are you?"

"Er, she wants to work."

"Roman," Nonna said, sounding horrified. "You should be waiting on her hand and foot at home at this stage."

"Of course, Nonna," he said, sounding chastised. "But she's never been very good at being told what to do." He shot me a cheeky look over Nonna's shoulder. I hid my blush. He's always been *very* good at telling me what to do.

"Who are we missing?" Nora asked.

"Sorry, I'm here," Father Laurence called as he jogged up the path towards us, his robe swishing around his ankles. There were more hugs all round as he joined us. He kissed my cheek and beamed at my belly. "Have you been taking those herbs I gave you?" he asked.

I almost laughed at the shocked look on both Roman and my father's faces.

I nodded at the Father. "The morning sickness is all gone."

"Well," my father said, his chest deflating with relief. "We're all here. Shall we begin?"

The six of us stood in a close huddle and sang "Happy Birthday" to the woman who birthed me, who loved me, and who, in a way, was the reason we were all standing here today. Even as the air was tinged with sadness for the ones who could not be here with us in person, I had never felt so happy.

It turns out that I was right all those years ago. Paris would never last. Paris *was* just a dream, a lovely dream. But this life, our *real* life, was so, *so* much better.

BOOKS BY SIENNA BLAKE

DUBLIN INK

Dublin Ink

Dirty Ink

Dark Ink

TBA (Liam's Story) ~ *coming mid 2023*

IRISH KISS

Irish Kiss

Professor's Kiss

Fighter's Kiss

The Irish Lottery

My Brother's Girl

Player's Kiss

My Secret Irish Baby

IRISH BILLIONAIRES

The Bet

The Fiancé

The Promise

BILLIONAIRES DOWN UNDER

(with Sarah Willows)
To Have & To Hoax
The Paw-fect Mix-up
Riding His Longboard
Maid For You
I Do (Hate You)
Man Toy (Newsletter Exclusive)

ALL HER MEN

Three Irish Brothers
My Irish Kings
Royally Screwed
Cassidy Brothers

BOUND DUET

Bound by Lies (#1)
Bound Forever (#2)

STANDALONES

Beautiful Revenge
Mr. Blackwell's Bride
Dark Romeo
Paper Dolls

ABOUT SIENNA

Sienna Blake is a dirty girl, a wordspinner of smexy love stories, and an Amazon Top 20 & USA Today Bestselling Author.

She's an Australian living in Dublin, Ireland, where she enjoys reading, exploring this gorgeous country and adding to her personal harem of Irish hotties ;)

tiktok.com/@siennablakeauthor
facebook.com/siennablakebooks